SHADOW WINGED

The Shadow Winged Chronicles: Book One

JILLEEN DOLBEARE

ICE RAVEN
PUBLICATIONS

The Shadow Winged Chronicles

Shadow Lair: Book .5
Shadow Winged: Book 1
Shadow Wolf: Book 1.5
Shadow Strife: Book 2
Shadow Witch: Book 2.5*
Shadow War: Book 3*

*Forthcoming

Shadow Winged
The Shadow Winged Chronicles: Book 1
Jilleen Dolbeare
Ice Raven Publications

Copyright © 2021
Editor: Cissell Ink
Cover Designer: Crimson Phoenix Creations
Interior Art: Rose Rasmussen

I dedicate this book to the people that have supported and encouraged me along the way. To my husband, Chad, who helped encourage me, helped me stay on track, and kept me in line with all the aircraft and pilot stuff. He knew I could finish a book, even when I didn't! To my niece, Baylee Rose, who read everything, and made suggestions. Also, for her brilliant art and help with every part of the book and novella. And to many others, I know you and I thank you!

Foreword

First, thanks for picking up this book, I hope you enjoy it! It's always tricky when a non-native writer writes about a native character. Living among the Inupiaq in Barrow, Alaska, I felt I could bring a native character to life while incorporating native Alaskan folklore.

Since Piper, having lived outside of her culture, gets to learn along with the reader about her background and traditions, I hope I will be forgiven for any unintentional slights as a non-Alaskan native. I love the rich history and traditions of the Inupiaq and learning their folklore has been enlightening and difficult since until very recently (in anthropologic terms) they were passed down orally.

I have used recordings from oral tellings; conversations from Inupiat friends, colleagues and neighbors; tales from the Arctic Inuit peoples; and other Alaskan native folklore to create Piper and her world. I hope that the stories I've spun will bring the folklore of the North alive. Good reading everyone!

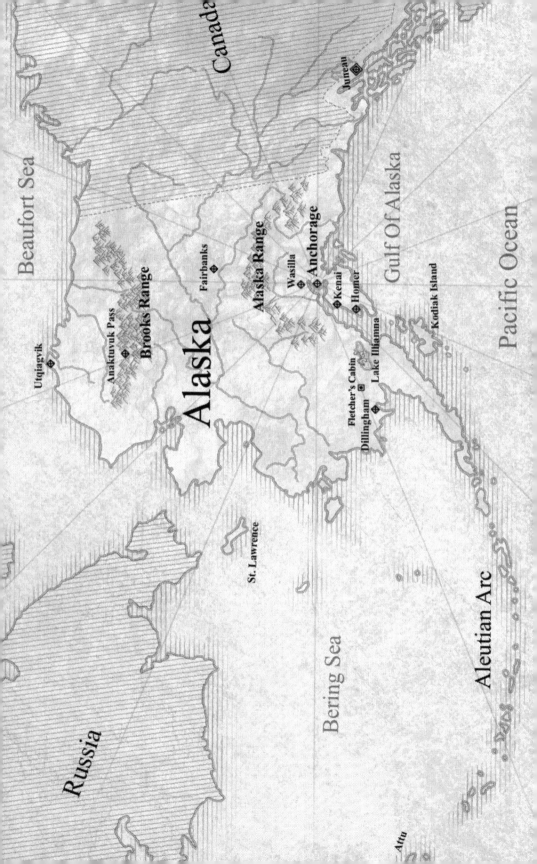

Chapter 1

The rugged cliffs of the Alaska Range darkened as the clouds pressed from above. I decreased my air speed and descended another hundred feet, hugging the right side of the steep mountain and giving myself room in case I had to turn around in the narrow pass and go back to Anchorage. We were close enough to the side of the mountain to observe a band of grizzlies under my right wing. Most of the animals cringed when we buzzed past, but a huge boar looked up, challenging us. My client barked out a quick laugh.

I'd already sunk four hundred feet on my way through the pass, and we flew along at an altitude of eight hundred. The lowering ceiling kept forcing us down as I raced an incoming front. I cleared the pass and zoomed out over open ground, trees, and tundra.

Suddenly, a black cloud materialized in front of me. I slowed further, trying to dip below. As I grew closer, I realized it was a cloud of dark birds. My heart sped up. I dipped my right wing to avoid them, but they moved almost as if they were *trying* to hit me.

I increased the dip further, and accidentally stalled the wing—losing lift. We dropped fast. My passenger gasped loudly. I grimaced; teeth clenched with concentration. After some quick maneuvering, I recovered from the stall, sweat running down my back.

A flash of black feathers and a loud whump were all I saw as the ravens bounced off the

plane. "Shit!" I yelled as I dove further to avoid the rest. We were down to three hundred feet. The clouds were still pressing on us, and I worried about the damage the large birds might have caused the cloth covered Super Cub.

"We're going to have to land." I straightened out and looked for somewhere to put down. "I need to assess the damage."

He grunted affirmatively. Rough maneuvering like that can leave your passengers a bit green, so I hoped he was doing well and wouldn't spray my cockpit with vomit.

Luckily, we were over a river and even though it seemed to be running higher than usual, there had to be a gravel or sand bar somewhere big enough to land a good bush plane on. The Cub bounced and swayed in the strong wind, and the sky continued to threaten as I located a potential landing spot on a gravel bar.

A quick glance back showed my passenger's white knuckles clinging to the back of my seat. I buzzed the gravel bar twice, mentally checking the length, and circled back to land. I came in at an angle, fighting the crosswind, and straightened at the last second to avoid the possibility of the wind flipping us. I could smell the sharp, quick scent of fear. Mine and the stranger's. It filled the plane as the sudden deceleration pushed us into the seat belts.

The Super Cub is the workhorse of the bush. It's small, likes to fly, carries a good load, and can take-off and land in a very short distance —luckily. I dragged my oversized Bushwheels through the water, slowing the plane, and bounced gently down the short, makeshift runway. I turned and maneuvered it for a quick take-off before I powered down.

"You doing okay back there?"

I got another affirmative grunt.

"You might as well stretch your legs; I know it gets a bit cramped back there."

I pulled off my headset and opened the door. The wind tore my long braids free and whipped them around my head. I cursed quietly and grabbed my red Tulugaq cap and jammed it down firmly, holding my hair in place.

"That was some pretty good flying." His voice was husky, deep, and rumbled from his chest.

I shrugged. I wasn't happy with my flying right now. "It's like they came out of nowhere." I scowled up at the darkened sky. "It's weird. I thought ravens were too smart to hit a plane," I spoke quietly, mostly to myself.

I didn't let on about it freaking me out. Ravens are a personal animal for me. Hitting them made me feel slightly nauseous and unbalanced.

I helped him remove the bags and gear that were pinning him down, and he stepped out.

A quick chill raised the hair on my neck and peppered me with gooseflesh. I looked around to see if anyone besides my passenger was around. No one. I brushed off the feeling. How dumb, by worrying about the ravens I'd spooked myself!

I frowned slightly at my passenger, trying to remember his name. He had a bemused smile on his face. He pushed his hat back a little. His auburn hair was peeking out, some pressed against his head with sweat. He pulled off his sunglasses and rubbed his face. When he looked up, his bright blue eyes immediately drew me in. Wow. He hadn't looked more than average at first glance, but those eyes were something. I looked away quickly.

He took a deep breath of the cool, clean air and looked around. "I can see how this country can get under your skin," he said. "Can I help you with anything?" he added after turning back to me.

"Thanks, uh, Vanice?" I stumbled through the name, hoping I'd got it right. I thought for a moment longer; no, that was right, Vanice Fletcher, but he had some kind of nickname. He flinched; I should have paid closer attention to dad when we were loading up.

"Call, me Fletch or Fletcher," he said. "Vanice was my grandfather."

"Okay, sorry. I'm Piper, by the way, like my airplane. It's a Piper Super Cub. Only I'm Piper Tikaani. I was a little distracted before. I don't remember if I told you my name." I was babbling. I shut my mouth, held out my hand, and we shook. "I'm good, with the plane, I mean. Why don't you have a look around while I check it over? Just keep an eye out for bears."

"Sure."

As he wandered away, I looked for damage. There didn't seem to be any marks, blood, or feathers on my propeller, which was good; I didn't think the ravens hit it, and I hadn't heard any change in the engine. I checked the leading edge of my wings. There was a small tear in the fabric on the right wing. I got out a roll of duct tape and fixed it. It wasn't pretty, but it would get me to Vanice's, ugh, Fletcher's cabin and back home. I didn't see anything else other than some blood down the side. I wiped it off. We were good.

I got in, pulled on my headset, tuned the radio to our air service's private channel, and pushed down the talk button on my throttle. "Tulugaq base, dad, pick me up?"

"Yeah, I got you, Pipe, okay."

"Hey, dad, we had a bird strike, Cub's fine. I had to put us down forty-two miles north- northeast of Clyde's. The front has pushed the ceiling and visibility down, and we're going to be hustling to the cabin. Would you please have mom or Baylee call and see if they can get me a later hair appointment tomorrow? I don't know if I'll make it back tonight, okay?"

"Sure thing, Piper, dad out."

I was delivering my passenger to an old family friend's cabin who had died this past fall. Fletcher had inherited it from Clyde and had never been there before. I turned off the radio and climbed back out.

I groaned inwardly. This was my third drop off flight of the day, and I was ready to be done. All I wanted was something warm in my belly and to stretch out on my comfortable bed.

The wind amped up even more. I looked up, concerned at what I saw. The clouds bore down, and the sky grew heavier and darker. I radioed Anchorage and got a weather report.

"Damn," I mumbled to myself. "Fletcher?" I called out tentatively, still not sure about his name.

"Yeah, I'm over here." He waved his hand at me from the brush over by the tree line about fifty yards back from the river.

His neutral clothing blended in well. He wore a tan shirt and faded blue jeans. He seemed to be five ten or eleven. I was average height for a woman, so he was probably only a few inches taller than me. He started back. Just then, I saw him jump to the side and whirl back to look at the tree line. I walked over to join him, concerned. I scanned the tree line to see what made him jump.

"Someone threw a rock at me." The sunglasses were back down over his eyes.

Raven gives me better eyesight than anyone I know, but there wasn't anything to see through the trees and the brush. I took in a deep breath to see if I could pick up a foreign scent.

Just then, a loud noise came from behind us and to the left, a *thwack* like wood being struck against wood. We both turned and faced that direction, spooked. I didn't have my weapon; it was in my backpack back in the Cub, but I reached behind me to the holster that I usually kept there when I was in the bush.

Thwack, thwack, thwack, again, this time rhythmically and quick. It was about five hundred feet in yet another direction; the wind had shifted, so I still couldn't pick up a scent. The hair on the back of my neck stood up. I was sure we were being watched.

"It's too loud for a woodpecker, or a ground squirrel," I mumbled.

He grunted an affirmative. We walked faster back to the plane. Fletcher's hand was behind his back, and I wondered if he had a weapon within reach like I should. I kept catching movement out of the corner of my eye, but when I turned to look, nothing was there. A large rock landed to the left of us. We picked up the pace.

"I think someone is screwing with us," Fletcher growled.

"Who?" I asked.

There wasn't anyone here for miles. No cabins. I hadn't seen any other aircraft from the air, although it was possible some hunters had this area staked out and were trying to scare us off, but I hadn't seen any signs when we flew over. Bears don't throw rocks, though.

I quickly got Fletcher resituated in the back seat, and all the gear packed back in. I climbed in and pulled on my headset, checked that Fletcher was wearing his, and flipped the intercom system on.

"The weather report stated that the ceiling is down to five hundred feet and visibility is below one mile, we're going to have to go fast or stay here for the night. It'll be rough. Are you ready?"

His answer was immediate. "Yes."

Just as I was about to shut the door, I thought I heard an unrecognizable, eerie howl. It sent a primal shiver down my spine, but I shrugged it and the feeling of being watched off as the wind and my overactive imagination. I pulled my door shut securely and fired up the engine. I blasted down the short gravel bar and the Cub lifted fast into the air, the wind screaming over the wings.

There are a few unwritten rules of the bush pilot. One is to never fly too low with a client. Alone, I had no qualms pushing myself or my ride, but it's safer to have extra air between you and the ground in case anything happens—like the raven incident.

I'd have to skim the bottom of the clouds to get us to the cabin, but I figured it was worth the risk to make it to shelter before the storm opened up and stranded us in the wilds with whatever had stalked us.

I fought the wind all the way to Fletcher's cabin. Luckily, I could see the landing strip before the low ceiling and the wind forced us out of the sky once again.

A landing strip in the bush is not a paved or even an oiled dirt road; it's equal to a cleared area where there may be a smoothed-out section, or it may just be mown grass, gravel, or a break in the trees. Clyde's strip was well used in the past, but it hadn't been tended to for over ten months. Granted, most of that was winter, and it was early enough that the grass that was growing wasn't very long. There was still snow hanging on in patches amongst the trees, but no brush had quite covered the strip yet. I circled it and scrutinized it thoroughly for branches or other debris before I put down.

Fletcher was quiet the whole way. Not because he was uninterested in talking, but to let me work through the turbulence. Now, we sat and listened to the pinging of the cooling engine. The trees blocked the wind somewhat, but an occasional gust would rock the small plane.

I radioed Tulugaq and let dad know we were here. The ceiling had dropped again, and it looked like the front that seemed to want to blow past had decided to drop a wallop of a storm after all. I'd be staying until morning. I sighed. Why did I bother making a hair appointment, anyway? I'd just make do, as usual, with hot rollers and charm for my date tomorrow night.

I huffed out a small laugh at myself, like charm was anything I had to offer.

I was shaky from fighting the stick the last forty or so minutes, and I was starving from the calorie draw. I pulled off my headset and opened the door to help Fletcher unload and get out. We secured the aircraft and started hauling his gear to the cabin.

The cabin was old, but Clyde had done some work to modernize it. It originally had one small window in the front by the door. He'd cut a window into each wall and added good, insulated glass, which slid open and had screens. The door was sturdy, handmade, solid wood.

Logs are naturally very insulating, but when Clyde had replaced the sod roof, he'd added more peak and insulated under the steel. He'd covered the inside of the roof with boards I'd hauled in with my plane. The floor was also wood, and since the cabin was older than Clyde's time, I'm sure that originally it had been dirt. He had a wooden framed bed in the far corner with a thick memory foam pad; I'd brought that to him. It was a lot more comfortable for aging bones than the old camp pads he'd used for years.

The other main corner had his stove. Clyde'd had steel flown in and built his own cook stove. Clyde liked to cook and can. He kept his kitchen area clean and neat, and the stove was a piece of functional art. You filled it with wood, and it doubled as a heater. He kept a small kerosene heater as well; I assume for when it got too warm using the stove. He had a small wooden table, two wooden chairs, and a wooden rocking chair next to a small bookcase, all hand made. There was electricity wired to the house, one outlet, an overhead light above the kitchen, and a lamp by the chair. He kept various things hanging on the walls, furs, a moose rack, some old photos—dad had taken most of those—and shelves with various things. It was a well lived-in home.

7

When we walked in, it smelled a bit musty from being shut up for such a long time. It was dusty and damp. Dad had locked everything up and taken care of any perishable foodstuffs by taking them out to burn, so it didn't smell of any rot; however, it was going to need a good scrubbing just the same.

I wrinkled my nose. "Maybe we should open the windows for a short time and air this place out."

"Good idea," Fletcher agreed.

I opened the windows. I knew we wouldn't be able to keep them open long, the temperature was dropping too fast, and the wind was still ramping up. I dug through my stuff for the matches and gathered wood to start a fire in the cookstove. Clyde had at least two years of split wood piled up along the house and shed, so it didn't take too much time or effort to build up a blaze. Clyde also had water piped to the house from the river, so I put a pot of water on to boil. Cocoa sounded good, something warm and sweet.

"I'm going to go have a look at that generator," Fletcher said after he finished stacking his gear neatly inside by the door. "I'll see if I can get it up and running."

I cleaned most of the surface dust away, washed off the table and chairs, and swept the floor while the water boiled. There wasn't much more cleaning that could be done without a day and a good scouring, but with the windows open and the bit of cleaning I'd done, the place smelled noticeably better. I have an extremely sensitive nose, so that was an instant relief. Plus, the cold wind dried out the collected moisture quickly. I was wearing my fleece-lined windbreaker, having left my heavier jacket in the plane. It was getting too cold to have the windows open, so I shut them.

Once the water was rolling in the kettle, I poured it into two mismatched, quickly cleaned mugs for the cocoa. The lights blinked on as I was stirring. Fletcher had gotten the generator running.

We'd brought up some lamp oil and candles, but we knew Clyde had refilled his fuel storage before he'd died, so we didn't need to bring any other fuel with us. The extra light unveiled the cobwebs in the corners, and the dust that had collected on the inside of the logs. I tried not to let it bother me. It wasn't my place; I could live with the dirt.

With the windows closed, the place grew toasty quickly. My stomach rumbled, and I had the beginnings of that grouchy, light-headed, "I need to eat soon" feeling. I don't let myself get too hungry; I have a lot less control over hiding my differences when I am. I pulled a military Meal Ready to Eat cheese tortellini entrée out of my back-pack. Fletcher walked in with a blast of icy air as I sorted through my backpack for a candy bar.

"Wow, it's really picked up out there," Fletcher said.

I looked around; it had grown darker. I could hear the brush of tree limbs against the metal roof, and the rattle as debris blew clear.

"Do you think it might snow?"

I frowned. It wasn't out of the question even in June, but I didn't want to get trapped here if a major snowstorm came through. "I hope not, but I guess it's possible. The weather service predicted wind, followed by fog with a slight chance of precipitation." I handed him the other mug of cocoa. We sat at the small table. "I just boiled water, and I was thinking of opening an MRE. Are you hungry?" I asked politely, although I planned to eat whether I had company or not.

"Starved. Let me dig something out of my stash," he replied.

I heated my MRE as he mixed up some of his freeze-dried food.

"Did Clyde ever mention being afraid of something out here?" he asked as we started tearing into the food like refugees.

"No, why?" I replied, curiously.

"Well, I've noticed a couple of odd things. First, look at the doors into this place." I glanced at the rear door that led to the woodpiles and outhouse, and then the door we had come in. "What about them?" They didn't look any different from the last time I was here.

"They're absolutely solid." He opened the door so I could see the edge. "They have a steel core. Look, why does he have these rein-forced bars?"

He lifted the wooden bar and slid it into its slots after he shut the door. Clyde's doors had those old-fashioned steel brackets bolted into them and the cabin, with thick boards that slid into them. I just assumed he liked that look, and it was cheaper to make them than to buy some deadbolt set.

"Why did he need floodlights?"

I thought about it for a while. Even having something that needs a light bulb, let alone a generator and electricity in the bush, is beyond extravagant. Everything that can't be brought by river had to be flown in and was extremely expensive.

Fletcher continued, "The windows are also too small to allow anyone to crawl through them. They should be bigger to let in light."

"I don't know, maybe he liked the way it looked?" I said uncertainly.

"There isn't another cabin or person for miles. He built this place like a fortress. Who's going to break in?"

"I guess I just assumed all gold miners are a little paranoid."

"The shed is the same way. It's also built from logs. He has enough steel roofing out there he could have much more easily built a metal covered shed. Yet, it has the same handmade steel core doors, and wooden braces, same with the outhouse. Also, both have food and water stashes."

I frowned; how had I failed to notice those things during the many trips I'd made here? Especially since I'd spent my growing-up years exploring every inch of the property in my various forms.

"I just never thought about it. That is odd. I'll ask dad when I get back to town if Clyde had ever said anything to him. They were friends. He hasn't ever said a thing to me, though."

I thought a little longer; my rational self overruling the nagging, instinctual alarm in the back of my head, "There is a rational explanation for everything if you think about it. In the winter, it is possible to get lost in a whiteout from here to the shed or the outhouse; there probably should be an emergency stash of food and water if you get caught in one.

Also, Clyde was a craftsman. He liked to make things; the doors could simply have been something aesthetic and functional to him. Same as the logs, they all match, and you have to admit the place looks good because it's not all mismatched and rusty.

"He also liked to work with metal." I gestured around the room at the various handmade metal objects, like the stove. "The windows are small to conserve heat and the bars, well maybe they were the easiest way to secure the doors, short of going into town and buying a lockset. It also gets dark in the winter, maybe he had the floodlights just so he could see from here to the shed."

There, that made me feel better. Everything could be rationally explained, even though it was totally impractical and expensive to haul such things out to the bush.

Fletcher frowned. "Yeah, you're probably right. I guess the way he died is making me suspicious of everything."

"No worries. I will ask, though. I'm sure there isn't anything really mysterious, but you never know." I paused for a moment, not sure if I should continue. The primitive urges to hide and flee, flirting in the back of my head, were making me uncomfortable and antsy. So, I shared them. Logically.

"On the other hand, this area, around the lake, has a history of strange happenings, unexplained lights, glimpses of unknown animals, disappearances, UFOs. Lake Iliamna even has a monster like Loch Ness!" I said lightly, jokingly, anything to lighten the mood. Clyde's place had never felt spooky to me like some places could, but these observations of Fletcher's were turning the tide on that. It was time to change the subject.

"You know, if you want to solve a mystery, here's a good one. Clyde always paid us in small glass bottles of flour gold." I paused for dramatic effect. "He didn't always know when we were coming, so I know he kept a stash somewhere that was readily available. Also, he mined all the time. So, where's the gold?"

"You think he found enough to bother hiding?" Fletcher asked.

"Yes, so does dad. We spent a lot of time trying to guess where Clyde had his gold stashed. It wasn't serious like we would look for it; it was just fun to guess. These old gold miners are notoriously paranoid and overly protective of their stash. Not that I blame them with the price of gold like it is."

"The attorney mentioned Clyde had paid him with gold. He'd left enough with the attorney for his burial, and the taxes on this place, so I didn't have to come up with anything when I took it over," Fletcher said.

"I guess it is possible he spent whatever he found to survive, but I bet he has something stashed around here, hidden. It might be fun to look." I shrugged.

"It will give me something to do after I inventory everything and decide what I need." Fletcher was quiet for a while, thoughtful, then he looked around the cabin. "I feel sort of strange going through this man's things, living in his home, talking about him, and I don't even know what he looked like, but here I am a stranger, dissecting his life, living in his personal space."

I threw up a hand. "Hold that thought!" I grabbed my backpack and dug around. I'd slipped in a couple of photos of Clyde, thinking it would be nice to show them to the new owner, who I thought would be a relative of some sort, but then in the midst of all that had gone on today, I'd forgotten. I handed them to him.

"This is a picture of Clyde and dad the summer before last. They were fishing on Ship Creek for kings." I lifted an eyebrow in question. I didn't know if he knew what king salmon were, but he nodded. I let him examine it. "This one is Clyde, here, in front of my plane." I watched Fletcher study the photos for a minute, and I tried to look at Clyde with fresh eyes. He had always appeared to be a man haunted to me. His mouth was smiling in the photos, but his eyes were always sad, in pain. He never spoke of what had driven him into the bush, but it must have been devastating to fill his eyes with such despair.

"I have dad's police statement, about Clyde's death. I'm not sure if you want to read it, it's a little disturbing, and since then, my dad won't talk about it. Reading it is better than me trying to tell you everything that happened, even though I know you know the basics. Dad was quite thorough in describing exactly what happened. I thought it may be something you'd be interested in." I was nervous about showing the report to him. It felt personal, because dad explained his thoughts and feelings as well as the details of finding his dead friend. Still, I figured it was more Fletcher's business than mine at this point.

He took the paper gently from my fingers, glanced at me a moment, and bent his head to read. His face remained stoic throughout —even though I knew the content was disturbing.

"Your dad is a descriptive writer."

"Yeah, he doesn't talk much, but he gets a little wordy when he writes."

"Thanks, Piper. I appreciate you sharing this with me." He handed it back. I folded it and stuffed it back into my pack. "Did the police ever discover any reason why he was on the roof?"

"Just guesses, but the fact he had pulled up the ladder throws all their guesses off." I shrugged, tired of guessing and of wondering what had happened.

I hurriedly changed the subject. "You said you were a stranger. I thought you were Clyde's relative?"

He looked at me for a moment. "No. Clyde left everything to my grandmother. I don't know how they were involved. I'm the only one of my family left, so I inherited everything by default."

I didn't know what to say, so I nodded. "Any particular place you want me to sleep?" I asked, although my heart was set on the foam bed.

He gave me a sexy crooked smile, mischief glinting in his eyes, and I gathered up a short retort, when he said, "You have your pick of any spot," he paused. "On the floor." He laughed as I turned pink, anticipating some chauvinist remark.

Realizing what he said, I opened my mouth to tell him what I thought.

He chuckled. "You can take the bed, but I'd like to know what you thought I was going to say."

"I bet you would," I mumbled as I spread my sleeping bag out over the memory foam.

The morning found me waking up disoriented, too hot, and trapped. I lay still and tried not to panic as I attempted to orient myself. Slowly, it

came back to me as I focused on the log wall. I was at Clyde's, no…
Fletcher's cabin, in his bed, with his arm around me. I relaxed.

"What!" I thrashed. "Get off me!" I wiggled my bag to the bottom
of the bed and stood up. "What do you think you're doing?"

"Well, I was sleeping, finally," He stated groggily.

"I thought you slept on the floor," I whined.

"I tried to," He yawned. "But between your snoring, and the stench
down there, I wasn't having much success." He rubbed his face. "Then
you turned over and faced the wall, and left that invitingly empty
stretch of bed, so…here I am."

"I didn't think you'd try something like that."

"Like what? You were in your sleeping bag, and I was in mine. It's
difficult to steal someone's virtue from inside a mummy bag."

I'd lost the argument. It was his bed, after all, and I was as alone in
my sleeping bag as he was in his. It didn't keep me from glaring at him as
I redressed in my bag from the clothes I'd shoved down at the bottom the
night before. Sure, they get a few wrinkles like that, but they're toasty
warm when you put them back on. After nearly dislocating my shoulders,
I was redressed and free of the bag. I yanked on my shoes and my jacket.

"I'm going out to check on the Cub and the weather," I said as I
pulled open the door. It was completely still outside. There was a light
fog, but it was enough to make the silence eerie. I'd grown up here
more or less. Never did I have as intense a feeling of being watched as
I did now. The eerie silence felt sinister.

My radio call ensured that Anchorage was clear, so once the fog
burnt off here, I was free to go. I took my time going back to the
cabin, embarrassed at how I'd acted. I was mad at being spooked by
the fog, and sad to abandon a place that felt like home to a stranger.
So, I took my time looking over my plane, did my preflight, and
checked on my repair job, all before heading back in.

"I'm sorry about the way I acted," I said as I walked in.

Fletcher was sitting on his bed, dressed, rubbing his hands over his
face and hair to wake up. "Don't worry about it," he replied.

"I can leave as soon as this fog burns off. Why don't I load our numbers into your sat phone while we wait, so you can get a hold of us as you need?"

"Good idea. Harder to lose that way," he replied.

I loaded the numbers to Tulugaq, my satellite phone, and my personal cell into his sat phone so he could reach our flight service anytime. I stuffed my sleeping bag into its compression sack and picked up my small mess. "Do you want me to help you check out the meat cache before I go? I could hold the ladder." I was still trying to make up for biting his head off for no reason.

"Sure, at least I'll have an idea what I'm up against," he said with a smile.

I peered up at the meat cache, a good ten feet in the air above my head. The wind had stirred and picked up, slowly clearing the fog. It was blowing away from me, so luckily, I couldn't smell it, but I could imagine that it wouldn't be pleasant. Fletcher leaned the ladder he had brought over from where it lay against the house onto the small ledge that ran in front of the cache. I held it steady as he climbed up and opened the door to glance inside.

"It's empty," he yelled down at me.

"What? That can't be! I know it was full before Clyde died. Was the door secured?"

"Yes, it has the same mechanism as the house, just on the outside," he started down. "Go have a look."

Curious, I started up the ladder. There was no way that meat cache should be empty, unless Clyde had emptied it shortly before he died. It should be full of meat. I looked inside. I believed Fletcher, but I was still surprised it was perfectly empty. Only the long-gone whisper of old bloodstains and the slight smell of old blood remained. I climbed down.

"Well, at least you won't have to clean it out," I said as I shook my head. "That's just bizarre."

"He could have just cleaned it out before he died, planning for new meat," Fletcher said.

"I guess, but I swear dad said he helped Clyde put some fresh moose up there only a week before he died," I replied, but I could be off by a few weeks. It was hard to remember for sure.

"Maybe it went bad, and he disposed of it."

"Yeah, I'm sure it's no big deal. At least you don't have to deal with the stench."

He looked thoughtful and glanced back up at the cache, measuring its height with his eyes. "I am curious about one thing, though. Last night, on the floor, I got a distinctly rotten odor—somewhere between dead meat, burnt onions, and skunk—coming in on the wind from under the door. It lasted for some time, so I climbed up into the bed. Last night, I told myself it came from the meat cache. The question is, what was it?"

Chapter 2

I looked at my phone and groaned. "Five o'clock already!" I mumbled as I juggled everything over to one hand so I could unlock my door.

Raleigh was picking me up in one hour, and I hadn't had a shower in two days. Then there was my hair. I threw my wallet and packages onto the couch and started stripping on my way to the shower. At least my new dress was made from that knit, shiny stuff that never seemed to wrinkle. He was taking me to a restaurant and then the theater, and I didn't even own a dress, thus the shopping splurge.

I left it in the bag as I scrambled to get in the shower as fast as I could. It took forever for my hair to dry. Once unbraided, it fell past the middle of my back, thick and wavy. I hated to blow it dry since that dried it out so much, but I didn't have a choice. I scrubbed and shaved as fast as I could and dressed hurriedly so I could do something with my hair and face. Luckily my complexion was good, clear, and slightly tanned from working outside. I could do with the briefest of eye shadow, mascara, and lipstick. I dried my hair while the rollers heated up and brushed my teeth. I checked the time on my phone, down to twenty-five minutes. After I rolled my hair up and left it to cook, I went to put on my shoes. That's when I realized I had forgotten to buy any.

I had planned on buying a pair of maroon short-heeled Mary Jane's I had admired in the online circular I'd perused over the weekend, or if that failed some black ballet flats, since I rarely wore heels.

"Dammit, dammit, dammit," I mumbled as I kicked my discarded clothes over to join the rest of the dirty laundry pile and crawled into my closet looking for something I could walk in. I came up for air with a pair of strappy red sandals with four-inch heels I'd bought once in a delusional state—and the encouragement of a friend—and never worn. *Great, after walking from the parking lot to the restaurant, and then the block to the theater, I'd have to be hauled home in an ambulance. What stupid things women do for beauty!* I thought as I frowned at the shoes in my hand.

After I removed the rollers and finished my hair, I walked into the dining room to look myself over in the full-length wall of mirrors. My house was built in the seventies; it wasn't my decorating choice. Although my hair didn't have the movie star waves I was going for, it looked fine, dark curls brushing down my back and framing my oval-shaped face. My new black, wraparound dress accentuated my small waist and softened up my curves. It had three quarter length sleeves and fell just below my knees. I had been putting fake tanner on my legs for a week, so they had a nice glow, and I didn't have to deal with hose. I wore my diamond tennis bracelet—a gift from my parents—and a simple long rectangular moonstone pendant hung from a silver chain to rest between my breasts. I actually looked feminine and maybe a little elegant. The red stripper heels were a bit much, but they made my legs look good, anyway. I was finally ready, and I had three minutes to spare!

I flopped down in my oversized leather chair with a sigh. It felt good to be home for a minute. I knew if I had to wait too long, I would talk myself out of going. I looked at the clock on my phone. I didn't really know much about Raleigh. I'd met him coming and going at the airport. He was also a bush pilot, but he worked for one of the top companies. He usually worked out of Talkeetna, but since he had family in town, I ran into him occasionally. He always went out of his way to be nice to me, which isn't always the case being a woman in a man's world, and he treated me like an equal. That was his major selling point.

His neatly trimmed hair was dark blond with that natural sun-bleached look that outdoorsy people tend to have. He wasn't much taller than me, which was another reason I hated the red heels. His brown eyes, nothing like Fletcher's bright blue, were nice, warm. He seemed to be well put together, as far as I could tell. Most of the bush pilots I knew weren't dressing to make a fashion statement at work, considering our business requirements.

I leaned my head back in my comfy chair, careful not to muss my hair. He was a bit thin lipped for me, I mused as I imagined the rakish, crooked smile and the sexy, upturned corners of Fletcher's mouth.

I shot up in the chair. "What am I doing?" I said aloud. Here I was thinking about one man and going out with another! Again, I checked my phone for the time; it was two minutes 'til. My palms started sweating.

"What am I doing?" I mumbled to myself, again. I don't go out much. Mostly because I don't get asked out. I'm not really a people person. I don't really trust anyone because of my little differences.

I can hide it. I don't have to shift; the moon doesn't affect me. I just have some odd quirks that are easier to hide if I concentrate, like that little bit of eye shine humans don't have in the dark and the extra senses. Sometimes I'm a little too quick or a little too strong for a human woman. But, like I said, if I'm paying attention, I can hide it. It's just that a real relationship would be difficult because I'd always be hiding the true me. Which is why I have no real relationships. Not that I've really had anyone knocking down my door. Still, I hope that someone might come along with whom I could share my secret.

I sighed. "Do I really want to do this?" I said aloud, seriously contemplating calling Raleigh and bailing. Fortunately, or unfortunately, I'm not sure which, the doorbell rang. I teetered over, grabbing my jacket as I went, and with a painted-on smile, opened the door.

Warm sunlight directly in my face woke me up the next morning. The sheets were tangled around me, and my hair was a noose around my neck. I was so tired last night that I hadn't bothered to braid it out of the way. I had to go into work at one, so this was my time to do what cleaning I felt like and wash my clothes. I contemplated going back to sleep as I lay there looking at the ceiling, but since I was out of underwear, I had to get up. The summer, even the beginning of the summer, was busy for bush pilots. I had to get up and at 'em regardless of the fact I didn't do mornings.

Sometimes I wished I had a useful power like telekinesis, so I could do everything from bed. Unfortunately, being able to change shape didn't do much in the way of help except eliminate the opposable thumb. Since I needed that thumb to pour in laundry detergent and turn on the washing machine, it was no help at all.

Before work, I pulled out my last load and got dressed in my "uniform," as dad calls it, which amounted to broken-in jeans, a t-shirt with a blue, checkered, flannel shirt over it, and whatever weight of jacket the weather demanded. I braided my hair, put on a battered Tulugaq cap, and headed over nearly forty-five minutes early—so not like me. I wanted to talk to dad about the odd things that Fletcher had noticed and see if Clyde had confided any fears to him. I had to do a babysitting job on a new pilot today so I wouldn't really get a chance later.

Dad was on the phone, flipping through his calendar when I got there. Even though we're small, we've developed a good reputation with a couple of local hunting guides and outfitters, so we were nearly completely booked for the season. It looked like dad was going to fill up the few remaining slots.

"How was your date, Pipe?" Dad asked after he hung up. This was an object of either amusement or torture for him, I wasn't sure which. It made both of us uncomfortable to talk about my dating.

"Fine, dad." I shrugged, as embarrassed as he was.

"Are you going to go out with him again?" he asked with a straight, but pained face, fulfilling his fatherly duties as outlined by my mom. I was definitely not, but I really didn't want to talk about it with anyone. Especially since it was an unmitigated disaster.

"I don't know, Dad, probably not. I promise I'll call Mom, so you don't have to know," I said vaguely.

"Good." He looked relieved. He glanced at his watch and back up at me.

"I wanted to ask you something," I said.

"I wondered why you were early." He smirked.

I winced. I did have a pattern. "Come on, I'm not that bad."

"Yes, actually, you are."

It was an ongoing family joke that I was late for everything. It wasn't exactly true. Things just ended up getting in the way of my attention—often.

"Fletcher, you know, the guy I took out to Clyde's place." I clarified for Dad; he wasn't great with names. "He noticed some odd things out there, and I said I'd ask you if Clyde had mentioned anything weird happening at his place."

"You mean other than him dead on the roof?"

"Yes Dad, other than that." I rolled my eyes.

"Why?"

"Well, for starters, the doors have a steel core, and he built everything unusually sturdy. The flood lights, oh, and the fact that the meat cache was completely empty."

This time he looked up at me. "What do you mean empty?"

"Just what I said. I held the ladder while Fletcher climbed up to check out the mess, and it was empty, not a scrap of meat in it."

"That is odd." He frowned to himself, thinking.

"Did Clyde ever say anything to you about anything weird happening, or being afraid?"

"No, sweetie, he didn't. You know Clyde, he was always high-strung, maybe even leaning to paranoid, but he never said anything out of the ordinary for him." He thought for a minute. "You know everything can be explained pretty easily, especially when you add in Clyde's gold paranoia."

"Yeah, I know, but Fletcher had me a little spooked when he started pointing things out. You're right, it's probably nothing." I could think that, but at the same time, Clyde's weird death pointed to something

21

not quite right. It was just hard to know, considering there could be a logical explanation for even the way he died. I pushed it to the back of my mind for a while.

"So, is the 206 ready?" Dad asked. We were trying out a new pilot today. He was a low hour pilot with a fresh commercial license.

We had one mail contract, and since it was approaching hunting season, we usually took on an extra pilot. Since our last guy had graduated on to his next big job, we picked up a low hour pilot to give him the experience he needed. It was cheaper for us, and a pilot could be paid to earn his hours. I was the lucky sitter today, so I got to fly with him to make sure he was competent, comfortable with the plane, and familiar with the route before we turned him loose.

"I fueled it up, but I'll let him do the rest, and see what he's got," I replied.

I sat in my favorite folding chair in the office as I waited for the new pilot and scrolled through my phone. I had a couple of voicemails, so I hit the call button to listen to them. The first one was from my mom, of course, asking about my date. I rolled my eyes; I'd have to call her when I got back. I erased that message and listened to the second.

It was my best friend, Branwyn. She probably wanted to hear about my date, but knowing her natural intuitive self, I bet it was more. I skipped it for later.

The last message was from Fletcher. "Piper, this is Fletcher." I sat up straighter, my interest piqued. It was just him calling in with his list, and I mentally kicked myself for reacting to his voice. I still had time, so I picked up my logbook to update my entries.

A logbook is a valuable tool for a pilot. There is the official FAA logbook that keeps track of aircraft engine hours and maintenance. Most pilots keep another one to track their flight hours for licensure. In it, pilots make record of essential details from each flight: takeoffs, landings, distances, passengers, etc. I checked my book and made sure I logged my last flight. I like to add notes about my days as well, and it's faster than a diary although not as detailed. I was finishing up when the new pilot finally walked in.

"Hi, I'm Steve." He extended his hand to Dad. Dad shook it.

"This is Piper, she's going to go up with you, show you the ropes." Dad gestured over at me, and Steve turned to look.

Luckily for him, he had a good game face. Most men—however modern they think they are—look disappointed at getting a flying lesson from a woman. At least, that has been my experience.

"Hey, Steve!" I stood and shook his hand. "Welcome. Do you have your charts?"

He nodded.

"I'm sure you're familiar with the route. I'll just show you some landmarks—check out some tricky wind areas. This is just routine; you should be comfortable by the time we get back." I could smell his nervous sweat, so I added, "It'll be fun!" I laughed, trying to put him at ease, although flying around in an aircraft I was not piloting was the last thing I wanted to do.

Dad threw me a strained look. He knew I was trying too hard, but as long as Steve didn't know, I was good.

"Let's go!" I pushed open the door into the sunshine, trying to think my happy thoughts while repeating the mantra, *Just another new guy, it will be over soon.*

The flight seemed to last forever, but once I got back, I reported to dad about the new pilot, got him squared away, and updated my logbook.

After work, I headed the fifteen miles to my parent's house to pick up my sister and head to the gym. I honked outside the house, trying to avoid a confrontation with my mom about my date. Luckily, my sister was on the same wavelength, because she came barreling out the front door, carrying her gym bag, her ponytails bobbing behind her. My sister is the fair Irish child my mother always wanted. We looked like we came from different planets.

My father's Inupiaq. I'm light-skinned for a part-native, but still a lot browner than my super fair, Irish born mother. Baylee looked like she fell off the potato wagon. The native genes she got from my dad had completely passed her by in looks and in the Raven's gift. She was strawberry blonde, with peaches and cream skin, and the personality and build of a cheerleader. The only things we shared were green eyes and naturally wavy hair. Her eyes were light-colored, like clear glass, and mine were dark green and stormy.

She tossed her bag in on the bench seat and bounced in. "You better hurry, before Mom gets to the door and waves you down."

I didn't waste any time pulling away from the curb.

"You owe me for one save from mom!" she said brightly as I pulled out onto the main road and headed toward the gym.

"You got it. What do you want?"

"I want you to fly us to the beach and spend the day with me!"

"You know I'd love to, but we're booked. I don't know when I could get a full day to do it."

"Please?"

"If I get a day off, and it's sunny, we'll go." I promised.

"So, how was your date?" Baylee asked, giving me a sidelong look.

She knew it was a painful subject for me because my mom was relentless in her pursuit of a son-in-law and grandchildren. Mom didn't think my issues were that much of an obstacle; she lived in her own world for sure.

"Ugh! Are you kidding?"

Baylee laughed. "No, I want to know. Did he kiss you? Did he bring you flowers?"

Sometimes I forgot the fifteen-year gap between our ages, and that my sister was in middle school. She thought dating was romantic, and magical. I have to admit—I liked to play that up somewhat and probably contributed to her fantasies. I wanted to tell her he brought me a dozen roses, but I didn't. She'd just want to see them.

"No flowers, and it was our first date!" I said subtly avoiding the topic.

"Is he cute?"

"Yes, but you don't tell guys they're cute." I winked at her.

"Is he going to ask you out again?"

"I don't know; he doesn't really live here."

"Do you want him to ask you out again?"

"I don't know, not really I guess." I really didn't. The date had been epically bad, and I didn't want to remember it, let alone talk about it with my kid sister.

"I can see why mom's always on your case, you're too picky!" she huffed.

I turned and stared at her, stunned. "How rude, I can't believe you said that! You know I have to be picky."

She blushed and hung her head. "I'm sorry, sis." She was quiet a minute. Then in a repentant tone, she said, "I know you have to be." Her brow creased with empathy, but her natural sunny disposition won out. "Come on and let's go see if we can get two machines together." Sometimes it's nice to hang out with someone who really has no worries.

Later, I snuck Baylee home to avoid my mom, and promised to take her to the movies on Friday.

Chapter 3

My daily routine in the summer is drop off hunters, pick up hunters, or drop in supplies. Since Alaska is so large, unpopulated, and unroaded, if that's a word, the primary form of transportation in the bush is by aircraft. So, during the good weather months, the airports are beehives of activity, and Anchorage airspace is the most crowded in the nation. Just in town you have Ted Stevens International Airport, Merrill Field, several private airstrips, and Elmendorf Air Force Base all within ten miles of each other. Lake Hood, where I fly from is nearly on top of the International Airport, with small planes coming in on wheels, skis, or floats. It's a carefully choreographed dance of disaster waiting to happen; it keeps my senses sharp, and I love every second of it.

My days basically ran from one to the other as I pick up or drop off. Before I knew it, a week had passed. It was Wednesday, and I was loading Fletcher's requested supplies into my plane. I hadn't even had time to analyze my attraction to him, so I was suddenly feeling odd about going back. I took firm control of myself and put my focus back on the task at hand.

Thankfully, my second flight to the cabin was uneventful, as most flying should be—one of those lazy summer days, when the sky is so blue it makes your eyes ache to look at. Bright sunshine, just the barest hint of a breeze, the lazy drone of an insect, and the slightest gurgle from the nearby stream made Fletcher's place an absolute picture of peace and contentment. That watched feeling wasn't evident today; the bright sunshine erased the sinister greeting the place emoted the first time I was here with Fletcher. In fact, I would have enjoyed stretching out in the grass in my swimsuit and working on my tan.

I sighed. If I wanted a tan, I had to go to a tanning salon in the fifteen minutes of free time I got during the summer, otherwise I had to fake it. I started pulling things out of the plane. By the time I finished, Fletcher had shown up, and I helped him carry his supplies to his cabin. Unfortunately, his eyes were still as blue, his sensuous mouth was still as kissable, and his jeans still fit too well. I was in deep trouble. As I was heading back out to get in the Cub, he cleared his throat. Neither one of us had said more than the usual polite greeting.

"Piper," he started, then fell silent.

"What's up?" I asked, conversationally.

"Do you remember you told me to look for Clyde's stash?"

"Sure." I nodded.

"Well." He stopped and looked back at the cabin. He pulled off his cap and scratched his head as if making up his mind. "Come with me." Putting his cap back on, he waved me back towards the cabin and I followed him in, curiously.

"You found it?" I asked.

He grinned, and I felt my breath catch.

He was silent for a long moment; I could only guess that he was having some internal dialogue about what to say to me.

"Yeah."

He paused for a while, and I waited. Something else was going on. I could feel it in my bones, an extra sense for trouble that came with my relation to Raven. I didn't say anything else. I was starting to think he was a man of few words.

He pointed to a small bag on the table. I glanced at him for confirmation, and then I opened it. Gold. Gold in small bars and coins. My brow furrowed. I looked at Fletcher questioningly.

"Where did Clyde get bars and coins?" I asked.

Fletcher shrugged. With the shrug, that itch of anxiety became more. The back of my neck prickled; my heart began to beat faster. A tendril of fear traced its icy finger down my spine. And the confirmation that something was odd, maybe even dangerous came with his words.

"Someone's been looking for it," he finally said.

I started as the gooseflesh erupted on my skin with his words. I looked around, letting the shivers settle.

Fletcher came back to town with me since he needed to do a few things and hadn't had a chance before. He was quiet as I loaded him in and took off. It wasn't until we were halfway back to Lake Hood that he opened up. It's hard to speak normally in a small aircraft. The engine noise is just too loud, so you have to speak through your headsets.

"Piper," he started.

"Yup."

"How private is the channel we're on?"

"It's not a radio channel, it's an intercom," I answered.

He was silent for a moment. "I found a lot of gold."

I threw a quick glance at him over my shoulder. "What do you mean a lot?"

"Bags of it, all kinds, flour gold, and nuggets, and…more, like you saw, all cleverly hidden around the property."

"How much?"

"I have no idea how to judge how much it is worth, but I'd say millions."

I was stunned. "Millions?" The only thing I could do was repeat what he had said.

"I think so." He was quiet again for a stretch.

"Back there, you said someone is looking for it. How do you know that?" I asked.

I couldn't guess how anyone would find the cabin or know about the gold. The cabin could be reached by air. Otherwise, someone could, with effort, bring a small kayak up the river. It was possible, especially in the spring. However, it was highly unlikely that Clyde's cabin would ever see another human being who didn't know it was there. It was remote. It was difficult to get to. His mining operation wasn't easy to see from the cabin and less likely to be stumbled upon. Clyde didn't know many people. The anxiety amped up again.

"There are places that look like they've been dug up, and I've noticed things moved or missing around the property," he continued.

"Have you seen anyone?"

He hesitated. "No, I haven't. I just have this feeling of being watched sometimes. I know it sounds crazy, and I'm sure you're thinking I'm being paranoid, but I'm not. Something is going on."

"I believe you." I really did. That weird extra sense screamed that something was wrong. It had been ever since Clyde died. I'd kept shoving it down or ignoring it since I had no way to discover what was wrong and no idea where to start. Now there was something out there to find. We finished the trip in silence, both of us lost in our thoughts. I couldn't let it go. Now I knew something was going on for sure, my Raven nature wouldn't let me rest until I had done something or knew what had happened. I resolved to do some research when we made it back. I wanted to know what killed Clyde. I wasn't sure how to go about it, but I had to get my hands on the autopsy report.

After I set the Cub down, and we were listening to the engine cool, Fletcher asked, "Do you mind giving me a lift to the library?"

"No problem," I replied, but I was a little hurt that he wouldn't confide in me further. I wanted him to trust me. I was already involved; what could more information hurt? Surely, he wasn't worried I'd go after his gold. My mind raced. I stopped in to let dad know that I would be back soon then took Fletcher to the library.

I needed some time on the internet, but I only had time to grab lunch, and take care of my next client. Since it was only a supply run, I made an impulse stop afterwards. It was early evening, but the light lasted a long time. I landed a few miles away from Fletcher's cabin after scanning the area for any spies. I took care of the aircraft, and after a few furtive glances around to make sure I was completely alone, I stripped off my clothes, placed them neatly in the cockpit, and changed into my raven form.

I flew to Fletcher's cabin to have a look around without disrupting any possible surveillance that may be occurring. Who would suspect a curious raven? The best thing about being a raven is that I can see much better. Ravens can see small objects at a half mile away, which was useful as I looked over the property from the air. It was easier from the air to see that Fletcher was right. There were some covered over holes around his outbuildings. They were old, but still visible from the air.

It looked like someone had tried to dig under the walls, which didn't make sense since the buildings weren't left locked, only closed. I scanned the woods and stream around the property, but only saw normal wildlife. I decided I could safely land and change again. I landed lightly, sheltered by the cabin, and changed into my wolf form.

In wolf form, I had the benefit of my extra strong nose. First, I sniffed around the holes I had noticed from the air. I smelled Fletcher and dismissed that. I searched under that but wasn't sure what I smelled. I picked up the scent of another wolf, but it was very faint, and overlaid by a strong odor of something I couldn't identify.

The worst thing about being a wolf is identifying the odors. If I hadn't smelled it before—and identified it—I wouldn't know what it was. The scent pinged something familiar in the back of my mind, but I couldn't pin it down. As I circled the property, I found the unidentified smell overlaying everything to the point that after a while I couldn't smell anything else. I finally sat down and sneezed with frustration.

I needed to find some clue to help me figure out what was going on, and my best weapons were turning up nothing. I rubbed my nose against my leg and trotted down to the river to get a drink. This might be my only chance to look around without being observed, and I was blowing it.

I would like to think I was deep in thought, because as a wolf, I should not have been caught with my metaphorical pants down. Yet, as I stood with my front paws in the cold water, taking my drink, a deep growl surprised me. I whipped around, planting all four feet in the water, as the fur on the back of my neck stood up. Standing at the top of a bank was the biggest wolf I had ever seen.

When I change into a raven, I'm a large raven, but well within the weight and average range of your general Corvus Corax. When I change into a wolf, I retain my mass. My dad thinks that the laws of physics don't apply in the wake of magic. I like to think that the laws of physics just haven't been discovered to explain the world of magic yet, mostly because who's studying them? Regardless, I weigh about 147 pounds as a regular person. I stay 147 pounds as a wolf. That's large for a wolf although Alaska wolves have been known to get over 150 pounds.

The wolf facing me probably had a hundred pounds on me or more. He was long and heavily muscled through the chest and shoulders, his legs were sturdy and thick, and even his head and jaws seemed thicker and heavier than a regular wolf. His fur was mainly tan with grey and charcoal points, coloring typical to this area. His freakish size, and uncharacteristically large chest, made me wonder if he had some sort of mixed heritage with either Saint Bernard or sled dog somewhere in his ancestry.

Studying him, I forgot for a moment that the other wolf's mouth was full of teeth, all longer and sharper than mine, and I was staring. In wolf language, that spells *challenge*. My human mind started repeating, "*Oh Grandmother, what big teeth you have,*" while jabbering to itself to run or get eaten. Luckily my wolf instinct took over and demanded I show submission. I lowered my head and body into the stream, tucked my tail, and waited for the big bad wolf to eat me. I knew I didn't have enough distance to run far enough away to change and fly higher than he could reach me, so I said a silent prayer that he would accept my submission and turn away.

He took a few steps closer to me, sniffing the air that blew over me directly to him. I tensed. I didn't know what a wild wolf would do if he smelled human on me. I didn't think that I retained any human smell, but my scent was too familiar to me to be sure. He must not have smelled anything odd, because he let me turn tail and retreat. I glanced behind me a couple of times, but he didn't follow. I hadn't picked up a scent from him, as the wind was blowing away from me. I itched to go back and see where he came from, get a good whiff to place his scent, but I was terrified.

Fear made up my mind. Once I judged that I was far enough away he couldn't grab me, I switched back to raven form, forgoing my superior nose for the safety of the air, and flew back to check out the wolf from the air. He was gone; at least, I couldn't see him. I thought I glimpsed fur deep in the woods, but it moved away quickly, and I wasn't sure what it was. It wasn't tan/grey like the wolf, so it could have been a bear or a moose.

I was feeling the strain of three rapid changes, and I still had to fly back to the Cub. I couldn't investigate much longer. My plan was a bust. I was more frustrated than before and had learned nothing except that Fletcher had a lot of wildlife around his cabin. Big whoop, there's a lot of wildlife everywhere around here.

Shape-changing, though natural and easy for me, sucked calories like crazy, so I was light-headed and starving by the time I hit Minnesota Drive. I grabbed a couple of burgers and fries and ate hurriedly in my truck. I wanted to get home to do some research. I didn't know when I'd hear from Fletcher again. I had him scheduled to go back on Friday, but I didn't know if he'd contact me before then.

First on my list, how do I get a copy of Clyde's autopsy? I opened my laptop and searched the internet. After looking around for a few minutes, all I could find was that only next of kin could get a report. There was a number to call at the state medical examiner's office. Since Clyde had no next of kin, I didn't know what to do to get one. Would Fletcher count as next of kin? As it was long past work hours, I couldn't call today. I wrote down the number and made a mental note to check on it during business hours tomorrow.

I wondered if Fletcher would mind sharing that information with me, or if he'd even find it important. He seemed so closed up about the gold; I was wary about asking him for fear he'd think that I was meddling in private things. I tried to push Fletcher to the back of my mind and looked up the wolf subspecies we had around Alaska. Something about that wild wolf I'd seen at Fletcher's was bothering me. At a quick glance, you would think to yourself, "*big wolf!*" but I had more than a quick glance. I wasn't a wildlife expert, but I knew a little about local wolves.

In my childhood I'd explored the area around the cabin and interacted with wolves and other creatures. That wolf wasn't normal. It took a couple of hours to find an animal that sort of fit the wolf I had seen. I tried looking under Alaskan wolves, wolves of North America, wolf species, I even tried wolf dogs and coyotes, and then I switched to large dog breeds. I didn't come close until I stumbled onto cryptids.

I found a drawing depicting Amarok, a large wolf spirit from Inuit mythology. That reminded me of the Inupiaq word for wolf, Amaguq and I leaned close to the screen, interested, but all the internet said was that Amarok was an Inuit legend for a large wolf-shaped trickster god. I pulled on my braids in frustration and went into the kitchen for a snack. I came back with a chunk of frozen chocolate chip cookie dough and potato chips.

As I investigated, I found a closer description of my wolf that matched that of an ice age relic called the dire wolf, thought to be extinct for nine thousand years. My wolf went from being a curiosity to part of the mystery surrounding Fletcher's cabin. I tried to find more about the creature on the internet, but there wasn't much that I trusted. I looked for local experts, someone to talk to who wouldn't laugh me out of the room and found a listing for a local cryptozoologist. It wasn't easy to find. I had to pick a name from an article and find out if they were local, and search for a phone number. By the time I finished, it was almost eleven o'clock and too late to call.

I'm the last person to judge what others believe in, and since I could be considered a "cryptid," I didn't want to assume this person was a kook. Still, I hoped that the "Dr." listed in front of his name meant he had a degree in something legitimate. I wrote down the number I'd found and exhausted, I headed to bed.

At nine sharp the next morning, I dialed the medical examiner's office. I was lucky and got someone on the first try, probably because I beat everyone to it.

"State Medical Examiner, this is Mary speaking." Her voice already sounded tired at the beginning of the workday.

"Hi, I have kind of an odd question."

"Yes?" Mary asked bored and uninterested.

"How does a person go about obtaining an autopsy report if the person has no next of kin?"

"That doesn't usually happen." She sniffed.

"But if it does, what is the procedure?" I pressed.

"Well, I suppose it would have to be someone who had power of attorney, or some legal right to the information." This stated as though I were an idiot. Which I probably was in this instance.

"Could it be a legal heir?"

"Yes," she drawled out, almost as though she weren't completely sure.

"Thank you very much!" I added hurriedly.

"You're welcome." The phone clicked; her last word cut off as she got off the phone quickly.

I sat alone with my thoughts. Now, did I dare bring it up to Fletcher? Would he let me in enough to work together on this, or should I attempt to proceed on my own? I pondered for a while but kept coming back to the fact that I had to know what the autopsy showed, and Fletcher was the only one who could get the information. I mentally put it aside for now.

Next on my list was to contact a Dr. Frederick G. Burns, my cryptozoologist. I was more than a little nervous about doing so since I wasn't sure if I was going to find a serious answer or a guy with a crystal ball and a divining rod. I didn't trust the information I would get over the phone, because I couldn't judge his character and seriousness by voice. I dialed the number on his website.

"Hello, Dr. Burns's office," a pleasant female voice answered. A good sign, so far. It didn't appear the good doctor worked out of an underground bunker, at least.

"Hi, my name is Piper Tikaani. I was wondering if the doctor was available to speak to me sometime today."

"Are you a student?" she asked.

"No, I have a question about…" I wasn't sure what to include here, so I tried to keep it vague. "Local wildlife."

"What is your contact information?" I gave her my name again, and my cell number. I could hear her pen scribbling on her desk.

"Is there something more specific you have a question about? A certain species?"

I scrambled for a moment to come up with something plausible that didn't make me sound like a raving lunatic, but then I thought, *"What am I worried for? The dude is advertising himself as a cryptozoologist!"*

"I saw a dire wolf!" I blurted out, a little ashamed of myself for not approaching this calmly and scientifically as I had planned. The secretary was quiet for a moment, long enough for a cool bead of sweat to form along my hairline.

"Dr. Burns is a respectable Wildlife Biologist at this University." I could hear the capital letters she added for effect. "We do *not* appreciate crank calls." A click and a dial tone followed.

Needless to say, I was confused. I looked up the website again to make sure I'd dialed the correct number. I checked the number with my cell phone log, and sure enough, it was the same. Shrugging, I began to search the internet for another "expert" when my phone rang. It came up as a blocked number, so I hesitated a moment before answering.

"Hello?" I asked tentatively.

"Is this a Ms. Tikaani?" a deep bass rumble asked.

"Yes, this is she," I said firmly.

"Ms. Tikaani, this is Dr. Burns. You just called?"

"Yes. I wasn't sure if I had reached the correct number. I found your name on a website for a Dr. Burns who is a cryptozoologist. I'm sorry I bothered you," I replied.

"No, no bother. I *am* a cryptozoologist." His voice was sure and firm.

"I'm confused. Your secretary said you were a wildlife biologist," I protested, not sure if I was being had.

"I'm both Ms. Tikaani. I'd like to apologize for my assistant. She is a department secretary, filling in for my usual assistant. She wasn't aware of my other, uh, hobby. I didn't realize my office number was still on my website. I'll remedy that immediately. I have a private cell phone for my other business. I believe you mentioned seeing a cryptid?" he continued.

"Yes, well at least I think I did."

"Would you like to tell me about it?" His voice was eager.

"Uh, I'd like to, but I'd rather do it in person. Is there a time we could meet?" I replied.

"Yes, my next class doesn't begin until this evening. How would you like to meet over lunch? Say noon at the pancake house on Benson and Northern Lights?"

"That would be great. I'll meet you there," I replied, nervous and unsure about doing this.

"How will I know you?" he asked.

"Oh, I'll be wearing a blue and black checked shirt." I hung up, my stomach churning with nerves as I wondered what I was getting myself into.

I hurriedly readied myself for the day, putting on my familiar 'work uniform.' I was nervous about the cryptozoologist meeting, but mostly I had been pondering Fletcher's revelation about the gold stash he'd found. It had been festering in the back of my mind since he'd told me about it. In no way, shape, or form, could I imagine how Clyde came by coins and bars. He always paid in flour gold. Stuff he pulled from right off his claim, from the stream right next to his cabin. How did he have it made into bars and coins? He only left the property if dad or I flew him out.

The more I chewed on it the more I was sure those bars and coins were marked. I had only glanced in the bag, but they appeared to have been minted. I didn't think Clyde had the money to mint his own gold or buy minted gold. So where did it come from? My vivid imagination sorted through all kinds of scenarios and all of them bordered on nefarious.

Yet I knew Clyde. He was kind and gentle. Odd, very private, and extremely paranoid, but not someone who would pull off the schemes I was dreaming up. The only thing that fit was that he found it, was given it, or uncovered a stash somewhere. That meant that someone else did something bad and Clyde was the one who ended up with the stash. It was only ten now, and I still needed to find as much information as I could about missing gold bars or coins or any thefts in the area. I started with the internet.

It took me a long time. I couldn't find anything about stolen or missing gold in the last fifty years, so I widened my search back to the gold rush. That seemed ridiculous, since no one from then would be digging around Fletcher's cabin now, but maybe they had relatives that had passed down the gold thieving gene. The topic was too large, and most of my hits were for books and media to buy. I made a note of a few things to check at the library. Frustrated about having no lead, I considered giving up when I ran across a story published in an Alaskan magazine. It was the story of how the Spencer Glacier received its name.

I knew the glacier; it was a popular stop on the Alaska Railroad for tourists. Apparently, a man named Edward Spencer oversaw paying the rail workers building the railroad in 1905. He was supposed to deliver the pay to Moose Pass, a twenty-mile railroad ride away, but an avalanche blocked the tracks. Foolishly, he decided to pack the payroll over the glacier to Moose Pass, taking only some light gear, and the payroll to be paid in gold bars. He didn't make it. His body was found one year later, in a crevasse near Milepost 53 of the railroad—but the cash box, filled with approximately one hundred pounds of gold, was never recovered.

I printed the story off to show Fletcher, hoping he would want to talk to me about it or tell me more about the gold he'd found. I looked at the clock and realized I was nearly late to meet the doctor.

I was expecting a nerdy guy with a bad comb over, or an old partially balding man with a ponytail and a bushy beard. I was pleasantly surprised with a tall, good-looking man, maybe thirty or fortyish, who looked like he'd be right at home at a logging camp, or commercial fishing boat in the Bering Sea. He was rugged and attractive and looked like he spent a lot of time outdoors.

We exchanged pleasantries, introduced ourselves, and sat down to order. He ordered the burger and fries, and I got the full breakfast platter with strawberry crepes, cheese omelet, bacon and hash browns with a large orange juice. He raised an eyebrow at my order, and I replied defensively, "I haven't eaten breakfast yet."

It was a stupid lie. I'd already eaten, but I was still hungry. Once the waitress finished, I had no more excuses to avoid relating my experience. I hadn't really thought through how to approach it, because I could hardly tell some stranger that I shapeshift. I decided to hold off a bit and distract him with the attack approach.

"How does one become a cryptozoologist?" I asked as he looked expectantly at me. He frowned. I could tell he was a little annoyed and eager to hear my story, but I needed to assess his trustworthiness.

"Well, there isn't an accredited school for it, if that's what you want to know. Most cryptozoologists are self-proclaimed. Personally, I have a doctorate in wildlife biology from the University of Washington, and masters' degrees in zoology and anthropology from Utah State and the University of Utah, respectively. I teach at Alaska State in the biology department. I study cryptids in my spare time. I publish a web magazine, which you've seen, and I'm working on a book about Alaskan cryptids. Does that answer all your questions?"

I was a little overwhelmed by the list of degrees he'd thrown at me, and I couldn't do much more but nod. He continued, "Do you want to tell me what you saw?"

Before I could answer, the server appeared with our food. We thanked her, and I delayed my answer by shoving food into my face. After I slowed down, I continued my story.

"I saw something that appeared to be a type of wolf. It was big, maybe 230 to 250 pounds. It was broad chested, like a Saint Bernard, or a Samoyed. Its head was heavy like one of those dogs, and its teeth were longer and sharper than a regular wolf. Its legs were shorter and stouter. It was tan and grey. It was definitely a wolf, but it wasn't at the same time. At first, I thought it might be some type of wolf dog mix that had gone feral, but when I looked up animals it might be, the only match I got was for the extinct dire wolf."

I pulled out a drawing I had downloaded off the internet. "It is close to this drawing, with the one exception that the head was slightly heavier, and the teeth seemed slightly longer."

He took the picture and studied it for a while. "How close were you to the animal?"

I continued to eat as I thought. This is where it got tricky. I had to let him know I was close enough for an average person to get a good look without giving away my secrets. "I was close, maybe ten yards?"

He narrowed his eyes. "How did you react and how did the animal react to you?"

"Well, I was frightened, and my initial reaction was to run, but I stopped myself, held still, and looked down at the ground. Once I did that, the wolf stared at me for a few moments, then trotted off into the woods and disappeared. After he disappeared, I ran to my plane and left the area."

"You said it was a he?"

"Yes, I could sm...see his..." I blushed. What did I say? Balls, nuts, gonads? I couldn't come up with the appropriate and accurate terminology. I cringed inwardly. I spent way too much time around full-grown men with the minds of pre-teens. "Umm...Walnuts, when he turned."

A slight grin crossed his face. "When did this occur?"

I thought for a moment, worried I'd give something away, but figured it didn't matter at all, as I was out flying in the area and there was no way to pin me down to a location by time exactly.

"Yesterday afternoon."

He drew back, but his face was unreadable. "Where were you at the time?"

I thought it was important to get the area near to my real sighting, but I didn't want to reveal Fletcher's cabin or anywhere very close.

"The northwestern side of Lake Iliamna," I muttered vaguely.

"Can you be more specific?"

"No," I stated firmly, with no explanation. We finished eating.

He studied me a moment, then took his laptop out of the computer case that sat next to him on the bench seat. He pushed aside our now empty dishes. He opened the computer and started scrolling through things for a minute or two. Eventually he turned the screen toward me. "This is a map I have made with sightings of various cryptids over the last three years around the Lake Iliamna area."

I glanced at the screen, expecting a couple of blips around the lake from people that usually sighted the lake monster or UFOs. I had to do a double take. There were thirty or more blips on the Northwestern shore of the lake.

"What does it mean?" I squeaked, worried about giving away too much about the location of Fletcher's cabin, even though the activity appeared to be miles away from it.

"It means the area around the northwestern side of the lake is busy with cryptid sightings. I'm trying to pinpoint areas for further field research."

"What kinds of cryptids? Has anyone else seen a dire wolf?"

"It's hard to say with the wolf. There are a lot of wolf sightings, and not everyone is as observant as you seem to be."

I blinked.

"Part of the problem with recording sightings is that people don't call me directly if they have a sighting. I must glean the information from news accounts or YouTube. Unfortunately, a wolf sighting is probably just a wolf sighting, and most people treat it as such. Consequently, I only have one other account of a quote 'dire wolf' being seen in the area."

He turned the computer so that we both could see it and began clicking on the marked points on his map. "Here was a sighting of a 'bear-dog,' here a sighting of the lake monster. Click around and you can see what's been spotted." He turned the computer back to me.

I clicked on a few other links and saw another lake monster sighting and bear creature sighting, one wendigo, several bigfoots, and finally the other dire wolf sighting. I breathed a sigh of relief; it was close to the lake.

"I only post sightings I feel are legitimate, and not imagined, hysterical, or god forbid, hoaxes."

I felt like I should question him more, but I couldn't focus. My mind kept going over and over the amount of weird animal sightings near the northwest side of the lake. Fletcher was still several miles away; however, he was in the unpopulated area, whereas the area around the lake had towns, cabins, and lots of people taking off for hunting and recreation. In my mind this was a hotbed of weird.

"What does it all mean?" I mumbled to myself again, lost in my thoughts and forgetting about my companion.

"Well, to me, it means that cryptids exist. I intend to gather enough evidence to prove it."

His words felt like icy water dripping down my spine. Something about the doctor chilled me—it was probably just dread that his research touched my secret world so closely. It might be the way the doctor looked at me, as though he knew I was hiding something, and if he stared hard enough, he'd see it.

I looked away and down at my phone, as though to check the time. He leaned forward, towards me, as though he were going to say something else, and my heart sped up in a panic. I scooted away from him.

"Thanks for your time; I've got to head to work soon. Would you mind sending me any information you have on the dire wolf? I'm curious about it." I spoke quickly, while writing my email address on a napkin and pushing it towards him with the computer. His hand reached out for the napkin, and his fingers brushed mine. I shuddered. "I really appreciate your time!" I grabbed my ticket and leapt up with the intention to pay my bill quickly and escape.

"It's probably not a 'dire wolf.'" I could hear the quotes in his voice.

I stopped. "What?"

"Dire wolves didn't grow that large. The only reason people think they did is because of *Game of Thrones*, you know, the TV show?"

I nodded, although I'd never watched it.

"They were probably only up to twenty percent larger than an average, modern, grey wolf. Also, recent research points to them being warm weather animals, most likely short furred and larger eared to aid in thermal regulation."

"Then what was it?" I turned to face him again.

He shrugged. "Could be an forebear of the extinct Alaskan wolf called a Kenai Peninsula wolf. They actually could grow close to that size, or something else. Thus the 'cryptid' designation."

I frowned. "I'm sorry, I've got to get to work." My mind was working furiously. What could it be?

"Do you mind if I call you with more questions sometime?" he asked.

"Sure, no problem!"

He sort of creeped me out. Although a good source of information, I would have to make sure and screen my calls.

I was running late for the distance as midtown was notoriously obnoxious to navigate, but because traffic was easy, I stumbled into Lake Hood at exactly 1:30. Dad raised his eyebrows, for me that was early.

"What? I can be on time." I grumbled defensively at his unspoken comment.

As usual, he was on the phone. He waved for me to wait before I took off to do my preflight. I sat in my usual folding chair and checked my messages. Nothing. I felt anxious about Fletcher. What had I done? I wondered. I thought we had a connection, and he'd acted like I couldn't be trusted.

Dad finally hung up. "Piper, I'm taking your route, today. I'll double up and do your drop on my way out. You need to go and help a client here in town."

"What are you talking about?" I was confused, because usually this meant doing some shopping or picking someone up. The way dad phrased it was odd.

"Uh." He scrambled at his desk and held up a sticky note. "That Fletcher guy called and asked for you to help him with something. He said he'd pay the full rate for your time. So, I sold you out."

"Thanks, a lot pimp daddy," I said sourly.

Dad just laughed. "How bad can it be? You chauffer him around town, go shopping with him, hold his hand so he can find what he needs, and drop him off somewhere. If he gets out of hand you turn into a wolf and rip his throat out, no worries."

"Glad you have full confidence in me." I could feel my blood pressure rising. I knew my anger was unreasonable, but why couldn't he just call me himself? Was the attraction one-sided? "Where do I pick him up?"

Dad handed me the sticky note with an address. I glanced at it. I was battling the indecision of how to feel. Should I be happy the guy called or pissed off he "paid" for my day? Why didn't he feel he could just call me directly and ask? I fumed for a minute, and then decided that maybe it wasn't that bad of an idea. I was busy and hard to reach. At least if he paid for my time, I would be around. The whole idea irritated me *irrationally,* though. I was a mess.

"You better get going, you're losing the company money," Dad remarked.

I threw a pen at his head, and he ducked, laughing. I made sure to slam the door on my way out.

Chapter 4

Fletcher was staying at the Salmon Inn, a European-style hotel in midtown. It was fairly new and cheap, but frankly, I like having my own bathroom. I picked him up in the parking lot. He was dressed in his same battered ball cap and sunglasses. I could tell from his white neck and even hair that he'd visited a barber while he'd been in town. He smiled when he saw me, and I wasn't sure if I should let the butterflies go to town in my stomach or snap at him for "buying" me.

"Where to, boss man?" I inquired.

My tone may have been a little icy because he gave me a double take.

"Are you mad about something?" was his surprised reply. He paused halfway to my truck.

"No, nothing. I love getting calls from my father telling me I've been purchased for the day." Even as it came out of my mouth, I cringed. I was acting nuts.

"Wait, I know you're busy, and I needed your help," he explained, chagrined. "I thought it would be better for you if I paid for your time." He climbed in and shut the door.

"Look, I know you employ me and my company, but I thought we were friendly enough you could just call me and ask if you needed help," I said.

He shook his head, probably confused.

"Piper, some weird shit is going on. I'm in over my head." He paused wearily. "I don't know who to trust or what I should do next. I didn't mean to hurt your feelings, I should have called, but I thought this would be easiest for you. I'm sorry."

Great. Now I felt like a schmuck.

I sat for a minute. "It's possible I over-reacted." I frowned and waved away my anger. "Forget what I said. You're right. It's a lot easier for me to be available if work is taken care of." I looked around and turned my blinker on. "So where are we going and what's up?" I pulled out onto C Street and was making my way over to Northern Lights.

"Pull into Wal-Mart for a minute."

I quickly made the lane change and turned left on Benson and made my way to Wal-Mart. We pulled into the parking lot. Fletcher directed me to a parking place away from the busiest section.

"Are we shopping?"

"No, I just wanted someplace public, yet private to talk for a minute." He fumbled around in his backpack for a few seconds and brought out a fistful of papers. "When you dropped me off at the library the other day, I found this." He started to hand them to me, then paused and pulled his hand back. "No, I think I'll go back a little in the story."

Sensing this was going to take a while, I turned off the engine and cracked the windows for air. I turned partway in my seat and drew up my right leg. I leaned against the door. Fletcher looked around nervously, watching for people nearby, I assumed. He brought out a small, flat gold bar. I had seen the bars the other day, but not closely. He carefully held it low, out of view under the windows, but where I could see it clearly.

"As you know, some of the gold is in these small bars. It took me a while to match the markings on them, but they were milled in the nineteenth century. I found over eighty pounds. That means this gold alone is worth over two million dollars. I took one out of curiosity into a gold assayer, and she told me the bars themselves are worth more because of their age and collectability. So altogether, I could be looking at five to six million dollars." He looked around nervously, but no one appeared to be around in the back of the parking lot.

He handed me the bar, and I looked it over. It had a maker's mark and another mark I couldn't make out.

I handed it back. "So, what do you do? Put it in a safe deposit box? Or do you just cash it in?"

"I already put what I brought, besides this bar, into a safe-deposit box. But that isn't the end. That wasn't all the gold. There are also stacks of old gold coins, and some raw nuggets. It's a bloody fortune. The problem is, like I mentioned before, I think someone else is after it. At first, I thought I was being paranoid, but too many weird things have happened. I don't know who it is, but someone has been looking around my cabin. I also think I'm maybe being followed."

"Maybe you should go to the police."

"I thought about it. I just don't know how things work up here, since my cabin is so remote. So, before I talk to the police I'm going to meet with my lawyer. That's one of the stops on my list."

"That sounds like a good idea. Are you going to tell him about *all* the gold?" The idea of him telling anyone the extent of his fortune gave me a weird feeling.

"I'm not sure. I don't think I should trust anyone; it's just too much money. Then I think about how Clyde died. Was it natural? Was he murdered? If so, who knew about the gold? Where did the minted stuff come from? How did Clyde get it? It's driving me crazy! What if the gold was stolen? What happens to me, the poor idiot who 'inherited' it? So, that brings us back to do I trust the lawyer? I just don't know. I have to trust someone." There was an edge to his voice, the stress showing through.

With that he looked directly at me, and I realized he was telling me he did trust someone, me. My heart raced, and my palms grew wet. My first thought was, "*He trusts me!*" my second was, "*Oh, shit, how do we figure out this mess?*" Of course, all of that came with the crushing guilt of keeping my own secrets from him, which I had to do.

I brought out my story of the Spencer Glacier gold and showed it to Fletcher. "I did a little research too after you told me you found some gold. This is what I came up with. It isn't much, there is too much information on one hand, and too little on another when you just look on the internet."

He looked over the paper I had printed. "This is interesting, it might explain the bar gold, I just don't know, we'd have to find some proof to link it, but if it is this missing gold, I don't know if it counts as stolen or found." I expected him to show me the papers from earlier, but as I reached to take mine back, he said, "Let's get out of here, someone is watching us."

"Who, where?" I looked around.

"Just go, it's that green Jeep over two rows. Don't look, act normal."

I pulled out and turned back onto Benson.

"He followed me yesterday when I took a cab. Every stop I made; I saw him."

"What should I do?" I glanced behind me and then kept track in my rearview mirror. Sure enough, the green Jeep appeared five or six cars back.

"Let's just do what we planned. I don't have anything on me but that one bar and we aren't doing anything secret. Let's just act like we don't see him and keep an eye out for what he's up to."

"Ok, where do you want to go?"

"I have an appointment with Clyde's lawyer at three. It's," he glanced at the clock on my radio, "Two-thirty. His building is just over there." He pointed down the block. After a moment, he added, "Have you eaten anything?"

"Umm, I had breakfast, but I could eat." I thought about my huge breakfast.

"Do you mind swinging through someplace?" he continued.

"No, just tell me where."

Five minutes later we were sitting in the parking lot of Fletcher's lawyer's office eating burgers and fries. I decided to stockpile calories because I had a green Jeep to check up on later if it continued to follow us. Ten minutes before the hour, we were in the elevator heading up.

Since the lawyer was in a fancy midtown high-rise, I guess I was expecting the whole TV leather office with expensive paintings and heavy books on expensive, exotic, wooden shelves. Instead, it looked something like a tasteful doctor's office. When we were escorted into the lawyer's office itself, his décor surprised me. He had mounts on the walls—moose and caribou—a bear rug, and pictures of him with various big game mixed in with his credentials on the walls. I saw a couple of shots of him next to a yellow and black Super Cub on the wall.

I pointed at the plane. "Is that your eighteen?" I asked him after we concluded introductions.

"Yes, do you fly?" he replied politely.

"I have a nineteen fifty-six; I fly out of Tulugaq Air."

"Really? Well, mine's a seventy-seven. Best plane made for out here. That," he gestured to the photo, "is my baby."

I smiled. I could like this guy.

He gestured for us to sit and positioned himself behind the desk. "What can I do for you folks?"

As Fletcher explained our reason for being there, carefully limiting the gold to the bars and leaving out the part about being followed, I studied the lawyer for any tells that he might not be trustworthy. He was younger than I thought he would be since he'd worked with Clyde, but he still had to be pushing forty or be young looking for his age.

He was maybe six foot, well built, neatly trimmed dark hair, and dark eyes. I guess he would be considered good-looking, but he was too polished for me, too precise. I continued to look around the room. It was hard to believe that the metrosexual man in front of me was a hunter, a Super Cub pilot, and a hard-core mountain climber, if the photos were any indication.

"Piper, why don't you tell Mr. Georgetti, what you showed me about the gold bar?" Fletcher's request interrupting my inner musings.

I retold the story about the Spencer Glacier gold mystery and my guess that this might be it. The lawyer's perfectly poised face looked intrigued.

"Of course, I have no proof, just a story and a convenient guess." I shrugged and leaned back in the chair, arms crossed to signal I didn't have anything else to add.

"So, I was wondering what I should do? Is this gold legal? Am I going to get in trouble if I attempt to sell it or cash it in?" Fletcher asked.

The lawyer thought for a moment, head bent slightly to the side, an almost imperceptible smirk on his polished face. I focused on that, concerned that it was a sign he wasn't trustworthy. After I moment, I decided it was just the natural way his lips turned up and shrugged.

"I think maybe you should let me see the assayer's notes and give me some time to do some research and I'll get back to you." He paused and cleared his throat quietly. "Initially, I would say you don't have any problems, as this was an inheritance, but I'm not positive. This is a little outside my expertise," he finished.

We ended up giving the lawyer our printouts and my numbers just in case he couldn't reach Fletcher, and we left. When we reached the lobby, we used the cover of the mirrored glass to look for our friend in the green Jeep. Either he wasn't following us anymore, or he was clever enough to stay out of eyesight for the time being. We walked quickly to my truck and climbed in.

"What now, boss man?" I turned to him.

"I just don't know. I'm working with nothing here!" He threw his hat onto my dashboard, frustrated.

I jumped slightly, surprised at his sudden outburst.

"I don't even know who Clyde knew besides you guys and this lawyer. I don't know who he could have told about the gold, or who might have guessed he had it. Did he sell some and tip someone off he had it? I don't even know for sure if he died of natural causes." He rubbed his hand through his hair, leaving it disheveled.

"I might be able to help with that at least," I said quietly, unsure if he'd be glad or upset I'd been prying.

He looked at me inquisitively. "How?" His sudden burst of temper controlled again.

"I called the coroner's office to see how to get an autopsy report. Basically, since Clyde had no next of kin, and he left everything to you, you are the only one who can get a copy. You need the will or something from your lawyer, and of course fill out a bunch of forms in triplicate, but you can get the report."

He looked at me, silent, both eyebrows raised slightly. "That's a start. Now if I can get something, anything, on Clyde's past or acquaintances, then we'll have something to go on. Do you think your dad would know anyone Clyde was friends with?" he continued, seemingly unconcerned with my prying.

"Sure, I know a couple of people Clyde knew. I guess we could try to pick their brains."

"Please, make me a list, and I can try to contact them. Maybe we can get some more leads from there. First, I'm going to get that autopsy report."

"Tell you what, I'll drop you at the library so you can print out forms, while I run to the airport and get our contacts. I can meet you back at the library in an hour, if that sounds okay, boss man?"

"Sure, sounds like a plan," he responded and pulled his hat back firmly on his head.

I was pulling into the library when I noticed the green Jeep was still tailing us.

"He's back," I said, and gestured low so that only Fletcher could see.

He nodded quietly and looked casually around, as though taking in the sights. "Is he anyone you've seen before?" he asked.

"I don't know. I'd have to be closer to see under the hat, but I don't recognize the car."

A terrible idea was percolating in my mind. I told Fletcher I had to use the bathroom and walked into the library with him. I wanted to get a closer look at the guy in the green Jeep but didn't know how in my current form. Needing somewhere private to shed my clothes, I walked into the ladies' restroom hoping there was a window, but there wasn't. I didn't know what to do because I couldn't just walk out to the parking lot, strip naked, and turn into a bird. That would definitely get people talking.

Also flying out of the library or walking out as a wolf would make quite the scene. So, I used the bathroom and went to the truck. I needed to find somewhere to change while I knew where the green Jeep was. I wasn't sure if he'd follow me since I didn't have Fletcher with me, and if he did, I didn't want to lead him to my house. I decided to just go to the airport like I told Fletcher I would and see what happened. I started my truck and wound my way through the growing traffic.

I didn't let myself look back to check if I was being followed until I was well onto Northern Lights. He was still there. I wasn't sure if I should be relieved or frightened. I wasn't sure what he'd do when we reached Lake Hood, since there wouldn't be as much car traffic to blend in with. I decided to ignore him and continue as though he weren't following. I'd worry about it at the air service office.

It was a busy day at the airport, but I could still see the green Jeep following five or six cars back. I wasn't sure if he was trying to be seen or was just inept; maybe he thought we hadn't noticed him. I pulled into my usual spot and tried to walk casually into the office. I'd forgotten dad wasn't there, so I had to unlock the door. I locked it behind me, something I didn't usually bother with.

The green Jeep had driven past as though he were continuing along the road, so maybe he didn't think I'd noticed him. I opened the small window that looked out over the lake, crouched out of sight, and stripped off my clothes. At least I felt a little safer in my office. I changed quickly and squeezed out the window.

My heart soared as it usually did when I took that first leap into the sky and stretched my wings. It was the incredible freedom and joy that could only come from flying under my own power. My Super Cub was a close second, but nothing beat the feeling of the raw sky under my wings.

I climbed just above the trees to stay out of the air traffic, yet low enough I could see the roads clearly. Stopped about a quarter mile from my office was the green Jeep. He had a pair of binoculars and was watching my office intently. I swooped down and landed directly on the hood of his Jeep.

I startled him as I passed right through his field of vision, and he jumped. I used his surprise to get a good look at him. I didn't recognize him, but he wore his hat low, and he was wearing sunglasses. Even though it was warm, he had his jacket zipped up under his chin and that partially obscured his lower face. I could see he wore a beard, but that was all. Frustrated, I turned to see what he was looking at.

With my raven sharp eyes, I could see the window I had just escaped from clearly. Had he witnessed my change? Dread tugged at my heart. I glanced at him again. He looked as though he were going to get out of the Jeep, so I squawked loudly and took off. I circled him once until he got out. He was trying to keep his eye on me, so I flew into a tree and hid there. I didn't have a good line of sight, but his movement or stance seemed slightly familiar to me, although I couldn't quite place him.

A few other ravens were close by, so I joined them and attempted to blend in and lose his attention so I could make it back to the safety of my office. I played raven games with my brothers for at least ten minutes before I noticed him watching the wrong raven at last. I made my break, using the tree cover to disappear and from a neighboring tree branch, waited to make sure he was looking away before I dived into my open window. Keeping well below the window, I changed and dressed quickly, then looked at the window, trying to spot my stalker. He wasn't there. I hoped he was chasing some random raven or had lost interest in the office. I grabbed the book for Fletcher, shut the window, and left.

As I turned right onto Northern Lights from Lake Hood, I realized he was still following me. "Shit, shit, shit!" I cursed aloud. Wonderful. Now I didn't know if he knew my secret and faked it so I would go back to the office, or he was only temporarily distracted by the ravens and had just watched me leave. Most people would tell themselves that they were imagining what he must have seen from my window. Maybe I'd just shooed that raven out and was out of sight for a while. But he had watched me so intently! I was running through scenarios in my head of what could have happened when my phone rang, nearly making me swerve off the road.

I looked at the screen; it was Branwyn. I hadn't called her back for a week or more, which wasn't that unusual in the summer. She usually just waited for me to call back. It was so unusual for her to call again that I answered it.

"What's up?" I asked as soon as the phone connected.

"I was worried about you!" she exclaimed. Branwyn is the only other person outside of my family who I trusted with my secret. She had been my best friend since grade school and had kept my secret since we were seven years old. I had entrusted it to her the day I had found out about her own secrets.

Branwyn had inherited some gifts, courtesy of her Irish and Welsh ancestry. She had the "Sight" as she called it, and some small control over the elements. Enough so that if this were the sixteen-hundreds, she would be labeled a witch. Of course, both of us studied everything we could about shape-changing or her gifts.

"I just felt the overpowering need to call you and see if you were ok."

"I'm fine, just heading to pick up a guy at the library."

"What guy?"

"Well." I wondered what to tell her. She was going to pick up that I liked this guy and want to ask a hundred questions, all of which I probably couldn't answer because they involved someone else's secrets. I must have paused too long because Bran sounded irritated when she cut in.

"What aren't you telling me, and how much trouble have you stirred up?"

"I don't stir up trouble, you know that. It just sort of finds me," I said defensively.

"So, you are in trouble."

I could hear the judgement in her tone. I had dragged her into trouble more than once and she was wary about future *adventures*. "No, not really, I don't think so," I replied, a little uncertainly. "I'm just helping a guy, a client, around town. We're running some errands."

"I do know when you aren't telling me the truth."

"Bran, I gotta go. Talk to you later. Believe me, I'm not in any trouble that I know of. If you want to help me out, see what you can find on dire wolf sightings in Alaska, and I'll call you when I have some time. I promise it will be soon!" I added.

"Ok," she said grudgingly.

"I promise! Just give me a little time to figure it out. Oh—Mom and Baylee don't know anything, so please leave them out of this. I don't want them involved."

She snorted an affirmative, annoyed that I knew her well enough to know she'd let go of the topic as well as a pit bull with a rump roast. I knew her M.O. If I hadn't warned her off, she'd hang up with me and be on the phone to Baylee or Mom inside of ten seconds.

We hung up. I had about forty-eight hours before she became really insistent and if I didn't come up with a realistic story by then, she'd call my mom and sister and I wouldn't hear the end of it.

Fletcher was already standing outside when I pulled up to the library. I could see he had some paperwork with him.

"I filled these out, but I need the lawyer to sign them and get them notarized. We need to go back over there," he said as soon as he shut the truck door.

I dropped him back at the lawyer's. A few minutes later, he was back in the truck. I lifted an inquisitive eyebrow.

"I left it with his secretary. She'll have it signed, notarized and sent over to the coroner."

"Cool, what's next on the list, boss?"

"Well, I need to do some shopping for the cabin if you don't mind."

"I'm at your beck and call," I said sarcastically.

"Cute." He snorted.

"Well, I'm bought and paid for. Do with me as you wish." That earned me a double take, but I kept a straight face, and he let it slide.

We spent the next several hours picking up supplies. Shopping is not high on my list of favorite things to do. I found it tedious. Unfortunately, I have to do it a lot in my job. If a client needs something, it's not always convenient to come into Anchorage to get it. The shopping generally falls on Mom, but I do it enough to hate it. Most of the stuff we bought was fairly mundane. Food, general supplies like toilet paper —which is one of those things you don't really think about until you need it—stuff like that. Then he had me take him to the sportsman's store.

"Getting some hunting supplies?" I asked.

He rubbed his hand over the back of his neck. He seemed indecisive. "I'm going to get some more ammo, but I want to pick up a couple of trail cams."

"That's a good idea," I said, nodding my head.

If he was really worried about people looking around his cabin, a well-hidden trail cam was a great idea. The only thing you'd have to worry about was keeping it stocked with batteries, well hidden, and able to view a good-sized area.

I didn't know much about trail cams other than what I'd seen advertised on outdoor programs on television, so I trailed behind as Fletcher chatted with the sales guy. He ended up buying six infrared trail cams that took digital stills and video, and a backpack's worth of batteries.

Shopping concluded I drove him back to his hotel. We left his supplies in my truck since we'd be flying back to his cabin the next day. When I pulled into the parking lot, the green jeep was parked across the street at a small strip mall.

I had put my hair in braids before I left to meet the cryptozoologist, but I hadn't re-braided it after changing at the office. It hung more than halfway down my back in thick waves. Once we stopped, Fletcher turned to me and reached out to smooth a strand away from my face. It was a gentle and completely unconscious gesture on his part. Once he realized what he had done, he snatched his hand back.

"I'm sorry. I didn't mean to invade your personal space," he apologized.

"No worries." I smiled at him to relieve the awkwardness of the moment. I hoped it covered up my quickened breathing and the hammering of my heart. He looked over my shoulder and straight at the green Jeep. The driver was leaning against it, staring directly at us. It was a challenge, and Fletcher was male enough to take it. He jumped out of the truck and started towards the road. The street was busy, so he had to wait to cross. Meanwhile, the man calmly climbed into his Jeep and took off. Fletcher gestured rudely at him before he came back.

"That bastard wants us to know he's following us, and he wants us to know there's nothing we can do about it, either." Frustration deepened his voice.

"I just wish we knew how he found out about the gold."

"I don't even know if he does. I just can't think of another reason for him to follow me," he replied.

"You don't have anyone that would send a private investigator after you?" I was stretching. It didn't hurt to know if he had a secret family stashed somewhere, though. My feeling was that the green Jeep's intentions were not benign. He had a feeling of malignancy about him that set my teeth on edge and lifted the hair on the back of my neck. Worst of all, he appeared to be persistent.

"No one." He shook his head in emphasis.

"You don't think he knows about your cabin?" I asked, the thought suddenly popping into my head.

"I just don't know, Piper. He might be the snooper, or he might be something else altogether. I just wish I knew what was going on." He held out his hands hopelessly.

"Maybe you shouldn't go back to the cabin." My breath was coming quickly, and I took a second to slow it down.

His glance brimmed with testosterone. He wasn't going to let this guy get to him. "He's not running me out of my place by following me around town. He might just be some asshole on a lark," he growled.

I decided not to say anything unless I saw him again and let it slide. "You're right; it's probably no big deal." We sat in silence for a few minutes. "Do you have anything else you need to do?" I asked hopefully. I was enjoying his company, and I didn't want it to end.

"No. Thanks for running me around," he answered tersely.

I watched him for a minute. The green Jeep had really messed with him. He was tense, maybe angry. I didn't know him well enough to judge his mood.

I put on my neutral voice. "No problem, boss man. You need a pickup tomorrow?"

"I can take a cab." He strode towards the hotel. I watched him until he entered. He didn't look back or even throw me a wave goodbye.

It hurt my feelings a little that he could dismiss me so quickly. I wasn't really trying to get him to ask me to stay longer, but it would have been nice if he had, anyway. I knew I was being ridiculous. He was a client. Maybe the attraction I felt was only one way, and he thought of me just as an employee. I left.

Chapter 5

I was too unsettled to go home. Since Branwyn was already upset at me, I figured I'd better stop by and talk to her. I didn't really like keeping my best friend in the dark. It was just that she tended to make a big deal out of things, sort of like my mom. I knew it was because she worried, and since she'd been knee deep in it with me a couple of times, the worry was probably warranted.

She owned a small bookstore and gift shop not far from Fletcher's hotel. It was one of those places that you could get touristy novelty items—candles, books, "I saw the Northern Lights" and "Los Anchorage" t-shirts—and other weird or fun stuff. Bran kept a fantastic supply of mythology and folklore books from all around, and I knew she had a collection of books about witches as well. Basically, anything we could get our hands on that was somewhat related to our abilities we collected and kept at Bran's store. Any duplicates were put out front.

Bran had developed a reputation as a good reference for anything obscure and a person who could find any oddity you were interested in. By doing this, she had collected an almost cult-like following of repeat customers looking for her odd and usually out of print books.

Summertime meant tourist season, and Bran's shop was hopping.

When I opened the door, the bell tinkled and a pleasant voice said, "Hi, welcome to the Lunatic Fringe." The girl behind the counter looked up and frowned. "Oh, it's you."

I grinned. She knew that when I came in, Bran usually went in the back with me, and she'd have to actually work.

People were milling about, touristy types, and a few Loonies— Bran's regulars—as well. There was a couple at the counter buying mugs and t-shirts and two people waiting in line. There were several looking at items.

The Loonies were at the back bookshelf where Bran stored her hard-to-find books and other rarities in locked cabinets. Bran was talking to a customer. She glanced up at me and motioned me to the back. I went through the beaded doorway behind the counter to the back room. Two of Bran's employees were sitting on the sofa chatting in their "Lunatic Fringe: Books and Oddities" t-shirts. I told them they were busy up front and they left. I wandered over to look over the folklore books—mainly to see if she had anything new.

Finally, Bran came in. She shut the door behind the beaded curtain to dampen the noise and for privacy. I usually didn't talk about things that just anyone should overhear. Bran was a stereotypical fiery Irish woman. She had a delicate build and seemed smaller than she was. She was five foot four and maybe a hundred and five pounds. She had dark hair, but the fair complexion of the Irish. Her skin was so pale it appeared nearly translucent, and she couldn't tolerate the sun for long without being sorry.

She was wearing a bright blue Lunatic Fringe polo shirt, and it brought out the ice blue of her eyes. She was a striking beauty and never seemed to act like she knew it. Right now, she had her long dark hair twisted up into a messy bun. Her make-up was basically worn off, so I knew she'd probably been at the store since early in the morning doing the books, stocking shelves, and taking inventory.

"How's business?" I asked as I flopped down on the couch.

"Crazy. The Loo...umm, my steady customers, have been hitting up different tourist sites and talking up the shop. This is going to be my best year ever!" Excitement for her business filled her voice.

She had been about to say Loonies, and I smirked at her. She pretended she hated the nickname, but eventually she was going to give in and call them that. I don't know why she insisted on avoiding it; even the Loonies called themselves that. Hell, they made t-shirts.

She walked over to the fridge and grabbed a couple of Cokes. She handed one to me, and then pushed my legs off the sofa and sat down on the opposite end. She stretched and sighed. Her eyes had dark rings under them, and her hair was a mess. She looked tired.

"Alright, spill it!"

I raised my eyebrows as if to say, "spill what?" but that just made her mad.

"Come on, Piper! You didn't just drop in for a Coke!"

I threw my head back and raked my hands through my hair. "I don't know where to start."

She gave a quick snort. "The beginning is always nice."

"Smartass." I stood up and paced.

"Whatever, Pipe, get on with it!" she demanded.

"Okay so, Clyde left his cabin to this guy." I paused. I just didn't know what to say about Fletcher. Bran could tell I was gathering my thoughts, so she just sipped her Coke and waited.

"His name is Vanice Fletcher, but he goes by Fletcher. Clyde left him everything, and he came here to see what was what and now, someone is following him and maybe me, and there's gold." It tumbled out of me with no cohesion or coherence. I don't even think I took a breath.

Bran calmly sipped her Coke and stared at me. Finally, she put it down. "Start with Vanice Fletcher and tell me who he is."

I sat down, took a deep breath, and told her the story from the time I put him in my Super Cub until I walked into Bran's shop. Bran had a calming effect on people. I didn't know if it was one of her gifts, if she was a super good listener, or if she just was a good manipulator, but for someone who was famous for her temper, she sure could settle you down quickly.

"Wow. Looks like you stepped in it good. At least there doesn't seem to be a demon involved." She glared at me accusingly. "Is there a demon involved?"

She was mad because the last time I had "stepped in it" a bunch of freaks kidnapped my sister and tried to feed her to a demon. Bran had helped me get her back. She hadn't gotten over it. Not everyone has the desire to mess with demons, at least no one intelligent.

"No, there is not a demon involved!" At least I hoped not. I really didn't know who or what was involved, but it seemed more like a greed problem than a supernatural one. Still, there was my cryptid wolf.

"You know I don't look for trouble. Right? This had nothing to do with me."

"That's what you always say," she replied, a glint of mischief in her eye.

I changed the subject. "I don't need anything, but I thought maybe I'd look up any myths or folklore on wolves in the area. Do we have anything on that?" I asked.

I didn't remember much folklore on wolves, but Bran brought in new books all the time, so I was hoping something would turn up. We had a better collection than the library, so if Bran didn't have it, it probably didn't exist.

"You're kidding right?" she deadpanned.

"What?"

"You dumped that whole story on me and expect me to just hand you a book and say g'day?" Her voice started to rise. She stood up and looked down at me.

"Why, is there something else?"

She slugged me in the arm. Even though I felt like an Amazon next to Bran, I was only two inches taller. I was built sturdier, but she was strong for her looks.

"Ow! What was that for?"

"You have a guy following you, who probably saw you change form, and you'll just take your book and go?" She was working herself up into a tizzy. "Oh, and I can tell you like this Vanice guy. Did you think you could breeze by that, and I wouldn't catch it?" Her voice was rising until it reached an octave that made my ears ache.

"No? Yes? Tell me what you want to hear."

She slugged me again.

"Now you made me spill my Coke!" I brushed the beaded liquid off my shirt onto the floor, looking down at the stain in dismay. I'd already done laundry, and I expected my t-shirts to last at least two wearings a piece.

"Oh, you big baby." She set her drink down and rifled through a box behind the door. She came out with a green Lunatic Fringe shirt, and I pulled off the wet one and put it on. "If you'd shop for yourself and not just clients, you wouldn't have to worry about not having enough clothes to make it to laundry day!"

"I know," I said sullenly as I changed my shirt.

"Your distraction attempts were weak. I want to know about this guy."

We settled back onto the couch.

"You're right. I think I might like, like him. But he's my client, and he hasn't given me any reason to think he likes me. So, that's it." I sipped my Coke and avoided her eyes.

"Is this the reason you haven't gone out with that pilot from Talkeetna again? What was his name?"

"Raleigh," I said miserably. "He won't be asking me out again."

"You never told me about that. I remember you were going all out, new dress, shoes, getting your hair done." She frowned. "You got away without telling me a thing about that date. How did you do that?" She looked genuinely puzzled, but I wasn't going to give my secrets away; it had taken me all of my twenty-nine years to put them in place.

"I missed my hair appointment, and forgot to buy shoes, and that's before it started. I should have just stayed home."

She tilted her head slightly, the universal sign for go on I'm listening. "Oh?"

"So, I had to wear those red strappy sandals I bought last year, remember?"

"The super cute ones with the four-inch heels?"

"Yep, that was a disaster waiting to happen. We went downtown and parked across the street from Sullivan's."

"Okay." She drew the word out to encourage me to continue.

"I made it across the street and into the restaurant alive, no broken ankles, and sat down. I did buy a new dress. It's cute. And it looks good on me. I only had a limited time to get ready, so I didn't really notice any issues with it until later. It was a wrap around and it sort of liked to gape in the front."

Bran frowned like she could see where this was going.

"I didn't really notice it, and I wore a black bra, anyway. So, dinner was going okay. We talked about flying and our jobs and it was comfortable, if not terribly exciting. I made the walk to the theater without disaster, and he acted gentlemanly and gave me his arm when I looked like I was teetering a bit."

Bran gave a little laugh, amused I'm sure because she knew how often I wore heels.

"Everything was fine, and I think we were both having a good time. I finally got over my jitters, and I even thought I'd go on a second date if he asked." I sipped my Coke, my throat dry.

Bran leaned forward looking concerned.

"Sooo, we head back to my place. I was going to offer him some cake and send him on his way since we had to hurry and missed dessert at the restaurant. You know, chocolate, right?"

Bran nodded. Chocolate was a universal food group.

"I invited him in, and I took off those ridiculous shoes, because they were killing me by this point. I got out a couple of plates and started serving up the cake. All perfectly innocent." I paused.

"That's when he decided I had invited him for more, um, carnal pleasures than chocolate and sugar. He started kissing me, and he had one hand down my dress and one up it before I could say, 'What in the hell are you doing?'"

Bran sat up shocked.

"I had to pull a knife on him to get him to stop. He wasn't a total jerk. It appears I give…" I held up my hand to make air quotes, "'mixed signals.' He thought the gaping dress, inviting him in for cake, and taking off my shoes were all a billboard for 'take me now.'"

"He was embarrassed, so he apologized and left. I won't have to worry about hearing from him again." I sighed, blushing.

I had to give it to Bran. She tried to look concerned for about ten seconds after my story before the Coke came out of her nose and she fell to the floor in hysterical laughter. She gasped out, "You pulled a knife on your date?" and continued to laugh.

I frowned unhappily. "I really don't see the humor. If I didn't want to be molested, why wouldn't I pull a knife if that was the only way to stop him?"

She laughed harder.

"Thanks a lot, Bran. I could have been raped and you're laughing."

My guilt trip made her laugh until she couldn't breathe. When she did take a breath, she gasped out, "You pulled a knife on your date!"

I still didn't know what the big deal was with the knife; didn't she think I wouldn't protect myself if I had to?

I frowned at my friend and contemplated planting a solid kick in her ass as she rolled on the floor. I decided she was meaner than me and went back to glaring at her. One of Bran's employees finally walked in because of the howling and frowned at Bran, who was a mess. She had been rolling on the not so clean floor. Her hair had come half down, and she had packing peanuts stuck in it. She had the Coke stains now from her initial laughing burst and had snorted some snot out of her nose with the soda. I handed her my dirty shirt.

"Should we close up? It's after nine," The salesgirl asked tentatively.

"Sure, go ahead." Bran waved the girl off and blew her nose. "That's the best laugh I've had in a while! Boy, we have to get you out on more dates!"

"Why? So, you can amuse yourself with my social graces?" I asked sarcastically.

"Yeah, that's a great reason." She smirked. I dumped the rest of my Coke on her.

"Hey!"

"You had it coming."

"It was worth it!"

"Whatever. Now tell me what you got on cryptids, dire wolves, or…" I couldn't remember what the crypto guy had called them, "Uh, some extinct Alaskan wolves?" The long day was starting to drag me down. "I should head home."

"Okay, let me towel off." She grabbed another t-shirt from her box and used her dirty one to sop up the Coke. Then she pulled a couple of new books down from a shelf.

I looked them over briefly. "Werewolves? Really? They aren't real," I said incredulously.

"You've got to be kidding," Bran said deadpan.

"Why?"

"I got them for you, dork. *You* are a werewolf."

"Not this nonsense again," I ticked points off on my fingers, "I wasn't bitten by some crazy wolf creature. I don't change into some furry man-beast at the full moon. I most certainly avoid eating people, and I do not have hair on my palms." I held them up for dramatic effect. "I'm a shifter. I can change at will and I turn into the 'real' animal," I stated indignantly with finger air quotes. "And don't forget, I'm a raven too."

Unimpressed, Bran continued, "You're a human who changes into a wolf. That's what a werewolf is."

"I disagree."

She sighed. "Read the books. I think there might be something that sounds close to your dire wolf in there. For a supernatural creature, you are very close-minded."

"Am not," I said sulkily. "And that's funny coming from a witch."

"I'm not a witch," she huffed.

"Who's close minded, now?"

"Knife." She snorted.

"Whatever." I took my books and grabbed a hot pink t-shirt from the box as I parted the beads. "I'm taking another one because you blew snot on mine." I pointed at her. "Oh, and one more thing, see if I ever tell you about another date!"

Chapter 6

I had to fly hunters and supplies before I took Fletcher back to his cabin, so I started early the next morning. After two trips it was mid-afternoon before I had the time to start stressing out about seeing him again. I had come to grips with the fact I was attracted to him, but I was worried he didn't feel the same about me. One minute he seemed into me, the next he was distant. Plus, the gold mystery was perplexing, and once I had time to think about Fletcher, that was the second thing weighing on my thoughts. The third was the green Jeep. I hadn't seen it on my way home last night, or on my way to work this morning, but I found myself looking constantly, my heart speeding up and my palms growing sweaty every few minutes as I expected it to come around a corner or pull out from behind a car that was behind me. If there was such a thing as a "chill pill," I needed it.

As I taxied in from my last job, I could see Fletcher standing outside the office, his face unreadable behind the sunglasses and cap. He stood relaxed though, his hands in his jean pockets, and a backpack slung casually over one shoulder. I topped off my gas tank and taxied over to my usual spot.

"Hey," I said as I walked over to join him. I pulled his enigmatic scent through my nose and over the back of my throat. Memorizing him. He nodded, silent as usual. I went into the office to check in with dad and came back out.

"You ready?" I asked him. He nodded again and followed me to the truck. He helped me unload his supplies and place them in the plane. I completed my pre-flight and when all was ready, we took off.

Once airborne and on our way, Fletcher asked, "Have you seen the green Jeep today?"

"No. I looked, but I didn't see him."

"Me either. Maybe he got what he wanted."

"Yeah, but what?" I asked. My head was swirling with reasons, but none I could pin down.

"Just watch out when you get back. He's up to no good."

"I will." I would too. The dude creeped me out. Plus, he probably knew my secret, and that really scared me.

We were both quiet, lost in thought for the remainder of the flight. Once we got there, I helped Fletcher unload and store his belongings.

"Did you get a chance to contact any of Clyde's friends?" I asked to fill the silence.

"No, I'm still at a dead end. I'm waiting to see what that autopsy says. Then I feel like I might have more of an idea what direction to go."

"Sure, sounds good." I paused for a minute, not sure how to prolong my stay any longer.

"Look, I gotta get back. I promised my kid sister I'd take her to the movies tonight. Would you please call me when you hear something? I'll keep looking for anything about missing gold."

"No problem, Piper." He pulled off his sunglasses. His eyes were bloodshot, like he hadn't slept well. He rubbed them and put the glasses back on. It wasn't that bright today, so I wondered if he used the sunglasses as more of a mask to hide behind then a shade from the sun. At least he seemed more comfortable when he wore them.

As I walked back towards the landing strip, I could feel his eyes hot on my back. I almost turned, but I forced myself to continue. Once I checked the Cub, I went to pull on my headset. That's when I realized it was missing. I looked around hurriedly, then climbed out and searched everywhere. I looked for Fletcher's headset in the back seat, nothing.

Did I accidentally take them into the cabin? I ran back, but Fletcher swore we had both taken them off and placed them in their usual spots. We both went back and searched again. I even pulled out my supplies and gear, nothing. Without a headset, I couldn't communicate with air traffic control. I pulled out my sat phone and called my dad's cell. It went directly to voicemail. I left him a message to call me back and hung up. I didn't need the headsets to fly. There were procedures if you lost your radio, but I didn't want to abandon my expensive gear without a complete search. Plus, my workday was done, and it was my own time. Fletcher was scanning the trees, His face a hard mask, a muscle twitched in his jaw.

"Somebody is here. He's watching us," he whispered in a low growl. The hair stood up on my neck.

Icy fingers gripped my heart, and it lurched into a frantic pace. I also began a desperate scan of the tree line. A half growl sounded deep in his throat, and he pushed me behind him. We walked that way to the cabin, he in a protective stance around me. I had my backpack in my arms, my hand resting on the .45 inside. Once we crossed the threshold, Fletcher closed the heavy door and shoved the bar across it with so much force the walls shuddered. He double checked the rear door and then looked through the windows. I backed up and sat down on the bed out of his way, as he prowled from window to window. At some point, I must have pulled out my gun, because it rested on my lap.

"I thought once I left to go back to Anchorage, this bastard would lose interest and leave me alone," he hissed out through clenched teeth.

"What do you mean? Who's out there?" I whispered, afraid to speak louder.

"I don't know. I think I see him sometimes in the trees, but I only catch glimpses from the corner of my eye. I know he's there. I can feel him, watching. Then something will be missing for a couple of days and returned to a new spot.

"He'll throw rocks at the cabin at night when I'm trying to sleep. I'm not sure if he's trying to drive me away or drive me crazy."

He had relaxed a little; the frantic pacing had slowed as though a great burden had been lifted with the telling of his experience. How did someone already know about the gold before Fletcher told anyone? How long had someone watched Clyde's place? Had they been threatening Clyde? Did they kill him?

"He took your headsets." He drew a breath to say something else when a large rock bounced off the metal roof.

I jumped.

"What does the fu..." He caught himself, old-fashioned manners kicking in. "What does he want?"

I didn't know what to do or say, but Fletcher's anxiety was affecting me. I didn't want to shift involuntarily, which doesn't happen often unless I'm extremely stressed. So, I started talking. Babbling tended to be my stress fallback.

"What's been missing? What has he taken? What has he returned?" I asked.

"Just small things. Like I had a red stress ball in my hand while I walked out to the shed the other day, and I had to use both hands to start the mower, so I set it down on the windowsill while I mowed the runway. When I came back, it was gone. A few days later, it was on that stump." He pointed in the direction of his chopping block.

"The same thing happened with a screwdriver, then my hatchet. They all returned two or three days later. Then I killed a few rabbits and set them on the porch while I went in to get a skinning knife. When I came back, they were gone. No sign of anyone."

"Why haven't you said anything?" I asked quietly.

He flushed slightly, embarrassed. "Until the rabbits, I kept telling myself that I was just imagining things, you know, mislaying stuff. But he keeps getting bolder, and I can't find excuses anymore. Someone is screwing with me. He lives in these woods, hell, he might have squatted here while it was empty, and I think he's trying to tell me to leave." He shrugged, helplessly.

A smaller rock hit the roof and rolled down. We both jumped. He threw me a glance as if to say, "see what I mean?"

"Have you tried to talk to him?"

"I sat out on the porch and yelled for him to come and face me. He didn't answer. Sometimes, though, I'll hear him talk to himself in the woods. I can't ever make out what he's saying, but nothing directly to me."

"Has he done anything malicious, or destroyed anything?" I was starting to sound as if I were interrogating him, and I cringed inwardly a little.

"No." He frowned. "Just stuff like this, things that mess with my head. I'm hoping I'll get something on those trail cams." He took off his hat and rubbed a hand through his hair, his tell that showed he was frustrated.

I screwed up my courage. "There's two of us, why don't we sneak out and try to corner him?"

"No, Piper. I don't know if this guy is dangerous or not, I'll go out there, but I want you to stay here."

"I can take care of myself," I said, hackles rising. My hand clasped the gun handle in my lap, and I saw his eyes drawn to it.

"You always carry that around?" he asked, pointing with his chin.

"Yup," I replied.

"Good, keep it trained on the door until I come back." He smiled at me and stepped through the front door.

I blinked. Then shot to my feet. I wasn't going to let the chauvinist go out there alone. With the gun firmly in hand and at my side, I went out the rear door and quietly closed and latched it. I sniffed the air and wished I could shift. My wolf was a better tracker. I could only smell Fletcher.

I walked stealthily around to the front. Fletcher stood there watching me, his mouth set in a grim line. He motioned for me to go back in. I shook my head.

We stood staring at each other for a minute, then I saw his shoulders drop, and I knew he had given in. He pointed to a spot in the woods, and mouthed, "He's right there."

I nodded. He turned his back to the woods and gestured that I should go right, and he would go left. I nodded again. The wind was blowing towards me, and I got a brief whiff of something, but I couldn't place it, maybe strong B.O. sort of like burnt onions? I'd smelled that before, when I was trying to find evidence that someone was after Clyde's gold. That made more sense. I imagine that some hermit living in the woods for months away from society might smell quite ripe.

The wind shifted, and the scent disappeared. One thing about this guy, he knew his bush craft. He always stayed upwind, except for that brief mistake when the wind shifted quickly and then back, because I didn't smell him again. Fletcher and I separated and moved towards the woods. There was a slight clearing around the cabin, but it only reached a small distance from the stump. When I looked back, Fletcher had already gone into the thick trees.

I couldn't see very far, once I entered the woods, and I contemplated shifting again. I had pretty much talked myself into it, but I worried about the gun. If the hermit saw it, he could just take it like he did my headsets. I stretched out the neck of my tee. I reassured myself, if necessary, I would shift out of my clothes in my raven form and get to safety. I hadn't done it for years, but I remembered how. I had done it a hundred times when Baylee was small. She would laugh every time my clothes suddenly deflated and fell to the floor, so anytime she was on a crying jag; it was my job to entertain her. She was a colicky baby, so I got a lot of practice.

I was getting a distinct feeling of déjà vu, the further I walked into the woods. I looked around. For some reason, I'd always avoided this small patch of ground when I was a kid. So, I was having a hard time deciding why it seemed so familiar. Memory tickled the back of my mind, but I thrust it away.

"Piper." A soft voice called to me from my left. I whirled to face it.

"Fletcher?" It didn't sound like him. It was a small whispery voice, so maybe he was trying to be quiet. I walked a few paces towards the voice. The woods thinned a bit.

A sense of uncontrollable fear washed over me, and I began to sweat. I panted, then I raised my gun, determined not to run. That's when he stepped around a tree and directly into my line of sight. An Urayuli, a bush man. He was easily nine feet tall, covered in thick dark hair. He was heavily muscled and if I hadn't recognized him in a flash, I'd have been paralyzed with terror. I dropped the gun immediately. Our gazes met and I had a flash of memory.

The childhood memory I had forced down for years came flooding back. I was small—maybe seven or eight—I still didn't have much control over my shifting. My parents had brought me here to stay with Clyde for a week while they were fishing. I'd been in this very spot, and I'd flown into a tree.

I'd lost control for an instant and shifted back into my human form and fell. It had felt like it took forever to reach the ground, and in my panic, I chose the wrong shape. Luckily, I never hit the ground—if I had, I would've shattered several bones, and maybe even died. The Urayuli had caught me. He'd petted my fur gently and set me on the ground. Then he melted into the trees, as he did now.

I sunk to my knees. I thought back to Bran's comments the night before. She was right—I was close-minded. I'd told myself I believed in other supernatural creatures, but I'd been lying to myself. I should have known the Urayuli.

Fletcher found me kneeling in the trees as my mind raced and years of self-lies erased themselves.

"Piper! Are you okay?"

"What?"

I looked up at him, confused for a moment as I re-oriented myself and my childhood faded away and back into the time it belonged.

"Yeah, I'm good." I said as I stood and brushed off the legs of my jeans.

"I've been yelling at you for a while. The guy is gone; I can't find any trace of him."

His sunglasses were pushed back into his hair, which made it stand all around like a halo in the light.

"I have something I need to tell you," I said, and then, completely out of character for me, I fainted.

72

Chapter 7

I came to as Fletcher pushed open the door of the cabin. He had carried me all the way here.

"Boy, you must be really strong," I said. I put a hand to my head, still a little woozy.

He stiffened, but then he laid me gently on the bed. "Are you okay?"

I sat up, and nothing swam. "I'm fine." I wasn't. I was seriously embarrassed. My cheeks felt like they were blazing red. I was truly grateful I wasn't as pale as my sister.

He snorted. "You're fine, and that's why you fainted? Crap, I don't have any way to get you to a hospital either."

"Believe me, I'm perfectly fine, I just had a shock. Pilots don't keep their license if they faint on a regular basis, and I've *never* done it." I clenched my hands into fists. I hated feeling weak or helpless.

He sat down next to me. I also hated that I still felt slightly confused and disoriented. It was if my brain had overloaded.

"What happened, Piper? What did you see?" he asked. His warm voice, full of concern, washed over me, and I threw a quick smile at him.

"It's not just what I saw, it's what I remembered."

He waited patiently as I gathered my thoughts. I didn't know how to tell him the story without giving away my secret. I wanted him to know, I trusted him. He had placed all his trust in me. I was sure he wouldn't betray me.

I took a deep breath, determined. "My dad is Inupiaq, and my mom is Irish." I began, "You can probably see that." I waved a hand down my body, indicating the Native Alaskan features I bore. "You've met my dad, so I know you figured out the native part already."

He nodded.

I looked at the floor and took a deep breath. Then the words rushed out, better organized than I thought they would be. "Alaskan natives have a few myths about a god, or a creature they call Raven. He is their trickster spirit, known not only for playing tricks on men, but tricks against the other gods or spirits in native lore as well. He is credited with many things like creating people and bringing them fire."

I paused and took a deep breath. "He is also a shape-shifter." I dropped my eyes to my hands in my lap. "He can assume any shape; human, animal, or inanimate object, and he uses this skill to fool the unwary for his own ends." I glanced at Fletcher and then back down at my work-worn hands.

"I wasn't raised in my tribe. I was raised a Christian, and I don't worship the gods of my people. Yet, I know there are truths in this myth at least and maybe others." I stopped and took a deep breath. Then with all the courage I could gather, I looked up into Fletcher's burning blue eyes. "Because, like my father, I can change shape."

The air seemed to freeze around us, as I watched the war going on behind his eyes as he tried to process and believe what I had said.

"What?" he croaked.

I stood and deliberately held his eyes. Then like I did when Baylee was a baby, I shifted into my raven form and flew out of my clothes. They fell in a perfect heap. I beat my wings and watched as Fletcher's eyes went from my clothes to my raven self, hovering in his room. I fluttered over and perched on the rocking chair.

"Piper?" He was frozen. Staring.

"Yes," I squawked in my raven voice.

Since he was already in shock, I dropped to the floor, and shifted into my wolf self. He jumped, startled, and then leaned forward, his eyes blazing. I trotted the few short steps and sat before him. Then I turned my back and stepped back into my human shape. I grabbed my clothes and dressed quickly, embarrassed. I sat down at the table and waited for him to speak. The sunglasses dropped back over his eyes.

When he sat silent for a few minutes, I decided to continue with my story. "It's considered a great blessing in my tribe to be related to Raven and have the gift to change shape.

"My dad was treasured and maybe spoiled as a youth. When he chose to marry a white woman, his people shunned him. They thought he wouldn't be able to pass his ability to his children, causing the gift from Raven to be diluted and lost."

I cleared my throat, to give Fletcher a chance to speak if he wanted to. When he didn't, I continued, "I believe even my father was shocked when I received the gift and it seemed stronger than it had in previous generations. Dad can change into a raven only after great meditation and effort and he can't stay long in that form. I can shift without any effort, and I can shape a raven and a wolf, just like I did now. When my parents were surprised by their toddler furry and running around on all fours, they needed a place out of the city for me to explore my gifts and have the space to run and fly without the danger of being discovered."

He nodded, a slight incline of his head as he continued to stare off into space. "Clyde's cabin," he mumbled.

I nodded.

I gestured to encompass the entire property, "It's the perfect place. Clyde was the perfect friend to tell the truth to. Dad had formed a special bond with him and had accepted him as part of his new family already, and Clyde agreed it was a good idea." I looked at Fletcher; his eyes behind the glasses still stared into the distance surrounding me.

"That's why we know your place so well. I spent my childhood here, and months in the summer being a 'wild thing.'" I used air quotes for emphasis. "It also brings me back to what happened in the woods a while ago." I recounted the story of my fall. "When I looked up, the Urayuli had me. He gently sat me down and then he melted away into the woods."

"Ur-a-yu-li?" Fletcher spoke, the question and awkward pronunciation in his voice.

"Yes, it's a native word for 'hairy man, bush man, or wild man of the forest.' You would know the word as Sasquatch, or Bigfoot, whatever you want to call him."

"Sasquatch?" He frowned.

"I should have guessed. I knew them once, and I study folklore, for heaven's sake." I stood up agitated and sat back down. "The signs were there. But I was blocking the stupid memory from my mind. He's been trying to feel you out with the missing items, the rock throwing. He's testing you."

Fletcher stood up violently and started to pace. His chair rocked with the explosive movement. "I have Bigfoot living in my woods?"

"Well, you probably have several," I said, not that it helped. "I played with his children for a short time when I was small." I paused. "In second grade, I told some kids that I played in the woods with bush men children. They laughed at me, and made fun of me, and told me I was a liar, Bigfoot didn't exist. I pushed it to the back of my mind and made myself believe I had imagined it. Then when I came back to Clyde's, I avoided the patch of woods where we had played. The Urayuli are very smart, they must have known that something had happened, and I never saw them again."

I took a breath, and looking Fletcher straight into the eyes said, "Until today."

He stopped pacing, turned, and looked directly at me. "You saw it?"

"*He,*" I emphasized, "showed himself to me, and when he did, all of my memories came back. He knew me. He called my name."

"You said you should have recognized the signs. What do you know about these things?"

"They are people," I emphasized again. "More than it seems since I didn't pick up the clues when it was happening. Being what I am, folklore is sort of a hobby for me and my friend Branwyn. People have researched these creatures for years, even though they get labeled whack jobs and kooks."

"Are they dangerous?"

"Not the bush men, not if they are left alone. At least no one has lived to say otherwise." I smirked but grew serious again when I got no reaction to my joke. "In my opinion, like most wild things, as long as they aren't bothered, they seem to be content to watch and make petty mischief. They don't like guns though, so if you point a gun at them, they are likely to respond.

"I suspect they've been feeling you out. See if you are going to try to hurt them or expose them. They do not want to be seen." I started to think out loud. "They know me though, I wondered what they thought when I dropped you here the first time. They must not have known what to think. First Clyde died, and then the place was empty for months." I slammed my hands down on the table. "They took the moose!"

"What?" Fletcher said, startled.

"They took the moose, you know, out of the meat cache?" I said triumphantly.

"Why do you think that?"

"They aren't animals, they're closer to men. They knew Clyde was dead, and he didn't need the meat, so they took it."

"What do you mean—men?"

"In all the native folklore, one thing they've agreed on is that the Urayuli are men. The natives of this land have a myth that the giant wild men followed them when they came to this land—probably over the land bridge. The natives had the tools to hunt the mammoths, and the wild men were more gatherers. To get meat, they lived on the outskirts of human society, taking what was left after a hunt. Always shy, they stay out of sight. Probably because when the natives saw them stealing their meat, they killed them."

Fletcher sat down on the stool next to me. "How do giant hairy men keep from being seen?"

"Magic?" I frowned thoughtfully.

77

"Really?" Fletcher lifted an incredulous eyebrow.

I just waved a hand to indicate my body and shape-changing abilities. He lifted his glasses briefly and rubbed his eyes.

"Even if they aren't magic, or only sort of magic, you've seen them, or not seen them, more sensed them, right?" I continued.

"Yeah, it's more like I know they are watching and sometimes I think I catch a glimpse from the corner of my eye."

"Well think about it. If you spent eons being murdered and trying to hide so you could steal what you needed to survive, wouldn't you evolve nearly perfect abilities to do so?"

"Makes sense," he conceded with a tired sigh.

"Researchers have noticed things about them. First, when they want to repel people, they can put off a nauseating smell. Do you remember that first night here? The smell around the place?"

"Yea, it drove me into your arms." He smiled and winked at me, I slugged him in the arm.

"They can somehow project a disabling sense of fear as well. They also have systems to warn each other." I thought back to the cryptozoologists map of cryptids and how they must have been around the spot we landed the first day we had met.

"Remember when we landed on the river that first day after we ran into those ravens? They were banging against tree trunks, wood knocking it's called. They do that to pinpoint where we are and warn others away. They are famous for throwing stuff to scare people away. The rocks on your cabin roof, and the rocks that same day we heard the wood knocking."

He was nodding, "It makes sense." He stopped and looked towards the door. "What do you think they want? Do they want me to leave?" he asked.

Like I had any real answers. I thought carefully, sorting through any esoteric knowledge I'd collected. "I think if they wanted you to leave, they would be much more persistent. People have written about them trying to break into their houses, destroying items, howling, and throwing things all night, anything to scare them away. That's not happening here. It's mild, like they're just trying to get you to react so they can judge your actions and make a decision about you. I think they decided today. That's why the big guy showed himself to me. It was his way of saying if you think the new guy is all right, we'll give him the benefit of the doubt."

"Well, that's good, I guess. Now what do I do?"

"Well, all good neighbors take gifts when someone moves in," I said with a smile. "You may be the one moving in, but let's take a welcome basket."

"I haven't been hunting; I don't really have anything that they'd recognize as food." He started sorting through his items. Finally, he drew out several large bags of Teriyaki flavored beef jerky. "You think this will do?"

I shrugged. "It does on the commercials."

His mouth quirked in one of his crooked smiles.

I grabbed one of Clyde's wooden mixing bowls. "Doesn't hurt to try."

We emptied all the jerky into the bowl and walked it out to the chopping block. We set it down, and went back into the cabin, careful not to watch out the windows or try to catch a peek. While we waited to see if our offering would be accepted, Fletcher asked me more about my childhood, and my abilities. Finally, the million-dollar question came up.

"What did your tribe do when they learned about you?" He asked.

"Nothing." I paused for a moment, the hurt and anger like a hand gripping my throat. "We've never told them." A certain harshness entered my voice, years of being ignored and shunned and watching my dad suffer the loss of his family and friends flaming the anger that moved from my throat to a burning brand in my chest.

Fletcher seemed to recognize it, and he let it go. "Oh."

"Only my immediate family, Bran, Clyde, and now you, know." I ran my sweaty hands down my jeans and stood up. "So, where did you find the gold?" I asked, effectively changing the subject away from me.

He glanced up at me, hot blue eyes blazing over the tops of his glasses showing me he recognized my need to move away from this current source of pain. After a moment, he covered his eyes again.

He leaned back casually in his chair, put his hand behind his head and laughed. "Wouldn't you like to know!"

I wasn't sure if he was being serious or not. I had told him my deepest darkest secrets, and he still didn't want to share about the gold?

He let me fret for a moment, then confessed, "It was in the toilet."

"Huh?"

"You heard me correctly; the bulk of it was hidden in the toilet. Think about it, where's the last place you'd look?"

He was right; I wouldn't look in the toilet. Although if I were looking hard, I might.

"It wasn't in an obvious place. If you looked in it, you wouldn't see it." He squirmed a little, probably wondering if he was going to gross me out. "I had to see how close the outhouse was to needing to be moved, so I was quite far inside. There's a secret compartment down there, separate from the waste, but still difficult to get too, well, cleanly."

I snorted.

"The old stuff, the stuff you couldn't pass off as mined, it was in the toilet. The flour gold, and nuggets, stuff he could say he mined, and wasn't as valuable was hidden in various places inside hollowed out logs all over the property. Once I knew how to look for it, I found most of that and I put it in here. He pulled a pot off the shelf and showed me the contents. It was a large soup pot, and it was full of gold. Some of it was already in little vials, or in cloth bags, but the bigger stuff was loose. That pot must have weighed quite a bit, but Fletcher carried it like it weighed nothing. He was strong.

"What about the old gold?"

"I left it where it was. It's safe there. I took just a small amount with us when we left. I cashed in some of Clyde's stuff and put the old coins and bars that I had with me in a safe deposit box."

"And you trust me with millions of dollars just lying around?"

"Yeah, I do. There's already more than I could spend in that pot and in the bank. Even if you cleaned me out, I wouldn't be hurting for money for a long time."

"Thanks for the vote of confidence."

"You're welcome, but since I also know you'd have to fish for it..." He trailed off and threw me his best rakish grin. He had pushed his sunglasses back again, and his eyes twinkled, the blue clear and innocent.

I stared at him for a moment too long, "Let's go check on our gift."

He shrugged, and we stood up and went to the door. The old growth stump Fletcher used as a chopping block was about thirty feet from the door. We walked over so we could see the inside of the bowl. I was surprised to see that the jerky was gone, and the bowl full of blueberries.

"I think you have been approved as the new tenant," I said and glanced at him.

He appeared to still be a bit dazed by the situation. I looked back down at the stump. My headsets were also there, leaning up against the stump. I leaned over and picked them up.

"I don't think Clyde was afraid of them." Fletcher said out of the blue. "They really don't seem to mean any harm, and he lived here for years. You said you played with them. That indicates that they weren't terrorizing Clyde, or he wouldn't have left you alone in the woods or let your parents think it was a good idea for you to be here."

I nodded, that made sense.

"So, I'm back to the things that show he was afraid. The door cores, the lights, the survival packs, and why did he pull up the ladder?" He walked around the stump, looking at it, then up at the roof. "What do bush men need of gold?"

"Absolutely nothing," I said.

"Exactly. Something or someone else has been here, they want the gold. They dug those holes, and followed us, or sent someone to follow us while we were in town. Maybe the bush men have kept them away, but it's only a matter of time before they get what they want. The answers to that have to be in Clyde's contacts, his past, or his death."

As he spoke, I searched the woods for my old friends. Deep in the shadows at the opposite end of the property from my childhood playground, I caught a glimpse of fur. Not the bush men.

The creature had accidentally given itself away.   In the quick glance that I got, I thought I saw grey and tan fur.   There wasn't a scent, I was facing upwind. It was the big wolf. I'd bet my plane on it.

I caught Fletcher's eye and drew his attention towards the animal. I knew he saw it when his eyes opened wide. I held up my hand to tell him to hold still and then like earlier, I shifted out of my clothes and stretched my wings to the sky.   Fletcher leaped to grab me, as I climbed out of reach.   "Piper, come back, it's not a wolf!" He yelled after me.

Chapter 8

His words worried me for an instant, but it's harder to stay focused when I'm a raven. I knew I wanted to see the wolf, so I flew for it. As I approached, it watched me, and then dismissed me. I perched above it in a tree. It definitely looked like the same wolf. I wished suddenly for my other nose but cut myself off before I accidentally shifted and fell from the tree. It looked even bigger than the first time. Again, I noticed the stockier build, the heavy head and longer, sharper teeth. Its paws were huge—the claws longer, thicker, and sharper than mine. It was a true killing machine.

It stayed hidden, the fact we'd seen it was just a fluke of the light and timing. I don't think it knew we'd seen it. I glanced back toward Fletcher; he was gone. He must have gone inside. I contemplated fluttering downwind of it and changing so I could scent him, but just before I jumped off my branch, I heard the eerie chorus of a wolf pack.

I leapt into the air and flew towards the sound. The air lifted me and burned through my feathers with exquisite pleasure. I dove and swooped with pure joy. Then I climbed over the treetops to view the pack. I couldn't imagine what a pack of monsters like the big wolf would look like, so I was almost disappointed to see a pack of average Alaskan grey wolves. There were maybe eight others in view, a normal pack size. They waited, and the monster joined them. Then they trotted away and disappeared deep into the forest canopy. I contemplated following them. Wolves and ravens have ancient ties, so it wouldn't be unrealistic for them to notice a stray raven following.

I couldn't follow them through the canopy, it was too thick. I dropped to the ground to change where I last saw them. The air was still thick from their scent, and I trotted after, not even needing to lower my nose to follow. Luckily, the wind was blowing directly at me, so I felt safe they wouldn't smell me before they saw me. I trotted slowly, trying to stay a safe distance behind them. I have a slight advantage when I'm in deep cover. My fur is raven black, and it's easier for me to blend into the shadows than other wolves.

I followed them in the ground eating trot of the wolf for what seemed several miles. Since I was so busy searching for them with my eyes, I didn't realize the smell had gotten thicker until I almost walked on top of them. They were in a small clearing in a loosely gathered group in various stances around the big brute. Those standing held their tails low and carefully kept their heads low as well. Classic submissive stance to a much more dominant wolf.

It was warm, and several were panting. Most gathered in the shade and sat or lay in the cool grass. I stayed under the tree I was at and clung to its trunk. The smallest wolf, grey with a white streak on her nose suddenly lay on her side and began writhing around as though she were ill. I watched, concerned as she contorted and thrashed about. Suddenly, she let out a piercing howl and I heard the distinct sound of bone breaking. Her back arched, and her limbs elongated. Her muzzle shrank and her hair receded. After several minutes, she curled into a ball, naked, and human.

I trembled and shook violently. I didn't know if I should run away terrified or jump out into the clearing in joy. These wolves were shapeshifters like me!

The woman sat up slowly. She was very small, her long dark hair tangled and matted as though it had been years since it had seen a brush. For me, other than being naked, I came out of my wolf and raven just like I went in. It is magic after all. So, I knew she'd been living in the woods a while to look so dirty and rough.

She was native, but unlike me, she had no other blood altering her genetic line. She was very thin, not emaciated or unhealthy, just sinewy and tough. She finally recovered from her change and walked towards the big dominant wolf, completely dwarfed by his great size.

She rubbed her face under his jaw, showing submission and respect and rolled over to give him her belly. He nipped lightly at her and licked her. Once accepted, she knelt before him with her head lowered and spoke in a raspy, unused voice. I wasn't sure what she said, her accent was thick, and her English was broken. She spoke what seemed to be some native words, but I couldn't place the tribal language either. I thought I heard the word "girl", but I just couldn't understand her well enough to be sure.

I found myself taking a step forward so I could hear more clearly. Hyper-focused on the clearing, I forgot to watch my feet; I stepped on a small, dead branch and it snapped with the sound like a shotgun blast. I cringed down; trying to hide myself in the shadows, but it was too late. Two grey wolves peeled off from the group and trotted towards the sound. They hadn't spotted me, so I slunk backward slowly, using my color to melt into the darkness of the tree shadows. I just needed enough space to change and fly. Keeping my eyes firmly on them and my ears pricked forward, I stepped back carefully, one, two, three steps.

The wolves in front of me didn't indicate that they'd sensed me. Attention riveted to my front, I jumped when I bumped into hard muscle and fur behind me. A deep resonate growl assured me that I had gone from the frying pan into the fire. I whirled around as the new wolf snapped at where my haunches had been. My hackles rose, my wolf responded. I've never been submissive as a human, which may be why my wolf instincts were not those of a submissive wolf. Backing down from a fight has never been the first road I've taken.

I lowered my head, my eyes firmly on my opponent's. We rushed together at the same time, the smaller grey wolf aiming for my forelegs, its powerful jaws sure to snap bone if they made contact.

Quicker than the smaller wolf, I overrode my wolf instinct and grabbed the smaller wolf's muzzle snapping my teeth with force and releasing. I knew that as a human, getting smacked in the nose took the fight out of you for a few seconds, and I had two other wolves coming in hot on my flanks.

I needed to get the space to be able to shift and fly. My first opponent backed away whining, then began rubbing her muzzle in the dirt. Unfortunately, my move didn't buy me any time. The other two were on me almost before I released my bite. If I couldn't get free, they would make short work of me. Unlike me, they knew what they were doing, and I was too afraid to let my wolf follow its instincts.

I dodged and attempted to protect my most vulnerable spots, throat, legs, hamstrings, belly and in doing so missed opportunities to inflict damage on the others. Slowly, I lost ground, my face and shoulders were bleeding, and my fur littered the ground like someone had blown up a pillow.

The first wolf recovered and joined the others. They circled me as I dodged and spun, running in, snapping, or slicing my flesh with their teeth. My fur dripped blood. I didn't see any way I was walking or flying out of the forest alive. In desperation, I considered changing and flying, but the wolves might be quick enough to snatch me the instant I changed.

A new louder growl came from a fourth wolf in the dark forest behind me. I could hear it pounding through the undergrowth, all stealth gone in its excitement to join the fight, to tear my flesh and destroy me. Desperate, with a dark snarl of my own, I used the distraction the charging wolf offered, and I rushed the largest wolf. It faced me and ran to meet me. As it lowered its head to protect its throat before lunging at me, I leapt, aiming for its broad back, planting my front feet, then pushing off with my back legs.

It tried to bend around, and I felt the heat of its breath as its teeth grazed my left foot. I leapt with all my strength off its back, the force pushing it to the ground, and at the summit of my jump, changed into my raven. I beat my wings furiously, rising ever so slowly into the trees, the fear roiling off my back and slicking down my feathers to fall away as I gained altitude.

I went straight up and landed awkwardly in a large spruce, gazing down, wounded and bleeding. The new wolf had distracted the others from my trick because I should have been an easy snatch and snack. He was in the middle of my torn fur, silvery white with darker points, another monster wolf like the first, but smaller than the behemoth alpha by a good thirty pounds. He was everywhere ripping and tearing.

The largest grey wolf, which had been distracted by my trick, lay broken and bleeding below me, his throat ripped open. The other two worked the silver wolf's flanks attempting to hamstring him. As I watched, he whirled and, in a movement, fast enough I could barely see it, ripped the throat from the second wolf. He pounced on the last, tumbling it over and ripping the tender belly flesh open. The last wolf, desperate to get away left a trail of its own entrails as it ran into the woods. It wouldn't go far. Finally, the silver wolf stood alone, its sides heaving, its head down.

It panted like that for a while, and then deliberately, it raised its head and stared at me through ice blue eyes. It knew I was a shapeshifter too. I shuddered, the movement shaking through my feathers and spraying blood over the branches around me.

Once it had assured itself that I knew it saw me, it turned and melted into the woods, not towards the group I had spied on, but away. Not wanting to follow it, I rose above the trees and headed back leaving the broken bodies of my fellow shifters lying below in their blood and fur.

I had lost a lot of blood, and I felt the loss as I flew. My wings felt heavy and beating them took willpower. I glided as much as I could, letting the wind lift and drop me, soothing and cool. My blood dripped steadily, soaking my breast feathers, spraying behind me. My vision was darkening when the cabin came in view. I aimed for the door, not thinking, and fluttered down in front of it.

It took the last of my energy to change into my human form and crawl through the door. I called for Fletcher but got no answer. Maybe he went searching for me. Naked, I dug through my pack for the first aid kit and a candy bar. I needed calories and water to replenish my blood and energy. I had changed three times, expended energy, fought and lost a lot of blood.

Some time passed before Fletcher found me slumped naked in the middle of his cabin, wrappers slung about, covered in blood, filth, chocolate, and sobbing in pain; I didn't have the strength to stand up let alone dress. He picked me up gently and laid me on the bed.

"God, Piper," he said, brushing my tangled hair from my face. He looked over my body in horror which wasn't an emotion I wanted to arouse in him. I didn't have the energy to look down but figured I was a mess. I whimpered.

"Just try to relax," he whispered. Then he got up and ran some water in a pan and put another on to boil as well. He gave me a handful of pain killers which I swallowed gratefully. He brought the first pan over to the bed and pulled over a chair. Gently, he began to clean away the dirt and blood from my wounds. I don't know how long it took, but it felt like hours. When he finished with a cut, he'd bandage it with some antibiotic cream. A few were quite deep. He'd apologize as he sealed them with super glue, and I'd cry out. Once he finished, he covered me in a blanket, and I dozed.

I heal fast for a human, but not anything outside the realm of natural. I'd never really been sick that I remembered, and I hadn't been wounded greater than skinned knees as a child. I wasn't sure how I would respond to infection, and from Fletcher's worried care, neither did he.

He made sure I drank water and added Gatorade packets to it for fluid recovery. Animal bites can be nasty, all kinds of bacteria stay on their teeth. I had several dozen wounds, some quite deep. The fever that set-in let us both know that I wasn't immune from illness.

I kept drifting in and out. At some point, Fletcher must have finally gotten a hold of my dad, because I heard a plane flying in low. Fletcher argued with him that I needed to get to a hospital, and I struggled for a minute, knowing I couldn't go and trying to stop him.

Dad was hurt once, he cut his hand badly when repairing an engine, and mom took him to the hospital for stitches. They did a routine blood test and got some anomalous results. Being human, they dismissed it as a contaminated sample, but dad and I knew the truth. We weren't human, and it was best if that wasn't proven by modern science. Since we were never sick, we made an unspoken decision to never go to a doctor again. I didn't relax until he explained this to Fletcher, and eventually Fletcher understood.

Dad had brought a vial of penicillin and some disposable syringes. I was aware for the first injection he gave me, and then nothing but heat, and rage, and blackness.

I woke up. I opened my eyes, and the searing light nearly made me cry out. My head ached, and I felt weak and exhausted. I tried to roll over because I had to use the toilet desperately. I couldn't move. My hands and feet were secured to the bed. I did cry out then, and Fletcher leapt up from off the floor to check on me.

"Let me up," I tried to shout, but it came out hoarse and thin.

"How do you feel?" he asked as he undid the ties around my ankles and moved to my wrists.

"What happened? What's going on?" I asked weakly.

"You've been very sick. You didn't react well to the bites." Free from the restraints, I tried to roll to my side, surprised at how much energy it took. Fletcher saw me and gently tucked his hand under my back and helped.

"Why am I so weak?" I asked.

"You've been sick for over five days," he responded. "You've lost a lot of blood; you've been delirious and fighting infection."

"Five days? I have to go to work." I tried to sit up but grew too light-headed and slumped back down. Fletcher gave a dry and brittle laugh.

"Uh, you aren't going to be working for a while." He pushed his bedding on the floor to the side and pulled over a stool. "Even if you were strong enough to walk to the plane, which you're not, you couldn't be seen in public. It looks like you were hit by a train."

I looked down. I was wearing an oversized t-shirt, not mine. My arms and legs were bruised and scratched and covered with bandages. I could feel the hurt spots I couldn't see under my shirt, and I could only imagine what my face looked like. I could also smell myself and feel the sick sweat that had dried over me which wasn't something I wanted to think about.

"Was my dad here?" I asked, wondering if I had imagined him.

"Yes, he brought medicine, and he's been helping me care for you. He had to go to town for more, and to do some work. He said to tell you not to worry; he has some guys helping out while you're sick. He'll be back tonight."

"I have to go to the bathroom."

I was embarrassed, but he half lifted me from the bed and held on to me. He tried to get me to use a bucket, but I refused and made him help me to the outhouse. Then I made him leave while I finished. He ended up having to carry me back, as all my strength was depleted.

"I'm so sorry," I kept saying to him as he carried me back as though I weighed nothing. My mind imagined what he had to do to care for me while I was sick, and the embarrassment gnawed at my guts.

He laid me down on the bed again. "Do you think you can hold something down if I bring it to you?" he asked. "You'll get your strength back sooner if we can get some food into you."

"I'm starving," I said and leaned my head back on the pillow. I was surprised to notice it was my pillow from home. Dad must have brought it with him and clean sheets from my house. Too bad I wasn't clean. My hair was greasy, and I smelled like sickness. There wasn't really any way to get clean here without a trip to the stream or a spit bath and I wasn't in any shape for either.

Finally, Fletcher brought over a bowl with some canned chicken noodle soup. I looked at him incredulously. "I was hoping for a fourteen-ounce porterhouse," I said and grinned.

"That's the second course." He smirked ironically.

I took an experimental bite. The soup was delicious and filled the empty space in my stomach with warmth. I greedily slurped down half the bowl before I realized I was full.

Fletcher watched me look at the bowl in astonishment when I couldn't finish it.

"You haven't held down anything but some broth the entire time you were sick. You're going to have to build up to solid food."

I nodded, and before I could say anything else, I fell back to sleep.

We repeated the pattern about three more times until I could finally stay awake for more than a few minutes. I had no idea what day or time it was. It was close enough to midsummer that the day was basically light the full twenty-four hours.

"When was my dad supposed to be back?" I asked.

"He called. Since you were better, he felt he better do some client runs. Don't worry, he's going to come and pick you up in the morning." His voice was rough. I was sure that he had had his fill of being a nursemaid.

"What?" I said, suddenly anxious. I didn't want to leave the comfort of this bed, but I realized I must have worn out my welcome a while ago. "Yeah, that's probably best. You kinda got more than you bargained for."

"It's not that Piper. It hasn't been like that. You just need modern conveniences now that we can move you. Somewhere there's a clean bed, a bathroom, and warm water; somewhere we can get bandages and supplies without flying two hours, someplace where even if your dad doesn't agree, we can get you to a doctor." He stopped and ran his hand over his face.

That's when I noticed that he also had half-healed cuts and scrapes, and his beard was growing in. His hair was wild and greasy, and I realized he'd been worried about me. "I thought you were going to die, and I had no way to get you to someone who could take care of you. It took eighteen hours before I got a hold of your dad and three more before he got here with medicine." He scrubbed his hands over his face and through his hair.

"Why did you chase after that creature?" he asked.

"The wolf?" I asked.

"It's not a wolf," he said. I remembered he had said that to me the day I had gone after it.

"Yeah, I know; it's a cryptid wolf. Possibly a Kenai Peninsula Wolf."

"What?" he shook his head. "That's not what I mean. It's not a Kenai wolf, or a wolf at all. It's a werewolf."

I laughed briefly but noticed that his face was solemn. "No, that can't be. He's just got to be a shifter like me. Like those other wolves."

"How do you know they change shape?"

"I saw a smaller grey wolf change and figured they were a group of shape-shifters like me."

"No Piper, they aren't like you. They are like me." He turned away for a moment, and I thought he said, "At least one of them is."

Chapter 9

My heart sped up. What was he saying? He was a werewolf? I remembered the other huge wolf, the one that had fought after I fled. I looked at his face and arms again and noticed the half-healed wounds. They looked old, but I hadn't seen them before that day, so I knew they had to be from the fight. Then I remembered the creature's blue eyes when it had looked at me and the fact that Fletcher didn't show up until sometime after I had returned to the cabin, and I knew I'd guessed the truth.

"You weren't sick because you picked up an infection in your wounds," he looked at me sadly. "You were sick because you've been fighting the werewolf sickness that is in your bloodstream."

"What do you mean? How do you know? Am I a werewolf now? How does it work?" The questions came tumbling out, panic at the possibilities and the unknown chewing an extra hole in my belly. I was a shifter. How could I be different than what I am? What would I do if I were to become a werewolf? Would I lose my raven? I sat up and put my feet over the edge of the bed. I was panting, my chest was tight, and Fletcher reached out to soothe me. He ran his hand over my hair and rubbed my back as I caught my breath.

"Piper, everything is okay, just lie down and relax. I'll tell you everything if you stay quiet."

My breathing slowed, and I let him comfort me for a moment. Then I stiffened. I had almost forgotten the worst part.

"You lied to me," I said suddenly, and as I did, I realized it was true.

I'd poured out my story to him, unfolded the greatest secret I had and handed it to him. In return, he'd said nothing. I'd trusted him, thinking he trusted me with his greatest secret, and I was wrong. He hadn't trusted me, not really.

"Why didn't you tell me, especially after I showed you what I was?"

"I didn't have time," he said weakly, at least he had the decency to look ashamed. He could've told me at any point during the time it took to tell him my story, he could've at least indicated that he had something to tell me instead of looking shell shocked and surprised like he didn't know that the things that go bump in the night existed. "I was still processing what you'd told me and shown me when you took off. I wanted to tell you; I just needed some time."

"Bullshit," I said quietly. My heart aching. "You weren't going to tell me." I was quiet, the truth in my words ringing between us. "Well, why not? Why is your secret so much more precious than mine?" I heard the hurt in my voice like a sob.

He hung his head. "I'm a monster, Piper. I didn't want you to know that."

"What are you talking about? You aren't anymore a monster than me."

"You don't know."

"Enlighten me," I snapped. I was angry, and I wasn't going to take his self-loathing as an excuse.

I hadn't seen a monster. I'd seen him help me when I needed it—consciously. It wasn't like he was rabid and eating babies under the full moon. At least I couldn't believe that of him. He was too calm, too focused too—I couldn't think of the word. Old-fashioned? Gracious? I shook my head. No, I couldn't believe he was any kind of monster. Even as a beast.

"You need to know. I don't know why I thought I could keep it secret; it's not like it's safe to be around me. I just figured I wouldn't see you enough for it to matter. But now you're helping me. You have to know, to protect yourself."

"Know what?" I asked, the hurt in my voice biting. I had no intention of letting him continue with his self-loathing.

"Werewolves aren't born, Piper. They are made."

"Okay, yeah, I've seen the movies." I lay back down—my outburst had been exhausting, and I could feel this wouldn't be a fairytale length story.

"Just listen."

I nodded.

"I told you I was teaching high school in Idaho?"

I nodded again. He'd mentioned it sometime when I wasn't really paying attention.

"Well, I taught history, and I was considering another degree. I've always been into the outdoors, and I decided that maybe I should try and extend my license into science as well, you know, use my love of the outdoors to get kids interested in the practical sciences. So, I signed up for some classes at the local university. Nothing heavy, I wasn't sure what I was going to pursue yet, so I was just taking a few general science classes. One of the classes had a backpacking element." He stood up, as though it would be easier to talk if he could use his body for emphasis.

"Okay. I know what you mean; I took one of those backpacking slash whatever classes for a creative writing course once."

"Yeah, so you know that part of the class is to go off and catalog and write about the things you see. So as part of the weeklong backpacking excursion required, we were to split up and take one day to explore and find something unique to bring back and share. I did this stuff all the time on my own, so I wasn't worried about it. In fact, I was looking forward to the solitude after listening to my classmates complain about their petty aches and ailments and how they would do things differently."

I grunted affirmatively. I would have probably been tearing out throats by that point.

"Since I was more woods savvy and I had spent time in the mountains around the area, I was comfortable going further afield than most. I went far enough I was sure I had put a couple miles between me and everyone else. I set up my camp for the evening and went off to search for my 'unique' item. That's when it found me. The werewolf. That big grey and tan monster you saw watching me that day you took off."

He walked over to the stove, checked the fire, and threw on a log. He put some water in the kettle. I tried to prop up my pillows so that I could sit up a little more and he came over and helped me.

"What happened?"

He sat back down and scrubbed his hands through his hair again. I was beginning to realize it was a habit of his when he worried. "I'm not an amateur in the woods. I always have a large caliber handgun for bears. I saw the wolf. It watched me for a while. I was startled at its size. I think I was even ruminating over how I could describe it to someone and how they wouldn't believe me. I've seen wolves before, even close, and I could generally scare one away. I had my gun out and I yelled at it, but it didn't budge. I was going to fire in the air and had the safety off. So, when the wolf charged me, I shot it. I must have put five shots into it before it hit me. There were bear rounds in that gun, and they didn't even slow it down.

"I won't go into the details, but I should have been dead. It savaged me. It tore my skin, it broke my bones, it exposed my organs." He shuddered with the memory, I gasped in horror and realized I had my hand over my mouth. He kept on. "I don't know what it wanted. First, I thought it just wanted to eat me. But I've changed my mind as I've thought about it." He looked over my head, reliving the moment. His voice became detached, cold.

"I lost consciousness sometime during the attack. I came to in the life flight helicopter. I had lain in the woods for two days before they found me. Miraculously, although my clothes were torn, and I was covered with blood and odd 'scratches,' I was only suffering from a fever and what they labeled 'exposure.' The bottom line is they didn't know what was wrong with me, and when I told them about the wolf attack, they didn't believe me. In those two days, I had healed from what should have been mortal wounds."

I hadn't studied much werewolf lore; I hadn't believed in it because it didn't match what I knew to be true about me. I also hadn't read Bran's book yet, so I wasn't sure about anything. But in the monster movies, you just needed to be bitten or scratched to turn. Then there was the whole moon thing. I must have looked like I was going to start in with the questions, because Fletcher held up his hand for me to wait.

"I didn't know what had happened to me. I even thought I had hallucinated on the brink of hypothermia or something, but that never rang true. I was prepared for the outdoors and the temperature was mild. I couldn't find anything that matched my symptoms on the internet, so I sort of put it in the back of my head and went on.

"Unfortunately, or fortunately, I'm not sure which; some of the things people assume about werewolves are true. The moon is one. The next full moon I was violently sick all day. I was fevered and cramping, and my head ached. As it progressed, I started having seizures. I was too ill to get to a phone by that point, luckily, so I lay on the floor in my bathroom in agony. Finally, I realized I couldn't fight the illness, and I surrendered myself to it, hoping that by doing so, I would die. I was that sick and in pain. That's when the change began."

He looked up at me. "When you changed for me, it was beautiful, graceful, and easy. For me, the change is white hot agony. That first change took hours. I don't really remember the end, but the next day I awoke covered in blood, the doors between the bathroom and the outside of the house were destroyed. I had killed and I didn't remember it. The full moon lasts about three days, and during that time I remember nothing except that people died."

"If you don't remember, how do you know that?" I asked, interrupting him.

He hung his head. When he finally answered, his voice was rough with emotion.

"After the moon cycle ended, and I knew what was happening to me was real, I tried to find out where the blood was from. There were three unexplained disappearances in my area. Two were joggers; one was a teenage boy walking home from his friend's house after a party. The joggers were never found, but the boy..." He trailed off, and I knew what he was going to say. He cleared his throat and looked down at his hands folded across his knees. "The boy was savaged by an animal, probably a wild dog." The way he said it, made it sound like a quote. I was sure he had it memorized from a newspaper article or something.

"Why do you think that was you?" I asked, never able to keep my mouth shut.

He was quiet for a moment, thinking, I thought, but maybe he was trying to bring his emotion back under control. "I was covered with blood, Piper. It wasn't mine. I killed and worse, I probably ate."

I wasn't sure I wanted to know that, but I couldn't believe that the wolf Fletcher I had seen would do anything differently than Fletcher the man. I told him.

"You don't know, Piper. My wolf isn't just primal and instinct driven, he is full of rage. Once I was able to remain aware during my change, I realized how difficult it was to control. I know I killed that boy and probably the others."

"Can you think as *you* while you're a wolf?" I asked.

He thought for a moment, "Yes, I think so, although it seems as though my thoughts are much more basic. More aimed at the moment than any deep thought. And as a man, I'm more volatile, quicker to anger."

"It's similar for me, but I *can* think, and I never forget that I am me."

He nodded. I felt a little triumph, shape shifters and werewolves weren't really all that different.

"Fletcher, in my other shapes, I still won't do what I wouldn't do in my human shape. I don't believe you would ever harm an innocent, especially a teenaged boy since you taught teenaged boys—you cared for them. Something else happened to him, either he was attacked by a wild dog or a wolf, or that other werewolf did it. I don't know, but I do know it couldn't have been you."

For a moment, a spark of hope exploded behind his eyes, but the despair dropped quickly back into place. "I wasn't me at the time. I can't remember, and I'm pretty sure I couldn't control it." He shook his head. "I know now, and I keep the wolf tightly reined in. I stay away from people. That's the best for me."

"Is that the real reason you came here?"

He ran his hands down his jean clad thighs, as though to wipe away blood. He tucked them into his front pockets. "It was my one chance to be safe, a place to be away from the fragile humans that I could hurt or kill. It was like it was meant to be."

"Hmmph." It was an involuntary noise, but it conveyed what a crock I thought he was spewing. "That's rather fatalistic," I said. "We make our own choices. Clyde would still be dead whether you were a werewolf or not. When this little mess is done," I waved my hand to encompass it all, my sickness, the werewolf problem, the gold. "Then we're going to find out what happened to that boy and the joggers so you can quit wallowing in self-pity." I sounded a little harsh, but he needed to be snapped out of it. "You are not a murderer, and I think we can probably find that out with some digging and persistence."

"You don't know me well enough to have that much faith in me," he said sadly.

"Bullshit." My answer was louder and firmer this time. I also added a half smile. He smiled, but it didn't reach his eyes. He sat back down.

"Anyway, I moved to Alaska soon after that. Doing odd jobs around the state. It's been five years now. I can change when I want too, and it isn't as bad as that first time, but it will never be fun." He flinched in memory. "I still have to change with the moon, but I don't have to stay wolf as long or change as early. Under the moon, is the only time the change is easy." He paused for a moment and made sure to hold my eyes. "The only other werewolf myth that seems to be true is silver," he added.

I didn't wear jewelry very often, because I sometimes forgot about it when I shifted, and I'd lost some favorite pieces that way. I have a lot of jewelry, ravens tend to like shiny things, but I didn't get to wear them much, so I tried to wear some if I had an excuse. Since I was bringing Fletcher out that day, I had dressed in my nicest work clothes and had worn a simple silver pendant on a silver snake chain, assuming that I wouldn't be shifting.

When I had shifted for him; it had fallen to the floor with my clothes, and I had tucked it in my pocket. He had seen me do it. My clothes were neatly folded on the rocking chair. He went to them and reached his hand into my jeans pocket and pulled out my necklace. He brought it to me and dropped it neatly into my hand. Then he showed me his. The necklace had burned his skin like acid. I could see its outline pressed into his hand and fingers. As I watched, the burns healed until no sign remained.

"I'm pretty sure I can only be killed by silver," he said, "Remember that."

"Do you always heal that fast?" I asked.

"Unless it's another werewolf bite, apparently." He smiled briefly and waved at the mostly healed cuts I had noticed earlier. "Piper, I didn't tell you because after I saw you shift, I knew for sure that I was a monster. I didn't want you to know that about me. You were so natural and beautiful, and by contrast, what I am is brutal and unnatural." He hung his head. "I thought I could stay away from you."

My heart skipped a beat and sped up.

He continued, "I couldn't let myself live if I knew I would ever hurt another human being. This cabin, this place gives me that insurance. As long as I'm here during the full moon, I am safe, and so are you."

We were both silent for a time, deep in thought. I was contemplating his revelations; still sure he couldn't kill. I was so wrapped up in his story, that the spot that had been itching in the back of my head was forgotten until the silence fell, then it came rushing forward.

"Who is the werewolf?"

"What?"

"Werewolves are only wolves part time, right? Otherwise, they're just wolves. So, who turned you?"

He looked at me. "I've thought about it a while. I don't have any way of knowing."

"Yes, you do," I said excitedly. "Think about it. You said, at first you thought he wanted to eat you, but that's not true or you would've been eaten. He wasn't disturbed, no one found you for two days. So, he did what he did to you to turn you. Sound right?"

He nodded; he'd thought this far at least.

"You were chosen." I paused for emphasis and watched the color drain from his face.

"The werewolf had to know where you'd be and when. He needed you isolated, in the wild and alone. Who knew this information?"

"The people in my class."

"That's right, the people in your group. He's male. We need a list of the men in your group, and we can find your werewolf."

"Why didn't I think of this before?" He paced violently. "I have a list of my classmates; I never erased my email from school." He was agitated. He started to pace again. He mumbled, "I don't even know why I saved it." He turned to me. "I need to get to a computer!"

We'd talked most of the night with brief stops for catnaps. I wasn't surprised when my extra sharp hearing caught the buzz of a small plane in the distance. When it got nearer, I recognized dad's Piper Super Cruiser. I hadn't remembered him here with me during the worst of my illness, but as I listened to the plane land, I felt a wash of safety and peace run over me. My dad would know what to do. I just didn't know what was safe to tell him. I opened my mouth to ask Fletcher, but he had been watching me and anticipated what I was going to say.

"Piper, he knows everything. I told him about you, the gold, me, the werewolves. He knows."

"Oh." I didn't really know what else to say.

My dad walked in. I didn't realize how scared I had been until the safety that parents seem to bring with them overwhelmed me. "Dad!" I said, suddenly having to hold back tears. I didn't know why I wanted to cry.

"Hey, baby." He came over and put his hand on my forehead, feeling for a fever. "You look a hundred times better. The worst of it must be over."

"She's still weak as a kitten," Fletcher added.

"I bet," Dad added. "You feel up to going home?" he asked me.

I didn't, but the idea of going home and laying in my own bed, having a hot shower and takeout food sounded like heaven, so I lied.

"Yes!" I said.

Dad and Fletcher exchanged a glance, I hadn't fooled them, but I think they were as anxious to get me home as I was to go.

Dad made Fletcher leave as he helped me get dressed, even though we both knew Fletcher had seen every inch. He had taken care of me after the fight, and I hadn't been wearing a stitch. But dads are dads, and he wanted to preserve what was left of my modesty.

"You really stirred it up good this time," Dad said while he was tying my boots.

"Dad, you know I never do anything. This stuff just happens."

He sighed. "This one is bad, Piper. This is serious stuff, and I think you may finally be in over your head. You almost died."

I rolled my eyes. "I'm fine. It'll be okay."

Neither Baylee nor I had told him about the demon incident. No matter how bad it got, it couldn't get demon bad. I tried to give him a reassuring smile. He was my dad, so he didn't buy it.

"Pipe, if there is any way to get out of this, I think it's time to pull your beak out of it. This Fletcher guy is a nice guy, and I want to like him because of Clyde. But I don't want to see you hurt again."

I didn't know what to say, but the stubborn set of my jaw must have let him know I wasn't going to stop. He slouched, defeated. "Just be careful, baby. I want you around stirring up trouble for a long time."

"I love you too, daddy."

I had to lie down for a while after I was dressed. Fletcher came back in and started packing up. I was beginning to wish I had his super nifty healing powers. That's when it hit me.

"I'm not a werewolf!"

Dad gave Fletcher a look. "You didn't tell her?"

Fletcher's face flared red. "No, I hadn't quite gotten that far."

"No, Pipe, you aren't a werewolf. We think you were so sick because you were fighting off whatever it is that makes a werewolf. Whether it's some type of magic, or a virus, we don't know. But you aren't going to stop being you."

I breathed a deep sigh of relief. I wanted to kick myself when I saw Fletcher stiffen.

"I didn't want to lose my raven," I said apologetically and watched his features soften as he realized what I was saying. I still didn't believe he was a monster, and he was clinging to that with all he had.

"I know." He smiled gently.

Dad gathered up our things, which were already packed, and Fletcher carried me to the plane. I watched my dad's jaw tighten at the intimacy of it. He had to let Fletcher take care of me while I was sick, but this last indignity must still bite. Apparently, werewolves come with extra strength because his breathing didn't even increase, and I wasn't light. His body felt steel hard next to mine.

Dad's Super Cruiser has a lot more room than my Super Cub—it has a captain's chair pilot seat and a bench seat in the back for two passengers. Fletcher put me in, and I scooted over. I felt like I could barely keep my head up, and I was shaking from the effort that one movement cost. When we touched down in Anchorage, I realized I was lying in Fletcher's lap, and I had slept all the way home.

Chapter 10

I collapsed the second I was tucked into my bed, and I must have slept the rest of the day because when I glanced at the clock it was after seven. I was able to get myself to the bathroom alone this time, and it was easier since I didn't have to go outside and walk as far. Fletcher must have heard me, because he came back as I was sitting back on the bed.

"Where did my dad go?" I asked. I thought he'd stick around, considering.

"He went back to work. He hasn't told your mom or sister you've been sick, he said he doesn't want them involved in this mess of yours." He grinned.

I was sure that's exactly what dad said, worse, he probably meant it.

"So, you've been really busy working with some new clients and that's why you haven't called or come by." He gave me a conspiratorial wink.

"Oh, are you my babysitter?" I lifted my eyebrows in a question.

"At least until Branwyn gets here." He smiled. "Your friend is a bit of a firecracker, isn't she?" he queried; his voice slightly wary.

I frowned. "Why what did she do?"

He shrugged.

"What have you told her?"

"Not much, just that you were really sick, and she wasn't to talk to your mom about it."

"Ahh, so do you have any ear left?" I grinned.

"Only because I hung up in the middle of the tirade." He smiled and shrugged.

"Crap, how long ago did you talk to her?" I sat up and looked around for my cell.

"I don't know, ten, fifteen minutes ago?"

"What can I tell her about this? She isn't going to wait long to get over here." I finally saw my phone and made to get up and get it off the dresser.

Fletcher saw what I was doing and picked it up and handed it to me. He looked apologetic. "Sorry, it's dead. It didn't have much juice, and it died right after Branwyn called. As for what to say..." He paused and gathered his thoughts. "I'll let you decide. I've already told you and your dad. I trust you, and if you trust her, that's up to you." He shrugged again and ran his fingers through his hair. His tell. He was worried about it whether he trusted me or not.

"She has kept my secret since we were children. I'd trust her with my life."

"Then you have your answer." This time his voice was firm.

"I really wish we didn't have to tell anyone. We may be putting them in danger."

He nodded. "Your dad and I agree. But we figured it was safer here in the city than the cabin. The werewolf isn't going to know what we're doing here or who we contact. I think if your dad and your friend stay quiet, they should be safe."

"I'm still not sure who knows about your gold."

He gave a weary sigh. "Me either. At least here in town, we can get more research done. Once your friend gets here, I'll go check into a hotel. I can get started in the morning." He took a step back, preparing to leave.

"Why? That's crazy. I have a whole unused basement and I have wifi. Just stay here. You'll have your own room and bathroom. It's a little girly, but it's clean and it's private." I think he must have seen it in my posture or read it through the tightness in my voice. Wolves are very sensitive to body language, so I knew he sensed my growing panic. I didn't have time to analyze my reaction, but I couldn't bear for him to leave.

My house wasn't big, but it had a large master bedroom and bath upstairs, and two smaller bedrooms and a bath down. I used the smaller bedroom for storage but kept the other one clean for guests. It had neutral walls and carpet, but currently had a purple and white striped comforter and a purple bed skirt, pillows, and accessories. The bathroom was lavender and green.

It was definitely on the feminine side, but I didn't think it would kill him. I had another bedroom set, but I wasn't in any shape to switch them out. I wasn't even sure where they were buried. I kept them for guests, but since that was a rare occurrence, Baylee's purple set was the one that got used the most.

He hesitated. I don't think he really wanted to leave; I know I didn't want him too. Maybe it was the shared experience, or the fact he had been caring for me for a week, but I didn't want to lose the comfort of his presence. I needed him.

"I don't want your neighbors to get the wrong idea," he said hesitantly. "Or tarnish your reputation." So, he was a gentleman at heart as well.

"No worries, I hardly ever see my neighbors, and I doubt they care or notice who I have over. Plus, I don't give a rat's ass what they think." I smiled.

He laughed. "Okay, I'll stay."

I didn't think he really wanted to leave either. Maybe he felt the same that I did. I know we had a connection, maybe it had started as an attraction, but it had deepened to something else over the course of this last mess. Now he had let me in, maybe he'd stop trying to push me away.

"Did dad say how he's covering all the routes?" I asked, worried because summer was our busiest time, and it was how we fed ourselves. My Super Cub had been gone from the cabin when we left, and I'd been worrying about it in the back of my head. I figured dad must have had someone pick it up, but it was my baby, and I didn't want just anyone flying it.

"He said he was using your mail guy for some, and he called in a favor or two with some other bush pilots for the rest. Plus, I think he's flying a lot too. Mostly he said not to worry, your Cub is fine."

"How's he keeping mom from being suspicious?"

"I guess he just told her you picked up some extra business and are just busier than usual."

Mom had been the wife of an Alaskan bush pilot for a while, and she knew that summer was crazy. She'd probably buy that for a while, but not calling her for over a week would be pushing it. I'd have to call soon, or dad and I would both be in trouble. I hated lying to my mom, but I'd do anything to keep her safe. She just wasn't that savvy about the supernatural.

Just then, the door slammed, and we heard Branwyn stomping up the stairs. The entryway to my house was badly designed. When you come in, there's a landing and then you either have to go up or down. There wasn't a main level. It's really a stupid design, and it makes it impossible to move furniture in and out. Luckily, I didn't have much and I wasn't planning on moving anytime soon. I looked at Fletcher. He had faced down a pack of werewolves and I swear he looked a little spooked at the prospect of meeting my friend.

"She's a witch," I said hurriedly, thinking that would put him at ease since I was about to spill all of his secrets to her. It didn't work.

"What?" and then it was too late.

Branwyn threw open my bedroom door, and tiny as she was, her presence filled the room. She took in my appearance with one searing look. Bran doesn't like to curse. She finds it crass and unbecoming. I don't have that filter. I work in a man's world, and it never occurs to me to hold back when a good curse just satisfies the need to express myself and whatever sticky situation I find myself in. So, I was slightly shocked when she bellowed, "What in the *hell* happened to you?" Hell is a mild word for me, but for Bran it was quite strong.

I had deliberately avoided looking in the mirror when I went to the bathroom but seeing my arms and legs which were covered with bruises, bites, cuts, and bandages, I'm sure I was quite a sight. She crossed over to the bed and leveled a devastating look at Fletcher.

"You said she was sick," she accused him.

He sighed.

She turned to me, "So did your dad." Her eyes narrowed, and she said quietly, "What is going on, Piper, and who the *hell* are you!" She leveled her glare at Fletcher, her finger in his chest. I guess the introductions never really happened on the phone.

"Well…" Before I opened my mouth again, my stomach let out a horrendous growl. I was starving, and I'm sure it took a lot of calories to heal. I had also been moving around a lot more than I had in the past week.

"I guess I have to feed you first." She wrinkled her nose. "It wouldn't hurt if you had a bath either."

I was embarrassed. I had been smelling up Fletcher's place with my stink of stale sweat and illness. I couldn't imagine what the combination must be like if he had a sensitive nose like mine.

Bran was usually more tactful, but I think my appearance must have scared and shocked her, and she always did better if she were busy. She sent Fletcher off in my truck to get food, and she got me into the bathtub, scrubbed, hair washed, and re-bandaged before he got back. She'd even changed my sheets which in the short time I had been in them were already covered with oozing blood and old sweat. I was beyond exhausted but feeling a hundred times better by the time he was back with the food.

It felt good to be in my own, clean, soft, and comfortable clothes with a full belly. I wanted to sleep, but Bran needed answers before she exploded.

After we ate, Fletcher took my laptop and disappeared downstairs —probably grateful to be off duty, and out of the line of fire. He was also dirty, and he looked tired. Before he left, I made sure he knew I wanted him to treat my place like his own. Since I heard the shower come on shortly after, I figured he felt comfortable enough to do so.

"I figured out who the hotty is. He's the guy you told me about at the shop," Bran said.

"Yup." I nodded.

"He's something. Hot bod, nice looking, and to top it off, crazy about you," she continued.

I cocked my head at her. "Why do you say that?"

"Duh, not only has he been taking care of you, he looks at you like a starving man. Trust me on this one." She put her hands on her hips with authority.

My heart had sped up at her revelation, but I didn't want to trust it quite yet. We had so much going on, it wasn't the best time to interpret actions and looks into anything but survival.

"You got a story to spill." She reminded me after I'd blanked out for a couple of seconds.

"I know. Let me think for a minute." I closed my eyes trying to find a starting point, but when I realized I was drifting off, I decided to just start talking and straighten out the bumps after.

"You were wrong you know."

"About what? I'm never wrong!" she said smugly.

"I am not a werewolf."

"Whatever, it's a dumb argument Piper, and you're stalling."

"No, I'm not. I was wrong too. There are werewolves. I'm just not one of them."

She squinted at me, trying to judge my announcement.

I took a deep breath. "This is what happens," I brushed a hand down my body to indicate my state, "if you meet up with a werewolf in a dark alley, or woods in my case…"

She looked me over, frowning. From there, I launched into the story I'd started at the store and filled in all the blanks until the time she came storming into my house. She sat next to me, her face a war of emotions as she took in the new mess I dropped in her lap. I hadn't seen her speechless very often, but she was for a few minutes after I finished.

"So now, you have unknown people looking for the gold, strange men following you, and a rogue werewolf pack out for blood?"

"As far as I know," I smiled. "It could be worse." We looked at each other and said in chorus, "There could be a demon!" Then we devolved into a girlish fit of frightened giggles; the kind that are one step away from hysteria.

Our first big supernatural adventure had started when I had insulted a shaman from a rival shadow clan. The shadow clans were the shamanic sect that had separated from the mundane Inupiaq centuries ago. They were the ones that guarded the shape-shifting legacy of my forebears. I had insulted Eagle. I belonged to Raven. In response, he and his buddies kidnapped my sister and tried to feed her to a demon for power. Even after that, sensitive to the supernatural, we didn't see much sign of it in our lives until now. Werewolves. Real werewolves who weren't native shapeshifters. Who would've thunk?

When we'd calmed down, I continued, "Bran, I can't help think that some of these things are connected. With so many things happening at once, it seems logical that they're linked somehow. We are looking at something wrong, and I don't know what it is. The werewolf couldn't possibly have known about the gold. He turned Fletcher way before Clyde died, in a whole different state, and before any link was forged between the two of them. So, what does the werewolf want? He obviously followed Fletcher here from Idaho; it's too big a coincidence otherwise to just show up in the same place."

"Here's another mystery. You said that Fletcher and the other *were* are 'dire wolves' or some other cryptid type wolf, so, who, or better yet, what are the other pack members? You said they looked like regular old wolves?"

"I saw that woman change. She didn't do it like me. She had to be a werewolf too."

"Okay, why the difference?"

"I don't know."

"We need to make a chart or something. If we can get it all down, maybe we can find a link."

"It's a good idea. We'll do it tomorrow." I was exhausted. I couldn't even think about it anymore and I wasn't up to making connections. I'd had a busy day and had done more than I had in a week. I think I fell asleep before I heard if Bran agreed with me.

Chapter 11

The next morning, my fuzzy head was gone, and I could make it to the bathroom without breathing hard. I was finally recovering. I even walked into my kitchen and sat at the table for breakfast. Fletcher was working on his list as he ate. Bran had made a full breakfast, waffles, eggs, bacon, orange juice, ham, and toast. I guess she knew that we would be starving. The hot food felt good going down.

"So, I've got the list of the men from my backpacking class. I'm going through and checking to see if any of them live here in Anchorage, or anywhere in Alaska."

"How many men are there?" Bran asked.

"Twelve, it was a small class, and it was mostly women."

She looked over his shoulder. "Was your professor male?" she asked

He frowned. "Yes. Why?"

"Well, you only have twelve names; you should have thirteen if your professor was included. Wasn't he on the trip with you?"

"Good point." Fletcher added the name to the bottom of the list of names, a few with check marks next to them.

"What do the checks mean?" I asked.

"I'm just putting a check next to them if they don't live in Alaska.

If none of them do, then we'll go back to the drawing board and try to find some other link."

By the time we were finished, Fletcher had finished his list with the names he could find. The rest were either too common to narrow down, or not easily found with just a simple web search. After a call to the school, he was able to cross a few off from the student directory, figuring if they were still at school in Idaho, they weren't living here. He did discover that the professor wasn't there anymore, but we still hadn't found where he or two other men were located just by a web search.

While Bran cleaned up, I took her laptop and searched for names on Facebook. I located one of the common names, Matt Porter, and although there were hundreds of Matt Porters, we eliminated him by profile picture as having moved to Florida. We also located a Scott Thomas who, finally, lived in Anchorage. He was pursuing a master's degree in biological sciences from the university, according to the school's website. Since we were on it, we searched for Fletcher's professor, Fred Burns. When I saw the name, I had a ping of recognition, but couldn't place it. After a quick faculty and staff search, we also found him living in Anchorage. We sat back; two names—one could be our big kahuna werewolf.

I closed Bran's laptop; a headache sprouting behind my eyes. "Hey, go back to the school's website." I said, "See if either of those listings has a photograph."

It took a minute to discover that the student listings did not come with photos, but the faculty one did. Fletcher stared at his professor's face for a while. Bran looked over his shoulder.

"He's a handsome devil," she said. "I don't remember having any good-looking college professors when I went."

Fletcher turned the computer around to me when I asked to see the photo, a twinkle of amusement in his eye. I knew he thought I just wanted to look at the handsome professor, but something kept itching in the back of my mind. I froze when I saw him.

"What's wrong, Piper?" Bran asked, more attuned to my body language than Fletcher.

"I know him."

"You do?" She squinted back at the photo as though there would be a reason for her to recognize the man. Fletcher also looked startled.

"Yeah, I do. Unfortunately, he's my cryptozoologist." I looked at Bran, her eyes flew open wide.

"What are you talking about?" Fletcher asked, and I filled him in on my first encounter with the wolf and my consequent search that had led to the professor. I ended with an apology for spying.

"That's a little too much of a coincidence," Bran said, eyes narrowed on the photo. "My bet is it's the professor. He was just a little too excited about the cryptid wolf, from your story Pipe."

"I think I should call him again, bait him a little."

"I should do it," Fletcher said. "If it is him, he shouldn't know that either of you are involved past the one sighting."

"Probably, but if it's him, we also don't want him to know that you are on to him, and if you call up or go see him, he'll know. Let me just give him a call, feel him out a little bit," I said.

His card was still sitting on the counter where I dumped my mail. I hadn't planned on talking to him again, I thought he was too persistent, and I'd ignored the one call he'd made after our meeting.

Fletcher wasn't happy, but I took the card and my cell phone into my bedroom and shut the door. If the professor was a werewolf, I was assuming he could hear as well as I could, and I generally could hear both sides of a phone call if I were in the same room. I didn't want him to know I had company or recognize Fletcher.

Luckily, the professor's cell number was on the card, I didn't want to have another run in with the bitchy secretary. Since I wasn't calling during office hours, I wasn't really expecting him to answer, so I was quiet for a beat after he answered.

"Hello?"

"Yeah, uhh, hello," I stammered. "I don't know if you remember me, Dr. Burns, but I talked to you a week or so ago about a dire wolf?"

"I remember, Ms. Tikaani. This is Ms. Tikaani?

"Yeah, Piper," I answered, flustered.

"What can I do for you?" He sounded impatient, and I didn't want to set him off. I only had a half-made plan in my head since I was counting on getting his answering machine and not his person.

"Well, I've been looking for other people who have seen a dire wolf, and I ran into someone on a crypto site I've been talking too." I searched my head quickly for a name I could give from Fletcher's list who lived far enough away he wouldn't be in danger if this was our werewolf. Who was the dude in Florida? "One guy," was it Mike, Matt, or Scott? "Uhh, Matt said he saw one in the mountains of Idaho a few years ago or so." I hope I'd guessed right. "Have you heard of any sightings there?"

I heard his breath catch for a moment, and I was sure I had him.

"Was that northern Idaho?" he asked.

I was startled, I wasn't expecting a real answer.

"Yeah, pretty sure, not far from the university."

"What was the man's name again?"

Before I thought it through, I answered, "Matt Porter."

"Ah, yes, I know him."

"You do?" I asked, getting worried I'd let a real name spill out.

"Ms., uh, Piper. Five years ago, I saw a cryptid wolf in the mountains of Idaho. Because of that, I have immersed myself in the study of cryptids. I saw it again a while ago, and once I heard of possible sightings here, I came here to follow them. I would really appreciate it if you could get me in touch with the young man."

I panicked. Could we be wrong? Was he lying? It didn't seem likely he was our werewolf. Maybe he really was just an interested party.

"How do you know him?" I asked, confused. I knew Matt Porter wasn't on some crypto site, which meant he remembered him from the infamous backpacking class. I wanted to know if he'd admit it or lie.

"He took a class from me. The last class I taught there in fact. It was a general science credit with a backpacking element and field research. Mr. Porter was in that class and that's the last time I saw the wolf. I'd really appreciate it if I could talk to him about it."

Shit, I thought, maybe this guy *is* clean. Since I was making up the lead, I gave him some general answer about asking the guy if I could release his number and hung up. Surely if he were our guy, he wouldn't have come up with such a detailed, honest sounding answer. He didn't know I was wrapped up with Fletcher. So, he wouldn't have had to tell me about the class. He could have made up any old story, not the truth. Fletcher and Bran came into my room, and I gave them the blow by blow of my call. We all agreed he sounded clean, and his story was plausible. That left Scott Thomas, the graduate student as our last lead.

Chapter 12

It took me a over a week to recover my strength, and in that time, we researched and came up with a plan to find out who the werewolf was. Fletcher had let his lawyer know he was back in town, so a few days after we were back, we were able to get Clyde's autopsy report. Unfortunately, it ended up being just as mysterious as the rest. Until Clyde dropped dead, he'd been the picture of health. No known cause of death was listed. I couldn't believe it, but weird as it seemed to me, a quick web search showed that people dropped dead all the time for no apparent reason. Go figure.

After pushing myself too hard and passing out, dad grounded me for another week. I was eaten up with guilt at the strain my illness had put on him and our business, but it probably wasn't all that safe for me to fly an aircraft. Since I couldn't fly for Tulugaq Air, I decided to try *Raven Air*. After locating the general place where our alpha werewolf prospect lived, I stretched my wings.

Anchorage is full to the brim with ravens, summer through winter and it's easy to blend in. Plus, I was itching to do something. I'd rested, driven by guilt, but I was at the end of my rope. I'd never sat still that long on purpose. We found and followed a couple of Scott Thomases of the age range of ours until Fletcher recognized the right one. Our prospective Scott Thomas had gone into an apartment complex by the university, but we had lost him. I figured I could follow much more discreetly as a raven.

Knowing that my compadres weren't going to let me go out on my own, I had to choose a time where my absence wouldn't be noticed. It was easy to avoid Bran. Since I was better and could be left alone safely, Bran went back to work during the day and was staying with me during the night. Fletcher was harder to avoid. He was staying at my house, and although we were researching, he was still around a lot keeping an eye on me. I needed to leave early in the day, so I would have the time to locate my student and follow him home. I needed to get rid of Fletcher for the day, and I wasn't sure how to go about it. Even if he went to the library, he wasn't likely to be there all day. Shopping would only be a couple of hours. I racked my brain for a couple of days when the opportunity presented itself naturally.

Fletcher had been acting oddly. He was naturally quiet, but it felt as though he was avoiding me, leaving a room as I entered it, keeping to himself in the back when I watched TV, etc. I figured that because Bran wasn't around, he was uncomfortable being alone with me because of the attraction we felt for each other. I wasn't quite ready to deal with it either. There was too much going on, and my recovery had put it firmly to the back of my mind, anyway.

I was sitting at the kitchen table, plotting my escape in my head when he walked in. He got a glass of juice and sat down at the table across from me.

"I have to leave." He looked up at me, his bright blue eyes intense. My breath caught. I was always a sucker for blue eyes, and Fletcher usually kept his hidden behind sunglasses.

"W-What?" I stammered when I got my breath back. I was a brilliant conversationalist.

"The moon is full in a couple of days, and I can't be here." He looked at me for a minute and dropped his gaze. "I know the timing is bad, but your dad is going to run me out to the cabin later today then he'll pick me up after the moon." He swirled the juice around his glass avoiding my eyes.

"I don't think you should be alone." I wanted to be with him during his next change to prove to him he could control himself and retain his hold on his humanity while his wolf was loose. I knew I wasn't up to it at the moment, and I felt bad that he would have to suffer another moon alone thinking he was a monster.

"I'm so sorry, I should go with you." Regret tinged my voice.

"I'll be fine; I've been alone so far. You should stay away from me during the moon anyway." His voice was rough. He didn't want to leave. At least I hoped that was the emotion I was reading.

I knew there wasn't any point arguing with him. He was determined to believe he was a monster and until I could be with him during the full moon, he wouldn't believe me. I let it go, which is something I don't usually do.

"Ok, I'll see you when you get back," I bit out.

He smiled at me. "Sure, thanks, Piper. I'm going to go. I have some things to do before I meet your dad."

"You can take my truck if you need it." I was trying to be overly helpful, hiding my emotions from him.

"No, the cab should be here in a few." And with that, he walked out of the kitchen, no goodbye. His shoulders slumped.

I watched until the cab was out of sight. Then I opened my second story window, changed, and flew out into the warm summer air. I dipped and rolled and soared and flitted with my fellow ravens, distracted for a short while by the utter joy of flying. Finally, I set off for the apartment complex that housed our possible werewolf. I found some other ravens near the complex, and I joined them for a minute copying their behavior and observing the area. I found a good perch where I could observe the entrance and settled in to wait.

I don't know how long I waited before I saw Scott Thomas getting out of his car. It looked like he was coming home from work, and I was disappointed because he'd probably go inside, and I wouldn't see him again. I decided to wait a while longer just in case he needed to make a trip to the store or go out somewhere else. I flew around the building and tried to see in his windows, but they were shaded. I went back to my tree.

I was almost ready to call it a night when he came out of the apartment again carrying camping gear. I was such an idiot. If he was a werewolf, wouldn't he also have to get out of the city during the moon? Even if he was the one who bit Fletcher, it didn't mean he wasn't trying to avoid people. Worst case scenario, he was an evil raving lunatic. Fortunately, even evil raving lunatics have to be out of sight to avoid being gunned down when they change into gigantic freaking wolves.

I needed to see where he was going, but I was exhausted and I didn't know if I could get back home in time to change, get my truck, and get back here before he left. I couldn't even call anyone until I returned home. I could probably peck out a phone number and speak enough to make sense, but I didn't have any pockets. I was growing punchy. I had over-extended myself.

I watched to see which way he was going out of town. There are only two ways, north or south. He was heading north. Once I was sure, I did the only thing I could and raced home.

I flew in my window, shifted, and grabbed the nearest clothing— old cut-off jeans and a t-shirt. I pulled on a ratty old ball cap to hold my hair back. I grabbed my cell, my wallet, and keys, and jumped in my truck. My arms were heavy and my legs like Jell-O, but I was hopped up on adrenaline, thinking that we finally had him. The quickest way to Glenn Highway was to go through downtown traffic and about a hundred streetlights. The only thing going for me was that I knew my target would have to face similar traffic issues on his end of town.

Once I cleared the lights, I pushed the old V-8 engine to its max, weaving and tailgating to make up time. I was silently praying I wouldn't run into any state troopers while I scanned for the white Subaru wagon Scott was driving, hopefully at or under the speed limit, because I was averaging eighty or higher. Unfortunately, it seemed like every other car in Anchorage was a white Subaru wagon, so I had to scan every car I passed that resembled his.

I finally caught up to him about a mile from the Eagle River exit. I had just settled into a comfortable position behind him when he took the exit. I was shocked. This didn't fit the pattern I expected for the big bad wolf. I followed him off the exit thinking that maybe he was stopping for gas, but he swung around town into the residential area. Maybe we were wrong again and someone else from the list was here in Anchorage or the surrounding towns.

Now, we were in a neighborhood, and I was starting to stand out. I wasn't sure what to do, sleuthing wasn't really my style. I was more of a "let's jump into the middle of it and see what happens" kind of girl. When he turned up the next street, I continued and flipped around. I got out of the car and strolled up the residential street until I could see his car. He was parked in front of a house and standing at the door. I walked slowly on the opposite side. I pulled my cap down low. He never looked over at me. Finally, a girl came out and hugged him. She grabbed some gear from the garage, and they loaded it in the car. I hurried back to my truck and started it. While I waited for them to finish, I sent Bran a short text so she would know where I was. Once they were on the main road, I pulled out and continued to follow.

What was he up too? Was this girl being set up for some kind of werewolf sport? A victim? I had assumed he would be going alone, but that was stupid! I had seen the alpha wolf with a pack of other *weres* or shifters; maybe she was part of the pack? That made more sense. Maybe the pack met for the full moon every month? I just didn't know enough. Plus, this girl was white and the other I had seen was native. I had just assumed that the rest of the pack was native, because they resembled her in wolf form. I guess I had silently imagined that they were shifters like me and since I was native, they would be as well. In truth, I didn't know anything except that the large wolf was like Fletcher, and I had seen one other wolf change into a human. For all I knew there were only four of us capable of changing—me, Fletcher, the alpha, and the girl.

My mind raced. With all the links and possibilities tormenting me as I followed the student and the girl with him, it never once occurred to me that I might be completely wrong about everything. I expected him to head to Denali, where wilderness stretched for miles and he and his wolves could run safely, but he took the turnoff towards Wasilla, and to my surprise turned into a popular campground at Big Lake. I continued, found a private place to park, and flew back to observe him. He and the girl joined a group of people. It was obviously a party with friends. They had fishing rods and tents and looked for all the world like average college students on a camping getaway. This could be his pack, but they were way too close to a population where people would shoot a wolf if they saw it. This was not our guy.

There was one sure way for me to know. I had a wolf's memory for scent, and I had smelled the alpha twice in his wolf form. I knew now from being around Fletcher, that he did retain some of his same scent as both human and wolf. If I could get close to the student in my wolf form, I would know for sure.

I hesitated. There had been recent sightings of wolves in the area, and I knew the residents were jumpy. I was extremely nervous about getting shot. I'd had a close call as a half-grown pup, and I retained a little anxiety about it. After the incident that also got me scolded by my father, I refused to change unless we were hidden deep away from the eyes of any people. I could wait for dark, but it didn't get super dark this time of the year, and only for an hour or two. I could wait for the moonrise, then they'd either change or not and I'd know for sure. I found a comfortable perch where I could watch the camp and settled in to wait. Either way, I'd check on Scott's scent.

I was starving and exhausted. They ate tin foil dinners and s'mores. The smell of food and the rich scent of chocolate filled the night. Even as small as I was in this form, I was ready to eat a horse. My stomach grumbled and my talons quivered on the branch. I wanted to buzz the camp and steal some food. I contemplated begging, as I knew ravens around town did, but I didn't quite dare. I shook out my wings and ruffled my feathers for warmth and hunkered down again, attempting to ignore the glorious food.

Eventually, they did seek their tents. When they were quiet, I drifted down to Scott's tent and shifted into my wolf. It took a minute for the smells of the food to clear from my nose as I sniffed around the tent. I could distinguish the differences between the male and the female, obvious now that they were a couple—the soft sounds of their lovemaking drifted to my sensitive ears.

I sat at the door and scented. I didn't recognize him. I didn't know his scent. I huffed, and plopped down, frustrated. Finally, I stood up and walked silently into the trees. I needed a drink and without thinking I trotted out to the lake. The water was cool on my hot throat after the hours of waiting in the tree without food or drink. I lapped it up. A river otter was floating close to shore, asleep on his back, head distinct, and paws relaxed above his chest. I considered giving him a scare and jumping at him, splashing and growling, my mischievous nature was more prevalent in my animal forms, and I chuckled inwardly at what he might do.

I inched forward—the water icy on my paws. The water climbed to my belly as I snuck close enough to leap and splash the creature. That's when I heard it; the distinct click, slide, snap of a rifle bolt being drawn and a round falling into place. No one should have seen me and even though I was wary of being shot at, I didn't really think someone would do it in a crowded campground in the twilight. Plus, my black fur should have hidden me some. Sometimes, I wished people wouldn't watch the damn news.

Instinctively, I ducked low, the water partially covering me. Fear cramped my belly. I had nowhere to go! I couldn't move fast enough in the water, and if I shifted, the water would weigh down my feathers and I wouldn't be able to escape fast enough. In panic, I reached out with whatever magic Raven had gifted me with and with senses I never knew I had; I gripped onto the mind and the essence of the otter and without a thought, I shifted.

I ducked lower in the water and swam hard. The first shot slid across my back parting my fur. It had lost some momentum and heat when entering the water and what should have cut me only stung as it touched my flesh. I sliced through the water, my sleek shape and oily fur letting me move faster than I had ever moved in the water. My webbed toes and short powerful legs pushed the water behind me as I dove deep below where the bullets would be able to reach. I was trembling. My new form was odd, and the sensations and sensory input were overwhelming.

My whiskers were ultra-sensitive, and I could feel the vibrations of the water current. My paws were very limber, and I could feel the dexterity in them so different from a wolf and much closer to my human form. I reached out and gripped a stone on the bottom of the lake and released it. My lungs felt comfortable, and I had no urge to breathe yet even though I knew I had been underwater far longer than I had ever been. Curious, I pushed off the bottom and swam gently through the cool water. Letting my whiskers guide me towards fish. I watched them with my new eyes.

In a few minutes, I had the urge to breathe. I wasn't sure if the rifle's owner was going to take pot shots at an otter, so I swam further before I ventured up for air. I quickly scanned the banks for my shooter. Otters seemed to have decent vision. Once the water cleared, I realized I could see as well under the water as above it. The shooter was either gone, or he was well hidden in the trees lining the lake. I allowed my entire body to pop up to the surface, and I lay on my back in typical otter fashion. I tried to relax and look normal, but I was on high alert, all senses scanning for danger. After a few moments passed, I relaxed some—sure that I either hadn't been seen, or I wasn't on the radar for another pot shot. Relieved, I relaxed some more and stretched my shortened limbs and long lithe back in total comfort.

With a sudden start, I sank and nearly drowned myself. I was an otter! How had that happened? In my twenty-nine years I had never been able to form anything but a wolf and a raven! I had tried when I was younger, not that I knew what I was doing. I forced myself to relax again. I wanted to wait and make sure the shooter was gone before I swam ashore. I needed to get back to my truck and my phone. Bran was going to be worried, and she was unpredictable when that happened. I didn't want her running to my family, calling the police, or worse, trying to find me. I calmly and cautiously made my way back towards the bank nearest my vehicle.

I had forgotten the other otter. He reminded me with a playful snout in my ear, and some cheerful chittering. My otter self wanted to play; I was nearly overwhelmed with curiosity and playfulness. I set my teeth and continue towards the bank. My new friend was confused and attempted to engage me with diving and splashing, but I ignored him. Finally, I was close enough to touch the ground. I thought for a moment that my furry companion would attempt to follow me, but he must have finally gotten bored and swam away. I looked around, and not seeing or sensing anyone, I stepped into the trees, shook off the water, and turned into a raven. I was starving and exhausted when I reached the truck, but at least we had eliminated Scott from the chase. That only left one other.

I drove home slightly slower, watching for moose, and thinking hard. When I got to Wasilla, I loaded up on fast food and gorged myself before continuing the trip home. I checked my phone and had a dozen texts from Bran, each angrier than the last. I rolled my eyes. At the next stoplight, I shot off a hurried, "On way home," and shut it off to avoid the inevitable call bombardment.

Bran was waiting in my house when I got home. I could tell she was ready to go after me with both barrels, but she stopped when she saw me in the light.

"God, Piper. You don't look so good."

I tossed my stuff down on the table.

"I don't feel so good either," I replied and threw myself on the couch. I could tell I'd overdone it. My legs trembled with exhaustion and my arms were heavy.

"It's not him, Bran," I said when she finished fussing over me. "The scent is wrong, it's close to the full moon, and he's camping at Big Lake with a group of friends."

"It's not whom?" she asked, confused.

"The student, Scott. He's not the werewolf," I answered.

"That leaves the handsome professor," she said.

"Yup." I groaned. I thought the professor, though handsome, to be creepy. I wasn't comfortable with the idea that Bran thought he was hot.

"So, what now?" she prodded since I'd allowed my mind to wander off for a minute.

"I don't know what to do about the teacher, but I think I need to go back to Fletcher's cabin and prove a point to him."

Bran smiled, "Oh, is that the reason? Because I've seen the way you look at him, Piper, and it might be more than that."

I blushed. My heart sped up a little. For the first time I paid attention to my reactions. I blushed again. Was I falling for him? Crap!

"Piper!" Bran snapped at me.

"What?" I looked up at her.

"I've been talking to you, and you just sat there off in space somewhere, again!"

"Sorry," I said sheepishly. "What did you say?"

"It doesn't matter, I don't like repeating myself anyway. You better get some rest and eat some more. Your dad won't let you fly in the state you're in now!" She smiled at me. "And you have to prove to that stubborn werewolf that he isn't a danger to anyone. If you want to train him to sit and stay." She winked.

I surprised myself with a girly giggle. "Sit and stay? He's not a dog!"

"I've noticed that myself!" she said with a leer and joined in my laughter. We spent a couple of hours talking boys and when she settled in to sleep on the blow-up bed in my room, I felt better than I had in a long time.

Chapter 13

The next morning, I awoke feeling stiff and sore, but more like me than before. When I went to wake Bran up, I realized I hadn't even told her about changing into a new animal.

After we ate breakfast, we went downstairs to the living room. I told her what had happened when I changed into the river otter. She sat back a little, her brow furrowed, thinking furiously. I waited; when Bran got into a deep thought zone, she was hard to distract.

"What did you do or feel right before you changed?" she asked.

"Uh, I don't know. I just didn't want to die I guess."

"Hmm, did you have any contact with the otter at all?" She was headed for full interrogation mode.

"No, I don't think so." I paused, thinking back, "I noticed him, I was paying attention to him, and then..." I let the images come back, another gift from Raven is an extraordinary sight memory. I replayed the events in my head, watching every move and action I made. When I got to the moment, I tried to dig deeper and look at what I did, what I felt. "I think that there was something," I said in a moment.

"Yeah, go on!" Bran encouraged me.

"It's like I felt him with an extra sense, and then I was him, or something like him!"

Bran jumped up and began pacing. She vibrated with excitement.

"Don't keep me in the dark," I mumbled, "What is going on Bran? What have you figured out?"

"Remember the stories, Pipe? What is unique about Raven?"

I cocked my head at her. She hated that move; she thought it looked inhuman.

"Uh, he's a trickster? Mischievous? Always getting into trouble?" As I mentioned a few things I remembered, she shook her head at each one. "Just tell me what you are getting at!" I finally shouted at her.

"Raven could change into anything."

I froze. "What?" I stammered, knowing what she said was true. Almost every legend involving Raven had him changing into something to fool someone or mess with them. He could change into non-living objects as well, although I didn't see how that was possible even with magic, but then again, I was up to three animals. A funny voice in the back of my head added, "And a butt load of werewolves." I grinned.

"What are you grinning about?" Branwyn muttered.

"Werewolves."

"Ah," she said as if she read my mind.

"So, I'm up to three. I don't think I can do any more. I used to try when I was a kid."

"Something changed, Piper," she started. "Don't you get it? You've found the secret."

"Having someone shoot at me? Because as far as I'm concerned, I'm not doing that again for anything."

"No, you pea-brain!" she yelled. "You reached out to that animal, did something and copied it. You just need to practice with other animals and see if you can do it again."

"Well, I'll have to practice that when I get some time," I remarked, deadpan. "I'm a little busy at the moment, but good talking to you." I held up a hand.

I thought for a moment she'd slap me. She got a little wound up when she had big thoughts, so I cringed a little. But then she started to laugh, and so did I.

"You're right, it's awesome, but completely unnecessary right now." She shrugged and changed the subject. "So, what are you going to do to that hunk of a werewolf to change his mind?"

"Well, sister, that's why I'm talking to you." I gave her a sly grin. She rubbed her hands together evilly and we sat down to plan.

Dad, not yet ready to let me fly on my own, agreed to drop me off at the cabin on his next supply run. He looked at me oddly but didn't say anything. He agreed with me, I thought, that Fletcher's wolf was in control. There was still one more night before the moon.

We flew in silence, not an odd thing when with my dad. He wasn't much of a talker on a good day, and he wasn't sure what to think of when it came to me and Fletcher. He probably didn't really want to know either. I think he respected Fletcher and knew he cared for me; he had seen it when I was ill. Still, I'm sure he didn't want to drop me alone in the wilderness with a man if he could help it.

Fletcher burst out of the cabin when he recognized the plane. I could see the firm set of his jaw and determination when he came up to meet us. Before the door was fully open, he was yelling.

"Take her back. You have to take her back!"

My dad refused to take off his headphones; he kept his gaze straight ahead. I climbed out and as soon as I was clear, he taxied away. He could also be stubborn. He had made up his mind about Fletcher apparently, and it seemed he approved of my choice.

"You should have stayed away," he started, then slumped slightly like a beaten man. "You just don't know."

"I may not know, but I trust you! I remember what you did when I was being attacked. You not only thought that through and came to my aid, but you kept me safe. You do control your wolf. You'll see."

"I was savage with rage; I was completely out of control. Once I start, I can't control it, and it's worse on the full moon. Before, I chose to change and chose what to do."

"You forget, I'm a wolf too. I'll be with you, we'll run and hunt together and you'll see that it can be wonderful rather than terrifying!" Fletcher shook his head slowly in resignation.

"When it happens stay locked in the cabin. Don't come out until I'm gone." He walked back into the cabin and refused to listen anymore.

I kept quiet about it the rest of the time. We tiptoed around each other, and he found a lot of wood to chop and repairs to do while I waited and watched. As the day before the full moon waned, I could see agitation and stress in everything he did. He was even quieter than usual, and everything was done with a hint of aggression. I was nervous but kept it tightly under control, so he'd be able to know that I still trusted him. When the moon began to rise, he finally spoke more than the past day's grunts and acknowledgements.

"I'm going to fight it as long as I can. Latch the doors and stay inside."

"Why?" I asked.

"Why what? So, I don't turn on you. Haven't you heard anything I've said?"

"Yes, I have heard, that's not what I meant, why do you fight it? Let it go. It may make it easier. I'm safe. You forget that I'm a shapeshifter. I can watch from the air if I wish."

He growled, and it wasn't a human sound. "Just do what I tell you!" he snapped.

And with that, he walked out the door and slammed it behind him. I looked out at him. He was taking off his clothes and folding them neatly against the cabin. I should have turned my head, but I was entranced with the lean muscled length of him, muscles rippling as he moved. His upper body was lightly tanned, as though when I wasn't around, he had been working outside without his shirt, and it stood in sharp contrast to the milky white of his lower body. Every muscle stood out with strain that only increased the perfection of his form.

I wondered about the rage he said the wolf brought out in him. I noticed irritation, even more aggression, but not anything crazy or uncontrolled.

When he finished, he walked slowly over to the stump where we had left the offerings. Only a few feet away, he doubled over as if in great pain. He fell to his hands and knees. His spine curved with a spasm, and within a few minutes, the beautiful, silver-grey wolf stood in his place. It shook itself, as though shedding the last of its humanity, sat back and let out a long and eerie howl.

I studied him for a while, marking the differences I had noted before between the two species of wolf. He was bigger than the natural Alaskan grey wolves, stockier. His legs were heavier and better proportioned. His head was heavier, the jaws wider and the teeth longer. He looked more like a wolf mix although a mix with a very large dog breed—maybe a Saint Bernard or a Great Pyrenees. His color was more silver and grey than tan and grey like the local wolves, and his eyes stayed their hot, bright blue.

He was watching me watch him, sitting there with the light of the sun and the moon spilling gently over his silvered coat, the tips of it ablaze with an unnatural glow. He was quiet, and I knew I was right. He would not harm me. I unlatched the door and stripped as quickly as possible and threw my clothes on the bed. I gave him one more glance, and watched his eyes scan my nude body like those of a man, not a beast. I leapt toward him and shifted in one move. I walked calmly, head and tail lowered in a submissive posture, and eyes not quite meeting his gaze. I could be cautious when I wanted to be.

When I reached him, I ran my head under his jaw. He nipped at my mouth and stood. He gave me a single glance, and then he bounded towards the woods. I yipped involuntarily, startled, and ran to follow.

I reveled a little in my superiority. I loved being right. Fletcher knew me. I didn't know how the werewolf thing worked for him, if he was a wolf and all humanity gone, or a human only wearing a form. But somewhere inside the great wolf body something of him recognized me and accepted me as pack. We ran together through the waxing night, black and silver weaving through shadows and drinking in the bright moonlight along with the dimmer sun. Finally, after the initial thrill of the run, we settled down to hunt together.

I had hunted as a wolf many times over the years, but as a lone wolf I was limited somewhat to what I could take down. A wolf will eat small game, but as a large predator, a bunny or squirrel isn't very filling and would make for a very lean time if that was all you could get. As a pack, even a pack of two, the choices increased greatly. Fletcher, perhaps closer to his wolf instincts than I, or just not as distractible, found them first. *Tuttu*—caribou.

Herds roamed around near Lake Iliamna constantly, not far in caribou travel from Fletcher's property. The lake was a very common stopping place for herd animals, giving up water and good feed. We set up an ambush on a caribou cow that was slightly apart from the group. Fletcher came at her right shoulder, causing her to veer away from the group, and run past me. As she passed me in the grass, I leapt out and caught her back leg in my teeth, tripping her and knocking her down. Fletcher was on her in an instant, his teeth around her throat. As she suffocated, she thrashed and twisted to shake him free. Finally, once she slowed down and I wouldn't get a hoof to the eye, I slashed open the tender belly, and the cow lay still. The warm blood splashed over my muzzle, and the rich scent filled my nose. We feasted together, enjoying the tender vitals, then the rich hams until our bellies bulged and the warmth filled us through.

We curled up against each other in the grass, the hot satisfaction in our bellies causing a languid exhaustion to wash over us. Fletcher lay his heavy head over my neck protectively, and I nestled against his warmth. We napped in the moonlight under the brief Alaskan night.

I woke suddenly when the warmth at my back disappeared. I snapped up to my feet as Fletcher's low growl sounded through my ears and echoed through my chest. I sidled up to him and pressed into his side. His size nearly doubled mine. He was gazing back towards the trees we had left on our hunt. I could see what had to be eye shine in the darker outline of the tree cover. I scented the air, but the wind was still and the creature too far away. I felt a flicker of fear lift the hair on my back, and my head and tail dipped in a natural reaction to danger.

Was it the big werewolf? Did he follow us, or was he also escaping the city for the full moon? Whatever it was, it stuck to the shadows and watched. Fletcher attempted to keep himself between me and the creature, but my natural curiosity won out, and I leapt over him and rose into the air as a raven, silent and dark as a shadow. I shot high in the sky, so my wing beats wouldn't disturb the creature and I could glide toward him from above, silent as any hunting owl.

Although I shuddered with terror thinking of the big bastard, as a raven I would only be a slight nuisance and hopefully, unnoticeable. The night air burned my lungs with a delicious tang, the silky wind flowed over my feathers. I finally reached the altitude I wanted and shot down, out of the eye line of the creature until the shadows fell away enough for me to see it. Startled, I back winged and gained altitude. I beat back to Fletcher and landed gently in the grass stepping down from the sky in my human form. He glanced at me, and for a moment I saw Fletcher, the human, in his eyes, not Fletcher the wolf.

"It's just a regular wolf, I think?" I heard the question in my voice as I remembered the pack of seemingly normal grey wolves that made up the cryptid wolf's pack.

He nodded his great head and sat on his haunches.

"What do you want to do?" I asked him and squatted back on my heels to read his body language.

He stood and took one step forward. He buried his nose in my unbound hair and leaned into the junction of my neck and shoulder, breathing my scent. I brushed my hand down his head and grabbed the thick fur. I also took in his scent, the wash of comfort, home, and pack breezed through me, warming me from the center of my belly and spreading throughout my body. I shifted into my wolf form, and we stood together for a moment before bounding off towards the other wolf, decision made.

When we neared the spot where we had last seen the wolf, Fletcher moved ahead of me, protective. I stayed behind him and to the side, my muzzle in line with his left haunch. I wasn't a submissive wolf, or person for that matter, but Fletcher wasn't either and it's hard to give up thousands of years of wolf instinct overnight. I let him take the lead and guide us. He was bigger and stronger as well, the wolf instincts sharper in him, and I recognized that.

We stopped a healthy distance from the strange wolf's last position. We lay down, alert, but non-threatening to see if we could contact whatever type of wolf we were seeing.

While we waited, we groomed the last of the blood off each other. I have a hard time judging time in my beast forms, their minds not adept at the abstract concept, but the moon had moved a great deal over the sky when finally, a small, naked female form walked out of the tree shadow. I jerked, surprised. So, she would feel less vulnerable, I shifted back to my human form and walked to greet her, with Fletcher, protectively pressed against my side, his growl echoing through the trees and vibrating up my body.

The woman was trembling, and when we got closer, she threw herself on the ground beneath Fletcher's nose, submissively baring her throat and belly to him as though she were still a wolf and not a human. Fletcher, surprised, quit growling and backed up a step before sitting down heavily.

The woman raised herself to her hands and knees and looked quickly up at me and back down. Not sure what to do, I also knelt, so I would be less intimidating. I could see this woman—thin, if thickly muscled—was filthy. Her hair was tangled and matted. Remembering the other wolf I'd seen, I wondered if she spoke any English.

"Hi, what's your name?" I said slowly and gently as though speaking to a small child. She darted her gaze at me again, then averted her eyes.

"You no wolf," she said softly. It took me a while to determine that she did speak English, though so heavily accented I had to think about it and translate it in my head. I tried to place the accent. The woman was clearly native, and although I wasn't a linguist and only spoke a few words of my native tongue, I had been around the various tribal languages and accents. I couldn't place hers.

Thinking she meant that I wasn't a werewolf like she and Fletcher, I said, "No, I'm a shifter. I can do other animals beside a wolf."

"He no wolf," she said pointing to Fletcher. "He other." Her English was not only heavily accented but quite broken, and I wasn't sure what she was trying to say. I was trying to formulate something in my head when the woman began to weep. Even her weeping was silent and as she wiped her face, she gasped to see the wetness on her hands. I cocked my head in confusion. I looked at Fletcher to see if he had any idea what to do, but he looked even more puzzled than I felt.

"Are you ok?" I asked and took a small step forward to lay a hand on her shoulder in comfort. I expected her to maybe wrench away from me, but instead she threw herself at my feet and wrapped her arms around my legs. Fletcher moved forward, teeth bared, but I waved him away and bent down to disentangle her.

"It's okay, it's okay," I repeated as I pulled her free and knelt next to her again, this time she pressed herself against me, frightened, but not of me.

"Has someone hurt you?" I asked, feeling strangely protective. "Is there someone nearby? Where did you come from?"

She continued to weep and cling to me for quite some time. Fletcher watched warily, ears searching the darkness for danger. Finally, she calmed enough or felt safe enough to attempt to speak again. After much faltering and guessing back and forth, she let us know she was alone. She hadn't had a pack for a long time. She was afraid and avoiding the pack with the large wolf. She acted like she was terrified of him, although her fear of Fletcher diminished minute by minute as he showed no aggression towards her. She had happened on our scent trail and was curious and hungry. At that, I told her she was welcome to the meat we had left, and she quickly moved to the carcass and began tearing the flesh with her hands and devouring it. I was, in my human form, slightly nauseated by the sight, but waited patiently for her to finish.

When she finished, she approached me again yearning for physical contact and clung to me. I held her briefly and asked her again who she was. Retaining her submissive posture, she pulled away from me, and pulling out some grass, she made a bare patch in the soil which she smoothed with her hand. Together with her very broken English and some native words I didn't know, she sketched out a story that had both me and Fletcher doubting all our beliefs in the natural and supernatural world.

Her drawings were crude, and reminded me of cave paintings or

petroglyphs, basic and raw. However, there was grace and expressive-
ness to them I couldn't explain. It flowed as naturally to her as though
it was a common writing system, and she was as adept at that as I was
at plucking away at my computer. Her body language also told the
story through her smooth movements, her dancing hands, and her
facial expressions as she drew and attempted to speak the English she
barely knew. She told a different story than any I had ever read in a
history book, and it thrilled and scared me as she knew the history of
my people unlike any I had ever heard.

It started out like the history books. A long time ago. She indicated that the land was empty of people, and it was covered with ice.
Her graceful arms wrapped around herself to indicate the cold to corre-
spond with her pictures. It was rich with animal life. She drew familiar
beasts and fishes with simple lines, but extreme accuracy, easily recog-
nizable. She drew bears, different from modern ones, horses, bison,
caribou, the mammoth, and other ice age creatures I knew had once
lived in my land. What surprised me was her accuracy and fierceness
when she drew the ancient wolves that once inhabited the area as she
threw suspicious glances at Fletcher under her submissive posture.

At one point she gestured to him and the picture, and I knew for
sure that his kind weren't dire wolves, but some ancient Alaskan or
ice-age wolves thought to be extinct, but somehow preserved in Fletcher's wolf form. I knew I was looking at a time in the ice age before
humans crossed the Bering Land Bridge and inhabited Alaska. I
nodded. She realized I understood and cleared her patch of earth
again.

She showed the first people here and showed crude dwellings and
hunting practices, her silent weeping leaving drops of water over her
sketches in the dirt. I tried to ask her if her people came then, but I
wasn't sure she understood me, she kept shaking her head and pointing
to her drawings. So, I let it go. If her people were the first in this
region, that would probably make her Athapaskan, but her accent and
few native words didn't sound like anything I knew.

So far, my small knowledge of history and her story seemed to be
meshing, making it easy for me to understand. She showed other

animals crossing with the humans, the smaller Eurasian grey wolves as well, and she pointed to herself and to me. We were the modern wolves to this continent, the invaders. I nodded. The moose came, and she showed countless pics of the good hunting the mega-fauna of the time provided for all. Her eyes lit up, and I nodded and smiled gently acknowledging her story telling. She cleared the ground again, solemn, she looked up and held my gaze longer than she had before. Her hand trembled. She drew.

Winged creatures descended to the land. I didn't understand. They appeared similar to birds, but were man sized and the people feared them. I stopped her and attempted to ask what they were. I didn't know if they were figurative, indicating gods, or literal creatures. She shook her head, not understanding. I let her continue. The creatures lingered with the humans for a while. They shed their wings and appeared human, they mated with the humans, they formed the humans into social groups, and they gave the people knowledge and showed them how to control the beasts. Everything was peaceful for a while.

The woman's face grew pale under her dark skin and the ground in dirt. She showed a war with a great slaughter as the people tried to throw off the rule of the winged creatures. The creatures, and in my mind, I assigned them to be the native gods of my people, were angry and unleashed terrible power in the world. It caused a great destruction. Many animals, plants and people died, and some were changed by the winged creatures forever. She showed the killing of the mammoths and the great Alaskan wolves.

Then she indicated that in the release of the destructive power of the winged beings, some people were changed into the animals, and she pointed to Fletcher. She also showed that some animals were changed into people, and she pointed to herself. I stopped her and sat down hard on the ground from my kneeling position. I looked at Fletcher. He had a startled look as well. Then he lay down heavily and sighed, eyes trained on the drawing.

This small woman was not human. She never had been. I was stunned. I'd never even read anything like this in my books of folktales and mythology. I studied her as I waited patiently.

I asked her again, "You are not a human?" I pointed to me and Fletcher. "You are a wolf?"

She nodded, eyes brightening as she recognized that I understood the difference.

Then as suddenly, she regained her submissive posture, terror oozing from her in a wide range of scents. How had I not noticed the difference in her scent before? She didn't smell completely human. I shook it off. Fletcher sat warily a few paces away, his gaze drifting between the woman and me, a low whine signaling his confusion.

The wolf woman slumped in exhaustion. My mind was stretched to its fullest capacity and even Fletcher's wolf appeared to have had all he could take. I gently took the woman's hand and stopped her.

"Thank you," I said gently.

She sighed and scooting over to me, relaxed against me. She fell asleep quickly as I stroked her matted hair, and after a while she drifted into a deeper sleep, her body slowly shifting back to its natural form. I shifted as well and curled myself protectively around her. Fletcher stood guard as she slept, and the moon slowly dropped low in the sky.

Nights aren't dark for long this time of the summer, so it was quite light when the wolf woman awoke. I indicated that she should come with us. She looked longingly at the woods but indicated she would follow us. Fletcher and I shared a look and headed back to the cabin. The brief night left a heavy burden on our hearts.

When we arrived, Fletcher laid by the stump and I looked away as his body distorted, and the grunts of pain indicated his shift back to human. I also changed and gestured that the wolf woman should join us in the cabin. She sniffed around warily, and then melted into the woods nearby, too wild for the enclosed space of the cabin. Exhausted, I pulled on my sleeping clothes and collapsed on the bed, almost too tired to notice when Fletcher's heavier form collapsed next to me, and I drifted off in the warmth and comfort of his arms.

After the brief but deep sleep of the mentally exhausted. I woke up, my mind still troubling out the history I had just been taught. I kept ruminating over the link between the big, newly minted, Alaskan wolf and the small pack of werewolves—werehumans? wolfweres? I needed to come up with a new term—that the big wolf seemed to be running with.

Now that I was pretty sure the big wolf was Fletcher's old professor, I had to start wondering what his motivations were. Why did he change Fletcher? It seemed deliberate once I sat back and thought about it. Also, why was he here? What was his connection with the odd pack of werecritters I didn't know what to call now? Ugh! My mind kept racing.

What if I was all wrong, and this was simply a lonely creature, who when attempting to make a companion, screwed up and was now simply looking for him? Maybe it was all friendly like, and I was the one making it all sinister? Then again, his pack did attempt to kill us. Not so friendly after all. So, if the good professor didn't know about the gold, what purpose would he have to search out Fletcher? Why was he haunting the area around the cabin? When did he get here?

That last question rattled around my brain.

"Fletcher." I shook him. "Wake up. We need to do some thinking. We've been looking at this all wrong."

"What?" he asked sleepily. He sat up and rubbed his eyes. He swung his feet over the bed and pulled his jeans up. "What are you talking about?"

"We've been trying to come up with why the professor is here, when we should have been looking at *when* he got here!"

"What are you talking about? Who is the professor?"

I blinked at him for a minute, having forgotten I hadn't filled him in on the past couple of days. "Uhh, well, I followed the college student. He isn't the big bad wolf, so our only other lead was your old professor. I guess we all assumed that he came up to Alaska following you, but what if he came before that, what if you didn't have anything to do with it all? That changes his motivation, and it changes everything."

He placed his head in his hands, his elbows resting on his knees, and scrubbed his face. He dropped his hands, and with his head still down said, "What are you getting at?" With that he looked up and caught my stare with the shock of his piercing blue gaze.

My breath caught for a moment, stunned by his beauty and the flood of warmth that socked me in the stomach. I stammered for a minute. "Well, uh, what if he is the one after the gold?"

He stood and paced for a moment. "How could that be? There's no way he could have known about it."

"I keep thinking that too, but we're letting that get in the way. We don't know all his connections. Maybe in his crypto research he found out about it, or he knows someone, or he has some link to Clyde. I don't know, but it makes more sense if he is involved in everything because otherwise, he doesn't make sense at all."

Fletcher stared at me for a while, as though trying to figure out my logic. Which to me was logical, but everyone's brain works a little differently. My wild conjectures and suppositions made sense to me—the little things adding up and making connections that weren't obviously there. He opened his mouth to reply, but a soft scratch at the door interrupted him. I had almost forgotten about our odd companion from the night before. Another tentative scratch. Fletcher motioned that I should open the door. He moved back as far as he could get. I opened the door slowly, so I wouldn't frighten the timid thing.

I was expecting the wolf, but the girl crouched there. I gestured for her to enter, and she glanced around skittishly, but trusting me, entered slowly, sniffing and alert. When she saw it was only the two of us, she visibly relaxed, her senses of sight and smell satisfied. Fletcher carefully handed me an old t-shirt and with a few minutes of verbal and tactile demonstration, I managed to get it on her. The poor little thing was so tiny my t-shirt reached her knees, and since I doubted she had any concept of underwear, I let that be good enough. I made some breakfast, apprehensive about whether the girl would eat it—curious if she would eat anything that wasn't familiar. I shouldn't have worried. Her thin frame should've prepared me for the way she inhaled her food, but she didn't appear picky or bothered by the mix of fresh and rehydrated foods I offered her. After Fletcher and I were through, we watched in fascination as she finished off all the leftovers on both our plates. Her fingers and her face covered with food, she finally sat back and licked her fingers clean.

"What is your name?" I asked her quietly, realizing that in all our discussion, I had never gotten a name from her. "My name is Piper, and this is Fletcher." I pointed to each of us.

She glanced furtively between us. Mouthing the new words as though trying them out before repeating them in her odd accent and broken speech. She dropped her gaze and sat quietly for a moment. Then pointed to herself and made an odd bark howl noise that I assumed was her name. Of course, why would she have a human name? She wasn't human. I tried to copy the sound of her name, but I startled her, and then amused her with my attempts. Finally, I gave up.

"How about I call you Jane?" I didn't really expect an answer because I doubted she understood me. I pointed to her and said, "Jane." I did this over and over until understanding brightened in her eyes and she repeated the name as best she could, looking proud and delighted. I wanted to question her about the professor, but I was afraid of her reaction. She had seemed so wary of Fletcher in his wolf form, and even I found the good professor terrifying in his ancient form. Fletcher beat me to it.

"Jane," he started gently.

She turned her head partially, so her ear faced him, like her wolf self would and kept her head and eyes down, submissively.

"Jane, I'm sorry to ask this, but what do you know about the other wolf like me?"

I watched her body language. I doubted she understood because it appeared she shrunk into herself and began to tremble slightly. She must be a very submissive wolf, or a very abused one, I thought. I leaned toward the abused. She was part human too, at least she had spent time as a human, or she wouldn't speak the languages she spoke or know the few human customs she adapted to so quickly.

"No, no," she whispered and shook her head.

"Is he your alpha?" Fletcher continued.

She shook her head. "I don't know word." She looked at me, confused.

I struggled for a moment, "Uh," I looked at Fletcher for help. "How do you explain alpha?"

He glanced away thoughtful for a moment, then gave me a few directions, and we stood up to act out the best we could. I assumed a submissive wolf pose in my human form, and Fletcher assumed a dominant pose. We held that position for a moment, then he pointed to himself and said, "Alpha."

Jane looked at us both quietly for a few moments, then understanding washed over her face. She smiled. Then slumped back into herself.

"Do you understand, Jane?" Fletcher asked gently.

She nodded, still closed off.

"Is the other wolf like me your alpha?"

"No. no," she said softly.

"How did he come to be in your pack?" Fletcher continued.

"No pack."

In the end, it was too much. She leapt up, threw off her shirt, and bolted out the door. She changed at the edge of the woods and disappeared.

I started after her, but Fletcher grabbed my arm. "Don't. She's frightened. She's been bullied and maybe abused. Let her go. If she trusts us, she may come back, eventually. But if you chase her, I'm afraid we'll never see her again."

I wasn't so stubborn I couldn't see the wisdom in that, so I stood with Fletcher and watched her disappear into the woods.

Chapter 14

I didn't know how to process everything Jane had told us. I'd never heard or imagined anything like it. I wondered if there was anything out there that was close to that story, anything to back it up in mythology or history. I fretted about it, and when Fletcher and I talked about it, he admitted he was just as baffled. Since his degree had been in history, I asked him to research when we got back, and he agreed. I also called Bran on the sat phone and told her the entire tale so she could also start searching for books or native stories, anything that fit or seemed to tie into the fantastical story we'd been told.

Once I'd done all I could about Jane and her story from the cabin, I was suddenly left with the realization that Fletcher and I were alone. No immediate problems, and no real worries about being a monster. He was quiet and had been sitting still in silence for a good stretch of time before I realized it. He'd come to that conclusion way before me. He'd been sitting and watching me for quite a stretch before I was aware of it.

I was standing by the door looking out, talking to Bran on the sat phone, when the weight of his gaze burned a hole in my back. I finished my call and stood still for a moment. I dropped the phone to my side and turned slowly. He was there in an instant. The chair hadn't even hit the floor from the force of his move before his hand was at my waist, and his mouth was hungrily on mine. I dropped the phone to the ground. My hands twined into his silky hair. My body burned with wanting.

He pressed me up against the door frame, his hard body molded to mine. The kiss was desperate; we were full of need. We'd been tiptoeing around our feelings for each other. Finally for a moment, we let go.

I don't know how long we kissed against the door frame, but it seemed forever and only an instant all at once. My hands moved from his hair to around the firm muscles of his back. His hands explored my body and ended up tangled in my long, loose hair. He pulled back and looked at me.

"You drive me crazy, Piper." His voice was husky, and his eyes burned with intensity.

My heart beat faster, and I struggled to get my breath. I felt so much, but I had no experience or ability to put what it was I felt into words. A knot of panic built in my gut and rose into my throat, nearly choking me.

I smiled, uncertainly, spun out of his arms and ran out the door towards the stump. I shed my clothes and changed into my wolf, daring him to follow. I knew a run would clear my head. I didn't know what else to do or what to say following our outburst of feeling and touching—thinking about it made my heart leap and race. So, I ran.

I ran so fast that the wind made my eyes water. I ran oblivious to what was around me, weaving through trees without thought, and letting my wolf instinct take me where it would.

Finally, I heard paws pounding the ground behind me. He had followed. I was fast, but he had size and reach on me and that made him faster. My heart leapt with joy when he drew alongside, and we raced abreast for a time—reducing all feeling to nothing but raw animal joy from the wind in our fur and the freedom of the wilderness.

The trees thinned, and I realized we were near the lake. We had run for several miles. Fletcher bumped my shoulder, and we tumbled out onto the shore, tangled up and panting. He gave me a wolfish grin, and I yipped in delight. Together we walked bumping shoulders and rubbing our heads together and drank from the icy clear water. Once our thirst was under control, he trotted back into the shelter of the woods looking back to see if I was following. I took another lap of the sweet water and followed slowly. I could hear him changing, the were-wolf change being a deal more loud and painful than mine. His bones crunched and then shifted under his skin with a wet sloshy sound. I slowed even further. I didn't want to talk; I didn't know what to say. I know that's what he wanted, because he wasn't going to be walking back to the cabin in naked human form.

My wolf-self drooped into submissive posture, as I dreaded what I was going to do or say. My tail tucked and my head down, I walked over to him. He knelt to be at my height and gripped my head in his hands.

"What's wrong, Piper? Why did you run away?" I averted my eyes since I couldn't move my head. "I'm so sorry, I didn't mean to over-step, or scare you. I'm just so attracted to you. I thought you felt the same, and that kiss..."

I shivered, he thought I didn't like him! I didn't know what to do. Part of me wanted to change back so I could reassure him that I *was* attracted to him. I almost couldn't stop myself during that kiss, but I was too inexperienced to know what to do next. Plus, I was suddenly shy about being naked around him while he was also naked.

Impulsively, I leaned in and licked his face. I just meant it to be a little lick, but it ended up being a long, wet, doggy lick. I sat down hard pulling my head out of his hands and hung my head. He drew back, startled. He looked at my dejected pose and started to laugh.

He wiped his face with his arm. I lay down and put my head on my crossed front legs with a sigh. He crawled over until he was sitting next to me and rubbed the soft fur of my ears.

"Ah, Piper, you are one of the most interesting people I've ever met." He continued to rub my ears and scratch behind them.

My eyes closed partially in pleasure.

"You just aren't ready to deal with this, are you?"

I laid my head in his lap and gazed up.

"That's it, isn't it?"

Without a thought, I shifted. I sat up. We were hip to hip facing opposite each other. I turned my head to face him. "I'm sorry, Fletcher. I panicked. I don't know how to do," I gestured between us, "this." I paused for a moment, swallowed, and looked away. "I've never had a serious boyfriend, hell, I've rarely gone on a second date."

His eyes never left mine, patiently letting me explain, but his hand seemed to have a mind of its own as it lifted a strand of hair from my eyes and gently caressed my cheek.

"I have so much feeling inside, and I don't know what it is or what it means, and when you kissed me, I was afraid of what I should do! I freaked out a little." I gasped for air, the words tumbling out so fast I didn't even get a chance to breathe. "So, I ran. That's all I could do to burn off this intense *feeling*. I'm sorry I didn't mean to hurt or confuse you. I *am* attracted to you; I *do* want to see where this will go. I just don't know how to proceed or what to do!" The panic started to build again in my chest, and it must have shown in my face.

Fletcher drew back slightly. "It's okay, Piper." His voice soothed me. "We'll take it slow. I didn't mean to frighten you before." I started to protest, but he stopped me. "How about we start here? I like you. I want to see where this goes."

He leaned in and this time, he kissed me so gently and sweetly, that my heart soared. He pulled back. "We'll go at your pace." He pulled away and smiled at me. "Come on, I'll race you back." And with that, he started his change.

I waited patiently, then changed, and we raced back. My heart was full, my mind quieter, and I trusted that even if I didn't know what to do, I wasn't alone trying to figure it out.

The rest of the time at the cabin was bliss. We talked, openly for the first time and discovered how much we had in common. We liked the same books, movies, music, we had similar tastes in food. We hunted together as wolves and ran for the joy of the chase.

We kissed a few times, but I could tell Fletcher held back like he hadn't the first time, and he respected my boundaries. We slept under the midnight sun and the brief flicker of starlight in our wolf forms, since that felt safer for now. And although a boundary remained between us, our feelings for each other grew and our attraction deepened.

When I heard dad's plane approaching to pick us up, dread rose in my heart. I flung my arms around Fletcher and this time I initiated the kissing. I threw all my emotion and all my feeling for him into it, and when we pulled apart, as the engine idled to a stop, both of us were panting. His blue eyes were dark with passion, and I blushed.

I grabbed my things and rushed out to the plane. He waited for quite a while, before he too came out carrying his bag. I smiled. The sunglasses were on, and the stoic expression was back on his face. I was still blushing and trying to hide it from my dad. Dad grunted a greeting to Fletcher and started the plane. The noise kept conversation to a zero, so both Fletcher and I were alone with our thoughts on our way back to Anchorage.

Fletcher was still silent when we walked into my house. He followed me to the kitchen, and I made sandwiches while I waited for him to speak. I could tell he was building up to something. Finally, as we began to eat, he picked up his sandwich, brought it to his mouth then set it down.

"Piper."

I glanced up at him inquisitively.

"I think it's best if I find somewhere else to stay." I opened my mouth to protest, but he shook his head. "Listen, I find you a great distraction, and I want to respect your boundaries. I just don't trust myself if I'm here with you all the time." He glanced at me to judge my reaction.

I just sat stunned. He flashed me his lopsided grin, his eyes twinkled. "Don't worry, you're not getting rid of me that easily, I won't be able to stay away." And with that, he dug into his sandwich. I laughed.

After lunch, he gathered up his computer and a few things he'd left in the spare bedroom, and I took him to a used car lot in midtown. Since he had plenty of cash, he bought a used SUV. I kissed him through the window, and we went our separate ways. He had house hunting and research to do, and he planned to return to the hotel where he'd stayed before.

My heart ached a little to see him drive away, but the thrill of butterflies in my stomach kept me smiling. I had to go back to work tomorrow, and I had half a day with nothing to do. I decided to check on Bran to see if she had come up with anything. Unable to wipe the grin off my face, I drove over to the Lunatic Fringe.

Even the obnoxious girl at the counter couldn't kill my good mood. I ignored her protests as I swung around the counter to the back rather than come up with a pithy retort.

Bran was sitting at her desk, her back to me deep into a mix of books and internet research. Her hair was twisted up in a messy bun with a pencil sticking out of it—a good sign she was thoroughly into her project. She hated her hair in her eyes when she was concentrating.

I grinned wickedly. I rarely got the chance to sneak up on her, and I was due a good show. Although I hadn't entered quietly, I quickly put on predator mode and slunk up behind her. I poked fingers into her ribs and yelled "boo" at the same time. She almost hit the roof she jumped so hard. Then she whirled around and zapped me with something. Whatever it was knocked me on my ass and rewired my brain for a moment. When I got my breath and brain back, I yelped, "What was that?!"

"Oh," she said nonchalantly, "just something I've been working on." Smugly, she turned back to her computer. "I figured I'd try to learn a defensive, uh, spell, for lack of a better word. Nice to see it works."

"That's an understatement," I muttered under my breath.

She whirled around in her chair and pointed her finger sharply at me. "You deserved it for scaring me!" The Irish temper flared, then she laughed. "You should have seen the look on your face!"

Grumpily, I conceded the point. I stood up slowly, rubbing my backside. I tingled all over as though I was getting a low dose of electricity coursing through my body. I still felt slightly disoriented, and I shook my head to clear it. "If you'd have amped up that 'spell' any,

I'm not so sure I could remember my name!" I growled. Bran needed to wipe the smug look off her face.

I looked around the room for another chair and found one buried under more books. I dumped them to Bran's annoyed huff and brought the chair over to join her near the computer.

"So, what's up? What did you find?"

She threw a sidelong glance at me. "Some things, but I don't know yet if they're really anything." She finished up her bookkeeping and closed the software program.

I waited for her to finish. "What does that mean?"

"Well, I've just been rethinking some of the Raven creation myths and researching them from different tribes."

"And?"

"Let me do some more. I may have something, but I'm not ready yet."

"You won't give me anything?"

"Your girl may have connected a lot of myths together. Enough to sort of scare me."

I frowned at her. Perplexed. "What do you mean, scare you?" I asked with a slight tremor in my voice that I hurriedly covered with a rough throat clear.

"You're just going to have to wait. A lot of the stuff I've been linking too is like a horde of tribal secrets. I'm sort of stalled out on what I can do on the internet. I need a good day in the library, and maybe I can get someone to talk to me at the heritage center." She turned and looked at me strangely for a moment. "I know your dad grew up in a village in your tribe. I bet he knows something too."

"No, that's crazy! He's never said anything like this, and he's told me a lot of what went on there." I shook my head, determined that I was right.

There was no way my dad knew some secret origin story he'd keep from me. No way! The thought ate at me. I drove home in a daze, the thought, like a cancer gnawing at my gut.

Did my dad know? The thought ate me up as I tried to fall asleep. He'd always been cagey when it came to talking about our abilities. I always thought it was too painful for him considering the abuse he had suffered in his tribe. But now I wasn't sure that was the issue. Something else was going on. I felt it. My dad knew something. And he had kept that something from me my entire life. Why? What? My troubled thoughts bombarded me until I got up and started to pace.

The wolf girl, Jane, had known the origins of her people. Why didn't my dad know? The only answer was that he knows. He must. He was with his tribe—that was the kinda stuff that got passed down. I knew it. Why not me? Why hadn't he told me? Was it some deep tribal secret? Even then, why not tell me? He felt no allegiance to them anymore. Was it because he thought I wasn't mature enough to handle it?

I paused for a moment in my interior monologue, hurt. But that couldn't be right. I worked for him at one of the most dangerous jobs in the country—the world. He knew I was mature enough to handle anything. Was he protecting me? I stopped again. Yes, that felt right. But from what? That was the real question. I shivered. What secrets did my dad's quiet demeanor hide?

Around and around I went. Yet, I kept coming back to the same question. Who or what was he protecting me from and why? I glanced at the clock, chagrined to find it was only three in the morning. I wanted to go directly to my parent's house and confront him. I just didn't dare. What if my mom knew nothing? What if there was true danger and asking brought it down on us? I didn't want to bring that to my family's home. I'd wait until it was time to go to work. I'd go in early.

Relieved to have a plan, I was able to go to sleep. The last troubled thought that drifted through my mind as I slipped down the well of slumber was where did the winged ones go?

I slept through my alarm. Panicked, I bolted straight up and flew out of bed. I threw on my nearest clothes, brushed my teeth and ran a brush through my hair. I didn't have time to shower if I wanted to have time to confront my dad. I grabbed a couple of breakfast meals from Mickey Dees. Dad didn't always remember to eat breakfast in the morning, so I hoped a little bribe would help pry the information free. I parked with twenty minutes to spare. Not as early as I had really wanted, but early for me.

Dad raised his eyebrows at me when I entered, so I tossed a greasy food bag to him, and handed him a cup of OJ.

"Thanks!" He smiled at me.

"No prob." I smiled back. We both munched for a minute, then I let it fly. "Uh, I ran into someone in the woods." I wasn't sure how to start my tale. "She told me, Dad. She told me and Fletcher."

His face was a mask of confusion. I knew I wasn't doing a good job of telling, but I just couldn't seem to spit out the words.

"She wasn't human." His brow wrinkled, but his eyes grew sharp and wary. "She was a wolf. One that could turn human." Dad stared at me for a moment then turned and looked out the window and ate his sandwich.

"She told me what I was." She hadn't, but I needed to figure out what he knew, or if he knew anything.

His shoulders stiffened.

"You knew," I accused him.

His silence stretched on. His back to me.

"Why?" I let the question sit in the air and fester.

He didn't respond for what felt like forever. Finally, he turned and sat heavily in his office chair. "It's not an easy question to answer. We'll talk later," was his response. And at that, he shut up, and I couldn't pry anything out of him.

To say that my day lasted forever would be an understatement. All I could do was think about what dad might say. I wasn't the best representative of the company to my clients because I didn't have the head space to think, fly, and answer all their questions with thoughtful responses.

When I finally landed at home, took care of my plane, and walked to our office, my hands were damp, and I was trembling with anticipation. I could hardly breathe. I was tense and scared about whatever he was going to reveal to me.

He looked up from the desk when I walked in, his face grim. "I told your mom I'd be home late." Fortunately, that was a common occurrence during the summer months, and she wouldn't be that curious about what we were doing.

"OK," I mumbled, wondering what he was planning.

He finished up his paperwork—waited for me to do the same—then stood and opened the office window. He stood there looking out for a minute, glanced at me, and in a sudden rush of movement, shifted into his raven. Then, flying up out of his clothes, he went out the window.

I stood there in shock for several moments. I hadn't seen my dad shift since I was a kid, and he'd convinced me he didn't do it because it was difficult for him to shift. What I had witnessed appeared to be as effortless as what I did. Apparently, my dad had kept *several* secrets from me.

My mouth was probably hanging open as I stood there frozen, still staring at my dad's clothing crumpled on the floor when a large raven flew past the window and squawked at me. I looked up, realizing that my dad wanted me to come with him. I shifted up out of my clothes and flew out the window towards answers, and maybe my new destiny.

Chapter 15

My parents lived in a small community just north of Eagle River called Chugiak. My dad had owned the home since they'd gotten married. It was a log cabin that had been added on to several times on about thirty acres surrounded by trees. It had a nice yard, great for growing up and having room to play, but not so big it was a pain to mow. Most of the landscaping was natural forest. In the back, surrounded by trees, was an outbuilding that my dad used as a shop. He was handy and creative, and the building had projects going from airplane parts to furniture. No one really went out there besides my dad, because it was a bit far from the house, cluttered, and there wasn't anywhere to sit or hang out, anyway. Only dad spent significant time out there.

I was intrigued when he flew the distance from south Anchorage to home, and even more curious when he flew into the trees, shifted, and walked through the rear entrance to the shop away from any possible view from the house.

I waited a few minutes, time for him to dress, and I saw him throw out some clothing. I swooped down, shifted, and dressed in what amounted to an old ratty robe Dad sometimes wore over his clothes for warmth when he worked. Once dressed, I entered the shop, bursting with questions. Before I had uttered a word, my mouth still hanging open to speak, Dad put his fingers to his lips in the universal, "Shut up!" signal and looked warily out the door.

He closed it, shut the blinds in the windows and walked toward the back wall where we'd entered. His desk sat there, perched below the window and to the left of the door. He pushed the desk over in front of the door, pulled up the tattered and filthy rug that sat over the cement slab and revealed a door in the floor.

I'd never known it was there, and I bet no one else, including my mom knew that it existed. That desk and rug had sat in that spot *literally* for as long as I could remember. The rug was so old, that the dust billowed out of it and the spot where my dad's feet rested beneath his desk was nearly see-through. I couldn't tell you what color it had once been.

Dad gestured for me to come closer. I approached and looked over the edge of the hole in the floor. It was large, nearly the full length and width of the rug, and plenty big enough for a medium-sized adult to enter. There was a ladder that reached down into darkness. I shuddered. Dad gestured for me to enter and handed me a Maglite. I shrugged and tied the robe tight and started down the ladder.

Once I hit bottom, I stood aside and watched Dad descend, closing the trapdoor behind him. Once he reached the bottom, he did something under the ladder, and lights flickered on. Again, I tried to speak, but dad shushed me and gestured for me to follow. He walked down a sloping tunnel. I brushed my hands along the wall to steady myself, and that's how I noticed when the man-made walls changed to those of a natural tunnel, probably volcanic in nature.

The tunnel gradually increased in size until dad stopped in the middle of a natural cavern. Even filled with fluorescent lighting, the cavern seemed to soak in the light and diminish it. The entire space was the blackest black. Crystalline structures on the ceiling and walls reflected some light, but mostly it was too black to make out any color. I twirled around slowly, taking it in.

Dad grabbed my elbow and led me further in towards an old couch. I recognized it from my childhood and smiled. It was a three-piece sectional, leather, and very comfortable, and it sat drowned in the darkness. I realized that there were other objects sitting around, other things from the house that had been discarded or replaced over the years, and some I did not recognize.

"It's almost entirely magnetite," Dad said quietly, startling me since we had remained silent for so long. "It's so large, it produces its own magnetic field," he continued. "It's deep enough that only the most sensitive instruments can see it exists down here. No known instruments can penetrate it, it is entirely private from prying eyes and ears. Especially of the electronic kind."

At this point, he turned, looked me directly in the eyes and said so calmly and firmly I couldn't doubt his next words. "I discovered it while gold mining in 1869."

I stared in disbelief. "What? That can't be!" I could feel my heart race and my breathing increase. "What's going on? Why am I down here, what are you talking about?" My voice steadily rose until I was close to shrieking.

"Piper, calm down." My dad's soothing voice and his gentle hand brushed over my hair.

"Dad, what's going on?" I asked again.

"First, promise you will be calm and listen."

I stared a while longer, not sure what to do or what to believe. His statement was so surreal. But I felt my heart slow, and my breath begin to regulate.

"Pipe, I really wished you could have had a normal life. I tried to give that to you and Baylee. I've kept these things from you hoping you would never need to know. Sure, I would've told you some things eventually, but truly the rest I intended to take to my grave. You girls are my life. I wanted you free of the burden I bear."

He stood, walked over to a crate huddled against some junk. He came back and handed me a familiar bottle. Coke, the real bottled stuff. It wasn't ice cold, but it was cool, and I suddenly realized I was parched. I popped the top off with the offered bottle opener and chugged half the bottle. He grinned at me and took a swallow of his.

He savored the flavor for a moment, and his face grew grim and serious once more.

"I went to live in an area that is now called Utqiagvik or Barrow in 851 A.D. A small fishing village."

"851? No. That isn't possible." I sat stunned, incredulous.

He fell quiet again for a while, sipping at his drink and looking contemplative.

I waited, knowing his silences. "The Inupiaq, our tribe, call themselves the real people.

There is a reason for this. We were here long before the others."

I blinked, not sure what others he meant. The other tribes? The other beings? I didn't dare interrupt him again, so I sat quietly.

He stopped for a moment, organizing his thoughts. "Some of the things I've told you about my past weren't really accurate."

I'd sort of figured this one out on my own, and I harrumphed in agreement. There's no way most of what he'd told us was true considering he was claiming to be roughly eleven hundred years older than he looked.

He threw me a sharp look. "What little you know about the Inupiaq, your tribe, is only partly true. As with most people limited in their knowledge of what you would call the supernatural, they have let themselves forget the truth."

He bowed his head. "I once told you I couldn't shift well, and I gave that as an excuse not to shift with you. The truth is more...*complicated*."

The tenor of his voice sent a chill through me. My dad never seemed to be bothered by anything. He had that native stoicism and quiet deep in his bones, and I had never seen him panicked or even more than mildly annoyed.

He settled back on the couch, sipping his Coke. "Long ago, many, many years before you were born, there was a shamanic class, a tribe within the tribe, secret and unknown but to those of us who were a part of it. As I've told you—we are the Raven clan." He glanced at me, mainly to make sure I was listening. I stretched and drank deeply from my Coke. "However, as far as I know or have been able to find out, all the shamanic inner tribes, the Eagle, the Wolf, the Bear, etc. are no more." I winced. I had had a run in with Eagle clan—at least three of them—but I didn't stop him. It didn't seem that important at the moment.

"As far as I can tell, you and I are the last shifters of all the clans. See, the shifters have been scattered, hunted." He looked at me to judge my reaction. Then he continued, "And others lost. The tribes don't know about us, and our feats have passed into mythic tales. That is the best thing that could have happened." He took a long swig from his soda.

"Now, about your question. If you have the power to shift, and do it often, aging becomes..." He looked at me and smiled comfortingly. "Slow."

My dad looked to be an age that was hard to judge. He could be any age between thirty-five and fifty. I'd assumed that since I was twenty-nine, he was somewhere in his early fifties. Eleven hundred and something was just not possible.

"That one I was going to have to tell you at some point." He stopped for a drink.

I wasn't sure how to deal with that. I felt shaky, uncertain. I set my coke down and hugged my arms around myself. I noticed I was breathing hard and worked to slow it down. I stood up and paced. Then I sat back down. How had he hidden himself so long? How was I going to do it in the modern electronic age?

Dad gave me a minute. Once I sat back down, he continued. "When I fled my village in the 1850s, shortly after the Yankee whalers came looking for the bowhead, I took you with me."

I shuddered, terrified, and leapt up. "No, that isn't possible!" I shouted. I finally had enough of this fantasy. "I don't remember anything past twenty-five or so years ago! I don't believe you!"

Dad threw back the rest of his Coke and strode over to get another.

"Our kind age slowly and strangely. Our children can take centuries to mature. You were quite precocious in many ways. You learned to shift very young, and you matured fairly quickly."

157

"Why don't I remember it?"

He ignored me and continued his tale as if I hadn't interjected. "You stayed about the size and maturity of a four- or five-year-old for nearly ninety years. Then your aging sped up. When you were close to the approximate age of a seven-year-old, I found your mom. The woman you think of as your mom."

The woman I think of as my mom? That felt like an arrow to my heart. I'd had another mother and my dad had taken me from her? I stood up, then sat down hard. I think my mouth dropped open.

Dad knew I was going to talk because he told me to wait until he was finished. "That took some explaining. But she wanted children so much, and I didn't dare try to give her any. Since we are long lived, and maybe a different species from humans, children are rare."

He was quiet a moment, drifting in his past. "My first wife, your biological mother was from the shamanic Wolf tribe. She was part human, having a Russian mother. She also had unique green eyes like yours. I left because even though we are mostly immune to human disease, she caught a fever and died when you were still tiny."

I felt a wave of grief. I would never know her. I loved my mom, the woman who raised me, but I still felt a sense of loss.

"Your mom, Shannon, took the weirdness in her stride. Luckily, you'd hit the turning point and started to age normally. We raised you as our mixed-blood child. At some point, I think you wanted to believe that was how your life had always been. We raised you with human children, you went to school, and before long you invented another childhood. We encouraged it. It was easier."

Tears formed in my eyes. My throat grew tight. I felt like I had lost a large portion of my life, and no one I loved cared.

"Your mom still wanted a baby, so she used modern science to get pregnant." I'm guessing he meant she had in vitro or artificial insemination or something with help from a sperm bank. "Baylee doesn't know and there is no reason she should. She is completely human. She is safe."

I probably should have told him about the demon, but it didn't seem like the right time now. At this point I was exhausted. There was too much information to disseminate, and I didn't know what to do about it or how to think. I walked over to Dad's crate of goodies. I picked up a package of jerky, one of cherry licorice, and another Coke and collapsed back on the couch. I couldn't keep my silence any longer, I felt cranky and wanted to just sleep.

"What is hunting you? Why did you leave the tribe? How did any of this," I waved my hands about, "come to be, and what are we? Why are we hiding in this cave?" I trailed off, out of breath, the questions bubbling up like hot vomit ready to spew out of my mouth.

Dad shook his head. He was only going to tell me what he wanted me to know and from experience I knew I could do nothing to pry any more out of him. I squawked a protest, but finally conceded and let him continue. I opened my snacks noisily and started to munch, doing anything to keep myself from jumping in with all my questions. Suddenly dad stood, and raked a hand through his hair, leaving it standing up partially on one side.

"This is hard for me, Pipe." He paced away from me, darkness eating at his figure for a moment before he turned and came back. "Tell me what you know."

I nodded and repeated what Fletcher and I had constructed from Jane's tale. Once I was done, he shuddered, but he came back and sat down. "I wish you hadn't been born shadow winged, baby. I'm so sorry." Then he took a deep breath.

"It is said that Raven made the world. When the waters forced the land up from the deep, Raven stabbed it with his beak and fixed it there. This first land was only large enough for a house, Raven and his parents. Raven's father had a bladder that hung above his bed. Raven was fascinated by it. He begged his father repeatedly to allow him to play with it. Finally, Raven's father agreed, and Raven played with the bladder until he wore a hole in it. From the hole, light appeared, and it filled the land. Not wanting the land to be light all the time, Raven's father took back the bladder so that the child could not damage it further. This is how the land began and day and night were created.[1]"

I narrowed my eyes. I already knew this story. I knew hundreds of Raven stories. I had grown up on them—some told by my dad, some heard at school, and some I studied because of who I am. I had no idea why he had told me this. I looked at him questioningly during his retelling. He shrugged. "There is truth in all the old tales," he said not meeting my eyes.

"You know too much, Piper." He looked up into my eyes, "Promise me—" he grabbed my hands; the sudden movement startled me, and I nearly jerked away "—promise me you will not look beyond what you already know. You will not look past the myths. They protect you. Keep yourself hidden always. Let no one know what you are, beyond those you'd trust with your own immortal soul."

"Immortal soul? Dad…" I couldn't even form what I wanted to say or ask so I ended with, "Why?" It was all I could manage to croak out.

My throat was dry and scratchy, and his fear had somehow leached into my bones. He ruffled my hair like he had when I was small. His face softened and I could see the love and concern there.

"It's my job to worry. It's my job to keep you safe. Just listen for once and do what you are told." His eyes hardened, and he got up to leave. I had no choice but to follow. I didn't want to be left behind in the black cave.

On the walk out, I realized he had not gotten my verbal promise. He hadn't pushed, probably knowing I wouldn't have given it to him anyway. The saying 'curiosity killed the cat' usually doubled for ravens and it was already eating me up. On one hand, I wanted to honor my father, he was truly freaked out,and that worried me. But I wasn't sure I believed him. It was one more mystery to add to my growing collection, and I needed answers like an addict needed a fix. Every beat of my wings seemed to increase that yearning as I flew back to the office.

Dad refused to speak any more about it and when I tried to bring it up in the days that followed, he'd just shake his head or change the subject. When he clammed up, he wouldn't budge. I finally stopped asking. However, it didn't stop me from telling Branwyn and looking stuff up on my own.

"Why that story Bran?" I asked her after I told her my tale.

She hung her head, her brow wrinkled in deep thought. After a moment she looked up. "I don't know, Pipe. I really don't. But you got a creation myth from your dad and another, in a way, from the wolf girl. With the rest of my research…I know there's something there. I still don't have my finger on it, but it must mean something. I'm more concerned with your dad saying you're being hunted considering what's been going on with the green Jeep guy. Do you think they could be related?"

"I don't know. That seems far-fetched since he didn't show up until the gold. If we could figure out who he is and what he wants, maybe we can find out," I said. "I just don't know how to do that. I'm a bush pilot not an investigator. I don't even know where to start!"

Bran smiled. "Too bad we can't just 'run his plate' like they do in movies and on TV. But I'm pretty sure regular people like us don't have that kind of pull. However, if you could draw him out of his car, I could probably sneak in and grab his registration?" She raised her eyebrows at me with the lift at the end of her sentence, like she was asking permission.

"How would you do that? I'm not even sure if he's following me or Fletcher. Plus, I don't know when he will be following me, or where I'll be or anything to set up that kind of thing."

I didn't realize that she was serious until her face fell. "You would really do that?" I asked incredulously.

"Of course," she replied with utter seriousness. "You know I would!"

"Still…"

"Yeah, it would take some planning, and we'd have to go fast the second you noticed he was following you again!"

"Okaaaayyy. I guess it couldn't hurt to give it a try, but I still think it's a long shot."

"Yeah, it might be, but it *would* give us a good start if it works."

"It would. At least we'd get somewhere on one mystery." I bit my lip. "Let's figure out how to do this."

We worked on it for the rest of the night and came up with a shaky plan. We still had to figure out who was after Fletcher's gold, who might have been involved in Clyde's death, and why my dad thought we were being hunted.

Chapter 16

The next few days were uneventful. I finally visited my mom, so that got her off the trail for a while. Baylee was harder to shake, but I couldn't have them involved in anything that wasn't safe. Nothing else could be done until I picked up my green Jeep tail again. I still wasn't sure if he was really following me or Fletcher, and I guessed my best bet to pick him up was if Fletcher and I were together driving around town. That was a problem. If I had Fletcher with me, I couldn't execute the plan. I knew enough about men that I knew he'd never agree to go along with it. So somehow, I needed to pick up the tail, ditch Fletcher, and pick up Bran for anything to work.

Another kink in the plan was that Fletcher had his own vehicle now and had found a place of his own. So, when we hung out, he wanted to take his vehicle. That was a problem—especially since twice when I had been out with Fletcher, we'd been followed by the green Jeep, and each time Fletcher had tried to force a confrontation with the driver. The green Jeep dude was too savvy for that and in an elaborate cat-and-mouse chase, always calmly pulled away until Fletcher was nearly howling with rage. I didn't think Bran and I would ever get a chance to put our weak, stupid plan into action.

The next delay was work. I was swamped for two weeks and the little time off I had I spent eating and sleeping. Fletcher went back to the cabin for his "moon time," and I didn't even have time to see him before he left. Dad took him out instead because I was tied up in the Brooks Range hauling in hunters and supplies for the start of the general season. Dad didn't trust our part-time guy in the difficult areas since he wasn't that experienced yet, so we were both run ragged.

Three days after Fletcher left, I finally got my chance. Our extra Super Cub had bush wheels on, and I hadn't had time to switch them out—although we needed it to have the floats on. It was a good half day or more job. Dad was helping me, and the plane was up on the hoist. Dad took off when we reached the point I could finish on my own since this was one of his rare days off.

I was nearly finished when I noticed him. He was subtle. He could have been watching for days, and I had barely noticed. I just happened to look across the lake and I caught a glint of sunlight. It caught my attention, and I stared for a moment to see what it was. It was him, lying on his belly in the grass, watching me through a spotting scope.

Since I was currently sort of hidden by my plane and the hangar we rented to work on them, I scanned the area for his green Jeep. It was off the side of the road. You aren't supposed to drive into areas that say aircraft only, so he'd parked on the road and walked in to where he could observe me without being noticed.

I took out my cell and texted Bran. This was our chance. I knew I had to keep him interested because it would take Bran at least fifteen minutes to get here and that's if she went directly to her car. It was a busy time of the day, so I had no idea how long it would take her. I needed to keep him on the hook. I moved out where I knew he could see me. I rifled through my tools and pretended I didn't have the right one. I grabbed my phone and put it in my back pocket and walked inside as though I were going to get a tool. Once I was out of sight, I called Bran.

"I know, I got your text. I'm just making sure I'm covered here." I could hear in the background that her shop was busy. "Give me five minutes and I'm on my way!" she said in between giving directions to customers.

"Don't hang up," I said hurriedly. "His jeep is on the road, he's watching me from across the lake, so I'm going to try to keep him interested. Just hurry. This may be our only chance!"

"Yeah, OK, got it." She sounded distracted. "Bye." She hung up.

I grabbed a bag of tools that I didn't need. I took off my flannel shirt and wrapped it around my waist and tied my T-shirt in a knot behind my back, so it was tight across my chest and showed my midriff. I laughed at myself, feeling ridiculous.

I didn't think of myself as sexy, mostly because that just didn't enter my sphere. I wasn't masculine, but I dressed practically most days. T-shirts, jeans, things like that. Today, I was wearing shorts, and I rolled them up, so they were even shorter. I had a figure, and I'd been told by different guys that they admired it. I shrugged. I may not know who the green Jeep guy was, but he was a guy.

It was hot outside, so it wasn't just to keep his attention. Once I was out, I made sure he got an eyeful every time I changed positions. I stretched my back a lot throwing my chest out, but there wasn't much left to do. I took a water break. I checked the engine. I oiled the door. All in slow motion. When I snuck a look, he was still there. Finally, I saw Bran's red SUV pull up behind the green Jeep. I wanted to cheer. I did the final tightening of bolts, faced the lake so he got an eyeful, and poured the rest of the water over my shirt. I was already sweaty, so I figured what the hell.

Bran snuck over to the Jeep. I didn't know what she would do if it was locked, and I couldn't see if she got into it or not since the side she was on faced away from me. All I could do was wait and not look directly in that direction too many times. I gathered up my tools and put them away. Then I went inside the hangar, where I could watch without being seen. I hoped she was fast. He'd probably pack up if I didn't come out soon, and I wasn't planning to come out until he left.

Finally, after what seemed like an hour, I got a text from Bran. "I got it! Come to the store!"

I waited until the green Jeep left. I didn't think he'd noticed that we were also spying back on him. My heart hammered all the way to the Lunatic Fringe. My throat was dry, and I had butterflies of anticipation as I walked in. The bell tinkled and grumpy girl, I think her name was Tina, glared at me. The store was busy, and she was sitting behind the counter with two other girls. I went around the counter and through the beaded curtain to the back. That earned me stony looks, and a soft, "bitch." I smiled. I don't know why they cared. I was always coming in and going to the back. It was probably because they knew I'd report that they were sitting down on the job.

Bran was huddled over her computer doing some type of research, maybe trying to find info on my stalker. Just as I was about to say something, her phone rang. The tinny sound made me jump. She picked it up and turned her chair around to face me. She raised her eyebrows and mouthed, "Mike." She was going to be awhile.

Mike was her sort of new boyfriend. He had a busy job so she didn't get to spend as much time with him as she liked, or I know she would have let the call go to voicemail.

While she chatted, I got a Coke from her fridge and plopped on the couch. I overheard something about fish. Since Mike ran the fish hatchery in town for Alaska Fish and Game, I sort of tuned out. He was always talking fish, fish counts, fish fry, fish stocking. I don't know how Bran stood the boredom.

In what seemed like an hour later, she finally ended her call. "Mike says hi!" she said brightly. I glared at her.

"Come on Bran! Tell me what you found out!"

She shuffled her feet and looked down. Her shoulders drooped. "Nothing."

"What do you mean nothing? Did the jeep have a registration?"

"Yes, but it belonged to a woman."

"Ugh, who?"

"Why? It doesn't matter since he's obviously a man!"

"Yeah, but he's had the car for a while. I doubt it's stolen. It could be a sister, a friend, a mother, a wife. Anyone. He's probably closely involved with the owner."

"I thought of that, Piper," she said condescendingly.

"In the fifteen minutes I've been back, I haven't been able to locate this woman on the internet. I realize that's not a lot of time, but I can't find her on google or social media."

"What's her name?" I asked impatiently.

Rather than tell me, Bran found a photo on her phone and handed it to me. It was the photo of the green jeep's registration. It was registered to a Gina Coullson. I didn't know her although, something about the name pinged something.

"Aargh!" I yelled.

Bran started.

"Nothing I've investigated has gone anywhere. I suck at this!"

Bran shrugged.

"I don't know what to do now, Bran. Do I dare go to the police?"

I dropped the idea almost as soon as I said it, and Bran's head shake reinforced what a bad idea that was. If the police looked too closely, what would they find out? Would they find my secret? I shuddered. I wasn't brave enough to face that.

"We have the address. We should go have a look. You know, just in case." Bran replied in her soothing voice. "We've already broken into his car. What's a house?" She turned calm blue eyes to look at me. My nerves were amped up, and her gaze steadied me.

"Seriously?" I asked incredulously. "We don't know this Gina Coullson from Adam. We can't break into her house. That would be wrong."

She gave a brief laugh, "Really? We broke into her car!"

"Yeah, but it's being driven by a stalker," I grumped, sulkily.

"Okay, but we should at least stake it out."

"Yeah, when? We're both so busy we don't have time to breathe."

I was working myself up again, frustration and anger causing my shoulders and neck to tense.

She sighed. "True. If we staked it out when we're both done with work, sane people would be home in bed. We need to do it during business hours." She grabbed a Coke and sat down next to me. "You should at least do a couple of flybys." She stated it like I could casually do those as often as I wished.

"You do a couple of flybys," I grumbled.

She looked at me and harrumphed.

"You know... You have employees, you could go stake out the house for a couple of hours during the day." I gave her an expectant look.

She mulled it over. "You're right. I'll try to get take a couple of hours off the next couple of days. I should make that new assistant manager work harder, anyway. She wants a business degree; she should see how hard it is to be truly in charge!" She grinned wickedly.

I nodded in agreement.

"You know, now is a good time for a flyby. I know you have a minute, or you wouldn't be here."

Her logic pissed me off, but it was sound. I was well aware it was payback for pushing her into a corner about doing a stakeout.

"You're right. I should go. Text me that pic with the address."

She did, while grinning at me and rubbing it in that she had the last word.

After a few minutes I stood up and stretched. "I guess I'll go."

Bran stood. "I need to go back to work too. Let me know if you see anything."

"You know I will." I grumbled again and walked through the beads and out the door.

I drove by the house once. I probably shouldn't have since the green Jeep stalker knew my truck at this point, but I was heartily sick of all the shenanigans. I parked two blocks away after determining no one was parked at the house. After a quick change below the windows of my truck, I took to the air on raven wings.

I know I've said this before, but it's easy to be a raven in Anchorage. They're everywhere. I can really access most places without being recognized as out of place or different in my raven form. There were two large trees near the house, so I found a nice perch that gave me a view of the driveway and front door, and I hunkered down. I told myself I'd wait half an hour and see what happened.

It was warm, and I was tired. I caught myself dozing several times. Finally, I decided I'd better go home and get some real rest when a dark green minivan pulled into the driveway. An attractive blonde woman exited and proceeded to let free a couple of children. One looked to be grade school age and the other closer to Baylee's age. Then, she opened the back and took out bags of groceries. I didn't recognize her. I sighed. No green Jeep. No man. Of course, if I had the stamina, I could have waited longer to see if he showed up, but my gut said that the green Jeep no longer lived here. It was possible it belonged to the woman's husband, but it was also possible she sold it to a stranger, and he hadn't had it re-registered in his own name yet.

I decided to come back the next night and see if by chance the Jeep was parked here just in case.

I was tired, my day off wasn't long enough, and my workday felt endless. I dreaded going back to watch the house, but Bran hadn't been able to get away during the day today, so I said I'd go after work. Again, same as last night, no green Jeep. Since I was later today than yesterday, I figured either no other car was coming home, or there was one out of sight in the garage. I sighed when I climbed into my bed. Dead end. I didn't know what to do next.

Luckily Bran said she could do some staking out the next couple of days. I was too tired to work all day and spy at night. I needed some real rest. So, I told her to let me know what happened, and I put it out of my mind.

A few days later, she called, and I met her at the Lunatic Fringe. Since it was close to closing, we ordered in food and ate in the back while her new manager closed and left. I was squirming with anticipation to see what she found out.

"Well?" I finally said after my pointed stare wasn't getting anywhere.

She put down her fork and took a deep breath, building the suspense. "Nothing," she said and slumped. "All I've seen is the green minivan and a white Prius."

"Dammit!" I shrieked, louder than I intended. "The Coullsons must have sold the Jeep to our stalker. We have no leads, again!" I threw myself on her couch.

"That was a good lead. We should have found something out about who he is! This sucks."

"I agree, this sucks." I sighed. Short of him walking up to us and introducing himself, we had zero ways of figuring out who he was. All I knew was he appeared to be about average height. His hair was sandy. He drove a green Jeep. I threw up my hands. "I give up."

"Me too." Bran's voice was a breathy sigh. "We are definitely not detectives."

"Nope," I agreed.

"Maybe we should hire one," Bran stated thoughtfully after a few seconds.

"No." I shook my head. "That's crazy, if we asked anyone, they'll just wonder why we didn't have the police do it."

"Really? You know what a private detective will say? Is that because you know all about private detectives?"

I rolled my eyes at her. "No, smartass, but that's what I'd say and wonder."

She shrugged. "Me too, probably, but I also wouldn't turn down a paying customer."

"I know we've talked about it before, but what about just getting the police involved?" I gulped, my paranoia and fear of being found out causing my hands to sweat.

If I was being true to myself, I had to admit that there's was no reason to look into my background. I wasn't the one doing the stalking. Really, my background should be the last thing they would think about.

Most people didn't believe the supernatural existed. I was an upstanding, tax paying citizen who ran a successful business. I could also play the weak minority woman who was being stalked. I had his vehicle's make, model, and license plate. Maybe they'd arrest his ass and solve all our problems at once.

"I don't know. I guess if you're comfortable with the possibility of being on their radar, then call them." She shrugged again.

I filed that away as a possibility for the next time I saw him. I was pretty sure he'd be surprised if I did. "I'll think about it. I really don't see much other choice since we suck at sleuthing."

Bran chuckled at this.

"We really do suck at it," she agreed.

"Let's work on something we maybe can figure out," I continued after a few moments pause.

"Like what? What else can we do?" She rubbed her neck.

"The big werewolf. Maybe we can find out what he wants." I worked my braids free. Thinking about the big wolf made my palms sweat, and I was trying to hide it.

"How do we do that? That sounds worse than trying to find the stalker. Plus, if we fail, he'll eat us." Her voice shook. She was also wary of him.

I put my hands back down. "Well then, if that happens, we won't have to worry about the stalker anymore," I said, deadpan.

"Piper, you come up with the dumbest ideas."

"I know. Isn't it great?"

She groaned. "So, what is your dumb idea?"

I swallowed. I knew this was an *extremely* dumb idea. "We know who he is. What if I just ask him?"

Bran looked as though I'd smacked her. As she flapped her mouth trying to find words to say, I turned as though to walk out the door.

Finally, her tongue untied, she ordered, "Don't you dare walk out that door."

I turned nonchalantly. "And why not?"

"Ask him? Really? That's your plan? He'll eat us for sure."

"I planned on talking to him in a public place while he's human. I'm not that big of an idiot."

Bran closed her eyes, threw her head back and sighed softly. "Sure, why not. What do we have to lose besides our lives?"

"That's the spirit."

"You know he's probably the one after Fletcher's gold."

I hesitated. "I don't think so."

"Why not? He's the one wandering around Fletcher's cabin. He's got to be the one or one of the ones looking for it."

"I suggested that to Fletcher, but it doesn't feel right."

She threw me a pointed look.

"Just a gut feeling. He couldn't have known about the gold when he turned Fletcher. At least if he did, that was some forward precognitive thinking since Clyde was still alive. I just don't think it's possible that his involvement has anything to do with the gold. I think he wanted something else from Fletcher. Maybe a pack, a friend? I just don't know."

Bran, not one to fly off on a lark like me, sat back down thoughtfully. I could see the wheels grinding in her head. After a while she turned a puzzled look at me. "He's the only one we know that has been up there. Who else could it be?"

"Well, that's why it's a mystery isn't it? We obviously know nothing except that only a few people know about the gold. There could be others because we don't know if Clyde clued anyone in. So, right now, we know for sure that only you, me, dad, Fletcher, and Fletcher's lawyer even know that it exists. So hopefully, Fletcher has tracked down Clyde's other acquaintances, and we can start to eliminate our other suspects. I still don't think the werewolf is one of them."

That was the most I'd spoken in a while, and my throat was dry. I grabbed another Coke from Bran's fridge and made a mental note to replenish her stock soon.

Bran huffed out a sigh, something she did a lot around me, mostly out of exasperation, I'm sure. "I'm too tired to argue right now," she said.

Frankly, I agreed with her. I'd been running on empty for a while. "Yeah, me too. We probably should get some sleep before we make any crazy decisions. I should really go this time."

"Piper, really sleep on it. Don't do anything rash or crazy. Maybe you should run your ideas past Fletcher or your dad first."

"I might," I said matter-of-factly.

"Piper…"

I walked out.

Chapter 17

I really did sleep on it and think it through. However, I wasn't about to ask Fletcher or Dad about it. I knew what they both would say. So logically, it didn't matter if I talked to them or not. Right? I decided that the next time I saw the green Jeep following me—I was becoming pretty sure he was following me and not Fletcher—I was calling the cops. Period.

Decision made, my mind felt more settled. I got ready for work, and another tough flight schedule for the week. Different hunting seasons brought in a lot of hunters and the flying in and out, dropping off and picking up, or dropping supplies left me in a fugue, zombie state with my brain on automatic. After work, all I could concentrate on was eating, sleeping, and driving home. A flying saucer could have been following me with every light on, and I wouldn't have seen it.

Bran checked up on me a couple of times, but I don't know what we talked about. When I finally got a three-day break, I slept through the first day. I hadn't talked or seen Fletcher for days, and I was missing him as well. I also hadn't heard what he'd found out about our mystery. He'd set up game cameras around his property, but I didn't know if he'd found any evidence of an intruder. Also, he was trying to subtly investigate Clyde's very few friends and acquaintances. After my long sleep, I felt up to working on the mystery again. I planned to get up, call Fletcher, and check in with Bran.

Early on the morning of the second day of my break he called. Finally.

"Hello?" I croaked sleepily.

"Hey beautiful," was the sweet reply in his warm and slightly husky voice. It sent shivers down my spine, and warmth throughout my core. Without meaning too, I grinned into the phone. The call had the added benefit of waking me almost instantly, unlike my usual groaning and moaning, and dragging myself around.

"How you been?" I asked, falling into the comfortable act of small talk.

"Fine, fine. I've been looking into things. I've also had to retain some services to help handle the money. I don't think it's going to stay safely hidden on my property. I'm going to move it."

"Are you worried about moving it? Or whether it's legal?"

"My lawyer thinks it's fine. From what he's researched, there isn't anything missing on the books, nothing reported lost or stolen, so I'm in the clear. It's on my property, so I own it. Frankly, the whole idea makes me sweat."

I could feel the stress in his voice as the timbre changed slightly. "Are you worried about moving it and being watched or attacked, or are you worried about being a millionaire?"

"I don't even know. I just have a bad feeling about the whole thing."

I agreed silently but didn't reply; there wasn't really anything to say about it. That much gold made me nervous too. Especially knowing someone or something was aware of it, and we didn't know what they wanted. What would they do to attain the gold once it was obviously out of hiding? My warm feelings from talking to Fletcher were slowly changing to a cold sweat and the chill of fear.

Finally, after an awkward pause I asked, "What do we do next?"

"Let's get together with Bran and compare notes."

"Sounds like a good idea," I agreed. "We could bring in some food and make it a party," I added lightheartedly.

He chuckled. "Sure. Why don't you two come to my new place?"

Sometime during the weeks I'd been busy, Fletcher had found a place to buy. It was amazing how fast you could finish up paperwork when you paid cash. Since it was empty, as soon as everything was filed, he had the keys and could move in. He'd only been there a few days.

"We'll barbecue. I'll supply the steaks; you guys bring the sides. That way, if you want a salad, you won't be disappointed."

"Sounds good." I paused for a moment. "I miss you."

His breathing turned rough, and the pause was longer than I was comfortable with. Finally, his gruff voice answered in a low purr, "I miss you, too." Then the soft sound of a cell phone ending a call. I sighed, a warmth suffusing my body with an indecipherable, but entirely pleasant *rightness*.

Fletcher had seen me in the very worst circumstances. He'd seen me naked, filthy, injured, and sick. I don't think he'd once seen me in full girl mode. Even though it was a barbecue, I made sure to bathe, and primped to the best of my ability. My hair was washed and brushed and curled into submission, and my raven dark waves were perfect for once. I did my makeup, subtle, but dramatic. I even wore a light, citrusy perfume. I wore tight jeans, my good ones without rips or grease and a soft, ruffled blouse, the kind that looks feminine and romantic. The green pattern in it brought out the green in my eyes.

Since I really didn't cook much, I picked up a macaroni and a potato salad at the grocery store. Bran said she'd bring a green salad with the fixings and dessert.

I have to say I was a little excited to see him again. I told myself it was mainly just excitement to have a normal, domestic, social evening that didn't involve a bad hamburger or TV dinner. But I was fooling myself.

Since we were going to talk shop, I was surprised to see that Bran brought her new boyfriend with her. I gave her a not-so-subtle eyebrow raise to indicate surprise and ask her what was going on. She just shook her head and smiled to say she wasn't going to talk about it right now. I groaned a little but smiled at Mike and shook his hand.

Fletcher displayed little emotion towards Mike's appearance, his stoic demeanor was back, and the sunglasses sat on his head. He greeted Mike as though this were a normal social gathering of friends, but I could feel the tension in the air build. As soon as it was socially acceptable, Fletcher slipped away under the guise of barbecuing the meat.

I was beginning to pick up his tells and his social anxiety, or the desire to be alone, was seeping through his pores—so to speak. He'd grown more comfortable with Bran since my illness because she was clued in on all the secrets we kept. Even though she could come off prickly, she had a way of putting everyone at ease when she wanted too. I always assumed it was the magic that leaked out of her, but it probably had more to do with how easily she read people and knew how to make them relax.

She picked up on Fletcher's self-deprecating personality and would rib him or tease him until he smiled. However, that didn't mean he would feel that way about a strange man in his territory, no matter how much he admired Bran.

I really didn't know much about Mike. During the winter when things were calmer at work for both of us, we would have spent hours talking boys, but we hadn't had much chance so far, so I only knew his name and that he managed the fish hatchery.

The ever so slight smell of fish clung to him, which made sense since I had a vague idea of what he did there as well. He was handsome enough—taller than Fletcher's average height—with brown hair, and dark brown eyes. He seemed to be well built, as much as you can tell just by looking at someone in their clothing. He was casually dressed in jeans and a button-down plaid shirt.

Bran had taken a page out of my current play book and dressed in jeans and a floaty, romantic top. Luckily the styles were different, or we would have looked like we coordinated. We gave each other the look and laughed. At least our shoes were radically different. I had chosen a pair of fashion cowboy boots and she wore strappy high heel sandals to add inches to her stature.

Even though he hadn't invited me to do so, I took it upon myself to play hostess and had the food brought out and sat everyone around the round deck table. Fletcher's house was furnished, so he had been busy since I'd seen the house when he moved in. It was basic and lightly done, but he had good deck furniture. A couch in the living room, a TV, a kitchen table, and a bed. I guess you don't need much else. Fletcher continued to work on the meat and ignore us, but we were fine talking and laughing without him. Mike ended up being funny and charming. I found myself warming to him and smiling as Bran looked at him with interest and a little possessiveness throughout the evening.

Unfortunately for Fletcher, the meat didn't take up that much time, considering that carnivores tended to like their meat a little on the rare side. He had also cooked chicken—well-done—and finally brought out a pile of steaming, deliciously scented meat and plopped it down in the middle of the round table. I think Mike was a little shocked at how much food there was, considering there were only four of us. His eyebrows raised even higher when he saw I was eating almost as much as Fletcher—who'd grabbed a large scoop of potato salad, chicken and two large steaks off the dripping platter. I only had one of each, but I filled up on the other sides.

During dinner there wasn't much conversation, as we all ate and mumbled how good it was. I didn't know how we were going to share notes with Mike there, since I didn't think that Bran had gotten to the stage in the relationship where she would share any preternatural secrets about herself or any of us. In fact, I'd never known her to have a relationship that reached that status, so I sort of wondered why she'd brought him.

It wasn't until about thirty minutes after we had inhaled dessert, that I found out why she'd brought him. He stood up and kissed her goodbye, thanked us for a pleasant dinner, and apologized that he had some sort of meeting at work and had to leave. I think that Fletcher and I breathed a sigh of relief, but I hope we weren't too obvious to Mike's face. He seemed like a decent guy.

As soon as his car door shut, she whipped around on us and nearly shouted, "Look we don't get to hang out very often. I just thought it would be nice to pretend we were all normal for a minute and have a double date!"

Fletcher backed up, hands up as though to deflect her outburst.

"That's cool, just give us a heads-up next time—that was awkward," I said.

"Well, it shouldn't be. Just relax sometimes. Damn. He probably thinks both of you hate him." She slammed her fists onto her hips and stared at us.

"Why? We were good," I whined.

"Maybe you acted normal, but you are both Scowly McScowly-tons," she replied with a straight face.

"A what, Mcwhat?" And at that, I couldn't help but laugh.

Fletcher smiled and Bran stomped her foot before she also started laughing.

"Come on, Bran. We'll do it again sometime when we can plan ahead and aren't wondering why you brought a practical stranger to our supernatural war council, OK?" I pleaded.

Fletcher left the room. Bran glared at me, hands still on her hips. I gave her my best puppy dog eyes, and she finally conceded. "Sure whatever." She sighed and put her hands down.

Fletcher returned a few minutes later. We heard him place a heavy plate on the kitchen table, so we moved to join him in there. He had the rest of the meat in front of him and was devouring it swiftly and neatly. "Do you want anymore?" he asked although he had an arm thrown protectively around it.

"I'm good. Bran?" I flashed her a smile.

"Are you kidding? I can't even keep up with you and he has you beat by a mile." She watched with respect as Fletcher ate. "Were you really still hungry?"

He nodded but was too busy to answer. Once his mouth was clear he said, "I was starving, but I held back at dinner when I saw the look on your boyfriend's face. I didn't want to have to answer any questions about how much I need to eat."

"I'm glad you showed some restraint," she mumbled sarcastically, and I chuckled.

"Let's not tease the werewolf," I reminded her. "Not when he's eating."

Fletcher added a very serious sounding growl as emphasis but ruined it by winking at us. We watched in silence as the meat disappeared from the plate. Bran and I had already cleaned up the rest of the meal, and it was easy to quickly finish the job after Fletcher quit eating. Soon enough it was just us around the kitchen table, an awkward silence filling the air.

Bran finally broke the ice. "Oh, for heaven's sake, let's get started. I'm tired."

I chuckled. "OK, maybe we should write some stuff down, see if we can make any connections."

Fletcher left the kitchen and came back with his laptop.

"I already started making some lists of things I've noticed, or wondered about," he said.

"That sounds like a good place to start." I nodded.

He opened the computer and found his document. "First, Clyde's death."

"The autopsy showed nothing," I said.

"True, but there were some mysterious circumstances. He died on the roof, true, but the ladder was pulled up on the roof with him. He was face down, which the expert I talked to said was odd and rare unless someone were elderly and had a cardiac incident. The ladder either suggests that he was escaping something, or someone threw it up there, which seems unlikely. And again, the autopsy showed nothing other than he was healthy when he died." Fletcher paused and yawned.

"I just said that."

"I know, but it didn't show anything that would prove it was natural or unnatural, so that leaves the possibility open," he explained.

I shrugged. "True."

"Bran, do you have anything to add?" Fletcher asked.

"Not really, other than I thought Clyde was healthy as a horse and I was completely shocked by his death."

I nodded. I had been too.

"Anything anyone can add to that one?" He looked at us. We shook our heads.

"Did you call that list of Clyde's contacts?" I asked since I knew he had been looking at it.

"Yep, nothing stood out."

I sighed.

"Next on the list, the gold. This is what I've got."

He proceeded to fill Bran in on the extent of his new fortune what it was and where it was found. I'd told her a little, but the size of her eyes made it clear I had understated it quite a bit.

"Also, there's been someone looking around for the gold on the property as evidenced by the dig sites, reinforced doors and windows, and some other small things. Here is my list of people who I know knew that Clyde had gold, even if they didn't know the extent of it."

The list included the contacts Fletcher had checked out, my family, Bran, Clyde's lawyer, the other bush pilots from our past that had been paid in gold, and even a few places in town where Clyde had sold gold for cash.

"Do you think that the merchants in town have any reason to think there was more than the stuff he mined? Is there anything that proves that he showed one of his coins or other minted gold to anyone?" I asked more to myself than to the others.

"There's no way for us to know," Fletcher replied, shaking his head. I sighed again. The Scooby-Doo gang, we were not.

"This is the main list our suspects should come from," he said and looked at us. We both nodded. "Any ideas?"

Bran and I looked at each other, then conceded we had nothing. We both shook our heads.

It was Fletcher's turn to sigh.

"Next, we have the other male werewolf."

At this, I cleared my throat. "Dr. Frederick Burns."

They nodded. Fletcher typed it onto his list.

"Your ex-professor, my cryptozoologist. He sure seems to have entangled himself in our lives." I brushed my hair back from my face.

Fletcher glanced up from his computer at me. "Yes, but is that because of the gold? If so, how does he know about it? If not, what could his other reasons be? He obviously has made himself a pack, or found a pack to belong too, so why would he still need me? Also, has he linked your crypto requests to my existence? Has he linked us together in any way? What is his agenda?" Fletcher added a couple of question marks to the name on the list.

"We know your werewolf form is ancient," I added helpfully.

He raised an eyebrow.

"You know from Jane's story."

He nodded his head. "What does that have to do with the gold?"

I shrugged. "Probably nothing, but I recently learned that shapeshifters," I pointed to myself and Fletcher, "may have very long lives. What if he is very old? Old enough to have known about that gold when it was lost or stolen and then he tracked it to Clyde?"

Fletcher's and Bran's faces showed surprise. About what, I wasn't sure—the aging bomb, or the conclusion I'd jumped to about the gold?

"We'll come back to that long life thing, but don't you think it's a bit of a stretch to try and put one coincidence into another? Even if he did know about Clyde's gold, how did he link it to Fletcher before Clyde's death? That doesn't make sense! Don't forget Occam's razor," Bran said.

"I know that it's a stretch, but we've got multiple mysteries going on. They should mesh together somehow." I huffed indignantly.

Fletcher laughed. "I agree with Bran, it seems farfetched, but at the same time, I feel like it should all fit together somehow, too."

The three of us pondered quietly for a moment, but none of us could find a way to make it make sense. Finally, Fletcher cleared his throat.

"Let's go to the next item on the list. The green Jeep."

At this, Bran and I looked at each other sheepishly.

"Do you have something to add, ladies?" Fletcher asked, a little danger entering his voice.

"Well," I started. "We might have flipped the spying thing around on him a little, broken into his Jeep, and staked out the address on his registration." At this, Fletcher's eyes glowed a little and his hands gripped the table hard enough that I swear I heard it crack.

"You don't know if he's dangerous, Piper. What were you thinking?" he growled.

At the moment, I was thinking that Bran should get her share of the lecture, but I kept my mouth shut for once. I knew he was worried.

"He could hurt you! What if he found out what you did, or worse, caught you in the act? We don't know what his agenda is! He could be a serial killer!"

At that I might have mumbled, "Bran helped," because I got an angry stare from Bran.

I wasn't used to being lectured. My dad's way of correcting my mistakes was quiet disappointment and redirection. My mom's methods were usually a quick swat on the bottom when I was small, and as I got older, guilt. I blushed, embarrassed by my chewing out. I was aware I'd scared him, and he felt protective of me, but I wasn't going to let it continue.

"Do you want to know what we found out?" I interrupted.

That earned me a glare with a little wolf behind it. But he shut up. I explained our little adventure and what we'd found out. Before I finished, he was up pacing.

"So, we still don't know who the Jeep belongs to, even after you two risked your safety?" Bran and I looked at each other and nodded. Fletcher threw up his hands in frustration.

"We do think that he probably isn't following you," I added sheepishly. Fletcher whirled and stared at me.

"Why do you think that?"

"Well…" I started. That's when Fletcher stomped out of the kitchen and walked to the backyard. He walked about fifteen feet, bent over, and started to breathe heavily, like he'd been running fast. Bran and I looked at each other, baffled.

"What do you think is wrong?" I asked her.

"I'm not sure. Maybe you broke him?" she answered.

I stared at her with disdain. "I don't know; he's very strong," I replied.

"Really? I don't think he handles being out of control very well."

We glanced over at him.

"Do you think that's what's going on? He's mad?" I asked, truly concerned.

"Maybe—although, he seemed sort of scared before," she said thoughtfully. "He could be mad. He's the only real werewolf I know, so he's hard to read."

I nodded along with her. "He's a guy. You're much better at guys than I am."

"True. I'd go with upset and leave it at that."

"OK. What do I do with an *upset* guy?"

She shrugged and stared out the back. "I'm not sure. This is starting to look like a werewolf problem."

I followed her gaze out the back door. Fletcher's body was twisting under his clothes. I felt a chill down my spine.

"Oh no, I did break him. He's going to shift. We need to stop him. He can't shift in the backyard of suburbia!"

I must have been approaching hysteria, because Bran threw me a dirty look, went to the refrigerator, and took out a pitcher of ice water.

She walked over to Fletcher and doused him. I froze. Terror seeped down my back, as I expected werewolf claws and teeth to dismember by best friend. Instead, his shift stopped, and he stood, fully human.

He stalked back to the door, silent, walked up the steps to the porch, stomped inside, and disappeared down the hall. Bran came back in, filled the water pitcher, put it back in the fridge, and stood next to me, both of us staring down the hall where he'd disappeared.

Fletcher came back a few seconds later, pulling on a dry shirt.

I glanced at Bran and mumbled, "Quit drooling. You have your own."

She stomped on my foot.

"Ow."

"You deserved it."

I probably did. I knew Fletcher had heard my exchange because he tossed me a quick grin. I knew I was forgiven.

"For the record," Fletcher started, then cleared his throat. "When a werewolf is shifting, it isn't safe to be around him. That trick might have killed you." He paused. "Otherwise, thank you. I couldn't bring myself back from the edge. The ice water helped me, uh, refocus." He shot Bran a look of gratitude. "That was pretty quick thinking. Just don't do it again. I couldn't live with myself if I hurt either of you."

Bran shrugged. "You were upset. Sometimes a slap in the face is all you need." She smirked at him. "You're welcome."

I threw my face into my hands. I wasn't sure how to continue with my story about the stalker. My body language probably showed my uncertainty. Because both Fletcher and Bran looked at me in anticipation.

I looked up from my hands, uncertain. "Are you back from your… upset?" I waved my hands, truly cautious and curious. "Do you want to hear the rest of the story? Or is it better to leave out the details?" I glanced at Bran as I said this. I really didn't know men all that well. I had no brothers, I hadn't ever had a boyfriend, and judging men by my dad was not really a good idea since he was obviously not a normal, modern, guy. I watched her body language to decide what to do. She seemed comfortable, so I assumed it was safe to continue before Fletcher answered.

"I have it under control."

"Ok, where was I?"

"The last thing you said was he was following you, not me," Fletcher growled.

I knew he wasn't angry at me, but at the situation. Still my heart gave a little leap, and I took an unplanned step back.

"Umm…" I looked at Bran for support.

"What she isn't saying so well is she's caught him following her on more than one occasion when she was alone. He may be watching to see if he can catch her shifting and may have done so once. And we took the opportunity to flip the switch on him." She paused, glanced at me, and when she saw that I had calmed down, gestured that I should continue.

I told him everything from sneaking into his truck to what we discovered. His whole body vibrated with his growling, but he didn't lose control again.

"I'm going to kill him," he said quietly when he'd stopped growling. A shiver ran down my back. The stoic history teacher looked like he could kill the stalker with his bare hands.

"It's OK; we've got it handled," I said quickly. I caught Bran waving and shaking her head "no" out of the corner of my eye. The growling started again.

"Umm, I'm sure he's harmless," Bran muttered and gestured for me to shut up. I bowed my head and took another step back to let her do the talking. "He's only watched. He hasn't done anything creepy."

"You don't know if he is dangerous. I want both of you to stay away from him. If you spot him, try to lose him. Do not snoop. Do not approach him," Fletcher said quietly, his voice deeper and rougher than normal. I could tell he was holding on with an iron will.

"Alright," I mumbled. But I kept my fingers crossed behind my back. I didn't want to scare or piss off my werewolf boyfriend, but I also didn't let *anyone* tell me what to do. Bran didn't say a word.

Chapter 18

I'd never been around a true werewolf before Fletcher. The protectiveness and suppressed violence were a little intense, and I wasn't sure how I felt about it. Fletcher tried to keep it reined in, and from what we had discussed about his past, this behavior came with the wolf, not from his human personality.

I really did not like being told what to do. In fact, it was a bit of a family joke that the best way to get me to do something was to command me to do the opposite. Like that really worked either. Good grief, just ask nicely and if I agreed, I'd do it. Idiots.

In this case though, I did not agree. I didn't think the green Jeep dude had done anything worthy of turning an angry werewolf loose on him. I didn't know if he was harmless, but he hadn't done anything violent yet. I really did think that Bran and I were fine doing our own little investigation, and I had no intention of stopping.

I would have enjoyed a goodnight kiss, but neither Fletcher nor I were very demonstrative in front of others, so he walked me to the door of his house and waved a friendly goodbye to both of us. Bran had come with Mike, so I drove her back to the shop. My insides seethed with undefined emotions.

We were quiet on the drive back, deep in thought I suppose,

although my thoughts were more chaotic than useful. When we reached the shop, we headed to the back. Bran spent so much time here, that sometimes it felt homier to hang out in the lounge in the back room of her shop than to go to either of our houses. We grabbed Cokes, our standard hang-out fare, and plopped on the deep-cushioned couch. After kicking off our shoes, we put our backs against the arms at the opposite ends, drew up our knees, and faced each other.

"So, that happened," Bran stated.

"Yep," I replied and slurped my Coke from the can.

"I know you aren't going to stop."

"Yep." I slurped again because I liked to slurp. It made the bubbles tickle my nose and throat, and because I knew it annoyed her.

"So... What are you going to do?" She took a dainty sip, to show me how to do it properly, I suppose.

I smiled and slurped some more. Truthfully, I didn't have any idea, only that I wasn't going to stop until I knew all the answers. It just wasn't my nature. I really couldn't stop that desire to *know* what was going on. "Keep at it until we figure it out," I said.

She nodded, having known me for as long as we both could remember. We sat in silence a while longer.

"Crap," I said.

"What?"

"We forgot to ask if he saw anything on his game cameras." I shrugged. It couldn't have been anything much or he would have said something. She agreed. I finished my Coke and went home.

The next day I woke determined to find answers. I had a shorter day, so when I finished work, I told myself I was going to confront the green Jeep guy as soon as I saw him. I was done playing the mouse to his cat.

Unfortunately, I didn't have a clue how to do it. So, I drove around for a couple of hours hoping to pick him up as a tail. I didn't see him every day, but he'd been fairly consistent. Of course, I didn't see him at all. I finally ran a few errands and headed home.

I repeated this the next time I had an early day off. Worried now that I *hadn't* seen him of all things. My garage emptied into an alley like most houses in downtown Anchorage. So, I passed my house on the way to park my truck around back when I saw him watching my house. I think he was trying to be discreet—he'd parked about three blocks down—but I knew the cars on my street and his stood out.

I suddenly felt anxious, sick. My hands trembled. Was I going to do this? Yes, I told myself. I was strong and fit. I hadn't learned to fight, but I'd taken self-defense courses whenever I saw them offered and had the time. I was armed. Or at least I had a gun in my backpack. I had a cellphone. I immediately put 911 in, so I just had to hit call then I stuck it in my bra.

I continued through the alley. I was now only one block down from him. I didn't want to give myself away too soon, so I crossed the street, entered the next alley, and circled around. I parked a block away, behind another truck which I hoped camouflaged me a bit. I grabbed my gun, racked a round into the chamber, double checked the safety, slid it with its holster into the back of my jeans, and pulled my shirt down over it.

I scooted out of my truck, took a deep breath, rubbed my sweaty hands down my jeans, and snuck up to the Jeep. I crouched low the whole way, using parked vehicles to hide my advance. The bastard wasn't getting away this time. I debated whether I should approach the passenger or driver's side. I had a better chance of being spotted on the driver's side, but if I was quick—I could be very fast—I might be able to open the door and grab him.

Sweat trickled down my back. I wished I was braver because I was so scared, I was panting, but I wanted answers and didn't want him to get away before I got them. If I went along the passenger side, I doubted he'd spot me since his attention was out the driver's side window. I could jump in that way, but then he could take off with me in the car and that was terrifying and way out of my comfort zone.

I slid in behind the Jeep, using it as cover and leaned out to glance down the driver's side. My heart pounded. I could see him clearly in the driver's side mirror. Same hat pulled low, dark glasses, beard. I didn't recognize him, but his face was almost completely covered. I slid back behind the Jeep before he could spot me. I tried to catch my breath.

A couple walked down the sidewalk. They saw me, looks of confusion passing over their faces. I smiled, waved, and put my finger over my lips in the international sign for "please be quiet" and winked. They smiled, thinking I was about to prank someone and walked off chatting. A woman walking her dog passed on the other sidewalk but didn't look at us. I braced myself against the back of the Jeep, my heart racing and breathing hard, gathering up my courage. Then I burst out, top speed. Two steps took me to the driver's side door, and I grabbed the door handle to whip the door open. It was locked. Of freaking course.

I hadn't really thought about that. The Jeep wasn't new by any means, but new enough to have auto-locks apparently. Startled, the man whipped around, horror growing on his expression. He had been looking through binoculars, and the sunglasses were perched above them on his forehead. Even though the door was shut, the window was open, and I grabbed his shirt. "Why are you following me?" I growled.

When I startled him, he immediately dropped the binos and his glasses fell back over his eyes. He pulled back away from me, but I kept a firm grip. I wanted to shake him until he answered, but I wasn't that strong. He wasn't a big guy, but he was stronger. The flesh under my hand was solid. This close, I could see that the beard was fake. He looked vaguely familiar, but I still couldn't identify him.

I pulled out my phone and held it up so he could see. One handed I swiped it open and showed that it was ready to call 911. "You better start talking, or I dial 911 and hold you until they get here. Stalking is illegal. I've been photographing you and I have proof!"

I didn't, but the bluff sounded good. His cheeks flushed, and then pulled some sort of move I didn't follow, disconnecting me from his shirt. He reached out with his hand and shoved me in the chest hard enough that I fell back onto my butt. He started the Jeep and raced down the road—tires squealing. I screamed in frustration and pain. The jolt from the pavement had gone straight up my spine in an electrical explosion and it took a minute before I could catch my breath and get up.

The dog lady rushed over. "Oh my, are you alright?" she gasped. "I was walking home with my dog and saw what that man did! Should I call the police?"

I shook my head. I think it was time I called the police, but I needed a moment to collect my thoughts.

"I'm alright," I slurred. "Just a little shook up. Don't call the cops, please. I'll deal with it." I waved her away.

She made some noises of concern but left quickly with her dog. Probably assuming I was an abused wife or something.

I pulled myself up, brushed off, and headed home. When I reached the gate in the front, I pulled it open, and sat on my front porch and texted Bran. While I waited for her reply, I walked back to my truck and moved it into the garage. While I sat there, the phone dinged.

"Ugh!" was Bran's reply.

I felt my color deepen. She was right. I had blown it. He wouldn't be as easy to access next time. He'd be careful and more watchful so I wouldn't get another chance to try to grab him. I groaned in frustration. I might have blown our only chance for answers.

Her next text was, "I'm coming over." That sounded threatening. She never left the store in the summer for longer than a run to the bank or to pick up lunch. I wonder what else I'd done wrong. I paced the floor in front of the dining room window facing the street. Fifteen minutes later, she marched up to my front door. We went downstairs to my living room where my comfortable, worn leather couch was. She plopped down and leaned on the arm, and I sat kitty corner from her in the matching oversized chair.

"I need more detail," she said.

"I don't know what else to tell you." I shrugged.

"Yes, you do. You may not realize it, but I know for a fact you have enhanced senses. You had to have noticed something you just aren't remembering."

"Then how do I remember? It's gone. I only know what I told you," I said, my frustration starting to leak out in a slight whine.

"I figured you'd say that which is why I came over. I'm going to help you remember!"

"What you gonna do? Wave your magic wand?"

She gave me a disgusted huff at that, but a secret smile lit up her face. "Yes." Then she laughed at the shocked look on my face. "You know perfectly well I don't have a magic wand and magic, as you call it, isn't like you see on TV. I'm going to help you remember through the simple power of suggestion, plus." She tilted her hand back and forth indicating that she couldn't explain what the plus was.

"You mean like hypnotize me?"

"No, I don't have any training for that," she said, shaking her head. "This is something I've read about in some old journals of my grandmother's I found last summer. It's more of one mind helping another. It should be simple and safe, and it might help. I've been dying to try it!"

"Does that mean you're going to read my mind? I don't think I'm OK with that."

"I can't read minds, Piper, I've told you that before. It's nothing like that. You'll see if you'll let me."

Frankly, I didn't really care if she could read my mind. I'd never kept anything from her for as long as we'd known each other. I just felt unsettled about allowing someone to muck about up there. Maybe something would break, who knew?

"Uh, OK, I guess. What do I have to do?"

"Not much. Get as comfortable as you can and try not to think of anything."

"OK." I slung my legs up over the arm of the chair and nestled in. I could sleep in the chair, so I knew I would be comfortable.

She walked around the chair and placed her hands lightly on my head. "I'm going to try to put you in a state of deep relaxation and then ask you questions so your mind will find it easier to recall."

I grunted an affirmative.

I figured I'd get a nap out of this little experiment. It wasn't that I didn't trust Bran to know what she was doing; I knew she had power. I couldn't really define what her power was, but I'd seen her do amazing things. It just seemed silly that she'd be able to pull more outta my head than I believed was in there. I have excellent recall. I just didn't think there was anything else there. So, I relaxed into her hands with a bit of a smirk on my face.

She just sighed. "I'm going to start, so just relax."

I answered by closing my eyes. It was easy. I quickly drifted into that place you go before true dreaming. Static trickled along my skin, and my hair lifted from my arms and my scalp slightly. Warmth came from Bran's hands and soaked through me with more liquid calm and comfort. I felt like I was drifting in a warm, weightless pool.

"Piper?" Bran's voice was far away. I heard her shifting and her clothes rustling as she changed position.

"Hmmm?"

Her voice was more warmth, more silky comfort and I felt myself sinking into it.

"I'm going to ask you some questions about today. You saw the man in the green Jeep, and you confronted him."

"Yesss." I felt my answer hiss off my tongue from far away.

"When you spoke with him, what did you see?" She moved again, her voice changing direction.

It took a lot of effort to answer, and my voice sounded like it was coming from someone else. "The man. He wore a disssguise." I was slurring. It was a little like being drunk, but much more soothing.

"Explain the disguise," she commanded softly.

"He had on a goofy hat, sunglasses, and a fake beard," I drawled.

"What else did you notice? Eye color? Hair color?"

This time it took longer to reply. It was like I wasn't searching through my brain files, but like I was observing the searching. "Umm, his hair was sandy. His eyes..." I trailed off. I had seen his eyes, briefly in between the time he'd dropped his binoculars and the glasses fell back over his eyes. My mind stopped there, the feeling of searching growing. "His eyes were green!" I paused a moment. "No, not green, green hazel!" My heart rate increased, excitement almost bringing me up from my half trance.

"That's good, relax." Bran's soothing voice calmed me back down. I relaxed.

"You have a very sensitive nose. What did he smell like?" she asked.

I wrinkled my nose as if I were sniffing something. Olfactory senses could be powerful in memory, and I'd smelled something. "The car had an air freshener. Very strong. I think it was vanilla?" I sniffed. "Yes, vanilla. His clothes were clean. I could smell the detergent and fabric softener." He used Tide Spring Meadows, and Fresh Linen Bounce sheets. I liked those scents. I sniffed again. "He was wearing cologne. I don't know the brand, but I've smelled it somewhere before." I sniffed for a while, remembering the scents from the man's car, but I couldn't place anything that tweaked my memory further.

"Piper," Bran said after a while, and I sunk back into comfort. "Do you recognize the man?"

Did I? That was the question. He felt familiar, but I couldn't recall a name or how I knew him no matter how I strained.

My breath quickened and my heartbeat sped up. I felt anxious, but the memory wouldn't come. Bran could see I was growing restless and must have realized I had nothing more because I felt the warmth leave me starting with my toes and working its way up to her hands. She lifted her hands from my head. I put my legs back down and placed my feet on the floor.

"That was sort of amazing, and I want you to do that when I go to bed, but it didn't help at all. We don't know anything real that we can use!" My voice rose in frustration.

"You're wrong. We know a lot more. We know you know who he is. Eventually, something will trigger that memory. Something more than my awkward first attempt at mind magic anyway."

"Mind magic? Is that a thing?" I asked ignoring her comment.

"My grandmother believed so. She had a few techniques listed in her journals. I'm sad I waited so long to read them." She paused a moment in contemplation. "I know what you're trying to do. You do it all the time and you aren't very good at it. You will remember who he is. And when you do, we're going to get our answers. It's all locked in that little brain of yours." She smirked.

"Ha, ha. I'm bigger than you, that means my brain is too. Joke's on you!" I stuck my tongue out at her. She repeated the gesture at me and before long, we were laughing like the idiots we were.

Chapter 19

I fell asleep wondering who the green Jeep guy was and why I couldn't place him when so much was familiar. I woke with the determination that I couldn't do anything about him. I'd probably scared him off, maybe for good, and there was nothing else I could do but let my subconscious brew on it.

Meanwhile, we had solved one mystery. I knew that Professor Burns had changed Fletcher. I knew he ran the weird shifter werewolf pack that attacked me. Hell, I'd had a pow wow with him. I wondered if he would talk to me. I wondered what he knew or suspected about me. How did you go about talking to a stranger and accusing him of being a werewolf? What if I was wrong?

I didn't think I was. The logic was sound on this one. There was a slight chance that Fletcher missed someone on his class list, or the wolf was a total stranger who happened to be wandering the woods that day. Yet, what were the chances of that? Then that same wolf hanging around Fletcher's cabin? Not good. I had to be correct on this one.

I didn't have much time to dwell on it. I was super busy. But as I flew, sometimes my mind would wander around what to do. Do you confront someone about this over the phone? Did I trust him enough to meet in person? What if he was some crazy psychotic? He was hunting cryptids for heaven's sake. He had taken a pack of cryptids and was leading them—or controlling them. Sweet Jane had acted terrified of him. Lots of questions. No answers that didn't require a confrontation.

I had a date with Fletcher. It wasn't our first date, and we had known each other now for almost three months, but it felt like the first real date we had been on because we were doing the whole show. Dinner and a movie. No mysteries to be discussed. The butterflies started before I made my final approach. I didn't know why I was so nervous.

I went home, showered, and dressed. Nothing like that disastrous first date I had before Fletcher. I *wanted* to go this time. I took care with how I looked, but at the same time I was comfortable in my own skin and with what I wore. No more heels for me. In fact, I tossed those red strappy sandals the day after the knife incident. I blamed them for getting felt up. I kept the dress, but now it had a permanent safety pin to keep it from gaping open. This time though, with Fletcher, I wore my best jeans. They fit like a glove. With those and a thin, long-sleeved sweater in a blue green that set off my eyes, I felt sexy. I put on a pair of motor-cycle boots over my jeans and a black leather jacket in a similar style.

He picked me up. He had bought an SUV when he'd decided he could live in town but had trouble with it. He had told me he was buying a truck to replace it. I assumed he'd buy new; he was a millionaire after all. But he pulled up in an older, serviceable full-sized extra cab Chevy. It was clean and seemed to be in very good shape. When I raised an inquisitive eyebrow, he shrugged. "What do I need with an $80,000 truck?"

I smiled. So true. That first impression I had of him months ago was *so* correct. He was completely real. There was no pretense with him. If I were my dad's age, I'd call him the salt of the earth. Heck, I just did. And he was. He was also mine. I claimed him. I felt the pull of that claiming reach from my heart to his. He must have felt what I did in that moment because when he opened the door for me and helped me up into his truck, his hands lingered at my hips and he kissed me gently, but with affirmation and possession radiating from him. He left me smiling and walked around to climb into the driver's seat.

He took me to Humpy's. Humpy's was an Alaska institution. A seafood bar and grill. I had the King Crab platter, and he took on the Kodiak Arrest challenge. You know the thing where if you can eat all the food in a certain time limit it's free? They should have made it with werewolves in mind. In his defense, he tried to slow down the inhalation to near human speed. He had it with a local specialty ale, but I had a Coke.

Fletcher took the t-shirt he'd won, laughed as they clicked his photo for the wall, and we left relaxed and in a good mood. The movie theater was mostly empty, and we sat in the back corner alone. I don't remember what we saw because once the movie started, Fletcher pulled me over into his 'luxury' lounger. I'd been shy about the phys-ical stuff between us for a while, limiting our contact to chaste hugs and kisses. Frankly, I wasn't sure how to advance anything and when I thought of it, my hands started to sweat, and I felt the edge of panic creeping up my spine.

At first, once we crammed together in the oversized chair, we were content to cling to each other, his arm was around me with my head on his chest, my hand on his thigh. We sat comfortably close, enjoying the few moments we had together. Soon, the arm around my shoulder pulled me in close, and he cupped my face with his opposite hand and tilted it up for a

gentle kiss. Maybe it was the warmth or the closeness of his body, or the dark comfort of the empty theater, but for once, I didn't pull back or end it after a few kisses.

I leaned into his hard body, my softer one curving to fit his. His lips parted, and we deepened the kiss. I didn't think that as an adult, I'd engage in a make-out session in a public theater. That was some-thing I attributed to horny teens. No one noticed us in our dark corner, but I slowly grew more uncomfortable with the extent of our touching and fondling in public.

Finally, I pulled myself out of his lap and took his hand. "Let's get out of here."

He raised his eyebrow questioningly. I smiled and swung my head in the direction of the exit.

We held hands in his truck on the way to my house. When we got there, we shed our boots and dropped our jackets at the door. We headed downstairs to my living room and collapsed on my big, cushy couch, hands searching and grabbing and caressing. Fletcher discovered my neck and the hollow behind my ear, and the intensity I was feeling increased tenfold. I gasped. My kisses went from eager to hungry.

I pulled him down on me until we lay on the couch. He braced his arm behind my head and rolled us over until we were side by side to take his weight off me. Luckily the couch was deep. The heat of his hand blazed up my side as he snaked it under my sweater. The rough texture of his hand from hours of work around the cabin took the intensity of my nerve endings up another notch. My breathing and heart rate had increased, and I yearned for him even though he was so close.

His scent poured into my nostrils. Male, aroused, salt, something I couldn't place that reminded me of the wild, and a subtle spice from his deodorant or cologne or something. It was maddening.

One hand was in my hair caressing my scalp and the other reached around and undid my bra. I gasped, unsure I wanted to take it that far, but then his fingers were caressing and teasing my nipple and the warmth built low in my belly and ached between my legs. I hungered for him. I needed him like I had never needed or yearned for anything before. I pulled away momentarily.

"Are you okay?" he asked, voice husky.

"Yeah," I gasped. "Yeah, I just don't know what to do."

"Do you want to keep going?" he asked, sounding unsure and sat up.

My bra was loose, and I could feel it bunched up under my sweater. I was suddenly embarrassed. "Umm." I crossed my arms over my breasts to rein them in.

"I promised you we'd go at your speed. I obviously want more, but

I have real feelings for you, Piper. I don't want to screw anything up between us."

"I know, I'm just new to all of this. I want you. More than I've wanted anything. But is this right? Should we be doing this? I don't know."

My breath came faster, but now it was because my anxiety was ramping up as embarrassment and uncertainty raged through me. Fletcher put his arm around me. I could hear his heartbeat. It was so loud I knew he had to be disappointed and frustrated.

Yet, he gathered me up and soothed me with a warm hug and caress. "Piper, calm down, everything is fine. We'll stop. Just breathe."

And I did. I let his voice and the cadence of his heart take my worries down until I was engulfed in the warmth of his touch. Damn, I was so lucky to have found this man.

He stayed until it was late. We ate ice cream and talked. We avoided the couch and the bedroom at all costs because I wasn't ready, and the temptation was too much. He left when I couldn't keep my eyes open, since he knew my schedule was busy.

I felt the connection between us was building and growing. I knew in my heart that he was filling the emptiness. Disappointment from the inability to connect to someone because of secrets, and the ache from believing that I'd always be alone were fading.

I dreamed that the cryptozoologist werewolf had answers I needed. I approached him and he told me everything I wanted to know. Of course, it was all nonsense since it was a dream, but I woke with a new determination to confront him. He had seemed so eager to talk to me during that first contact. I had been wary, but no more so than with any stranger. So, I convinced myself that a direct confrontation was best. I'd make an appointment and ask him straight up what his game was.

He had to know that it was me he saw that day at the cabin when I was standing in water, and he approached me boldly as a wolf. So, I was pretty sure he knew something about me, since like an idiot, I went right to him and said I saw him in the woods.

He had to know about me. How much did I dare say? Should I feel him out about how much he had guessed about me? Did I dare give away Fletcher's secret? What was my approach? My mind went round and round over these questions with no answers or direction popping up.

I couldn't ask direction from Fletcher or my dad; they would both try their best to stop me. I didn't want Bran dragged in since there was no way he knew about her. By the time I was taxiing back to Tulugaq Air, I still hadn't made a plan.

Dad noticed my distraction and questioned me, but I blew him off, and he didn't press. We hadn't really talked since the big reveal, and I think he was giving me space to process. Plus, we were both exhausted with our schedules being like they were.

He did pull me in for a hug before I got in my truck to leave. "Pipe, I know you're about to do something stupid, just be safe."

I did a double take. "How do you know that?"

He grinned. "Because you're my girl, and I know that determined set to your jaw."

I relaxed my face. I had just that moment decided to go straight to the school and confront Dr. Frederick Burns in his office. Maybe Dad was the mind reader, not Bran.

"If you can't be good, be careful?" I winked.

Dad laughed. It was something Mom liked to say to me growing up when she knew I was headed for trouble.

"Exactly." He shook his head as he turned back to the office.

I climbed in my truck and opened google on my phone. I looked up the professor's office and searched a campus map until I was sure I could find it.

His office hours were listed for today from 2:30 to 4:30, and it was a lot closer to 4:30. I knew I had to hurry to catch him. In fact, I'd be lucky to make 4:30 since I had to maneuver through town to get to the school. My sweaty palms attested to the fact that I wouldn't be that disappointed if I didn't make it.

Unfortunately, things aligned. The lights all seemed to coordinate so I hit them green, the traffic was light and the visitor parking closest to his office had open spaces. I approached his office at 4:27, and the large shadow through the glass of the door attested to the fact that he was still there.

I swallowed hard, wiped the sweat from my hands by rubbing them on my jeans, and knocked timidly on his door. I heard a muffled sigh, but only because my hearing was extra, not because he was loud. I chuckled to myself imagining that he was hoping to slip out soon and not be trapped by a student asking for a grade change, or extra time on an assignment. The shadow grew larger, and the door swung open. I swallowed again. The handsome face was turned away still focused on the computer screen that wasn't far away in the tiny office. When his eyes landed on me, there was a very definite look of surprise in them.

"Ah, Ms. Tikaani!" he stammered. "I wasn't expecting you; did we have an appointment?" His composure settled and he looked past me, probably to see if the department secretary was still there. Since she was walking out as I was walking in, I knew he wasn't going to find her.

"No appointment. May I come in?" I asked, firmly hoping boldness would increase my courage.

He hesitated. I shifted my weight from one foot to the other, ready to flee if rejected. Instead, he opened the door wider and waved me in. The office was hardly big enough for his desk, his chair, and the additional chair for one visitor. The rest was full of shelves, books, and paper. He had been grading it looked like from the mess.

"Please, sit down." He gestured to the extra chair, then hurried to clear it of books.

I sat and shifted uncomfortably.

"How may I help you? Do you have more cryptid sightings?" he asked somewhat eagerly.

My mouth, always slightly disconnected from my brain, blurted out, "I know what you are." I almost clamped my hands over my mouth. However, I maneuvered them under my legs so I couldn't. That way he wouldn't know that I surprised myself. I'd worked myself up so much that I had no control over the output.

"Excuse me?" he exclaimed with a frown, still slightly distracted by his task.

I fidgeted. Sweat started to soak under my arms and I could feel it beading on my brow. The cat was out of the bag so to speak, so even though I hadn't been planning to be quite so blunt. I barged ahead.

"You're my wolf. The one I saw."

He blanched; I could see it even through the facial hair. But I saw him form the lie before he spoke it.

"I don't know what you are talking about, Ms. Tikaani. Perhaps you should leave."

I stood so suddenly, the sturdy chair I had been sitting in rocked back. "Look, *Doctor*," I over emphasized his title to show my disdain. I don't know why. "Cut the crap. I know what you are, and you think you know something about me. Both of us will know more if we stop lying. I have serious questions as I'm sure you do. Maybe if we stop, we can help each other out."

He faced back to the computer. He was chewing the inside of his cheek on the side near me. His hand on the arm of his chair clenched and unclenched. His presence seemed to swell and overpower the small office to the point I wanted to pant and make myself small.

I considered bolting and forgetting the whole thing. I even threw a furtive glance at the closed office door behind me. Finally, he turned towards me. I expected sharp teeth to have formed and claws to burst forth from the hands gripping the chair, but he rocked back and clenched his hands together in his lap—a forced relaxed state. The air cleared and the weight in it disbursed. I hadn't noticed that I had been holding my breath until then. I let it out with a louder than desired sigh.

"What exactly do you think you know? I'd really like to hear you spell it out."

I swallowed. His tone and ease of manner both caused me a moment of doubt and confusion, but I was sure that he was our wolf. I didn't see another answer to the riddle that we hadn't thoroughly investigated already. He had to be my "dire" wolf. I straightened my shoulders and spine. "You are a werewolf. Some kind of ancient throwback as I've recently discovered."

He chuckled. "Really?"

He wasn't giving an inch. I wasn't reading his body language well. I was sure. I *thought* I was sure. I sat back down and copied his fake relaxed pose. I crossed one leg over the other, and I relaxed my hands in my lap.

"So, if I'm a werewolf, why are you so calm?" He leaned forward suddenly and snapped his teeth.

I jumped. I couldn't help it. I instinctively pushed back as far as I could in the chair. His eyes had gained an element of...something. I wouldn't say they were glowing, or changing, but they became more. More predatory, more focused, I don't know, but it was intense. Sweat started to roll down my back and my throat tightened.

"What is it you want from this little revelation, Ms. Tikaani?" He leaned back into his chair and turned to his computer.

What did he mean what did I want? I was confused. I thought he'd flip it on me and accuse me of being—whatever I am. I shook my head. "What do you mean?" I asked.

He clicked something in the program he was using and glanced down at the paper in front of his laptop. He was quiet for a moment, and I thought he wasn't going to answer.

"I mean, Ms. Tikaani."

I was starting to flinch every time he said my name like that.

"What do you want? Exclusive rights to my story? A werewolf change on camera? A confession that the cryptids of old have always been around? What do you want?" He turned back to me with a glare, and the oppressive feeling in the office began to build again.

To break the mood, or just be generally obtuse, I said, "Call me Piper, please."

He gave me a brief, tense smile as he realized how ridiculous our conversation must appear.

"I don't want anything from you but answers, Doctor. I'm not a reporter. I don't even own a camera that isn't already attached to my phone. I have no desire to tell your story to anyone." I kept my eyes open and looked at him directly, innocent so he could judge I wasn't lying.

He didn't suspect that I was the other wolf or that Fletcher's cabin was where I had seen him. I was about to either trust the wrong guy or make the biggest mistake of my life.

I lowered my eyes and leaned over my knees like I was confiding, "I know someone like you."

The shock was immediate. It was like getting shot. He reeled back and almost went over in his chair. Then he stood suddenly and backed away from me. "How?" I heard his heart rate increase; it was so loud. The pulse pounded in his throat.

"Fletcher, Vanice Fletcher. You know him."

Then the realization hit his eyes and lit them up, "You, you." He pointed his finger at me. "You're the black wolf!"

In for a penny, in for a pound as the story goes.

Chapter 20

He started to pace in the tiny space that was left in the office. I gave him a few moments because that was a rather large shock for anyone. My fear of him had settled. I didn't think he was dangerous in this setting. I wasn't sure of his agenda, but I knew that here, in his office I was as safe as I could be. He was tied to the social rules that made him a professor, and I felt like that was important to him.

Finally, I couldn't wait anymore. "I guess my main question is why did you change Fletcher? It was deliberate, but then you abandoned him without any direction or explanation. Why would you do that?" My question was harsh, direct, and sincere. I really wanted to know, and I felt like Fletcher deserved to know.

He whirled on me, hands brushing back his hair. I had hit a nerve. "It was a mistake," he practically growled. "I wasn't going to change anyone. Why would I curse anyone with this life?"

He sat down, arms on knees, head down, in despair. He sat like that for a moment, then spoke, "I was so alone. So lonely."

I thought he would tell me more about himself and what had happened with Fletcher. Instead, he raised his head and looked me straight in the eye. "I know what you are, too."

He relaxed in his chair. He had read me, and even though I tried not to show any reaction, he knew he'd hit a nerve and was back in control. His announcement sent a tendril of ice down my spine.

"What do you mean?" I managed to spit out.

His mouth curled up, a cruel edge to it.

"You know nothing," he stated coldly.

"I'll gladly acknowledge that. Please tell me what you know." What I thought I knew had proven that I was probably wrong on all fronts. "I know you and Fletcher are not common wolves. I don't even know your species."

He waved his hand as if to dismiss my comment. "I'm an ancient type. My wolf was particular to this land."

"A dire wolf?" I asked, confused.

"Nothing so common. The modern remnant of the species was called the Kenai Peninsula Wolf here in Alaska before it went extinct over a hundred years ago, but it had been here from before the ice age."

The professor did like to teach. Maybe I could use that to get the information. He paused, but he wanted to tell me. I felt the shift in his intention right before he started to speak.

"Fletcher. I didn't intend to change him. We were backpacking, a class I was teaching. It had a solo aspect. I planned that during the full moon, so I wouldn't be around any students. It's hard, you know, being, and hiding, and trying to interact like your human half wants. I've had a long time to practice, but even I struggle."

I shrugged and kept quiet, hoping he'd continue his monologue.

He shuddered. "I cut it too close. The wolf is lonely too. I didn't get far enough away. When I realized what I'd done, I watched from afar to see if he would change. It doesn't always work. I couldn't remember how badly I'd savaged him. It usually takes a near fatal attack and even that isn't a guarantee that a new wolf will be born. I didn't see the signs in Fletcher. Either I wasn't persistent enough in my observation, or I missed it. Fletcher is different. He's a loner by nature, so it's hard to see the personality changes that usually persists when a *were* is first changed. Anyway, I missed it. I didn't know. I was so relieved when I thought he was unchanged."

"If that's true, why were you snooping around his cabin?"

He shook his head. "When I heard he was here, in Anchorage, and had inherited a cabin, I wanted to double check. I didn't have an opportunity before to search his house or look for scent markers because he lived in town in a neighborhood with very nosey neighbors." He half laughed and shook his head. I imagined he must have been caught. "Once I found his place, I checked it out. It wasn't until then that I knew. I didn't know how to approach him after that." He had the decency to look ashamed.

"Well, you can now," I stated bluntly. "I can set it up. It's the least you can do."

The guilt at his deed lingered in his posture a few beats, then his back straightened and he made a clear decision. "You're right. I need to put aside my own shame and talk to him—if he'll see me."

"I'm sure I can make it happen." I sniffed. "I also want to know about your pack. They aren't natural wolves either. What are they?" I cocked my head, curiosity burning in my chest. I had so many things I wanted to know.

He shrugged. "They are like me and you."

I sat up straighter and interrupted. "What do you mean?"

He looked confused, lost in memory. "We were made."

I jumped in, "By who?"

He shrugged. "I don't have a name for them, not in this language. At the time, so long ago, my people called them something like 'sky people.' I really have no other reference for them.

"Even though I was in the group that was first changed, a lot has blurred from my memory, and from the difference as language has evolved. My people are gone, and those like me, scattered if they still exist at all." He paused.

I was itching, a feeling of anticipation growing. Something in me told me I needed to know this, it was the key linking everything together. My heart started to pound. I felt the sweat start to bead on my forehead and upper lip. Waiting.

"To us, it was magic. Even now I'm not so sure it wasn't. Maybe you could call it genetic manipulation or engineering. I don't know.

207

They weren't human. But I can't tell you what they are. Aliens? Demons? Angels? Gods? They wanted us. They wanted to be with us and belong to our world. I think at first, it may have been benevolent. Finding something they thought beautiful and wanting to be part of it. But over time, it became warped. They were powerful, gods among us no matter what they actually were." He stood and stretched his back and then sat back down. His chair looked uncomfortable for a man of his size.

"They had abilities we couldn't understand. They could control the elements, the weather, the very heavens. They could transform things and people, and the very substance of the world obeyed them. At first, they just interbred with the humans. Their children were magnificent. They inherited the power and beauty of their godly parents. They were taught the secrets of the universe by their parents. Their creations were wondrous. You've seen those remnants scattered around the world."

My eyes grew huge. I imagined all the grand structures from the ancient world. I leaned forward even further, engrossed in his story.

"Anyway, that wasn't enough. Just like all civilizations, even among the gods, apparently, it couldn't last. Most of the sky people grew bored and left. Those that remained formed factions, and inevitably, it led to war. Soon, their power to change and manipulate nature was used to create the monsters. Those like me who began as human and were given the ability to change into something else. It wasn't just wolves like me. It was all predators, anything to give an edge in the war.

"When that wasn't enough, they took the beasts and gave them the ability to become human, because the humans wouldn't always fight, and the animals were easier to motivate with cruelty. See, those previous humans rebelled against the enslavement that came with the power. Eventually the world was destroyed, and the power they had released flooded the earth. Most were destroyed forever. Only a few of us remained. Then the endless millennia followed." He stopped, swallowed, and looked at me. A horrified expression crossed his face. "I didn't mean to say all of that," he started. "I... It's just been so long." He hung his head.

I understood, I thought. Who could he have told in this modern age? Only his kind. I surmised it had been a while since he had any of his kind to share with. "Is that why you search for cryptids? To find your kind?" I asked gently.

He nodded, misery outlining his eyes. I paused for a moment acknowledging his grief and longing.

Finally, I continued, "I don't understand. How am I like you? I already know I'm different from Fletcher. What am I?" I was too curious, too lost to feel his pain in that instant. I couldn't give him whatever he needed from his confession. What did he want, absolution? I couldn't judge.

He scrubbed his hands over his face. "I spoke out of turn when I said I knew what you are." He studied me for a few moments. "I was in the group of humans changed into this. In fact, I may be the first werewolf. I don't remember for sure. However, as far as I know there were three main classes of beings. Beings like me, humans that changed into predators. Later, during the first war, there were the predators that could transform into human. The third were the overlords. Those that were a mix of the two races. A mix of sky people and humans. Powerful, beautiful, and completely, utterly, evil." He paused again and looked me straight in the eye. "Can you identify the group you come from?"

I reeled. My stomach roiled and kicked, and I felt sick. Could my ancestors be these evil hybrids? Was it possible to be born evil? Why would he think that? I must have uttered some of that out loud, because he answered me.

"I don't know if just being a mix, a hybrid, made them inherently evil. I just know that their parentage seemed to give them the desire and the power to try to control the rest of the world."

I still felt sick. My mouth filled with saliva, and I looked around for his wastebasket just in case.

"It is evil to take away the free will of other intelligent beings. They ruled this world for millennia, ruled over the millions of slaves whose will they'd stolen." His eyes were red, as though from lack of sleep, and I could see the memories flash over his face, causing him pain.

I didn't know what to think or do. I wanted to hear more, but at the same time, I couldn't stand to hear more. My reality was too strained, my soul too raw. I rushed out of the room, horror pounding in my heart, bile in my throat, and my eyes burning with tears. As I raced down the hall, I could hear his voice, echoing in my ears. "They are still here, Piper. They would be very interested in you."

Chapter 21

There were only two people with whom I could seek solace—Fletcher and Branwyn. Mom and Baylee were too vulnerable and best left out of my mess. My father had either lied to me or kept me in the dark, and right now my ability to trust was broken. I knew he'd been keeping things from me, but I didn't know how much. How much of this new information did he know? I couldn't even stand to look at him at the moment. My heart wanted Fletcher, but he wasn't answering his phone, so I ran to the Lunatic Fringe.

Bran took one look at my face and pointed to the door to the back room. I went in, still stunned, and collapsed on the sofa. I didn't even grab a Coke. I pulled my knees up into my chest, wrapped my arms around them and buried my face in them. It seemed like forever before she hurried in. I think I must have said something out loud, because she replied that she'd closed and sent everyone home with full pay. My face must have shown the shock I felt at that, because she shrugged and quietly said, "I've never seen that look on your face before, Pipe. You scared me. What's wrong?"

My eyes welled again with tears. Bran looked shaken. She didn't know what to do. She looked like she wanted to come over and hug me, but I wasn't much of a hugger, so she went to the fridge and grabbed two Cokes and handed one to me. I sat it next to me on the couch, unopened. I wiped my eyes with the bottom of my shirt, sniffling.

"What's going on?" she asked.

I stared into space for a few moments, not sure what to say. Then I started with Jane, my dad, and his secret hideaway, and finished with my discussion with the cryptozoologist—for lack of a better term. The whole time my eyes burned, and my throat felt like sand. When I finished, I looked up at Bran, afraid I'd see fear and loathing in her expression.

Instead, she looked thoughtful. I was mystified.

"Why aren't you cringing away from me? You know what this makes me!" A surge of despair ran through me, and I buried my face again.

She didn't reply, so I looked over at her again. She was still sipping away, nothing but a contemplative gaze on her face. I didn't say anything else. She was the better scholar between the two of us. She knew what I believed about myself, and she still didn't seem affected by my revelation.

Finally, she remembered I was there. "I don't think you're a demon, Piper." She waved a hand as if to wipe that silly thought away from me.

"How can you say that? You did hear what that, that, thing told me?"

"Yes, yes, and we'll get to that. Did you ask him about the gold?" She asked absent-mindedly.

"Gold? What are you talking about? We already talked about this. We decided there was no way he could have anything to do with the gold."

"I've been thinking about it. Piper, if he's Fletcher's maker, the other werewolf you saw at the cabin and the one whose pack attacked you, then he or a member of his pack may be the ones searching the cabin for the gold."

"That doesn't make sense. How would he even know about it, or want anything to do with it? He's ancient. He probably has more money than he knows what to do with!" I scoffed.

"Why would he have a ton of money?" she countered.

"I'm sure he's collected treasure over the millennia he's lived. You know like in vampire stories and stuff," I said a little more uncertainly.

"Perhaps, who knows? But where did the treasure come from? Couldn't he possibly be trying to get it back? Or having spent endless swaths of time as a wolf, not saved? We don't know. But we do know he's been there. We know his pack has been near there. Isn't the most obvious answer usually the true one?" she asked.

Probably, although I didn't say that. However, it didn't feel right. I saw absolutely no link between Frederick Burns, professor, cryptozoologist, and ancient werewolf and Fletcher's gold.

When he turned Fletcher, he didn't know Fletcher would inherit a remote Alaskan cabin. There was no way Burns would know that with that cabin would come millions in gold. It was an absurdity to believe he'd have the slightest idea it even existed unless something happened recently.

Fletcher said that someone had looked for the gold or had been searching the property long before he arrived. I shook my head. "It's not him." I paused, but before Bran could argue, I put up my hand to stop her. "Quit trying to distract me and tell me why you don't think I'm a demon. Didn't you realize what Jane, Burns, and even my dad were hinting at?"

Her mouth quirked into her irritated expression. "I think so, but you better spell it out so we aren't talking past each other," she said resignedly.

"The winged beings, Raven, Eagle, Thunderbird, whatever in Native traditions throughout the Americas…" I trailed off.

She nodded. "The sons of God came in unto the daughters of men, and they bore children to them; the same were the mighty men of old, the men of renown."

"Yes, that!" I said miserably. "That horribly unexplained piece of scripture."

"Genesis six."

I threw a dirty look. She sniffed and mumbled, "Well it is."

"The winged creatures both Jane and Burns talked about, those were fallen angels." I faded into a whisper. "Demons."

She snorted softly. It was an old argument over what the "sons of god" were, so I ignored her. There were tons of theological arguments over that one Biblical passage and its apocryphal buddies. I had always leaned toward the explanation of the "watchers" being angels that disobeyed and were thrown out, but Bran had a different interpretation. My new revelations may be proof I was right.

"Piper, what do you think evil is?"

This was also something we'd discussed in the past, and she knew what I believed, so I answered sort of grumpily. "Come on, Bran, this is stupid. You know what I think. Evil is taking away other's choices." That was the short version.

"Would you ever take away someone's choices to hurt them?"

I felt affronted. She knew I wouldn't out of meanness. Sure, if I had to save someone, or protect someone, but not just to take their choices away to hurt them or torture them.

"No. You know this."

"Wouldn't a demon be inherently evil?" She also knew what I thought about this. We'd had a run in with a demon once, and that was enough to convince both of us that true evil could exist.

"Yes," I replied without hesitation.

"There you go. You can't be a demon. So, stop thinking that way."

"Then what am I?" I begged her.

"You are you. My friend, a good sister, a good daughter. Your family, your friends, and your life haven't changed from before you found this out. It changes nothing. We can figure the rest out later."

The Scarlet O'Hara defense I thought ruefully. Something my mom always said when she couldn't deal with something right then. It meant that tomorrow was another day. It helped.

"We'll deal with it after we figure out the gold and who is stalking you. It just doesn't seem that important for now." She stated it with finality. A prescient chill slid down my back and goosebumps prickled my arms. I picked up the Coke.

"Better?" she asked as she sipped daintily from her own can.

"No, but calmer. You didn't—you know." I wiggled my fingers at her.

"Don't be ridiculous," she said. She looked away but didn't deny anything. I didn't really think she'd zapped me with anything witchy, but her calmness and logical thinking had helped to relax me and soothe my fears.

After sitting quietly my heart finally slowed, and the panic eased. I felt like I could face everything again. "Frederick Burns is out as a suspect for the gold."

Bran shrugged, she didn't believe so, but I felt it strongly. He wasn't a contender for either the stalker or the gold sneak.

"Could he be the stalker? Maybe he was checking up on Fletcher or you?" I looked at her sharply, she had done that mind reading thing she said she couldn't do.

"Nah, the Dr. is too tall." I shrugged. "He's like Viking big. Plus, his beard is real, not fake." I slurped my Coke. "I'm out of ideas on who the stalker could be. What do we do now?" I looked at Bran directly. "You have any ideas?"

"Not really, there's something tickling the back of my mind. I am not ready to let the cryptozoologist off the list of suspects. As you know, he's the only suspect we have."

My shoulders sagged, feeling despondent.

"However, I've been thinking that maybe we overlooked something obvious."

My face must have pulled some sort of weird questioning look because she rolled her eyes.

"We keep trying to find people who knew Clyde and may have known about the gold. But who knew for sure about the gold, or at least had been paid with gold?"

"Me and my dad, so what? You know we aren't the ones." I shook my head in exasperation.

"Don't be daft. Who else got paid in gold and knew about the inheritance?"

I thought for a moment, going through a list of services and items that Clyde had paid for and coming up with nothing. In the last few years at least, he hardly left his property, and anything he wanted, he gave us gold to buy for him. I couldn't think of anyone, except, "The lawyer?"

"Yep. Why haven't we investigated him? We've talked about it." She stood up and stretched her back.

"I don't know. We've talked about it, but we've been wrapped up with the professor and the stalker. Plus, he's the one helping us. It's stupid when you think about it. I guess I assumed he had money. Why would he care about more? I assumed he was ethical. I don't really know. I'm starting to feel foolish."

"It's just a thought. He may be totally innocent, but maybe we should dig into him a little deeper."

I thought while I finished my Coke. My stomach burned with the Coke, my emotions, and the lack of food. I rubbed it distractedly. "OK, what should we do first?"

"Google?" Bran said.

I accidentally snort laughed. "We both need to keep our day jobs. Solving mysteries is not our thing."

Bran got out her laptop, and we started googling.

Enthusiastic as we were, we forgot the most important thing. The lawyer's name. So, the googling took a little longer than we planned since we had to search Anchorage lawyers until something triggered my memory. It helped that I remembered the approximate location of his office and that his name sounded foreign. Finally, I identified the lawyer as Mr. Georgetti. Then we were stymied by the fact that the firm was a father and sons outfit. There were actually three Mr. Georgettis. I was frustrated by this time, but Bran, intractable as always when it came to research, told me to calm down and we were getting close.

I told her that I remembered Fletcher's Georgetti was an outdoor type, metrosexual, and owned a Super Cub. I wanted to kick myself. I should have paid closer attention to his photos. If I had his "N" number, I could have learned a lot about him immediately. At the time, I hadn't thought much about it, other than that Clyde and Fletcher were paying him for a service. I hadn't thought to check him out. He seemed to know what he was doing.

I needed to talk with Fletcher. He knew more about the lawyer than I did, if we were going to find anything else out, we needed his help. I turned to tell Bran just as she said the same thing to me. We both laughed.

"If we could get his plane's N number, that would give us a good source of information," I said when we were done laughing.

"What's that?" she asked distractedly. For my best friend, she'd been almost pathologically unwilling to find out anything about aviation. She was terrified of planes and flying, and that led to an almost psychotic ability to block anything about them out of her mind. I shook my head.

"Seriously? You know those numbers printed on the side of a plane? In the US, they start with an N. That's how you identify the plane. It's sorta like a license plate on a car, but anyone with google can look you up." I gave her my Super Cub's "N" number. We plugged it into the computer.

"Huh," she said.

I glanced over her shoulder. Sure enough, it mentioned me, where I lived, who had owned the plane, and where it was located. She could even view its last flight path.

"You're right, that's pretty good info." She looked over her shoulder at me. The blue glow from the computer lit up her blue eyes and made them eerie, almost cat like.

"What can I say. If you own a plane, or an air service, you have no privacy."

"That must suck, Pipe, sorry."

"My choice." I shrugged. "I have other secrets, more important than who I work for and where I live. Like hiding in plain..." I trailed off and stared off into space. I came back to my surroundings with Bran shaking my shoulder. "I had an idea or epiphany or something."

"I noticed," Bran said ironically. "Your brain was overtaxed and shut down."

"Ha, ha." I looked at her, she grinned. "Very funny." I squinched up my eyes since it seemed to help me think.

She gave me the hand gesture to go on.

"'N' numbers made me think that maybe we're overlooking something obvious. Even more obvious than the lawyer." I took a deep breath. This was a real leap. It was probably dead wrong and way off base, but it felt right. Like when you find that puzzle piece that doesn't quite look like it fits, and you try it anyway and clicks right in smooth and easy.

"I think I know how to find out who the green Jeep guy is."

Bran gaped at me.

"We were scared that someone would find out we were following them, but no one knows about you." I pointed to her. "You are going to talk to the owner of the green Jeep."

"What? I can't, Piper, you know I'm not good at stuff like that," she whined. It was true, she tended toward bookish and would rather do things over the phone or the computer. However, when you got her out there, she was bold and capable. She'd proven that when she snuck into the Jeep and stolen the registration information.

"Not the guy in the Jeep, the woman who is on the registration." She didn't look very relieved, but she nodded.

"It makes some sort of twisted sense." She sighed. "What do you want me to do?"

We came up with a very loose plan—sort of like the last one, not very good—but we were winging it outside of our safety zones.

We planned it for my next day off which was four days away. It gave me a chance to forget about everything for a little while, except for work, and I was surprised at the relief I felt at that.

The next day, Dad and I ended our day early because we were going to see Baylee try out for the high school cheer squad. She was excited and since I barely got to see any of my family except Dad during the summer rush, it was something I looked forward to. Fletcher was going to accompany me, and it would be the first time he'd meet my mom.

I don't know why, but I suffered a million degrees of uncertainty and fear at that one. Mostly because I didn't know what she was going to do. Either a) scare him away, b) smother him, c) embarrass me, or d) all the above. I raced home and changed five or six times. I don't know why. Fletcher had seen me at my very worst, and mom and Baylee didn't care, but the pressure on my chest that made it hard to breathe kept making me do weird things.

I stopped, took a deep breath, and pulled on jeans and a cute knit top that was casual and flattering at the same time. Since it was the first thing I'd tried on, I sighed and brushed out my hair, wavy from my work braids. I pulled on a pair of boots and ran to open the door for Fletcher when he rang the bell. I let him in, panting, "just a minute," and ran back upstairs to smear on some lipstick and grab my bag. "Sorry, I wasn't ready," I apologized exactly one and a half minutes later as I paced down the stairs more sedately.

The quirk of an eyebrow was the confused reply. He lifted his ubiquitous sunglasses. "You have to be the quickest date I've ever had to wait for." He winked. "No apologies needed." I thanked him, and we headed out the door.

Soon after he pulled his truck out onto the street, I started, "So, my mom..." I trailed off. How was I going to warn him without making my entire family sound nuts? "Well, she gets a little excited about the prospect of me dating." I looked down at my hands curled tightly in my lap. I relaxed them.

He looked over his sunglasses at me.

"See, I know you know this, but I haven't dated much, and she's, well, she's a lot more social than you or me." I took a deep breath, keeping my vision focused on my hands so I didn't have to look at him.

He gave a small grunt of acknowledgement.

"She just projects a little, uhm, enthusiasm." I finally gasped out. Mortified about what I knew was about to ensue. "Baylee will love you no matter what, so no worries there," I added with a hopeful lilt to my voice. I finally looked over at him.

He pulled up to a stoplight and stopped. He pushed up his

sunglasses and looked me right in the eye. "Babe, you don't have to worry. No one is going to scare me away." His mouth quirked up at the corner.

I slapped him playfully on the arm. "You haven't met my mom."

"I've met your dad; he likes me." He preened in the rearview mirror.

"Stop. My dad could make you disappear if he wanted too, and no one would ever look twice at him. They're not even remotely like each other. Just, be prepared. Oh, and you can't get away with your one-word answers either. I'm just warning you. You may not want to date me after tonight." I swallowed and wondered if that would happen.

I wasn't good at this, and Mom scared me sometimes at how tenacious she was. "After, I have something to talk to you about." I planned on telling him about Dr. Burns and my confrontation. I hadn't wanted to talk to him over the phone, and I wasn't sure about his reaction considering how he had responded after our dinner party. Either he'd be better while driving the car and having to focus on that, or he'd crash, turn into a werewolf, and expose all supernaturals in one night. I liked a gamble like that.

He frowned. "Is it something important?" There was the very tiny hint of a growl in his voice.

I wondered if men had the same insecurities as women, or if he was expecting another bomb drop like before. Probably that.

"Nothing important." I waved it off, so he wouldn't worry all night. "Take this turn." I directed him to Baylee's high school. It was in a copse of trees and hard to see from the road. I noticed he had a bead of sweat running down the side of his face and smiled to myself as I realized he was nervous. His knuckles were white on the wheel. I turned away so he wouldn't see my smile.

The parking lot was half full, so it was easy to find a spot. We walked in the side door and up the stairs to the gym. He held my hand, and before we entered, he pulled me to the side out of the sight of others and kissed me thoroughly.

After I caught my breath, I asked, "Not that I'm complaining, but what was that for?"

His voice was raspy, but he said with emotion, "So you know nothing will scare me away."

I looked in his eyes. He had left the sunglasses in the truck, and I saw the truth of that statement flash across his eyes. I nodded.

"Ok." My voice wavered slightly, and I cleared my throat. "Ready?" He took my hand and led me in.

Mom and Dad were already seated about three rows up on the bleachers. Mom saw me first and waved us over. She wasn't a very big lady. She was probably the same height as Baylee, built like her, with that sturdy cheerleader build. Now that I knew, I realized that other than green eyes, we had no physical likeness.

She and Baylee had heart-shaped faces—mine was oval—and they had similar builds. I wasn't exactly built like my dad, but even though I had a figure, I tended toward willowy, where they were more voluptuous. I was also the tallest in my family, which wasn't saying much. Other than my obvious native features and coloring, you'd never believe I belonged to either of my parents. My mom jumped up and hugged me, and then to his chagrin, hugged Fletcher before I even had the chance to introduce him.

"Mom, this is Vanice Fletcher." I introduced him. At that point a handshake seemed awkward, so he nodded at her.

"Call me Fletcher," he said quietly.

"Nice to meet you, Fletcher," she answered exuberantly. "Baylee is warming up on the floor." She pointed at the gym floor, where girls of all sizes tumbled, jumped, and practiced cheers in a variety of dance and workout clothes. The varsity girls wandered around, correcting forms, and answering questions, dressed in their blue and gold uniforms. We sat down in the bleachers.

"I see her." I showed Fletcher where to look.

Baylee noticed us and waved enthusiastically. I knew she was dying to come up here, but she got back to her warmup, all business.

Mom chatted with Fletcher, which I found astounding. She was so sedate and natural, and he seemed relaxed. I found my gaze wandering, watching the girls warm up on the floor and gazing around the bleachers to see if I knew any of the other families.

I waved to a few of Baylee's friends and stopped my roving in shock when I saw Raleigh, the date that ended in disaster. He hadn't seen me, and I looked away quickly. What on earth would he be doing here? He didn't live in Anchorage, or at least hadn't the night of our one date.

I threw a couple of more glances over there, but he was talking to a woman seated next to him. Was he on a date? My heart jumped. If so, she looked a little tame for him. She had perfectly done sandy colored hair, her outfit was precise and fit her tiny, toned form to perfection. He started to look around. I looked away and turned to the front so he wouldn't notice me.

The competition started with an announcement by the principal and the playing of the national anthem. I tried to forget Raleigh sitting in the bleachers and enjoy my time with Fletcher and my family.

Somehow, I managed to avoid Raleigh, since he either didn't see me, or had no interest in an embarrassing reunion either. Baylee bounced over and met Fletcher after the tryouts, and of course was completely happy for us. Just like I told him. He took to her easily, the ex-high school teacher falling easily into a rapport with a teenager. Baylee was totally charmed. She invited him to her first game as a full JV cheerleader since she'd made the squad. He graciously consented.

When we got back in Fletcher's truck, I told him he'd made her day. He smiled. We were about to drive across the street to meet them at one of the restaurants there. I was still tense, but Fletcher seemed more relaxed having gotten the hard part over. "Are you ok?" I asked. "This isn't too much for one night?"

He turned on the truck and put it in drive. "No, your family is lovely. Don't worry." He smiled at me.

Like that ever stopped anyone from worrying. I was nearly thirty —or at least felt like I was nearly thirty—and I still felt like a sixteen-year-old taking her boyfriend home for the first time before a school dance.

He may be relaxed, but I was wound all the way up past the breaking point. I had sweat dripping in places I didn't want to think about. I fanned myself and lifted my hair off my neck.

"Are you hot?" I asked.

He graciously turned on the AC for the three-block ride, a sympathetic smirk on his face.

Dinner went well, and by the end, I think my mom liked Fletcher more than me. It was obvious Baylee did. She may have had a full-blown crush going on, which I could totally understand. I know I had one.

He was charming and vivacious. He was social and gracious. He could talk about politics and sports, and anything outdoors. He of course knew a lot about high school and could even talk to Baylee about her interests. I was amazed at how much depth my Fletcher had. I felt lucky and my heart swelled with pride.

"Oh, I almost forgot. Baylee, Bran said she's sorry she couldn't make it. Her new boyfriend invited her to a work thing."

Baylee sighed a little, but then perked up. "Are they official?"

I laughed. "I don't think so yet, but close!" I smiled at her.

She got a wicked glint in her eye. "Are you two official?"

I choked a little, caught off guard.

Fletcher smiled and looked her straight in the eye. "Yes, we are very official."

She squealed gleefully and bounced in her chair a little.

I melted. I think my mom did too. When I got up to go to the bathroom, she followed me. I did an inward shrug, knowing I was going to get questioned the second she had me alone. Once she made sure we were the only people in the bathroom, she asked me, "Does he know?"

I deflected. "Don't you and dad talk at all?"

She swatted at me playfully. "Of course, we do! You ungrateful child!" She groped in her bag for something.

I went into the stall.

"He told me you'd tell me if you wanted me to know." She huffed indignantly.

"Yes," I replied quietly. "He knows everything."

I heard a gasp. She knew that meant we must be serious. "So, how official are you?" she asked, trying to keep her excitement in check.

"Come on mom, if you haven't figured it out by now, which you have, we're serious."

I heard another happy little gasp. I rolled my eyes. I left the stall and washed my hands. When I looked up at her in the mirror, she wore a grin, and her eyes were full of unshed tears. I dried my hands and hugged her.

"I'm just so thrilled for you. Plus, he's really neat."

I may have giggled a little in pure joy. We fixed our faces, got ahold of ourselves, and went back out to finish supper together.

Fletcher and I were comfortably solemn on the drive back home. I was dreading the information I had to give him, and he was probably solemn because he had just met my parents. We both started talking at the same time, then laughed and he indicated I should go first.

"No, no, you go on. Mine can wait."

He glanced over at me and nodded. "The full moon is approaching. I've got to go back to the cabin."

"I know. I put you on the schedule."

He grinned at me, so I qualified it. "It doesn't mean I don't think you can handle yourself. Just I know it's easier when you're in the wilderness."

He nodded. "What did you want to say?" he asked.

I hemmed a bit, then just spilled it all out. I told him about meeting the werewolf and where and why. I watched his hands the whole time, not willing to meet his eyes. They clenched and unclenched, but he kept control. I did tell him my reasoning, that we were on campus, and if he wanted to stay hidden, which by all accounts seemed to be true, he couldn't do anything to me. He did swerve a bit when I told him that Dr. Burns wanted to meet him. I finally looked over to see his jaw was tight and his breathing accelerating.

"Are you OK?" I lifted my hair again, the nervous sweat beading and running down my back.

It took him a moment, and I could see his iron will take control. "I'm fine."

It was still a little growly, but I didn't push him.

He was silent until he pulled up to my house. I wasn't sure he was going to say anything. But he turned off his truck and bowed his head while maintaining a firm grip on the steering wheel.

"He wants to talk?" he snarled. Then he slammed his fist into the steering wheel. It bent and twisted, and I jumped, surprised. Then he threw his head back, eyes glowing, and a vicious howl full of rage and loneliness tore from him. I couldn't believe such a sound could be ripped from a human throat.

He curled into himself for a moment, and I kept my eyes down on his hands that hung limply to his sides. Watching to make sure he could contain the wolf. He was panting quietly. Finally, the pressure I hadn't realized had been building since I told him my story started to dissipate from the cab of the truck, and his breathing slowed.

He glanced at me from under his lashes. "I'm sorry I lost control, Piper. I never claimed to be that good at this anyway." He reached for my hand, and I slipped it into his. "I just…" he trailed off, at a loss for words. "I'm not even sure how I'm feeling. I had no one to teach me this, this way of living. I've been walking the edge so long, and I can't decide if I'm pissed off, or happy he wants to finally tell me what I am. I have so many questions. Still, I don't know if I can see him and not try to rip his heart out."

I rubbed my other hand up and down his arm, the flesh-to-flesh contact helped to calm the wolf. I wasn't sure what to say to help him. "You know I'll be with you, no matter what."

He nodded, stiffly.

After a few more moments, he said, "Even though I'm not sure I care anymore, I think I should speak with him. If what he said about the Sky People being interested in you, is even partially true, between what he said, Jane's story, and your father's vague warnings, it sounds like you and your family could be in danger." He reached out with the hand not holding mine, caressed my cheek, and leaned in and gave me a gentle kiss.

"This bastard who cursed me may know what is out there. He's the only one who seems to know the past and origins of what we are. He may know how to protect you if the danger is real. I can't turn away a possible ally. I have a feeling—" he looked out the side window as though to check our surroundings "—we need to find all the allies we can.

"If these 'Sky People' do know about you, and if it's true that they were battling for dominance over this planet at least once before, we don't know what they could want from you. We have to be prepared."

He looked straight into my eyes, and a wash of fear, not of him, but of the unknown entities that may want more from me than I wanted to give, washed over me, and I shivered.

I bowed my head to him. "I'm sorry, Fletcher. I didn't mean to get you involved in a planet wide disaster."

He scoffed.

"I'm being serious."

"I know." His voice was soft and loving.

"We may be acting ridiculous you know. There isn't any proof, other than the stalker, that anyone knows anything about me other than you, Bran, and Professor Burns. This is an ancient story. It's like expecting the boogey man to get you."

He nodded. "Yes. But the possibility remains."

"If you want, you could walk away now. I wouldn't blame you or think less of you." With that I made to slide away from him.

He growled slightly. Then his grip tightened, and he pulled me as close to him as possible in the tight space of the truck cab. He pulled his hand free of my waist and grasped the back of my head. He tilted my face to his. Then he bent and kissed me, claiming my mouth with his and in his own way claiming me as well.

His kiss was fierce, and I felt like melted wax all the way to my tightly curled toes. When he pulled free, he lifted me from the truck as though I were as light as a feather. I thought I'd float all the way into my house. This time, I didn't hesitate, and he pulled me all the way to the bedroom and then proved to me he wouldn't leave, and nothing would separate us.

Chapter 22

When my alarm went off early, I stretched my sore body, and ran a hand down Fletcher's gloriously naked body. He grunted something and rolled over, still sleeping. I grinned to myself and hurried to the shower, knowing I was going to be late as usual. I didn't know how to modify the look of wonder and joy on my face and knew that anyone who saw me would immediately guess what I had done the night before. I reached down inside and decided I really didn't care.

This was the man I wanted in my life, forever, and I had no regrets. I leaned down to kiss him on my way out the door and was rewarded by an obviously happy man who pulled me down and almost made me later. I pulled away from him reluctantly and promised to see him that night, since he was going to be leaving the next day. He gave me a hungry look, and I forced myself to leave.

When I got to the office, Dad mumbled, "You're late," and handed me the already completed flight plans for the day. Luckily, he'd filed my first one already. When he looked up at me, I blushed. He grunted and looked away, and I knew he knew.

I felt a wave of shame, and then shook it off, and threw back my shoulders. I shouldn't feel like that. I was a full-grown woman in charge of her own destiny. Plus, I had no intention of stopping what I started last night. It was too incredible and felt so right. I could see he wanted to talk about it but couldn't bring himself to do it. I shrugged him off and went to check the weather and do my pre-flight check.

The hunter was already waiting in his truck, and since dad had done some prep work for me, I wasn't that late anymore. We did our weigh in, and the client had to move things around. Tulugaq planes had all the mods, which made us a more popular transport service than most, since we allowed more weight. It always seemed that hunters always managed to fill that extra poundage too. Finally, he was loaded up. My long day began.

That evening, as I taxied back to the office, I was exhausted, but excited to see Fletcher. The thought of another night together kept the adrenaline rushing and butterflies flitting in my stomach. I kept randomly blushing at the memories of last night, and then would roll my eyes at my weirdness. People had been having sex since they were first created, why should I be so special? It was hard keeping my mind in the game, and concentrating on my flying, which was foolish of me. I had to keep reminding myself to stay focused.

I was flying our "spare" Super Cub, not my personal one. I had one tricky crosswind landing in the bush that helped snap me out of my musings for a time. I was relieved when I coasted in on my final water landing at Lake Hood. I pulled up and tied off. When I looked up, I saw the green Jeep. Light glinted off his binoculars. A shiver raced down my spine.

A wave of absolute fury built from my core and the heat rose through me. I ran at him. I wasn't careful at keeping a human pace, and I saw him startle as I got closer to him than he expected. He started the engine and raced off, but I got within ten feet before he was able to do that. He kicked up a lot of dust, since he was parked on the side of the road, and he caught the notice of a few other people, including my dad. He ran out to meet me.

"What was that all about?" he asked.

I blanched a little at his question, since I hadn't informed him about my stalker, and knew he was going to be upset.

"Umm," I mumbled. "That Jeep has been following me."

He grabbed me by the shoulders, so I had to look at him.

"How long, Piper?"

"Since around the time that Fletcher found the gold," I replied quietly.

"Are you sure he's following you, or Fletcher?" he asked urgently.

"It was hard to tell at first, but I'm pretty sure he's following me," I answered, looking
him straight in the eye.

He shook me a little. "Why didn't you tell me sooner!" he whispered harshly, then pulled
me into a tight hug. "This could be very bad." He turned and walked quickly back to the office.

I had no choice but to follow, especially since we'd drawn a few onlookers. I waved, smiled stupidly, and continued into the air service office.

"What's going on Dad? And no more cryptic tales and protecting me from whatever." I put my hand on my hip and glowered at him.

"The less you know, the better, kid." He searched through his desk.

"Of course," I said sarcastically. "What *are* you looking for?" I asked curiously.

"Nothing important," he hedged.

He was going to put me off again.

"Should I be worried about something?" I asked.

He looked up from his searching. "No, but if you see him again, call the police."

I rolled my eyes. "Ok. Really, that's all? You had a panic attack that I'm being followed, and you aren't going tell me what freaked you out?" I shouted my last words which finally drew his attention. We weren't really shouters in our family.

"Of course, I'm worried my baby girl is being stalked. That's why I told you to call the police," he responded coolly.

"Fine, Dad." I walked away. I was too mad to talk to him, and completely aware that he was lying to me.

I called Bran on the way home. I was livid as I explained every detail. She was thoughtful on the phone. "Do you think your dad knows something about the green Jeep?" she asked.

"I don't know, but I think he suspects something he's not telling me," I replied. "I can't wait to see what we find out. Will you be ready when it's time?" I asked her.

She snorted. "Yes, Piper, I already told you I'd go through with it."

I nodded even though she couldn't see me. "Thanks." And since I didn't feel like I'd been a good friend lately, everything being about me, I followed up with, "How's it going with Mike?"

She paused, noticing my sudden change of subject. "It's good. He's a little different, but very nice." Her tone was formal, and I couldn't read her.

"How was that work thing you went to last night?" I continued.

"You know how it is... Acting like you were happy to be there among a bunch of strangers, all talking shop you know nothing about. It was a riot." She sniffed.

"Sorry." I paused, but when Bran didn't add anything else I forged ahead thinking about what Baylee had asked the night before. "Is he someone you're planning on getting serious with? You have been dating for a little while now."

"Are you feeling guilty? This is the most you've asked about Mike since I first started going out with him."

"Maybe?" I replied.

She laughed, then added more seriously. "I don't know. I want to like him, and he's a lot of fun. He seems to really like me and wants more, but I feel like something is slightly off. Maybe it's because he's so focused on fish and work. I don't know. I can't put my finger on it, and it's sort of a ridiculous reason to keep someone on the hook but at arm's length. It's not like I have a ton of men beating down my door."

"Bran, I can't tell you what to do. And you wouldn't listen anyway. However, we both know that you of all people should listen to your feelings. I haven't known them to be wrong."

"I get that, Pipe, but I'm not sure if my 'feelings' are because there is something wrong with him, or because I'm nervous about letting anyone into our inner circle."

"I get that. You know my past. Before Fletcher, I never let anyone in. It's scary. But I trust you to make the right decision." I tried to reassure her.

"That's the problem, Piper," she replied. "You trust me with a lot of dangerous secrets, so I have to be one hundred percent sure of him. I'm just not there yet. But I'm having fun, so here I stand."

"Ok." I couldn't really say much else about that. She asked me about my big meet the parent's night, and I summarized it, leaving out my nocturnal activities. I could tell she picked up that I didn't tell her everything because she was my friend and since everything appeared to have gone well, she didn't push. She'd find out soon enough, it wasn't like I could really keep it to myself for too long. I grinned as I hung up.

I would normally stop and pick up something to snack on before I got home, but Fletcher invited me over for dinner, and since I knew there would be more than enough to satisfy me—I grinned to myself— I didn't stop. I rushed home, showered, changed, and threw some things together to take with me. I guessed I'd be staying the night, and since our relationship had just entered that stage, I didn't have anything at his house to allow me to do so.

When I got there, I felt a little shy about bringing in my big bag. I didn't want to seem presumptuous.

"I thought you'd want to stay over?" he said, when I showed up with nothing.

I looked down, suddenly shy. "I do, I just wasn't sure..." The hunger in his eyes was enough to stop me, and the flush I felt this time was pure heat. I was the inexperienced one. I had no background in relationships, beyond the little flings and stolen kisses of a schoolgirl. I knew that wasn't the case for him. He hadn't grown up having to stay hidden from the world, and he was a man solidly in his thirties.

He must have had relationships before me, and what he'd done to my body last night proved he was very experienced in that regard. Maybe I should have been concerned about his pre-werewolf past, but

I felt secure in knowing he was mine now and more importantly, he thought of himself as mine. A wave of contentment settled over me. I melted in his arms and his kisses consumed me. Dinner was very late.

It probably wasn't the best time in a new relationship to start lying, but I saw no other way to go through with Bran and my plans. If he knew, he'd try to stop us or make us wait until he was back, and frankly I wanted to get it over with. So, I told him I couldn't stay with him on my day off at the cabin because we had a new client, blah blah blah, and I was on call.

I think he knew something was up, but he let me get away with it. I'm sure he knew how sore I was, and probably thought I was trying to not hurt his feelings. I was sore, and I did need a day off from our nightly exertions, although I wouldn't have ever admitted that. I dropped him at the cabin, we set a time for pick up after the three moon nights, and I flew back to enact my plan with Branwyn.

After a desperately needed good night's sleep, I met Branwyn at her house. She'd left her store in the hands of a new day manager, and although I knew how hard it was for her to give up that kind of control, it was nice to have her free for the day.

We drove to the address we had for the green Jeep. This was going to be tricky. It relied on the fact that Bran looked totally harmless. She had braided her hair in two braids, and she looked like a college student. Her height and cherubic, youthful looks were what we were betting on since she was about to lie her face off. She wore jeans, a tight dark green t-shirt, and black, knee length, high-heeled boots. We'd found an old ad online for the green Jeep that led to this house. The poster of the ad hadn't listed the address, but we were hoping that a simple, "I looked up your phone number" would get us by without setting off any alarms.

Bran wiped the sweat off her palms before she rang the bell. After a few moments, a harried looking woman opened the door. I couldn't see her clearly since Bran was blocking my view. I saw the woman pause as Bran did the spiel that we'd rehearsed a million times. Then Bran turned, waved, and walked down the street. The woman watched her a moment before she shut the door. At that moment, I saw her clearly and froze. I recognized her.

I pulled out and picked up Bran a couple of blocks down. She hopped in and took a deep breath. She wiped her palms down her pants again. "Well?"

"She was a little hesitant when I said I basically stalked her home address and the fact the ad was over three months old," she said. "But I think you were right about acting small and young."

"You are small," I said.

She hit me; it stung.

"Ouch, oh mighty one," I said.

She glared at me. "Do you want me to finish?"

"Yes, go on, sorry, I won't interrupt again." I mimed bowing down to her.

She huffed.

"I told her that the ad was still active, which is lucky that it was, and she seemed mollified. I said exactly what we rehearsed, I told her I knew the Jeep was probably not still available, but I lived on the other side of the neighborhood so I decided I could walk over and find out. I figured it was probably gone since it wasn't in the driveway, but I had to ask since it was exactly what I was looking for." Bran took a breath. "She smiled and told me she'd sold it to a family member. She was sorry, she'd take the ad down. Then I said some nonsense, like oh it must be nice to have a family close, and she said something like it was nice, although it was her brother who bought it, and he didn't live that close, and she wished he lived closer. I said thanks, and you saw the rest."

My mouth was dry. I recognized the lady, and knowing that the Jeep belonged to her brother, pieces started dropping in place.

"I know her," I choked out.

"What?" Bran wheeled on me and grabbed my arm.

"Her brother. I know her brother. I recognized her from Baylee's tryouts. Her brother is Raleigh." Bran's eyes were huge. She made a gasping sound.

"Oh, my lord," she strangled out.

I knew exactly how she felt. I was processing it.

"What do you think he wants?" Bran asked.

"I don't know. It's weird. If it was for romantic reasons, he could have just asked me out again. I didn't throw him out, we just sort of *awkwardly* parted."

"I know."

"He really started following Fletcher, I think," I said thoughtfully.

"Are you sure?" she asked.

"No. I just don't see any reason for him to stalk *me*." I was truly confused.

"He's probably just some sicko," she growled.

"I think it's something more than that, but I don't know what. You may be right." I shuddered. "Now that I know this doesn't have anything to do with the gold or the supernatural, I'm calling the cops next time I see him."

"You probably should have done it already anyway," she mumbled.

I gaped at her. "You agreed it was a bad idea!"

"I can be wrong," she said sheepishly. "But for the record, I don't think there's a box for 'what kind of supernatural are you' on the police report. So, you should have done it earlier."

"Whatever," I grumped.

"Yeah, yeah," she shot back.

I brushed her off. "Well, since we've solved one mystery, let's solve the other. Have you found any dirt on the lawyer?"

"I don't know if it's important or not, but the lawyer Fletcher is using has only been working for his dad in that firm for the last three years. He may have been Clyde's lawyer when he died, but he wasn't for very long. He's also a bit of a playboy, lots of social media stuff with him and gorgeous women. Other than that, I couldn't find much else about him on the interwebs."

"So, suspicious? Or another dead end? We know someone is after Clyde's gold. I know in my gut they are responsible for his death. The lawyer obviously has money. He has a plane; he has high class girl-friends. We have to keep digging."

"You're coming at it wrong, Pipe. He could be overextended. Those are expensive habits," Bran replied.

"Yeah, but we currently don't have any proof. Just suspicion."

"I get it, Piper. I just don't have any other ideas. Unless you think Raleigh is involved with the gold."

"I don't know how. I'd just met Fletcher when I had my one disastrous date with Raleigh. He couldn't have thought I had anything to do with the gold."

"Yeah, maybe, but you did know Clyde, and he was a very good family friend. You knew the property. You had access to the property. He may have even thought you might inherit the property. Did you ever think about that?"

I thought for a moment, surprised I hadn't put that together. "I didn't think about that."

"I know," she said with an air of superiority.

"So, Raleigh, having somehow found out about Clyde's secret gold, thinks I'm going to be able to get close enough to the property either by helping out or inheriting, so he takes me out, attempting to get close to me by any means." I threw her a meaningful look. "He feels me up, because he thinks he can, and by so doing I'll want him so bad, I'll give him the gold I just inherited?"

"Maybe? I could be wrong, but it doesn't mean he isn't involved in the gold scheme," Bran said.

"I guess." I thought for a while. "Maybe he and the lawyer are besties."

"Don't be ridiculous. Now you are just making fun of my theories." She huffed.

I laughed at her chagrin. "It all seems ridiculous. Nevertheless, someone wants the gold, someone caused Clyde's death somehow. We have three players in some weird game. The wolf, the lawyer, and Raleigh. They may all be involved, none of them may be involved. We suck at detecting." I rolled my eyes.

"I don't think we're that bad. We solved two mysteries. That's two more than we've ever solved before," she said.

"Sure, I guess."

I felt defeated. We'd solved two worthless mysteries. We didn't know why or how Clyde died, we didn't know who was after the gold, we didn't know why Raleigh was stalking me, we didn't know what the old werewolf wanted for sure either. We knew barely anything. Sometimes it's just best to let things happen as they may.

Because I'd worked last night and didn't need my phone alarm for the morning, I'd turned it off. Now that we'd finished our spying, I turned it on while I was driving back to Bran's store and was immediately pinged by several notifications. I grimaced, annoyed. Someday, I was going to go in there and turn off all notifications, but I was lazy. Mainly I just frowned grumpily at my phone every time I got an unwanted ping.

Since I was driving, I had Bran check my messages. I had a few work-related texts and voicemails, no big deal. There was one from Fletcher, but it was a simple "call me" so I shrugged it off for later. I had Bran text back on the work texts. Nothing on voicemail was too urgent so it could wait until I got home or to the office. It was mainly questions about gear from new clients. I wanted to call Fletcher back when I was alone, because I had no idea if it would get steamy or not. I smiled to myself.

"Wanna stop for food?" I asked Bran. She shrugged. She was a more salad and chicken girl than I was, so I followed that up with, "Where do you want to eat?"

She thought for a moment. I figured fast food was out with her, so I prepared myself mentally for a sit-down restaurant with other people and waitstaff. Not usually my scene. We were close to Midtown, and I figured she'd pick somewhere close to the area.

"Let's go to the Roadhouse."

I swung my head to look at her, my mouth open. I was surprised. The Spenard Roadhouse had rabbit food, but it was more a "bacon of the month" type of restaurant. I didn't want to appear too eager, but the drool I had to slurp up probably gave that away.

She laughed at my surprise. "Mike took me there the other night. I hadn't ever been, and it was really good."

I blinked. "Wow."

The restaurant was always busy, and today was the same. The parking lot isn't that big, and I had to park as far from the door as possible. As we walked around my truck, my phone rang. I swiped one-handed without looking and put it to my ear. Bran threw a quick look at me, and we both paused behind the truck.

"Piper!" it was Fletcher's voice. It was strained, gruff, and faint.

"Hi!" I said warmly, excited to talk to him. Bran looked at me and rolled her eyes. She took a few extra paces to get ahead of me for the relative idea of privacy. I turned my back to her.

"The gold. They're here for the g—!"

I assumed the last word was gold, but it was cut off somewhere in the middle and the line went dead. I felt a shiver of fear and the hair lifted on my arms. I whirled around, my eyes round. Bran looked at me as though she were going to say something snarky but stopped when she looked at me.

"What's wrong?"

"Get in the truck," I yelled.

She paused, reading my body language. Both of us frozen in time for a split second before we barreled into the cab in tandem. I was panting. My anxiety pushed me to break all the traffic laws on the way to Lake Hood. Bran sat, staring at me, and questioned me steadily as I drove.

"What's wrong?" she asked. I could feel her pressing in on my awareness, her magic trickling around my edges trying to calm me and settle my nerves. It didn't work.

"Something is going on at Fletcher's. He said someone was there after the gold. He didn't say much because he got cut off. I don't know what's wrong." The last words were nearing shouting level. I was starting to sweat. My body ached with the desire to change, to fly, to get there faster. My reason and humanity worked to keep me grounded, alert, and rational.

My mind raced. I thought he'd removed the gold. He said he was going to put it in a safe deposit box. Then my mind searched for an actual event or something he had said that confirmed he had done so. Nothing. Was the gold still there? It had to be. My fear spiked another level. What would someone do for that amount of gold? Were the interlopers human or supernatural? I didn't know. I gulped air.

I had to calm myself, to concentrate. I ran through things I needed to take. If I succumbed to my raven, I would have no clothing, no tools, no weapons. Someone or something was there. Fletcher had said, "They're here!" So more than one. My handgun was in my backpack in the back seat. I should grab dad's rifle from the office. Bran, what should I do about her? On one hand, she hated flying and wasn't really an "outdoor" girl. She was most definitely a city girl. I glanced at her feet. She was wearing high-heeled boots for the love of Pete. She noticed my look.

"What? I know what you are thinking, Piper."

I shook my head.

"I don't think so. I'm thinking you need to decide if you are going with me. You can take my truck and go right back to work if you want." I was dead serious.

She was quiet for a beat. "No, you might need back up."

I thought of the ridiculous boots and her lack of practical bushcraft. Also, Bran didn't handle guns. She was my pacifist friend. Then I thought of the zap she gave me when I scared her once, and the insight she had into situations, and her ability to sense what was going to happen. She had saved me once from a demon with her quick thinking, a real-life evil who wanted to kill us and suck our bone marrow, *demon*. Those things outweighed the others.

"It's rough and primitive and I don't know how long we'll be there. I also don't know how dangerous it will be. But I could use the help if you're willing," I explained with a sigh.

"I'm willing." The stubborn cast to her jaw attested to that as well.

I started adding other supplies to my mental list to grab from the office. I kept survival gear in my plane, but I could grab the second bag from the other Super Cub and the bear spray from the office supply. Bran barely weighed a hundred pounds; I could carry a lot of gear added to her slight weight.

Bran would need a coat; I'd grab dad's spare from the hook by the door. All the preparations were running through my head, anything to keep my mind off the bleak despair I'd sensed in Fletcher's voice. I clung to the words that he'd told me once when he'd been afraid of being out of control as a wolf. He could only be killed by silver. I prayed he was right and that whoever was there didn't know it. When my mind turned to him there alone with unknown assailants, I would chant the mantra in my head, "Only silver."

I screeched to a halt in front of the air service office, my truck crooked. Bran and I bolted out. I went straight to the office to grab Dad's coat, the rifle case that contained dad's rifle, and the bear spray. I handed the coat and bear spray to Bran. I knew she had no problem with using bear spray when needed; it had saved our butts once before. I checked the desk drawer to see if dad had extra rounds for his Browning A-bolt. There was a mostly full box. I grabbed it and stalked out.

I walked down to the water, and out onto the float of the other Super Cub. I opened the cargo storage door and pulled out the emergency backpack. Then I returned to the office. I needed to fly fast, so I had to cut as much weight as possible. Guns, ammo, and survival stuff stayed. I shed as much of the other collected junk, like my tools, that I dared. I did a quick fuel calculation. Just enough to get there and back, no reserves, and I fueled up. Then I loaded Branwyn and the added gear into my plane. I strapped the rifle to the wing and began my pre-flight check.

My hands were shaky with anxiety as I tried to keep my mind on the items I was checking off. Fuel, flaps, ailerons, and rudder were all in order. I continued after I started the engine with instrument checks and fuel mixture until finally my list was completed and I was ready. I radioed the tower and taxied to the small Lake Hood runway. Once I was cleared, I asked Bran if she was ready. She whispered, "Yes" into her headset, and I hit the throttle.

Chapter 23

You know how if you drive the same route every day, you sometimes forget how you got from point A to point B? Your mind knows the way so well you go into autopilot. I'd like to say that flying to Fletcher's cabin was like that, but it wasn't. Every minute was agonizing. I no longer had a list to rely on, so I struggled to keep my mind off the what ifs—the biggest of which was what if I'm too late and he's dead?

That was the one that drove me to push my plane to its limits. I flew low, I turned my carburetor heat on, I quartered into the winds, every trick I had to shear off a few seconds here and there. My plane made me proud. It leapt at the controls as though I had finally freed it from its constraints, and we raced together like we were a falcon diving on its prey from the clouds.

I didn't check on Bran, but I knew she could sense my growing panic. I wasn't helping her hatred of flying on this trip. I think the last time she went with me we flew like this—reckless and rough. Banging through turbulence and swishing side to side to avoid obstacles and shave time.

She probably thought this was what flying was like every day. I'd have to remember to set her straight when this was over. I dove down the side of a mountain to gain airspeed and continued my nap-of-the-earth route. I heard her gasp through the headsets; I'm sure she felt her stomach drop as we barreled down. I realized I was now chanting "silver, silver" over and over out loud, and wondered if Bran had picked that up. I stopped myself. Instead, I started praying soundlessly that Fletcher was still alive.

My mind wandered to Clyde, lying face down on his roof, ladder pulled up—dead. Only it wasn't Clyde in my mind, it was Fletcher. Sweat drenched me. It slithered down my scalp and onto my forehead and down my neck. I couldn't force one more millimeter of speed from my plane. I was forcing it with my body, my mind, I felt melded to it. Its wings were my wings. The propeller was my beak, screaming into the wind.

Bran's hand on my shoulder brought me back abruptly. A few black feathers drifted loose in the cockpit.

"What?" I grumped.

"Your hands. I could see them fade. There were feathers, and I was afraid you were going to shift."

I glanced at the feathers. "Oh." I paused, confused. "I don't think that's ever happened before. Thanks." I had never partially shifted or hung between forms. It was always one or the other. I shook my head, distracted for a slight instant. I frowned. I took a breath and centered myself. The feeling of being one with my plane faded, and I was present in the moment again.

"Thanks," I said again.

She squeezed my shoulder in acknowledgement. "You aren't going to be any help if you don't get control of your emotions," she said.

I rocked my head back and forth to loosen the tense muscles of my neck. I knew she was right, but it was hard to calm myself and stay centered with the panic gnawing on the edges of my mind.

"You're right." I responded. I continued to deep breathe. I rotated my shoulders. We were getting closer, and I needed to be able to think and act.

I burst over Fletcher's clearing low, engine growling. I tilted my wing down to view what was happening. It was a mess. I wasn't sure what I was seeing. I checked the runway and noted another Super Cub and a Cessna Skyhawk parked in my usual spot.

I buzzed to the end of the clearing, swooped up and swung around to view the scene again and land. I wasn't looking for a subtle arrival, not that it was possible in a noisy single engine plane. I flew even lower to get a better view. It looked like at least four men visible in the clearing. I couldn't see Fletcher. There could be more in the cabin or any of the outbuildings or trees. The Super Cub could carry two and the Skyhawk four. So, there could be six. My count of four wasn't reliable.

The Super Cub was a traditional yellow with black, a common color and sight at any local small airport. The Skyhawk was solid black with white N numbers—a unique paint job that should stand out anywhere it was kept. I didn't recognize it. I wasn't sure who or what we were going to confront. Two of my suspects flew—the lawyer and Raleigh. The lawyer was a Super Cub owner. Who flew the Cessna? Maybe Raleigh, but he flew a black and white Maule M-5 not solid black. The black plane was definitely a Cessna, tricycle landing gear, dragonfly body shape and all.

Because both planes were parked near the end of the short runway by the cabin, I was severely limited in space. I was flying into the wind, so I skimmed the trees and dove down into the clearing. I pulled up to flare into the wind for a super short landing, coming down on my front wheels with the plane level and then allowing the tail to touch as the plane stopped. I was well-versed in the maneuver. Many of our hunting drop off spots were very tight—on a hill or mountain in a space no larger than a mall parking spot.

The plane bounced slightly on the oversized Bush Wheels. Bran gasped, then breathed out a relieved sigh. I switched off and ripped off my headset. We jumped out. I grabbed my backpack and took out my handgun. I pulled back the slide slamming a round into the chamber and checked that the safety was on. I shoved it back into my holster and tucked it in the back of my jeans. After removing the rifle case from the wing, I opened it, and removed the rifle. I'd filled the magazine before we left and shoved a handful of cartridges in my pocket. I slid back the bolt, loaded the chamber, and slung it over my shoulder. Bran took the bear spray from my hand when I offered it. She threw me a questioning look.

"You never know," I said and shrugged.

She also shrugged and tucked it in the back of her jeans. It was the large bottle, so she couldn't really put it in her pocket. She rubbed her hands together.

"Are you cold?" I asked. I was beyond feeling the weather, although the wind was blowing stiffly, and I was damp from my nervous sweat.

"Nah," she said, "I'm preparing my zapper."

"Oh." I wasn't really focused on her. The yellow Super Cub blocked my view of what was happening, and I was struggling to stay in the moment and not race ahead with the worst-case scenario. She reached a single finger out to my arm and a small tingle of electricity zinged through me. I jumped.

"What was that for?" I exclaimed, rubbing my arm.

She frowned at me, "You aren't concentrating. You need to be calm and focused. Pull it together."

I stopped and shut my eyes for a moment. I breathed, opening my senses, and letting the information that they were giving me flow in.

I couldn't see, but I could hear and smell. Voices were shouting. Under them a growl. Somewhere close to Bran and me, I heard shuffling feet. My nose brought me different scents. The strongest was an expensive smelling cologne. Under that, several male bodies; I could always smell the difference in sex by the pheromones given off. Males had a salty, slightly musky odor. Individual scents were more difficult; they were coming at me together as I faced into the wind. I smelled local animals, including a very strong salmon bear.

Bears that eat a lot of salmon smell very strongly of fish on top of the rank bear smell. It was so strong I wasn't sure of the species. In this area you could run into large grizzlies or the smaller black bears. I was hoping for a black bear. I smelled wolves, too, but I couldn't tell if it was an old scent or new. The scents were becoming muddy in my mind. Too many at once in this shape and my ability to parse them was less accurate. I shook my head to clear it.

"Ok. I saw four men when we came in. What did you see?" I should have asked her in the plane, but I wasn't thinking right. She should have told me, but I'm sure she was more worried about my ability to land than what we were landing in the middle of.

"I saw the same," she agreed, nodding.

"I'm going to go straight in. I think you should go around the yellow plane and into the trees. They know I'm here; the plane is a dead giveaway. You should stay hidden. I doubt they'd guess you're with me."

She nodded, her worry framed by the deep crease between her eyebrows, a sure sign she was thinking hard.

"My 'magic,'" I heard the quotes in her voice, "only works if I'm really close."

I shrugged.

"I have no weapon to help you with but this." She plucked the bear spray out of the back of her pants and wiggled it before tucking it back. Bear spray could be very effective. Generally, most cans say that it is effective within nine feet. The truth is it can shoot up to forty feet in the right conditions. Bran knew this well.

"Just remember, don't shoot it into the wind." My attention was already jumping ahead, secure in my knowledge that Bran knew what she was doing.

"I won't," Bran promised. Any other time, she might have returned a snarky answer.

"How fast can you move in those boots?" I asked.

She looked at them. "Fast as I need too," she said.

"OK." I gripped her elbow and guided her to the side of the yellow plane closest to the trees. The scene we'd viewed above the clearing placed the four visible men in front of the cabin. The cabin's rear had about a ten-foot cleared space. The outhouse was just inside the tree line behind the cabin and about one hundred yards further was the small river that Clyde used to mine.

There was a very defined trail leading from the cabin to the river, but the rest was heavy brush and trees. It should provide Bran good cover if no one was lurking there. When we got to the tail of the plane, I peeked around it.

"It's clear, run!" I whispered.

"Good luck," she whispered and ran into the trees.

Once she disappeared, I took a deep breath and prepared my next steps.

I slunk around the yellow Super Cub and rushed into the shadow of the black Skyhawk. I slithered to the front and peered under the propeller to see what was happening. Four men were standing like sentries, waiting. That meant the action was occurring either in the cabin, or behind it where I couldn't see.

One man had a handgun held loosely at his side. I couldn't see if the others were armed because of the angle, but I had to assume they were. Two of the men were native, and by their build most likely either Inuit or Inupiaq like me. The giveaway was their stocky build with long body and short sturdy legs. One was very bow-legged. I couldn't tell what the other two were since they also had dark hair, but nothing else to distinguish them by.

They all wore black jackets—maybe a uniform—and blue or black jeans, so any skin I could see was covered. None of them seemed familiar, but I couldn't see their faces. Did this mean we had the wrong suspects all along?

No one was paying attention to me, which was odd, since I had just landed a plane—that wasn't something you could hide. Whatever they were watching must have been much more interesting. Or they recognized my plane and figured I wasn't a threat. Why men always seemed to dismiss women as a threat was a mystery. I could wield a firearm as effectively as any man. That seemed like a great equalizer to me. I shook my head. Or—I whirled around—someone was behind me, and I was the fool. Sure enough. I was the idiot. A black clad arm came down on my head, and I was out in an explosion of stars.

When I came to, I was lying by the stump where we'd left the offerings to the Urayuli months ago. From the ache in my shoulders, I'd been dragged here. The rifle was gone, but the ache in the middle of my back let me know they hadn't bothered to search me. That meant they really didn't think I was a threat, or they didn't expect me to wake up soon.

It took me a while to get oriented. My head ached and my vision swam. I saw everything in photo negative for a couple of minutes before it snapped back into focus. I felt vaguely nauseated as well. Definitely going for full concussion here. I blinked to clear my eyes. A few moments later, voices replaced the white noise I'd been hearing. I moved my head to pinpoint the scene. That was a mistake; pain shot through it again. I didn't want to make any sudden moves—I didn't know who was watching me—but I didn't see anyone nearby.

They must have thought I was out of the game for a long time—or forever. I raised my hand to the side of my head and felt the partially dried blood congealing there. I could also feel it in the collar of my shirt. I began the slow process of rising to a sitting position, using the stump to support my back. The effort left me panting with pain.

There was an impressive pool of blood where I'd been lying. The sight of it increased my queasiness. They must think I'm out for good. Head wounds could bleed impressively, but it was still a lot. Once my head felt like it wouldn't explode, I looked around. I didn't see anyone, but I could hear voices.

The four, no five, men dressed in black must be in or on the other side of the cabin. I eased my way up the stump until I was sitting on it. The throbbing was still there, but it was tolerable. I guess my mom was right about my hard-headedness.

After a few deep breaths, I slowly stood. I swayed a few moments on my feet, but the throbbing in my head didn't increase. This was probably as good as it was going to get. I walked away from the cabin into the trees. At some point they were going to notice me missing, and I wasn't in any shape to go up against them without time to regroup. I also needed to find Bran. Did they get her too? I looked over my shoulder. They still didn't know I was gone. Good. I faded deep into the shadows. I had one great advantage—I knew this property very well.

I hiked back to my tree. When I was small, I had a hidden place where I could put my clothes when I shifted. I also left my childhood secrets and favorite things there because I knew the place was only known to me. It was an ancient, burned-out tree. Most of it was gone, just a tall, hollow stump remained. Who knows why it still stood at all? It was approximately eight feet tall and the back of it was mostly gone, leaving a perfect hiding spot, ideal for a five- or six-year-old to reach into and leave her treasures.

I placed the handgun in my spot and covered it with my clothing. Unless you knew this was here, you'd never find it. I hoped my shift wouldn't aggravate my wounded head, but this was life and death, and I had no choice. I had to find Bran and make a new plan. I crouched and leapt high, shifting at the zenith, and stretching my wings for the sky.

I could ignore the pain in my head better in my raven form. Maybe it was the smaller wound, although I couldn't believe it wasn't proportional, or it was the animal ability to stay in the moment and focus on the action being performed.

I pumped my wings, gaining height to get above the trees. Usually flying left me euphoric; the air was the natural place for me, and I felt at one with the world. Now, I struggled. Whether it was the pain or the blood loss, I didn't know. It could be the worry, but that was a small nagging beneath my immediate needs. I had to stay focused on my task, which I struggled to do with my head injury. Raven was always distractible outside of eating and flying, so I struggled a little bit with her intentions.

First, I needed food. I was weak, and sick. There were granola and protein bars in my plane. As a raven, I was fairly adept at getting in and out of it, since that was something I'd practiced many times. I landed on the wing and walked in towards the door. Super Cubs are high winged aircraft, meaning the wings are above the door.

Using my talons, I flipped myself over and grabbed the strut with my beak then flipped down. Then I hopped to the door handle and pulled it down, and the door popped open. From there, it was simple to pull a granola bar from my opened backpack and open it. I didn't have time for the calories to hit my system, so as soon as my belly was full, I reversed my ingress and leapt from the wing.

There weren't other ravens nearby, but I doubted that my raven self would be recognized as a shapeshifter. Two of the men I'd spotted, though, were Inupiaq. That didn't mean they knew, but it made me nervous. I'd have to be cautious—not really a word in my vocabulary. I stretched my wings until I was over the trees. I swept back and forth, my sharp eyes watching for Bran. She was roughly in the same spot where I'd left her, curled up in a ball. I dove down and landed near her. She didn't notice. I pecked her lightly with my beak. She swept her hand at me automatically, before jumping up.

"Piper?" she whispered.

I cocked my head. "Yes." One benefit of my raven shape is that I don't lose the ability to speak. Ravens are fantastic mimickers, and their voices are very hard to distinguish from humans.

Her eyes were red-rimmed, and I could tell she had been crying. "I saw that man hit you and drag you away. I thought you were dead," she sobbed.

"Not dead, but my brains got scrambled pretty good," I replied. "They dragged me up by a stump in front of the cabin. They must have thought I wouldn't wake up because they left my handgun. I think there are at least six of them, maybe more. I didn't recognize anyone, but I didn't see them all." I fluttered my wings.

"What do we do now?" she asked.

"I'm going to fly around and see if I can get more intel," I said. "Then we'll decide."

"Okay," she said slowly. "Do you think that's a good idea?

"I don't have any others, unless you do?" I asked.

She shook her head. She didn't know this property. I had sketched her a very rough map once, but that wasn't the same as having walked it.

"I'll be right back."

I leapt up and climbed above the trees again. I was beginning to tire and hoped that the energy from the granola bar would kick in soon. I circled high above Fletcher's clearing. I caught a nice thermal, and it helped with the fatigue as I could glide and rise with very little effort. My raven eyes are almost as good as a hawk's. I can see small objects from nearly two miles away. The cabin was much closer, so I could see quite well.

There were men on the side of the cabin away from the planes. The four men that I had seen initially stood spread out, all armed. I still didn't recognize them. Two men stood over Fletcher who was lying on the ground. His hands and feet were bound, and he had been beaten and shot. I could see the blood and bruises.

Both men wore baseball caps and black clothing. I didn't understand the black clothing, it was bright daylight. This time of the day in late summer, the light lasted long, faded into a long twilight, and true night only lasted a few hours, why black? I kept thinking it looked more like a uniform, but there weren't any identifying badges or marks on it. My hearing was good, but nowhere near as good as my eyesight, so I dropped lower.

Fletcher's body was curled up, tense, his eyes tightly closed. I wondered why he didn't shift, but maybe it was because his hands were tied behind him or he didn't want to do it in front of them, I didn't know. I could see his wounds closing slowly and wondered why the men hadn't noticed. The taller of the two men, suddenly kicked him in the gut, and I could finally make out what they were saying. It was something about me.

"Go get the girl," the tall man commanded one of the four. The jig was about to be up.

I must have missed something before this because he was telling Fletcher I was dead. I saw Fletcher tense. They didn't know him well if they thought killing me would encourage Fletcher to reveal where he kept the gold. I had to get his attention. I cawed as loud as I could. Fletcher's eyes opened and he saw me. His eyes blazed. I was low enough now to see that his hands were bound with zip ties.

My caw gained the attention of the tall man that had ordered my death. He looked up at me and raised his gun as if he were going to shoot me. "Bang!" he yelled, and laughed, amusing himself. When he looked up at me, I saw his face under the hat. It wasn't who I expected or even suspected. It wasn't the lawyer or Raleigh. It was Mike. *Bran's* Mike.

If a raven could trip while flying, that's what I did. I fluttered a moment and lost altitude. No one on the ground really paid attention to me, so I was pretty sure they didn't know about my ability to shift. I lunged for the nearest tree and landed. I could see well from here, and the men had already lost interest in me. I blended into the shadows and watched. My raven self was quickly forgotten by all but Fletcher. His eyes followed me and marked my location. I nodded to him, the only thing I dared do, and he winked at me. Winked. I cocked my head at him.

Finally, the men sent to retrieve my dead body came running back with the inevitable news that I was missing. Fletcher tried to hide his grin but was too slow and earned himself another burst of vicious kicks to the body. I flinched with each one. No matter if he could heal the injuries quickly, they still hurt. His grunts and panting increased my worry.

Mike ordered the four armed men to search for me, and I had a moment of fear for Bran. I had to have faith that I had hidden her away as best I could. I didn't have the time or ability to worry about both of my friends. The granola bar was finally hitting my bloodstream, and I felt energy like warmth fill my small form. I stretched my wings and shook my feathers out. I settled, and my feathers smoothed down.

I watched Fletcher and the scene before me. I couldn't understand why he hadn't broken the zip ties. He was strong enough to do so, and those men wouldn't stand a chance against an enraged werewolf of Fletcher's size and strength. What was he waiting for?

My attention wandered, as happened easily when I was a raven. I snapped back to Mike questioning Fletcher about the gold. Fletcher didn't answer, he just laughed, and that *bastard* shot him in the leg. It wasn't the first gunshot wound I had noticed on his body. I assumed they were healing like the other wounds I could see on his skin, but it was hard to tell, since the blood soaked his jeans. Fletcher howled at the pain, then closed his eyes and curled back up, completely ignoring

Mike and his demands. Mike kicked him repeatedly again, but no answer or response was forthcoming.

Mike's companion spoke to him harshly, "You're going to kill him. and then we'll never find it!"

Mike laughed. He kicked Fletcher again and again. "It's nearly impossible to kill a werewolf."

The other man drew back, apparently shocked. I nearly fell out of my tree. They knew? How? How did Mike know? Had Bran spilled our secrets? No. I couldn't believe that. It must be something else. Was he working with Raleigh? Did Raleigh know about me, about Fletcher? Was he part of this?

He had been following us and spying. There was still another man I hadn't identified. Was that him? I couldn't really judge well from this angle, but the other man just seemed too tall for Raleigh who was barely taller than me. Still, what was his angle? Why was he following us?

I couldn't wrap my head around it, and it wasn't relevant right now since Fletcher was in deep trouble. If they knew he was a werewolf, it was an easy jump to think they knew about silver. Silver, the hope that had kept me sane while trying to get to him. It was now his bane. Were they shooting him with silver? I checked his wounds, but it was hard to know since his clothes were bloody and I couldn't see the gunshot wounds themselves.

His bruises were healing. That might mean he was silver free, but why wasn't he breaking his bonds? I leapt up into the sky, frustrated and able to do nothing. I needed to check on Bran, maybe lead her further away from the men searching for me. She was my secret weapon. I just didn't know how to use her.

I circled around the men. If they knew about Fletcher, they may know about me, although it wasn't likely since they were searching for me on the ground. I spotted my hiding place and dove down. Bran was huddled against my tree.

"Piper!" she whispered at me.

I needed to speak to her, but I needed more than a voice, I needed to be able to give her comfort from the news I had to share. I shifted, and since I was naked, I covered myself the best I could with my hands. Bran stared at my face, confused as to why I wasted the energy to shift. I knelt by her.

"Bran, I don't know how to tell you this." I looked earnestly into her confused face. Her body tensed with new fear. She figured it must be bad. "It's Mike. He's the one after the gold."

She gasped and blinked. "What?" she mumbled.

I knew that was rhetorical because her eyes told me she understood. She ducked her head down for a moment, then raised it.

"That bastard."

Now the worst news. "He knows that Fletcher is a werewolf," I said flatly, watching her reaction.

She jerked like I had slapped her. "What the hell?" She was swearing a lot. I knew she was really upset since I was the one that usually had the mouth like a sailor, and she was the one correcting me. "You can't possibly believe I told him, can you?"

I saw the hurt in her eyes. I blinked. I really hadn't thought about it for more than a split second. "No," I said it savagely, and she nodded, mollified. "But Mike and his buddies know and Mike's torturing Fletcher. He's shot him multiple times and kicked him. They bound him with zip ties, and he's not escaping. They must know about the silver." I paused and as an afterthought, added, "They also know I'm missing, and they're looking for me. We need a better hiding place."

My friend, eyes full of compassion, hugged me, and I choked up. Before she could notice my weakness, I shifted back into a raven. A wolf may have been more useful at removing Fletcher's bindings, but being a wolf would probably get me shot, and I could be killed by any bullet—silver, lead, or steel.

I led Bran deeper into the woods, heading toward the tree I had fallen from in my youth and hoping the Urayuli were watching. I spoke quietly on the wind so they would hear me and know I sought their help. Shy creatures, yet so strong. If they agreed, I knew Bran would be safe until I needed her. So, I begged the wind. Once there, I cawed once and directed Bran to lean against the tree. I didn't get much of a reply, but the oppressiveness of the woods decreased, and I thought I heard the whisper of my name. "Thank you," I whispered to the wind.

"I'll come back when I know more," I said to Bran before I flew off.

She nodded and sank down. She was shivering. I'm sure she was scared since it wasn't cold. Then I remembered the Urayuli used fear as a weapon. She must be feeling the remnants of that emotion as it faded from the grove.

As I flew, wind burning my feathers and the sun on my back, I tried to come up with a plan of action. I couldn't get close enough to Fletcher to free him. As a bird, my beak was the only weapon I had, and I didn't think even my powerful beak could chew through a zip tie. If I shifted into a wolf, I'd be shot.

They knew about werewolves and would be suspicious, plus even a normal wolf wouldn't be tolerated. If I shifted back to human, they were already looking for me. I'd have to be very fast, and I'd have to sneak around six men. I went round and round, and no option was getting clearer. I was back in my tree where I could see Fletcher and if he looked up, he could see me.

The sixth man, the one whose face I hadn't seen, kept his hands loosely on his gun, obviously left to guard Fletcher while the others searched for me. Fletcher didn't move at all. I thought he'd fight those bindings, so something must be very wrong with him. They *must have* used silver in their guns.

His breathing was also shallow, and I was growing more and more concerned. I was afraid I'd have to make an impulsive move and try to free him in my human form. At least I'd have thumbs and be able to use a tool. The next obstacle was that I'd left my clothes and gun with Bran. I'd have to fly back, change, and sneak back here through the guys searching, distract this guy, find a knife or other cutting instrument and then free Fletcher. Ugh.

I was about to launch myself from my roost when I saw a flash of grey fur to my left. I swung my head to focus on it. Ghosting through the trees in utter silence, was Dr. Burns. I didn't know what else to call him in his wolf form. Big wolf, I guess. The biggest wolf I'd ever seen, anyway. An irrational fury filled me. That's how they knew about Fletcher. He was working with them. Just when I'd thought that maybe he was on our side, he came to steal from us too.

If I were bigger, I'd dive down and peck his eyes out. The rage that blew through me was so intense, I thought I'd burst into flames. I wanted to scream and fight and cry all at once. It wasn't fair that they had a werewolf and a bunch of guns on their side. How was I going to save Fletcher now? Plus, he knew what I was. The second he told them; they would find me quickly. He finally stopped, nearly invisible in the trees. He could see Fletcher clearly. I saw his muscles tense. Then ever so slowly, he scanned the trees.

His gaze was heavy when it struck me, and I bowed under its weight, defeated. In a moment, he would rush out and reveal me. Then both of us would be captured, and our lives worth only as much as the gold could buy. Probably absolutely nothing. I fluttered down to the giant wolf. At least my death would be quick, and my life wouldn't be used against Fletcher. It might give him a slim chance of escape. The big wolf watched me and as I glided down, he backed up deeper into the darkness of the trees. I followed.

Chapter 24

I landed near him, near enough it wouldn't be much for him to reach out and snap me in two with his powerful jaws. "Make it quick," I said softly and stretched my neck. The large wolf backed up a step and sat down heavily, confused. I hopped closer. "If you care for Fletcher at all, kill me, don't let me be used against him," I said. No answer from the big brute. Of course, wolves couldn't speak. Instead, he lay on his side, and I watched as his body began the change.

It was loud, and I looked around to make sure no one had heard us and was heading in, but the old wolf's wood sense was impressive, and no one could smell us from the position he'd brought us too. The stream noise covered any sound. I watched as his bones rearranged themselves and his fur melted away. He lay still for a moment, then sat up, carefully covering himself. He was a very polite robber and murderer at least. I kept my eyes glued on his face.

"I'm not with them. What happened?" he asked once his voice recovered, and he was able to speak.

It took me a moment to relay the events leading up to this point—I could speak as a raven, but long speeches were taxing—taking time to decide if he was telling the truth. In the end, I had to go with my gut reaction that he wasn't involved, only concerned. I ended with, "I'm pretty sure they shot him with silver."

He drew in a quiet breath. "When we are young, we are quite vulnerable to silver," he said softly. "He needs help as soon as possible."

"No shit," I said angrily. I was at the end of my patience, and here was a werewolf, more than enough of a weapon to make things happen. "Look, dude. I have no clothes, no weapons. You're it. Get him out of there."

He blinked. "I'm going to shift back. You've got to listen to me. I'll go get him. You've got to get the silver out of the wounds and make him shift. It's the only way to save him. You have to do it quickly. I don't know how long I can hold off the four shadow winged guards. So, it's up to you to save him!"

I nodded confused.

Dad had used the term shadow winged. Or maybe it was Burns when I spoke to him at his office. I shook my head, focusing. "I'll try," I answered.

He had already started his shift back. I watched over him as he completed his shift and shook out his fur. He stretched.

I could only imagine how much it hurt for him to shift like that. Fletcher had described it as excruciating. The big wolf had done it twice in less than five minutes for Fletcher. He must be a better person than I gave him credit for. I launched myself back up into my viewing tree.

Dr. Burns threw me one last look and leapt through the trees towards Fletcher's location. He made no secret that he was coming in hot. He crashed through the brush, snarling. His lips curled back, and his fur rose along his spine. He looked enormous. The man guarding Fletcher, took one look at the huge werewolf and backed up, fast. He fired three shots into the massive body and fell hard on his ass. The shots, most likely silver, hurt him. He cringed hard. Then his body ejected the slugs and his wounds healed. It was fast.

The man watched as well, stood, and retreated, calling for his buddies. Dr. Burns grabbed Fletcher's bound feet by the straps and pulled him away from the cabin with his teeth. I fluttered my feathers nervously, terrified for Fletcher.

Before the huge werewolf had pulled him into the trees, I saw men running from across the clearing towards the cabin.

"Hurry!" I squawked. Hopefully, I hadn't given myself away. The first two men who made it to the werewolves, emptied their guns at Dr. Burns. He growled, and although hurt, he never stopped dragging Fletcher away. Once their guns were empty, I watched them strip. They were shapeshifters like me.

These were the men the cryptozoologist was afraid of. I partially stretched out my wings, although I didn't know what I could do. I needed to get the silver out of Fletcher and make him shift. That was my job, I had to stay focused.

The first man finished as Dr. Burns pulled Fletcher into the woods. He shifted into a gigantic grizzly bear. I gulped. How could the doctor, large as he was, fight that? No wonder he was worried—and there were four of them. Once he'd dragged Fletcher far enough away, he ran back to intercept the grizzly and another large wolf, although not the same type as Dr. Burns. I couldn't concentrate on the fight; this was the distraction so I could save Fletcher. I had to work fast.

I fluttered down and examined him. I didn't think I could snap his bindings with human hands, so I worked on them with my beak. I was able to snap them. Then I had to decide how to get the silver slugs from his flesh. Whatever I did would hurt him, so the faster the better. My fingers were too large, and I didn't have any tools.

The bullets weren't that deep. His body had attempted to push them out but had stopped as the silver poisoning progressed through his system. I could probably reach them with my beak, but my beak was large, and thick, and would tear his flesh. I didn't see another solution. I plunged my beak into the first hole in his flesh. I grabbed the slug and yanked it out and dropped it to the ground. Fletcher grunted but tried to stay still and quiet. I reached for the next.

With each one, I felt Fletcher's life slip away. The blood loss, the silver, it was going to be too much, I had to be faster. I pulled out another, and another, faster and faster, not caring anymore if I hurt him, just worried he wouldn't last long enough for me to pull the poison from his system. Finally, I pulled out the last one. Seven. Seven silver bullets in his body.

I breathed for a second. The next thing Dr. Burns said was that he had to shift to survive. I'd removed the bonds, and he had survived my awkward surgery. His wounds were slowly closing. But Fletcher lay still, exhausted, life force drained. I didn't know if I could get him to shift, and my heart filled with despair. I shifted to my human form and took his face in my hands. "You have to shift, Fletcher. Please! You have too, I need you. Please don't leave me."

His head was heavy in my hands. He couldn't lift it on his own. His brilliant blue eyes gazed up into mine. He tried to speak, but nothing came out. His eyes glazed over, and I knew he was giving up. I set his head down gently. I rocked back on my heels and glanced up to see the fight. Dr. Burns had lost ground, and the fight was getting closer. This was it. If he didn't try now, he wouldn't make it.

I leaned back in. "Fletcher, you have to try. I'm not going to let you give up, so you man up and shift!" I yelled, then I slapped him.

His eyes popped back open, and the anger built on his face. His teeth sharpened, and his face began to elongate. I pulled his clothes off, to free him. His feet under his shoes and socks lengthened, his heels turning into hocks, and his body started to grow fur. I heard the bones changing, breaking and reforming, and his back arched with pain. Finally, he lay there, in his wolf form, panting. He would live. I breathed a sigh of relief and turned to the fight. The doctor was losing. There was no other word for it. He was fighting a giant grizzly, a wolf, a wolverine, and a giant eagle. Strange animals, they looked unnatural. All shifters. I tried to find a form that could help. My raven wouldn't do a thing, and neither would my river otter. The wolf, maybe, but I was out classed in weight.

I had no other animal. But Fletcher wasn't in any shape to fight. Frustration and fear were clawing at my guts. I reached and reached for a form I could command that would help in the fight. I needed to save my love, myself, my friends. I reached with all my soul, and the reaching touched something. Knowledge snapped into my body, and I shaped the greatest creature I could find.

My body stretched, and reformed. I grew and grew. My body was covered in thick fur, my arms stretched and became heavily muscled. My hands had hard and thick nails. I looked down and realized I had to look a long way down. I took a few awkward steps, my stride immense. I was an Urayuli. I roared my anger. The combatants froze. Their heads swiveled towards me. When the sound from my throat ended, they continued fighting, but they were aware of me, and the fight was now aimed in my direction.

This body was odd. I felt its incredible strength, but it also had some other abilities. I wasn't even sure what they were, but they tickled my awareness. I ran towards the fight. The wolverine was closest. I grabbed it by the tail and hurled it towards the cabin. It slapped into the wall and crumpled into a heap. They were tough little animals, strong and like a miniature bear in nature. It lay stunned.

I lurched back into the fight, grabbing at the animals, and thrusting them away from Dr. Burns's wolf. He shook blood free from his fur, and head down, panted for a moment. I stood in front of him, facing the grizzly—the biggest threat in my mind. Unlike me, the grizzly had huge claws for tearing and grabbing. I had very large human-like hands; the nails were thick and strong, but they were blunt. I didn't have a muzzle, although I could feel large canines with my tongue. I would have a harder time biting than the bear. My only weapon seemed to be my ability to grab and throw with my great strength. I charged the bear.

He growled a low warning at me, his paws reaching and slashing. I roared back and grabbed one of the clawed paws. This form was fast. I could see the speed of the bear, and I could respond. The bear was also incredibly strong, and I grappled with it, unable to stop its lurching motion. A loose paw raked down my side. The pain angered me, and fire burned along the scratches. I grabbed his other paw.

That didn't stop him; he still had the ability to move his head, and I couldn't get far enough away to avoid his teeth. He bit down on my shoulder, and I screamed. It felt like he was trying to rip away my flesh, and I couldn't let go, or I'd be unable to avoid the claws. I screamed again, and I hit something—a note or a tone—and the bear froze unable to move.

I let go with one hand and removed his teeth from my flesh. Then I grabbed him around the chest in a hug. I squeezed until I heard his bones snap, ribs and probably spine, and I let go. If he was like me, he wasn't healing from that. The bear lay crumpled at my feet, and I screamed at it again, that tone reaching throughout the clearing around the cabin.

I turned and saw that all were frozen in place, waves of fear were tumbling through the air, and I could smell it on the breeze. I stood, confused for a moment. The heat of the fight had ended, and my side ached. I could feel blood crusting my hair and reached a hand to survey the damage. Suddenly, I was utterly exhausted and found I couldn't hold my form. The landscape changed perspectives, and I was myself, my own height—nothing but an average, naked woman—standing wounded in a field of enemies.

It seemed like minutes, but it was probably only seconds before the others started to fight again. I stood, unable to move, wearing nothing but my long hair and unable to shift. I swayed on my feet. I'd burned through all my energy reserves and had lost blood. If someone wanted to kill or capture me now, nothing could stop them. I sank down to my knees.

Dr. Burns's massive wolf made short work of the eagle and the other wolf. The wolverine hadn't gotten back up, so maybe I had done more damage than I thought. Maybe I had killed two of the shape-changers. I wasn't sure how I felt about that. I was too tired now. I'd think about it later. I struggled up to my feet. I had to get to Fletcher. There were two men left, and they had guns loaded with silver.

I shambled, that was the only word for it, around the dead animals, and the slavering wolf. The armed men were currently out of sight, but I knew they were around somewhere. Obviously, their silver rounds didn't do the damage to the older wolf that they'd done to Fletcher, and they were afraid of him. If they were fully human, they were no match for the massive werewolf. I stumbled to Fletcher, who still lay on his side in wolf form. His breathing was smoother, and his wounds were closing. I wondered how fast his healing would be now. Would he snap back soon? Would he need time to heal internally? I put my hand in his warm fur. His eyes snapped open, and he attempted to sit up.

"No!" I whispered. "They're still out there with guns!" I warned.

He whimpered but continued to sit up on his haunches. He was still struggling, but he couldn't even lift his head minutes ago. Maybe his healing would accelerate now that the silver was removed, and the wounds were closing. He'd have to replace blood and I had no idea how quickly his body could do that. I wrapped my arms around him, so grateful he was still alive, that my heart filled my chest. He licked me. I didn't even mind.

We were both wobbly, but we walked to the edge of the woods together, so we could see what was happening. Dr. Burns joined us. He was covered in blood. I couldn't tell what was his. His wounds were healed, but that didn't mean that the blood soaked into his fur wasn't his own. He'd made a mess of the remaining animals, having torn them apart. Most of the blood on his face and chest was probably from that.

The armed men weren't in my line of sight, but I knew if we didn't stop them now, they would be back with more reinforcements. Fletcher and I weren't going to be much help in a fight, but maybe we could fake them out. I didn't think I could shift again without refueling, and I desperately wished I had my clothes and my gun. I needed to get Bran because another person would be helpful in finding the missing men.

First things first though. I had to stop them from leaving. I used the cover of the trees, to make my way back to the airplanes. I needed to disable them. Without the power of flight, they weren't going too far. I was an A&P as well as a pilot, so I had good knowledge of airplane mechanics.

I should be able to pull the spark plugs without too much trouble, although reaching into the engine would probably require more energy than I had. I usually needed a step ladder. Tools were important too, and I had pulled mine from my plane before taking off. Hopefully, I could find what I needed in the other cockpits. I needed to remove them and place them where they couldn't be found.

Fletcher stayed close by my side, unwilling to let me go alone. His fur brushing my leg was welcome and soothing. Dr. Burns led the way, his bulk a welcome sight since he was our only weapon. We slunk through the trees, heads on swivels as we scanned for the missing men. Nothing.

That worried me, and I'm sure it worried my silent companions. I figured they may be by the planes, attempting to escape, but no one was there. That worried me even more. What were they planning? What were they up to? We didn't have much more fight left in us. I searched the nearest plane for tools. Nothing. The next had a few. I grabbed a pair of pliers; I didn't intend to do this precisely, just get it done.

I quietly eased up the engine cover and yanked out the spark plugs. I had to hold them in my hand since I didn't have any pockets. I took them from each plane, including mine, although I did that one much more carefully. When I finished, I had more than I could carry in just my hands, so I had Fletcher dig a hole under my wing and bury them.

Unless someone was watching, there was no way to see the hole in the grass, particularly under the shadow of the wing. We also searched the planes for food. All three of us were suffering from calorie loss. I had another granola bar in my plane, but only protein would work for the two large predators.

I opened the cockpit of the other Super Cub. I found some jerky, but it was more like a snack. I offered it to Fletcher. He took it gently, inhaling the small offering. The next plane had a bag of sandwiches, several ham and cheese, and one tuna. I offered those to both wolves, and they consumed them in a few bites. That was all I found. It would have to do, but it wasn't nearly enough.

My small pack followed me to my secret tree where I'd left Bran. She took one look at us, covered with blood and gore, and gasped. Unlike the other two, my wounds were still breaking open and bleeding some, although not severely. My Urayuli form had been heavily muscled, and the wounds hadn't been as deep as I'd feared. I pulled on my clothes, gratefully. I tucked my gun back into the back of my jeans. Then the four of us headed back to the cabin to find the true monsters of the hour. The men who had tortured and tried to kill Fletcher. Mike and his companion.

I didn't think the two men were any match for us, wounded and exhausted as we were, but they were armed, they were fresh, and they were smart. A silver bullet to any vital area would effectively remove Bran, Fletcher, and me. I wasn't sure about the doctor. He seemed to shrug off silver just fine.

The large wolf seemed to know the woods well. That made sense since he'd been watching Fletcher, and his bushcraft was ancient. I let him take the lead. He was amazing to watch. He moved like liquid and could melt soundlessly through the tree shadows. In contrast, Bran and I sounded like a herd of caribou crashing through the underbrush.

He was patient with us. We couldn't move as quickly as he did. Fletcher was still struggling, and I wasn't much better. Bran helped me along when I stumbled. A thought kept tickling the back of my mind as we walked, as stealthily as we could, back towards the cabin. They knew about werewolves. How? Mike and his unknown companion weren't in our secret circle of the knowing. Also, they had four shadow winged companions. How did they find them? My dad hadn't known of others. He thought those like us were dying out.

Who was behind this? Mike? Did he go after Bran because of me? Who knew about me that would have informed them? Raleigh? How did they know about Fletcher? They were obviously surprised by Dr. Burns. These thoughts roiled around in my mind, and all I could do was guess. All my guesses did was make my head ache and my guts grip with anxiety. That weird extra sense I attributed to Raven was pinging hard and telling me that we had stumbled on something a lot bigger than gold thieves.

I was panting and Fletcher's head was hanging when the doctor stopped. We drooped into the shadows, and I heard some distant voices. The big werewolf looked back at us and gestured with his snout that we should stay. We all slumped down as he melted away to spy.

I caught my breath and checked on Fletcher. He appeared to be healed, but I could tell that the healing had seriously sapped his ener-gy. I wish I had more food to offer him, but all I could do was pet his head and rub his ears, so he knew I understood. He laid his head in my lap. Bran also leaned against me. She was the freshest, but the stress was getting to her. We had given our safety wholly to the doctor and his strength and experience. I didn't feel right about that. I still wasn't sure how far we could trust him.

"Bran," I whispered.

"Yeah?" she responded when I paused, trying to fully process my thoughts.

"I think we should circle around behind the planes and come from the other direction. Dr. Burns shouldn't have to do this alone. We don't know if they have any more men, weapons, or what kind of traps they could have set. We should hedge our bets."

"Sounds good. I've got a bad feeling and it won't go away. I think we need to do something," she responded.

Fletcher nodded his head and stood stiffly.

I started to head in the same direction that the professor had gone, but Fletcher grabbed my sleeve and pulled me further back into the woods. Bran nodded and followed. I let him lead us. Even though I was very familiar with the property, his wolf form had better senses, and I felt the zing that told me this was the better path. Bran grabbed the back of my shirt, and I pulled my gun out and held it down to my side. My other hand was buried in Fletcher's fur as we followed him into the deepening twilight.

Part of me wanted to join Fletcher in my wolf skin as it grew darker, knowing my senses would be well needed, but the feeling that seemed to be on overdrive told me I needed to stay in this skin. I gripped my gun and prayed that we would all be safe. At this point, I just wanted us to escape and go home, but I knew that wouldn't end this. I was afraid that only death would. These people knew about supernaturals, and I couldn't help but feel that the gold was only the tip of the iceberg. The supernatural thing was important to these people, and we would never be safe from them.

Once we were deep in the forest, Fletcher turned us around until we were headed back towards the landing strip. I yearned to leap in my plane and fly away but shook myself out of it and followed Fletcher back around towards the cabin side. The forest was unnaturally still. I wondered if my Urayuli brethren were watching, or if their shy nature had caused them to escape deeper into the forest. I wished I dared to ask for their help again, but this wasn't their fight. They had long forsaken the company of the human world, and they owed me nothing.

In the far back corner of the landing strip, the land cleared where it joined the stream, and we had a stretch to traverse that offered no cover. We crouched in the tree line to make sure our way was unobserved. The planes were parked more than a football field away, so they offered little cover. The darkness was still not complete, so we'd be walking in full view of anyone that was looking. The best thing to do was to fly above and look for observers, but I didn't know if I could shift twice more on my reserves.

This was our very lives. I didn't have the option to wimp out. I had to find the will to continue. I set my gun down on the ground under the tree, Bran looked at it fearfully, like it could leap up and start shooting on its own. I rolled my eyes.

"I'm going to scout ahead. Stay here," I whispered.

Fletcher growled in response, trying to tell me no, but at the same time sat down heavily and hung his head in submission. Even growling was exhausting to him. Bran grabbed my sleeve.

"Are you strong enough?" she asked. Concern darkened her eyes, and her hand on my arm trembled.

I sighed wearily. "I have to be."

With that, I surged out of my clothes, wings beating heavily and dragged myself towards the sky. The darkness wasn't much of a deterrent to my sharp raven eyes. Even though ravens aren't considered nocturnal, I could see far more of the light spectrum as a raven than a human. There was enough light that my raven could see clearly and far away.

I strained to gain altitude quickly so I could rest and glide. Usually flying was joyful. The wind and the sun were my sisters, and they bathed my feathers with light and life. Now, exhaustion hung from every feather pulling me to earth like slowly hardening tar. I beat my wings through will only and rose slowly into the darkening void above me. Finally, I rose high enough that I opened my wings and let the wind bear me. My shoulder and wing muscles burned and if I survived, I was going to be very stiff and sore tomorrow.

I circled above the landing strip, searching every inch of the area. I could see it clearly, and it was empty of human life. A squirrel raced across and leapt into a tree, chittering his fear and warning to his family. A porcupine lumbered at the tree line; seeking food, this was its favorite time—that crossover to the night. Other than vaious small creatures, I saw no life. I looked for the professor, but I couldn't find him either. I hoped he was hidden and watching, safe. I couldn't see anything that should stop us from crossing, so after another pass for safety, I headed back to my friends and my clothes.

I landed heavily, utterly exhausted. My arms were lead as I clumsily pulled on my clothes. When I finished, I barely had the strength to sit down and rest. I put my head between my knees for a moment to stop the buzzing between my ears, then I shook out my arms trying to relieve the numbness that was building. Bran and Fletcher gave me the time to recover as much as I could. I did need to hurry, or my spying would have been for naught.

"It's clear," I finally managed to mumble. "We should go now."

I stood shakily and Bran took my arm. Fletcher heaved himself up and our poor little pack started to move across the empty landing strip to the safety of the next patch of woods.

If I thought I was tired before, I was completely nuts. I could barely lift my feet, and I stumbled several times. I was leaning on Bran's slighter figure too much and she was also starting to strain. Fletcher wasn't much better. My wounds ached to the point I couldn't put the pain aside, and I was growing scared that I wouldn't be much help in the coming struggle. I needed to recover my strength faster, and it wasn't happening.

We made it back to my original spying hole without incident, and we all rested. I could see the back of the cabin again, but still no one else was in sight. No Mike, no unknown bad guy, and no Dr. Burns. I was growing concerned. Did he make it here safely? Was he observing somewhere unseen? It was like he'd disappeared. Also, where was Mike and his toady? In the cabin? They had to be. We could see all around the clearing from here, except for immediately in front of the cabin, and we could no longer hear voices. I was going to have to go look around the corner of the cabin to see. That meant I was going to have to leave the cover of the trees. I told Bran and Fletcher what I wanted to do.

"No!" Bran said softly. "It's my turn. I've done nothing while I've been here but shuttle back and forth from hiding. Both of you are wounded and exhausted. Piper, you're so tired you can barely walk. I can do this."

I knew she was afraid because her voice squeaked and wobbled during her speech.

But I also knew she was right. She was competent, and we had treated her like a child, keeping her out of danger. I'd brought her because I knew her to be formidable. I had to let her go. I nodded. Fletcher growled in disagreement, but he had little choice, being nearly out of the fight as his body used his reserves to heal his internal injuries.

She stepped out of hiding and crouched low to run across the small space to the side of the outhouse toward the cabin. She crouched under the window and snuck up to the corner. She peered around it and quickly drew back. She did it one more time and then slunk around the corner out of our sight.

I wanted to yell, "Come back!" and my heart sped up quickly.

Fletcher stood as though he were going to race after her, and I grabbed his ruff.

"No!" I whispered.

We had to trust her instincts now and wait. It was nerve racking worrying about someone else. My worry for Bran started the sweat pouring off me. I scritched my fingers through Fletcher's fur, and he leaned heavily against me.

I heard voices and tensed. Fletcher stood, and I felt his readiness quivering through his fur. The two men came into view. It looked as though they were headed towards the cabin, and I swallowed in fear for Bran. Where was she? Had she gone in the cabin? I wished we could see her or warn her. I lost sight of them. I started to walk towards the cabin. Fletcher grabbed my hand and pulled me back.

We slunk back under cover just as Bran burst from the back door and ran to our side of the outhouse. She leaned against the back wall and glanced around. Then she made a dash back towards us using the outhouse as cover.

"They weren't in there. They have Dr. Burns!" she panted. Fletcher moved us deeper into the woods, worry scrunching up his wolfy face. I nodded and grabbed Bran's elbow to lead her with us.

"He's tied up in some kind of net thing," she said when her breathing steadied. "I tried to get him free, but I didn't have time." She took another breath. "I think it's enchanted somehow."

I started in surprise.

"I could feel it vibrate in my hands," she continued. "I tried to deactivate it, since I think he could rip it free with his teeth if I could, but I didn't have enough time." Her frustration was clear. "He looked miserable. I didn't know what else to do to help him," she said dejectedly.

I shrugged, helpless. "We need to know what they're doing, what they're saying," I responded. It was the only next step we had.

"I'll go back," she said. "The window on the plane side is open. Maybe I can hear something that will help."

We had no choice. We had to accept her help. So back to the cabin she went, staying low and keeping to the deepening shadows. It was growing dark enough that walking without being observed was easier. However, I was beginning to wonder if our aggressors were even human themselves.

I was getting my second wind. Although not filled with energy, I felt stronger and more rested. I think Fletcher was too. Both of us needed some serious calories, but we were going to have to worry about it later. We needed to make a plan. This sulking about in shadows was wearing on us. I could feel Fletcher's need to do something. First off, we needed Dr. Burns. He was the best resource we had.

It was taking Bran forever. I was growing restless. Just as I was about to run into the dark after her, we heard her rustling in the brush.

"There you are," she said, breathlessly. "It's getting too dark for me," she added.

"What did you hear?" I interrupted, impatiently.

She sighed, her usual response when she thought I was being rude. I smiled, it was a normal thing, it relieved a slight amount of pressure from my brain to see this expected response.

"I didn't understand some, but this is what I did put together." She took a breath. "Someone hired them to catch a werewolf. They'd planned to take Fletcher, but they must not have anyone who'd seen his werewolf form before."

"Why do you think that?" I interrupted.

"Because they don't recognize Dr. Burn's form. They were excited about it. They know he's a werewolf because of his healing and the net working like it does. They were arguing about it. But they aren't exactly sure what kind of werewolf he is." Another breath, a swallow. "They definitely don't know who he is. They dismissed you, so I don't think they know you're a shapeshifter, either."

I was surprised. They had those other shadow winged men, so it wasn't a stretch they'd know about me.

"They were lent the shape changers by their employer who is on his way."

"How much time?" I demanded.

"I don't know, sounds like it could be any time between now and morning. No one said exactly."

"Was there any indication that they might be…more than human?" I asked nervously. She shook her head.

"Sorry. I'd say they could be anything, but I dated Mike. I thought he was one hundred percent human, but then he tortured and tried to kill Fletcher, is trying to rob him, and has a bunch of supernatural hitmen working for him, so my judgment is way off," she retorted with steam.

I put my finger over my lips to remind her to be quiet.

She shrugged sheepishly. "I wish I'd never met him," she added.

I nodded sympathetically. I was sure she was feeling guilty right now, but it wasn't her fault. He seemed like a decent catch—no pun intended—from the outside. A tall, good-looking man with a decent job. You just don't expect a psychopath to have a good job. Particularly at a fish hatchery. He was perfect on paper. The only thing I would have said was *off* was the fact he always smelled slightly fishy and was a little boring, but that made him feel even safer. She couldn't be judged on her choice. He fooled us all.

"Could you see who he was with? Who's the other guy?" I asked.

She shrugged. "I don't know. He has dark hair and Mike called him something that I couldn't hear. Maybe started with a G."

"Huh." I was still uncertain who he was. The lawyer's last name started with a G, but that wasn't a definitive reason to think that it was him. Could be G for George or Greg or Gus. I gave a mental shrug. "Any mention about the gold?"

"Yes, they appeared to be arguing about it before they came in. The other guy seems to think that's more important than capturing the werewolf. But Mike seems to think it's just extra. He'll look for it, but he doesn't seem to care either way. I don't know what that means or how it helps us."

"Me either. It's just something gnawing in the back of my mind, and I can't seem to figure out why," I replied.

I shuddered. Goosebumps pimpled my skin. Fletcher growled lightly. He plucked at my sleeve with his teeth. I looked down at him. He was scratching something in the dirt. I crouched down so I could see better in the dark. He was writing clumsily with his paw. "Kill" was all it said. I nodded.

"I agree." I looked at Bran. "We're going to have to kill them."

She looked stunned, but I saw her nod. It was almost imperceptible, but I knew she understood. They'd already tried to kill or capture us. My conscience was clear.

Bran was shaking. I could hear her teeth chattering. I grabbed her arm and squeezed. When we woke up this morning, none of us had remotely contemplated having to take a life. It wasn't even the beginning of a thought. It was intimidating, and it made my stomach churn. But I also didn't think that anyone would be trying to kill me or this group of people I loved either. I found I had real space in my head where killing was an acceptable solution. I'd analyze that part of me later. I knew Fletcher would agonize over it, and Bran definitely would. She wouldn't even hunt. Well, we had to survive before we could tear ourselves apart with it. That was the bottom line.

Fletcher licked my hand. I must have been frozen in thought for a moment.

I smiled down at him. "Well, I have no plan, you can't talk, and we're all scared. I guess we should just go while they're trapped in the cabin and there are more of us."

They nodded.

"So, Bran and I take the front, and you take the back?"

Fletcher nodded again.

"Can you handle the door in this form?" I directed to Fletcher.

Again, he nodded.

"I'll whisper when we're ready so we can go in together. That alright with everyone?"

More nervous nods.

If they were prepared, someone, maybe all of us were going to get shot. We couldn't leave the professor alone, and we had to end this before we got killed or captured, anyway. I took a deep breath.

"Bran, it's your job to deactivate the net."

She nodded.

I looked at Fletcher, he met my eyes. We were thinking the same thing. "Okay, let's go." And we walked quietly towards the cabin.

Chapter 25

Bran and I slunk up to the outhouse, peered around, and slid along the back of the cabin until we were by the door. Fletcher had trotted boldly right up along the side since his back was below the window, and he hardly made a sound. I waited a moment, until I was sure he was in position, and I had my hand on the pull. I whispered, "Now!" knowing Fletcher could hear me and yanked on the string that operated the latch and pushed my way in, Bran on my heels.

It was a large cabin for a bush cabin, but with the furniture, the stove, the two men seated at the table, and the very large werewolf, there wasn't much room for a fight. Fletcher flew in like he was possessed. I led with my gun and opened fire at the men, careful not to hit Fletcher.

Bran was at the net, behind the wolf and out of the mess. I wasn't watching her. I hit the man closest to me in the thigh. He had sprung up right before I fired, and I didn't have time to adjust my aim. He went down hard, screaming in agony. Fletcher had the other man pinned to the ground, his teeth around the man's face and throat. I grabbed the men's guns and pulled them out of reach.

A popping noise behind me made me whip around. Bran was calmly pulling the net off of a very pissed off werewolf. He stalked over to the man I shot. I backed out of his way. He grabbed the man around his bleeding leg and bit down hard. The man screeched briefly and passed out. He let go.

I glanced over at Fletcher. He was still holding the other man by the face, and I realized that his instinct was to suffocate his prey like a wolf would in the wild by grabbing the animal's snout.

"Fletcher," I said softly, and his eyes flicked to mine. "We should probably ask him some questions."

Fletcher's growling faded, and he let go. He padded to my side.

I grabbed a knife from Fletcher's utensil collection and began cutting up the net. I used it to bind both men where they lay. The one Fletcher had tried to suffocate was awake, and now that I could see his face, I realized it *was* Fletcher's lawyer. That sniveling little *bastard*. He didn't look all slick and professional now. He looked like the weasel he was. His face was bloody where Fletcher's teeth had scraped and pierced the skin, and he was crying, snot bubbling out of his nose. Mike was still passed out. It didn't matter. I was putting a bullet in them the second we had the information we needed.

I heard shifting—that nauseating sound of breaking bones and sloshy fluids and watched, fascinated, as Dr. Burns shifted back to his human form. He was quick. Much quicker than Fletcher. What took Fletcher minutes only took him seconds. I looked away when he finished and lay panting naked on the floor. Fletcher thought faster than me, and drug over a pair of his stretchy athletic shorts to the naked man. He thanked Fletcher and pulled them on.

I know Fletcher was nervous to change back, I could read it in his body language. I shook my head at him when he looked at me questioningly. Dr. Burns was so much bigger than I remembered. I'd only seen him sitting before. Now, he tried to stand. The cabin that accommodated Fletcher's and my average heights was not as kind to the doc's massive form. He must have stood over six feet six inches and that was probably the height of the cabin roof on the low ends of the very slight pitch. He wouldn't be able to wear shoes and stand straight.

Fletcher's shorts were nearly obscene on the man, and I had to keep forcing myself to stop staring. He was insanely muscled. I had never seen a human that was so cut. His muscles had muscles. It was amazing and disturbing. I wondered if it was natural or part of his engineering. He had indicated he was *made*. I wondered what that really meant.

His skin had ever-so-slightly crisscrossed marks over it that matched the pattern of the net. I wondered what the net was made of, or what the enchantment was that the big wolf couldn't heal instantly from. The marks already looked old though, so he wasn't going to scar permanently.

"Bran," I shouted suddenly, "Did that net mark your hands?"

She looked down quickly at her hands and shook her head. "No." She double checked after seeing the doctor's skin. "It just felt tingly, no burns or anything."

"Are you okay?" I addressed the professor. He nodded and rolled his shoulders. His muscles popped and stretched under his skin.

I watched boldly, fascinated. I pointed to the marks.

He looked down and frowned. "I don't know what that net was. It didn't burn me or hurt, but it drained all my energy. I could barely raise my head."

"Yes!" Bran exclaimed. We all looked at her. "Sorry. It was like a kind of electrical field, or something." She put her hands on her hips, her thinking stance. "Not exactly, but like that only magical. Anyway, I used my new zapper to short it out."

"So, it could come back on?" I queried, looking at the mess I had made tearing it apart.

"I don't know. If it could, it probably won't now that you cut it up," she replied, a little snippy, like I had torn up a favorite toy or something.

Mike groaned.

We turned to him. The lawyer was watching us, and Mike was struggling up to full consciousness. Dr. Burns dragged both men and sat them up against the front door. I couldn't remember the lawyer's first name, not that it was important. He tried to say something, but the instant sound came out, Dr. Burns cracked him across the face with an open-handed slap that rang through the cabin.

"You may not speak until I tell you you can," he spat out. "First, who are you?" He folded his arms over his chest.

The lawyer stared up with defiance, but when Dr. Burns raised his hand as though to slap him again, he quickly responded, "I'm Antony Georgetti, Vanice Fletcher's lawyer."

Mike wasn't defiant, but his voice was sullen. "Mike Evans, manager of the Anchorage fish hatchery." He didn't mention Bran.

She glared at him. I knew she was hurt and deeply disturbed at his betrayal. I'd have kicked him if I were her.

"Who do you work for?" Dr. Burns continued with his questioning.

Both men were silent. The wolf raised his hand again, before he could strike Mike blurted out. "We can't tell you, or they'll kill us."

The professor was quiet for a minute, then he let out a loud guffaw. "I'm going to kill you as soon as you answer me. I'll make it quick though, a bullet through the brain. If you don't answer me, I won't make it quick." His face was chilling. He meant every word, and none of us doubted he'd do it. They also read his face and the truth ringing in the air.

You could almost read the decisions being made on their faces. I would have held out for as long as I could, hoping for a miracle, trying to prolong my life to the last, but these two men were scared. You could see they had no hope for life, and the best they could do was a bullet to the brain. The only choice they had was the measure of pain they wanted to endure.

Mike straightened up. He was still bleeding, and his face was pale. "We work for the Silla Corporation."

A chill ran down my spine. I looked at Bran, her face was white. She mouthed, "Silla?" to me, and I shuddered. There were a lot of Alaska native corporations. That's how the money paid to us in 1971 by the United States government was handled. There were thirteen initial corporations and others formed to handle that and oil money. I hadn't ever heard of the Silla Corporation. It had to be a native corporation. Silla was a god, for lack of a better word, of my people. It was funny, but the gods of the Inupiaq and Inuit were quite similar. And none of them were completely benevolent. Most had a dual aspect. Silla's was all-powerful but completely amoral. I hoped fervently it was a weird coincidence.

"Who are they, what do they do, and what do they want?" Dr. Burns continued.

Mike sighed, pained.

The lawyer answered, "They are everywhere, and they want to control everything if they don't already. You can't escape them."

I shuddered again all hope snuffed by that statement. Bran looked at me. Both of our eyes were wide with fear.

"Who do you report to?" He continued.

"A man named Aningan Silla."

A human? My mind raced.

"Who is coming, when will they be here?" the old wolf continued.

"We don't know. Someone with a helicopter to transport the wolf," the lawyer continued, then gulped as he realized a wolf was the one who was going to end his life.

"So, a worker bee, not a power player," Dr. Burns stated.

The lawyer and Mike nodded.

"How do you know about us?" He glanced around the room indicating himself, and Fletcher.

Mike started, "We, or rather, Tony knew about your gold from before. He's been up here several times looking for it. I've helped him once or twice, but it must have been hidden really well. Tony saw him," he pointed with his chin at Fletcher, "change." He paused and swallowed. He was fading fast, blood pooling under his leg. "He told me, and I mentioned it to one of my higher ups in the corporation. They're always searching for supernaturals. They ordered me to capture him. I didn't know about you. They never said that you weren't really wolves. I don't know what you are." He gulped.

"We are wolves," the professor said blandly. He didn't bother explaining more. "You work at the fish hatchery, how are you involved with this…Silla Corporation," Dr. Burns spat out as though it were an evil taste in his mouth.

"I was recruited as a scout. I'm one of many that search for supernaturals and report to them. I get a commission if they are proven to be true supernaturals. It's a way to earn on the side for little work."

"How did you get involved?" Dr. Burns kicked the lawyer's foot, so he knew he was asking him.

He skulked and answered sullenly, "I did because of him." He gestured towards Fletcher. "I just wanted the gold. I didn't want any of this."

The huge wolf regarded him, then dismissed him with a snort as the greedy trash he was. Georgetti hung his head. He was going to die for his greed and getting mixed up in something that was well out of his league.

Meanwhile, Fletcher found a space by the bed and began his shift. I watched, worried about his strength. I realized he probably had questions of his own, so I grabbed his clothes and waited for him to finish while the professor continued his interrogation. Bran huddled close to me, her shivering telling me she was frightened too.

"Do you know why they want supernaturals?" Dr. Burns asked after a long pause.

"No," he scoffed. "I'm not important enough to know those details. I only report and occasionally help with a capture."

"You do know they are kidnapping people then," the doctor stated coldly. No answer was really expected. The men just nodded briefly.

Fletcher finished and lay panting for a few moments as the questioning continued. I tuned it out, mostly disgusted and frightened, my stomach churning. When he was strong enough to stand, I helped him over to sit on the bed so he could dress. I found some food, more granola bars and jerky. We ate greedily. No matter how upset or scared, the body had demands that had to be met.

I could compartmentalize my needs, and right now calories were high on the list and fear low. We were safe for the next few moments; we had to prepare for later. Bran looked green when I offered her some food. So, I set some aside for her and Dr. Burns. He acknowledged it with a nod.

Fletcher seemed to recover his strength somewhat after the food hit his system. I felt better too. I wasn't keen on running any marathons, but I didn't feel weak or wobbly anymore.

The interrogation had continued, although I missed some of it as I couldn't stay focused for long. There was more about the Silla Corporation I'd have to ask about later. Apparently, they knew Fletcher was a werewolf, but no one knew about me or Dr. Burns except for the two we'd captured and the dead men outside. I wondered where Raleigh fit in. Was he another scout for them? Had he turned me in, or was he still unsure?

The werewolf finished his questioning. He turned to us and asked if we had anything we wanted to know. I was wrung out. I'm sure I had a hundred questions, but I couldn't think of one.

Fletcher stood up and walked over to the men. "Why me?" he asked. A simple enough question.

Mike looked at him for a moment with a sneer. "You're isolated, mostly alone, you have no family." He paused to take a breath; he was easily winded. "The corporation thought you were unique since all the werewolves we have captured were animals that could sometimes take a human form. You seemed to be human most of the time. Now that we've seen your animal form, you appear to be some other species of werewolf we haven't studied." He shrugged.

Then his eyes flicked to me. "You would be a great trophy. They collect the shadow winged at every opportunity." He looked me up and down like a prize cow at a fair.

I shuddered in disgust. How did everyone in the world know about shadow winged? I just barely found out. I still wasn't sure what it meant other than a descriptor for shapeshifters like me.

"What does shadow winged mean?" I blurted out. I hadn't even planned to ask.

Mike looked at me in surprise.

"It's what you are," he said simply.

"But what does it mean, why that term?" I asked again. Everyone was silent, watching me and waiting for Mike's response.

"I'm not sure, but all the others like you I have met, can shift into a winged form." He shrugged.

It wasn't an answer. It appeared he didn't know much more than me. I felt an incredible wave of disappointment. I supposed we weren't going to get much more out of the grunts of the operation. I looked at Dr. Burns, so he knew I was done. He looked at Fletcher, Fletcher shook his head. He looked at Branwyn.

"What did you do to that net?" she asked.

Mike shrugged. "I don't know. We were just told to use it for werewolves."

Bran continued. "Did you know how it was spelled?"

He looked surprised. "You mean like magic?"

She nodded her face purposefully blank. She was trying to keep all emotions in check.

He shrugged. "Don't be ridiculous. Magic isn't real."

She shook her head. "Yet you believe in werewolves?" she asked quietly.

"Werewolves are constructs, made with science. Some crazy scientist mixed human and animal genes and wham. Animals can turn human. That's not magic. That's hybridization."

I wasn't that educated in the sciences, but I still didn't think that could be true. Something else was at play here, nothing so simple as someone playing Dr. Frankenstein in a lab.

I used to think Mike was smart. My opinion took an even further dive at his ridiculous statements. I guess it was true; people only saw what they wanted to believe in. If they didn't believe, it didn't exist. I saw similar thoughts cross Bran's face. She walked over to him, the first time she even looked at him for more than a second. She put her hand on his shoulder and zapped him. He jerked, and his body stiffened. She must not have given him much because he recovered quickly, weak as he was. Then she smiled, the smile that is all teeth and no eyes. She showed him her empty hands.

"Was I made in a lab too?"

He looked startled. "How did you do that?" Then he calmed down. "So, you can use a taser," he snapped.

She rolled her eyes and walked away. "I don't have any more questions," she said softly to Dr. Burns.

He nodded. He looked at all of us and I knew what he was going to do. I felt a little sick about it, but I couldn't see another way. We weren't going to be safe if these people were alive.

Just before he moved, I blurted, "Did you kill Clyde?"

Both men looked blank, either they didn't know what I was talking about, or they were deep in their own psyches as they faced their deaths.

Mike stated simply, "Who?" and the lawyer said, "No," at the same time. My jaw dropped in surprise.

The big werewolf picked up both men, one under each arm. I started. It was an amazing feat of strength. He took them outside with the other bodies. To their credit, they did not beg for their lives, they had after all bargained for an easy death, although I did hear sobs.

I waited until I heard two sharp shots, and I knew they were dead. I glanced at Bran and watched as she melted to the floor. I pulled her into a hug. She didn't cry. I think she was as stunned by everything as I was, and whatever she felt for Mike fled when he'd tried to kill us. She clung to me for a moment then pushed me away and stood. The doctor walked back into the cabin. His face was stone. I wondered if killing was hard for him. He seemed to do it so easily. He had an armload of guns. He dumped them on the table.

All of us just stood there, quiet. I think we were in shock. Maybe even Dr. Burns. He and Fletcher started sorting through the guns and assorted ammo. There wasn't much ammo left. I saw Dad's rifle. I grabbed it. It was still loaded.

"I don't see any silver rounds," the doctor said.

Fletcher nodded. "Me either. They mustn't have had much."

"Maybe the grunts don't deserve much of the expensive ammo," I suggested.

Dr. Burns shoved the worthless guns off the table in a fit. He gripped the table with both hands. I heard it creak. I shook myself out of the remaining shock. I had to know if we could trust the old wolf.

A sudden thought gripped me. "What did you do to Jane?" I demanded.

Everyone looked at me.

"Who?" Dr. Burns asked.

Idiot. He wouldn't know her name. I gave *it* to her.

"We ran into a wolf, very timid. We assumed she had escaped your pack. She seemed to know who you are." I continued my description and explanation of Jane.

"My pack, as you are calling them, is not 'my pack,'" he said coolly. "They are descendants of the old wolf bands that were used by the shadow winged in the wars. Most are ignorant of the past. I run with them because we have some similarities, and they accept me. I haven't been back in Alaska long, and it's been at least a hundred years since I was here before. I don't know a wolf that has left the pack, but I don't spend much time with them."

I was confused. How did Jane know him then? "She acted like she'd been abused," I accused.

He shrugged. "I truly don't know."

"What if she were really old like you?"

"There aren't many left as old as me."

I glared at him. "Old as in from the wars."

"It's possible. I was the equivalent of a general. I commanded many. She could have been from an opposing side, I guess."

It was all guessing. I fell silent. He had some loyalty to Fletcher. That was all we had as assurance he could be trusted. I still wasn't sure what had happened between him and Jane. She'd recognized Fletcher's wolf type and was afraid. She seemed to know Dr. Burns—at least his wolf—and was specifically terrified of him. Until we could get them together, we'd never know. The silence stretched.

There was one more elephant in the room. "What do we do now?" I let that float out there before continuing. "They know about Fletcher. I have to assume they'll try again. They have a helicopter coming to pick him up. We have no idea how many more men are coming.

We have six bodies to hide or get rid of. Any suggestions?" That was me. I had a gift for stating the obvious. It wasn't much, but I was good at it. "Oh, and there are two extra planes to make disappear too," I added.

"And a helicopter," Dr. Burns said quietly.

I nodded. "And a helicopter." I knew I could get rid of the planes easily. We had to cross the Alaska Range, a set of rugged mountains to the northeast of the cabin to head home to Anchorage. Many small planes were lost there. It wouldn't be a problem to fly them into a hard-to-reach peak where no one would spot them. The trick was making sure they were off the recorded flight path. Since I doubted they had submitted a flight plan because what they were doing was illegal, I figured if it wasn't along the obvious route, we were good. I could do that easily. Fly the plane, aim towards a certain peak, and then fly out in my raven form before the crash.

I didn't know how to fly a helicopter. I was stumped. "Uh, I can't fly a helicopter," I said. Since no one was listening to my inner monologue, it took them a minute and some explanation to catch up.

"I do," Dr. Burns said softly.

"You do?" I raised my eyebrows in surprise.

"I've been around for a very long time. It leaves time for various pursuits. I flew for the military for many years and privately as well. Helicopters and planes," he answered simply.

Bran, Fletcher, and I looked at each other and back to him. He shrugged, he wasn't trying to brag, just stating the facts.

"Huh," I said. "I guess that answers the question why we keep seeing you out here. You must fly out on your own. Where's your plane?" I asked, suspiciously.

"Well, I bought some land not too far from here. I cleared a runway. There isn't anything much else there. I'm hauling in materials as often as possible to build a cabin and eventually a single hangar."

"Wow, that's ambitious," I said.

"I have a lot of time and patience," he replied without emotion.

"Why here?" Fletcher demanded angrily. Probably because he knew the answer.

The professor shrugged and looked at Fletcher apologetically. "I wanted to be close to you," he answered simply.

"I'm a stranger. A man you had in a class once. I'm nothing to you!" Fletcher continued.

The old werewolf was quiet for a while, contemplative. He was probably searching for the reason, or he hadn't really thought through his motivations before, I didn't know.

"When I learned you'd been changed, I was devastated that you were alone for that. I had wanted a companion, but I never intended to leave that companion alone to navigate this," he swept his hands up and down his body, "alone." He paused, and this time emotion did sweep over his face.

"Long ago, when another of our kind was created, the creator was responsible for them as if they were their child." He looked at Fletcher gently. "Children made this way bear the genetic heritage of their maker."

I was shocked by that, and Fletcher also looked like he'd been smacked. It made some sense to me. Fletcher was an ancient looking wolf breed in his other form, just like the doctor's. I guess it made sense that whatever genetic changes were made that enabled the shift to happen would come from the werewolf "parent" who made him. Fletcher turned away. I'm sure he was feeling some sort of emotion. I couldn't even guess what.

He was without family. This must be overwhelming. Add to that the attack, the torture, the kidnapping, and then all the killing we had to do. I couldn't imagine where his heart was. I wasn't dealing with it because I was compartmentalizing and putting off feeling for later. I was pretty sure that was what Bran was doing as well, since I'd known her longer than I'd known Fletcher. We coped the same. We buried it and let it out in private.

He turned around after a few long moments. His eyes were red-rimmed, but he seemed to hold it together. He looked at the doctor and nodded. Acceptance? Perhaps, I'd have to ask him later. It was also hard to read the Professor's face. He had that stern, stoic look that almost echoed Fletcher's. Where Fletcher's eyes gave things away,

Burn's did not, but he had millennia of practice controlling his face and/or his emotions. These two had a lot to deal with and a rocky road ahead. I suspected a fight—either in wolf or human form—in the future. Men. I shook my head.

Before I could say anything, we heard and felt the heartbeat pounding of helicopter rotors. Whump, whump, whump. We shouldn't have been surprised, but we hadn't been paying attention, deep in our own drama.

The bodies were still laying on the side of the cabin. If the helicopter spotted those, we would lose our slight element of surprise. We should have already hidden them away. Anything we did now would just draw the attention of anyone in that helicopter. Luckily it was dark. The long, late August twilight had finally ended. Maybe they would assume any bodies they saw were us and not their own people.

The men we killed were wearing black uniforms. Professor Burns took dark clothing from one of the larger bodies, I didn't ask from which one. He could probably pass for Mike. Mike was tall, although not as large as the professor. Perhaps from the distance, Fletcher could pass for the lawyer, and maybe if we stood far off and in shadow, Bran and I could pass for the other shadow winged henchmen. Bran, Fletcher, and I were all wearing blue jeans. Bran had those ridiculous boots. True, she got around in them okay, but they wouldn't pass for what those men were wearing. All we could do was pray they didn't notice the difference.

The Doctor had to take the lead; he was the one most passable. As we walked out, he leaned down and swiped a cap off one of the bodies and put it on his head. It didn't quite fit, but it would pass in the fading light. We followed his lead and grabbed caps from off the other bodies. Then we dragged them as close to out of sight on the side of the cabin as we could, praying fervently that we couldn't be seen. We stood away from the lighted cabin in the deepest shadows we could find and waited.

The helicopter landed on the far side of the planes in the middle of the runway. It was the only open spot that was large enough. We heard the rotors wind down as they were turned off. Dr. Burns whispered, "I can't be sure, but I think that's a Bell 212. It can hold up to ten." It was a warning to be ready for any number of hostiles.

My heart sped up even faster as I contemplated having to face ten new enemies in our weakened states. I wiped my hands down my jeans. I swallowed. I could hear the others shifting around, probably doing similar things to me as the adrenaline hit their systems. I pulled my gun out of its holster in the back of my jeans and clicked the safety off. I held it down to my side, slightly behind my hip, finger on the trigger guard. Fletcher did the same.

Strangely, the doctor didn't have a weapon, but then he probably was the biggest weapon of all. I shrugged to myself. Bran stood behind me and to the right, trying to hide since she was the most vulnerable, but also obviously not one of the dead men. I had braided my hair back into a single braid, so in the gathering dark you couldn't see my long hair with the cap on. Bran had done the same although her boots and her small stature were a dead giveaway. We listened for the men to clear the runway and head our way.

They crashed through the brush. They must not have waited for the rotors to wind all the way down. There were three of them. I wondered if the pilot was still on board. My bet was probably. He wouldn't be doing grunt work if there were three, plus the six others they'd assume were on the ground already. Once they were close enough to see, I was surprised one of them was a woman. She wasn't a petite woman either, but a brute as tall as the men with her. All of them wore black tactical gear, including bullet proof vests. I groaned. My gun was a .45 caliber, and it was packing bear rounds, but I didn't know if that would go through a Kevlar vest. That wasn't stuff I studied.

I kept a big handgun for bears, not for heavily armed and armored people. It probably would just hurt like hell. I didn't know. Everything like that I knew came from action movies. Fletcher tensed though, and I figured that wasn't a good sign, even though he was a high school teacher not ex-military. These people looked way out of my league. I wondered if they were shadow winged to boot. Probably not, since they were all geared up. If I were being used for a weapon, I'd be wearing clothes that were easy to get out of.

We had two werewolves, me, a couple of guns and a can of bear spray. They had armored clothing, and a lot of guns. I sure hoped someone in our group could outsmart them or only the old werewolf would be walking away.

"Where's the cargo?" The woman yelled when they were close to speaking range.

"In the cabin," Dr. Burns replied.

"Why didn't you bring it closer to exfil?" she yelled back, sounding annoyed.

"No time. Just got it trapped and secured," he answered. Soon they'd be close enough to see us.

She approached Dr. Burns. "Are you Evans?" she asked when she was standing close enough to converse normally.

"Affirmative."

I remembered the professor had confessed he'd been in the military. What military or when he hadn't added, but it seemed to be working. Hopefully he remembered Mike was a dude who worked in a fish hatchery. She hadn't recognized him, so maybe she had no idea who he was or what he did. That was fine with me, maybe we could fake our way out. At least until they discovered there was no werewolf.

She turned. "Go back and get the sled, and another one of those nets," she ordered. The two men turned obediently and headed back to the helicopter. She turned back, "Have your men drag the cargo out of the cabin."

I followed Bran to the back of the cabin, blocking the view of her the best I could. Fletcher was close behind me. We might have a chance to overwhelm them if we had a werewolf to deal with. Once we were out of sight I whispered to Fletcher, "Can you shift?" We should bring them a werewolf.

"The food helped. I think I can handle it." His eyes glinted in the low light. A feral growl rumbled from his throat. He wanted payback; I could sense it. The dead men were lackeys, these people knew what they were doing, they knew why, and they had no qualms about getting what they wanted at any cost. He stripped quickly and started his shift. Bran and I waited.

Soon he was panting on the floor, his beautiful silver coat gleaming. He scrambled to his feet and shook out his coat.

"I guess we act like you are knocked out and drag you out?" I asked and looked at Bran.

She thought for a moment. "This is your idea."

"Well, we obviously don't have the net, so we better come up with a reason why not. It's probably best if you stay in here. I'll drag him out."

"This is the worst idea ever," Bran snarked.

Fletcher huffed in agreement.

"I'm open for suggestions," I retorted.

Bran stayed back and crossed out the back to stay in the shadows. I pulled the wolf out the front door and out of any stray light. I dumped Fletcher as close as I could while remaining in shadow.

"Where's the net?" the big woman demanded. Luckily the professor was quick on his feet.

"It was ineffective. Something was wrong with it," he answered nonchalantly.

"Where are the other men?" she followed up, sounding suspicious.

"They're cleaning up and gathering their gear." He turned around. "Brower!" he yelled.

I jumped a little. I hope that was someone he'd identified in the pile of dead men. "Bring

that net as well!"

Just then the two new men and a sled came into view. The big woman motioned them around her, and they headed towards Fletcher's prone form. "What did you do to him? They want him alive," she said coldly.

"He's alive, just knocked out," the Doctor said just as coldly.

The men looked to her for instruction. She gestured, and they moved the sled closer to Fletcher. I could see the net resting on the sled, a simple wheeled vehicle for transporting heavy items. We couldn't allow them to touch Fletcher with the new net. That would remove him from the action. My gun was back in my holster, as I couldn't drag Fletcher with it in my hands. If I reached for it, I didn't know if I'd have time before they started shooting. Their leader was already suspicious. I looked to the professor for guidance, but his back was to me. No help there. I reached around my back and lifted my shirt.

My hand grasped the handle, warm from my body. Just then one of the men noticed me. He dropped his hand and grasped the gun that was on a sling tight to his body. I was screwed. No way could I pull my gun free and flick the safety off before he could shoot me.

Just then Bran stepped around me and blasted both men square in the eyes with bear spray. Unfortunately, Fletcher got a whiff and while they writhed on the ground in agony, he scrubbed his muzzle in the dirt, also in pain from the powerful pepper spray. I closed my eyes and looked away until the breeze dissipated. Still, it made Bran and me sneeze violently. One of the men vomited.

The woman turned and ran. She gained some distance before we could react and turned and began firing short bursts behind her. The professor was hot on her heels. Bran and I grabbed the men and disarmed them. Since they were equipped with zip ties, we used them and secured them to the sled with the net. Fletcher's eyes were swollen almost closed and his breath came at a wheeze.

With his accelerated healing, as soon as the pepper spray was rinsed out of his eyes, he should recover quickly. I ran inside the cabin and filled a cup with water. I poured it into his eyes. He sighed with relief once the pepper spray rinsed away. He'd just gotten the over-spray. The other men had gotten the full blast. They still writhed in pain, coughing and sneezing.

He ran after Dr. Burns since Bran and I weren't immune to bullets like the werewolves. We huddled together in the dark, waiting. Shots continued. I heard the helicopter rotors start back up.

Crap, we couldn't let that helicopter pilot leave or radio back. If he did, we were all toast. Bran and I looked at each other.

"Go," she said, eyes wide.

Chapter 26

I flew out of my clothes and then switched to my wolf. I was black, and difficult to see in the dark. Immediately, my surroundings lightened as the ambient light lit the landscape to my wolf eyes. I ran as fast as I could towards the helicopter. I dodged the fighting and took the path between the planes. Since the other two wolves were engaged with the woman, I blew past their position. The helicopter side door was open.

When the men had removed the transport contraption, they'd left the side door open out of sheer laziness. I ducked under the front and leapt into the body of the helicopter. The pilot didn't even know I was there. He was already on the radio. I grabbed his arm. The seatbelt harness kept him secure, and I couldn't rip him free. He scrambled for his sidearm.

I reached around his neck and throat with my teeth and bit down with all the force of my jaws. I felt his neck snap as blood flooded my mouth. I gagged and pulled back. After a moment, I gathered my wits. I couldn't fly a helicopter, but I could turn one off. I looked at the cockpit controls. No digital screens, just regular instruments, and toggle switches. I flipped the appropriate ones with my paw and powered it down.

I hadn't wanted to move the dead man, so I left him sitting in his seat, still strapped in. I glanced at him. He stirred. I jumped back. Shit, he was a *were* something or other. I jumped at him and snapped his neck again. This was going to suck. I had no silver bullets, or gun to deliver it. I was going to have to remove his head. That was as permanent as you could get. I closed my jaws around his neck and bit through flesh and tissue and bone. When his head separated and fell to the floor, I gagged and vomited on the floor. I never imagined I'd ever have to do something like that, and I never wanted to have to do it again.

I hopped out of the helicopter and ran back to the cover of the woods. Intermittent gunfire was still going on in the distance, and I didn't know what was happening. I thought only one person was left, and she must be formidable if she was holding her own against two werewolves and a witch. I circled around until I was behind the cabin again. I slunk around the outhouse and the far side of the cabin, out of the line of fire.

I peered around and couldn't see anyone. I cautiously headed towards the sled where I had left the two men and Bran. Everyone was gone. Since I could hear gunfire, I knew they had to be somewhere close. I went back to the cabin and peered in. Bran was there, crouched low in the dark. She had my clothes. I jogged over to her and shifted back.

"What's going on?" I asked.

"That woman tricked Fletcher and Burns and came back. I hid. She let her guys loose. They are all out there, armed."

"Shit."

"Yeah."

"I think that Fletcher and Dr. Burns might be in big trouble," she whispered.

I nodded. "Do you know where they are?"

She shook her head. "Everyone went the same way you did, back towards the planes."

I'd circled around and behind the planes, not back the way I had initially gone.

"I think that the men we tied up are some kind of *were* creatures," she added.

"Yeah, so was the pilot," I said flatly.

"Was?" She picked up things too easily.

I shuddered. "I had to kill him—with my teeth." I gagged again and started to shake. I had to pull it together. I'd think about it later; I couldn't now. Now I had to stay alive and keep my friends alive too. "I chewed his head off," I stuttered.

She grabbed my hand to comfort me. Concern lined her face. What we had to do tonight would haunt us all for a long time. I knew it would probably affect Bran worse than anyone, since she was much more empathic than me. So, I appreciated her ability to offer quick comfort in the midst of this horror.

"What can we do?" she asked. She could offer me comfort, but she knew that in this instance, I would have to face the danger and find a way to end it. That was one of my gifts for whatever reason.

"We can hope they can't fly a helicopter," I said, trying to alleviate some stress.

She huffed a partial laugh since it wasn't really funny. "True."

"I guess the only thing we can do is find Fletcher and the doctor." I thought for a moment. "I'll have a better chance with the rifle, I doubt my handgun will work against their body armor unless I am really close, and you probably used up your bear spray." I paused. "Quick thinking by the way. If they hadn't been *were* things, they might still be out of the fight."

She nodded in acknowledgement. "Thanks. Uhm, I think I might be able to disable one if I got close enough to touch them," she said thoughtfully.

"It's something. I don't know if a regular bullet to the brain will kill them or just disable them for a minute. I think a close enough bullet might penetrate their armor or knock them down for a time, but I don't have any silver rounds." We looked off in the distance for a moment. "We have to get close to do anything, but only the werewolves might be able to kill them. I don't think I can do that again," I finished up, softly.

She nodded, understanding that what I had done to the helicopter pilot was dark and haunting.

"Can you do any kind of hiding spell? Invisibility? Anything?" We needed something. We were severely outmatched by the *weres*.

She gave me a dirty look. "I'm not a witch, I can't cast spells." She rolled her eyes.

"Okay, not a spell, but anything?" I asked.

She stood and put her hands on her hips. Then she frowned. "Maybe?" she said uncertainly.

I smiled. We might have some hope of sneaking up on them. Her magic seemed to be, for lack of a better word, natural. It was stuff that you would expect from anyone with mental abilities. Telepathy—which she denied—some telekinesis, clairvoyance, control of elements, etc. It seemed less supernatural and more within the realm of recorded human abilities. So, I was happy, but surprised and uncertain about what it was she could do.

"I think I can make myself less noticeable," she said tentatively.

"You mean invisible."

"That's not a real thing," she scoffed. "I'll just put out a thought that I'm not really there." She was growing frustrated. "It's like a suggestion or..." She trailed off for want of words.

"Invisible."

"Sure, whatever—you aren't listening anyway!"

"Will you bring my clothes and guns, if I go wolfy?" I asked. "Can you make them invisible too?"

She sighed. "Yes."

"Cool. Go ahead, invisible yourself."

She glared at me. Then she stared off into space.

It took a while, and I lost interest and looked away. "Are you ready yet?" I asked after a few minutes had passed.

"Yes, go wolf yourself," she said, annoyed.

I huffed and stripped. I could still see her, so I was a little worried about going

out into the bullets. She didn't appear to be worried though.

"I can see you," I said as she gathered up my clothes.

"Of course, you can. I'm not invisible," she snapped.

"Ummm."

"Piper, you notice me because we're talking, and you know I'm here. I'm tricking their minds, not going invisible. It's some of my grandmother's mind magic."

I shrugged.

"So, it's like I'm sending out a field that says I'm not here don't notice me," she explained.

I smiled, then shifted. She put her hand on my back since she couldn't see as well as me. The area was forested, so in the dark it was easy to stumble around.

I guided her, careful not to run into obstacles. We went as fast as I dared. I thought Fletcher and the professor could hold their own against three humans, but they were potentially up against three *were* creatures who weren't vulnerable like the shadow winged were. That meant the same fast healing that our two werewolves had. And if they were old like the professor, they also had some immunity to silver. Not that it mattered since we didn't have silver ammo anyway.

We could stun them, and take their heads, that seemed to keep them out of it for good. I didn't know if our werewolves had figured that out. The least we should do was warn them. And to warn them, we had to disable the bad guys.

We came in behind them. I could only see the woman and one of the men. I looked around to make sure we weren't in between the enemy party. Nothing. I couldn't see the werewolves. There was still intermittent gunfire by the bad guys. They must have brought a lot of ammo. I wondered if it was all silver. That might solve an issue if we could get a hold of their weapons. I hoped that the noise, and the effect of noise on the ears might help cover us. I also wondered if Bran's invisibility spell extended to me since I hadn't thought to ask. I hoped so.

If the three were all *weres*, which I was pretty sure of, they could probably see as well in the dark as me and the other wolves. I sighed. Bran's hand tightened on my fur. I shouldn't do that when I can't talk. She didn't know what I was thinking. I stifled another sigh.

I walked slowly to get us closer to them. Bran needed to be in touching distance. I needed to be human so I could use a gun. I kept going back and forth, teeth or gun, teeth or gun? I dragged Bran back behind cover. I shifted back.

"What's going on?" Bran asked quietly.

"I'm not sure what to do," I answered. "I could use the rifle, but I see better as a wolf."

"Wolf then," she commanded.

"Yeah, but then I don't have a gun to help disable the bad guys," I explained.

"Well, neither of us can see out here, so wolf," she replied. "What did you see when you sighed and dragged me back?" she asked.

"I could only see one guy and the woman," I answered. "Then I was wondering if your invisibility spell covered me too."

"It's not..." she trailed off. "What does it matter," she scoffed, throwing back her head. "Yes, it's telling them that we aren't there. It's kind of a short-range thing, so it only works if they don't spot us before we get like within fifteen feet or so. I'm not sure. I just know when I've tried to project ideas before, that seems to be my range."

"Oh."

"Now you have all the facts. What are you going to do?" she asked.

"I think that I'll have to wolf it. Put my clothes down." She did. "I'm going to lead you to the man I saw. He is behind and to the left of the woman. You zap him with all you've got." I cleared my throat. "When I killed the pilot the first time, he healed in like twenty seconds and that was from a broken neck. I think the most we're going to get is fifteen seconds, tops." I fought down a wave of nausea. "So, in that fifteen seconds, I'll lead you to the woman and you do the same to her. Then we'll call the boys and have them dispatch these two."

She nodded. "What about the third?" she asked.

"I don't know. I didn't see him," I replied. "We'll just have to hope he's already gone or out of range until we kill these two."

"So, we're hoping for luck?"

"Yup."

"Of course." She sighed.

I shifted. I was tired, but I had no choice. I'd sleep for a week after this if I made it. Not that I could, because I had to work. Sometimes owning a business was a drag. I shook my head and then my whole self. Focus. Bran buried her hand in my fur again, and I led her to the first guy. Her spell thing must have been working because he didn't notice us until she put her hands on his back and zapped for all she was worth. He hit the ground like a brick. I rushed her over to the woman.

It was only about four steps away, judging in human strides. But the man falling must have drawn her attention. She saw us. Bran's "spell" wasn't foolproof apparently. I whirled and pushed Bran down then shielded her with my body just as the woman sprayed the area with bullets.

Bran yelled, "Fletcher!" which was quicker thinking than I had.

I leapt off Bran and toward the woman. I had zero plan, but I couldn't run off and leave Bran, and if we stayed here and I did nothing, we were both going to be suffering severe lead poisoning. So, I jumped at her. Luckily, my move startled her enough that I crashed into her and knocked her off her feet. My body weight kept her gun flat against her. With the gun fire ended, the professor leapt into view. They must have been close and taking heavy shots to their bodies. He was covered in blood and gore.

The woman struggled to free herself. I was heavy, but she was very strong, and I didn't know how long my weight would keep her down. I saw the doctor rip the head off the man who was coming out of his stunned state. Bran crawled towards me. I leapt off the woman as Bran's hands came down and zapped her solidly. Her body twitched and lay still.

Before the doctor could dispatch her like he had the other man, the strangest thing happened.

The woman's body began to shift. The force of it ripped through her clothing and body armor. The only things that remained were her gun harness and rifle. The harness must have been attached with some kind of elastic. She grew and grew into something I'd never seen alive before. Her body stretched until she was standing on four overly long legs. Her body sprouted dark fur and her huge head sported an ugly squashed looking face. I only knew what I was looking at because I'd been to the Anchorage Museum recently with Fletcher. She was a short-faced bear. A leftover, ice age, megafauna freak. She must be ancient like the professor. An original shifter.

We backed away. She was quiet for a minute, still partially stunned by Bran's zap and her change. Then she shook, the immediate impulse we all had after a shift. Her fur settled. She looked directly at me and huffed. She lifted up and slammed her paws into the ground. I swallowed. I'd seen this type of behavior before with modern bears. She was going to charge. With those legs, she could probably outrun me.

I was normal sized for this era, and she was not. Those long legs and slim build made her look like she was built for speed, and even a normal bear was fast over a short distance. I looked around, desperately. The professor, huge as he was, looked small next to her. I saw no way out. I didn't have time to shift into a raven, and this was my next fastest form. I'd have to run. She clacked her jaws. This was it; I could see her gather herself. I spun and ran.

Chapter 27

I tried to run through the trees that were closest together. The only thing I had on her was size. Her speed, her reach, and her strength far surpassed mine. I was only quicker because I had less mass to maneuver. I twisted, I turned, I went over, under and through tight spaces, and still, I could feel her breath coming up behind me.

I hesitated at one spot, and her claws separated the fur along my flank. I couldn't afford any more damage. I was weak and tired, and hurt already. I raced for my life. I tried to see each move ahead of time, letting the wolf instincts go like I never had before. For a moment, I was flying through the forest on four feet instead of wings.

Coming up, I saw a tree with a few low branches. I might be able to leap up into the tree. The bear, if standing, had to be close to twelve or even fourteen feet tall. I'd have to get high or get ahead of her enough to make it up. With the reach of her legs, and the ability of bears to climb, it was a desperate thought. I saw no other way. The wind rushed through my ears, and bit at my eyes. My breath burned my lungs, and my legs were starting to feel like lead weights.

I bore down, and with a burst of speed, pulled ahead. I hit the branch, front feet, back feet, and I leapt high with everything I had and shifted to my raven at the apex. I beat my wings harder than I had before and rose slowly up the tree.

Stroke, stroke, stroke, I chanted in my head to force my wings to comply. I felt like I was going backwards. My panic dragging me down as surely as gravity. I could see the bear. I had confused her for an instant, but not long enough. She stood up, and up, and up. I barely stayed above her, but then she lifted her giant paw, and I realized I wouldn't gain enough altitude before she swatted me out of the air and crushed my delicate bird bones with her enormous paw. I pushed even harder as that paw came towards me.

From the right, a streak of silver launched itself at the side of the bear—Fletcher. He hit her with a tremendous force; it echoed through the trees and vibrated the air. Her reaching had unbalanced her enough that she fell hard and ugly.

I looked away long enough to choose a perch out of reach of the gigantic bear. Fletcher must have been truly fast because it took a few moments before the professor reached him. While the bear fought to right herself, the huge werewolves harried her, leaping in and taking chunks of flesh from her body and leaping out of reach of her vicious claws. In and out, working with that wordless efficiency of a wolf pack. Tearing vital parts, ripping at the belly, the hamstrings, the tendons. Her body had to try to right itself, heal the damage, and stop the ravaging of her flesh.

A massive paw raked the doctor. He yelped and as he was flung into a tree with a hard thump. I heard the crack of bone. He lay still for a moment. It was long enough that the bear was able to right herself with a roar. The horrible sound echoed through our bones.

The bear went after Fletcher, who jumped back. I heard a groan from the professor, and he staggered to his feet. His healing factor catching up fast. Fletcher dodged great swings. The bear was slow because of her damage, although she was healing quickly.

The doctor was back in the fight, ripping her hamstrings. Her back leg buckled. Fletcher grabbed the other and her back end collapsed. They continued their systematic attacks, trying to overload her healing by inflicting damage faster than she could heal.

Desperate to help, I looked around. The woman's gun was close. It must have been ripped free during the fight. Unfortunately, the fight continued in that area, and I didn't trust my timing to get there safely.

I kept looking at it. Did she have silver ammunition? They were trying to capture a werewolf, so wouldn't they be prepared in case something went sideways? Also, it may not matter against the ancient form; silver didn't seem to affect the professor.

I wondered how long it would take her to heal a bullet to the brain. I wasn't sure I could place a bullet accurately if I could get to the gun. Could I lift it in my raven form?

The most I had ever tried to lift was less than two pounds, and the lightest rifle I knew of—from weighing tons of them for my job—was a gun with a titanium action and a carbon fiber stock. It was still around six pounds. I was a large raven though. Maybe I could lift it.

The boys were getting slower. They were tiring. The bear was slower too, but she was still fresher than they were, even wounded. Both wolves were bearing multiple claw wounds now as well. The bear's back end hadn't yet healed, and she was dragging herself with her front paws. Her swipes weren't as vicious as before since she had to support her weight with one leg to swipe with the other. Now was the best time to end this before the wolves were too tired to end the fight for good. I watched until they were as far from the rifle as possible.

I dove down, a black arrow focused only on the rifle strap. I back winged and grasped the broken strap in my beak. Then I beat my wings. I rose quickly until the weight of the compact rifle tugged me down.

The fight was rotating my way again. I struggled to rise, the weight of the gun straining my neck muscles and my wings ached with the added drag. Slowly, I rose, only will power dragging that gun up and up until I was a safe distance from the fight. I chose a sturdy limb to perch on, close to the tree, then shifted to my human form.

I'd done this in the trees before, but as a child, so I was out of prac- tice. I lost my balance briefly, and in trying to regain it nearly dropped the rifle. I bore down with my teeth, knowing the only way to save Fletcher was to keep that gun. I found my balance.

The bark was rough on my naked back and legs as I braced myself against the trunk and balanced by wrapping my legs tightly around the limb. I had to wait as the fight rotated back to give me a clean shot. I exhaled, aimed, and fired.

The bear dropped like a rock. Her front feet went out, and she went down belly first. The boys went to work separating her gigantic head from her body. I looked away. It took a while, because her body fought to regenerate, and they had to rip and tear chunks of flesh from her to beat it. It seemed like forever before the forest grew still and I made myself look down.

Both wolves panted, heads and tails down, but the bear lay still, head several feet away. We had finally prevailed. I looked around for Bran. I hadn't seen her since she'd zapped the bear woman. I didn't have the strength to shift again, so I had to climb down the tree naked, gun strap in my teeth. Luckily, I hadn't gotten up as high as I'd thought.

Apparently, ravens do have weight limits. I stumbled back the way I had come, worried for Bran. Either she was dead or had chosen to stay out of a fight that was far outside of her weight class. I hugged the gun to my chest, the only thing I had to cover myself with. Going back furless earned me a smattering of scratches and abrasions. Finally, I broke through the brush to our last location.

Bran lay on the ground. I ran over to her. She was bloody, but I couldn't see the wound well. I searched her body with my hands. It looked like she had hit her head on something, and the blood had come from that. I remembered my own smashed head and in response, it started to pound again. I raised my hand to my scalp and flinched.

I felt around her head wound, but the bone felt sound to my touch. She groaned. I squatted back on my heels and sighed with relief. She had just knocked herself out in her fall, probably when that bear brushed past her when it ran after me. Maybe I had knocked her down when I took off.

"Piper," she whispered.

"Yeah, I'm here," I said.

"Did you get her?" She asked and sat up. "Ah," she groaned. "Why did you let me do that?"

I chuckled.

"You gotta get up some time," I replied. I took a deep breath. "She's dead."

"Good." She sat holding her head.

I looked around for my clothes and found them right where Bran had left them. I dressed. The two werewolves were sitting patiently, looking away respectfully as I did so. When I finished, they led us back to the cabin with their much better night vision.

We were all exhausted. The wolves had fully healed by the time we got back, but Bran and I were beat up. She with her head wound and various scratches, me with my head wound, bites, scratches and scrapes, and claw wounds. Even my eyelashes hurt. We all needed calories.

I lay on Fletcher's bed with Bran, and he warmed up MREs in a huge pot on his stove. Fletcher and the professor shoveled several into their bottomless stomachs while Bran and I attempted to keep up, an impossible task. We ended with cups of hot cocoa, we needed the sugar load and for me it was a comfort thing, so I made it even though I got odd glances from the professor, who was probably expecting coffee. Bran and Fletcher knew better.

I knew the night wasn't over for me, being one of the two pilots in the room and we had several aircraft to dispose of. It could probably wait, we were out of the way here and rarely did Fletcher get an unplanned fly over, but this organization that was after him was an unknown.

"The pilot was on the radio when I got to the helicopter." That brought all discussion to an end suddenly.

"What?" Fletcher said.

"I don't know what he was able to communicate before…"

"We should get out of here to be safe," Doctor Burns said.

"Should we…clean up first?" Bran added.

The professor shook his head. "We need rest. I don't think anyone will come tonight. They'll assume their crew is cleaning up and they probably won't be missed until later."

Everyone looked relieved. If they were half as tired as me, they didn't want to do a single thing.

"Let's load up the big helicopter and we can stay on my land. It should be safe," he said.

Even though it was a good plan, we spent the rest of the night, after a brief rest, completing the task of ferrying Fletcher's gold, his belongings, everything that was his, from the cabin and sealed it up the best we could. We couldn't remove smells, or tracks, or fingerprints, but we tried.

Once everyone was settled in the new location, I put the planes back in working order and moved my Super Cub to the doctor's property. Then I collapsed. Since we were sleeping rough, I used the very last bit of energy I had to slip into my wolf skin, curl up with my head on Fletcher's flank, and pass out.

Epilogue

The sun woke me. Not the brightness, but the heat of it on my side. Fletcher was still in the shade, but the sun had moved around enough that part of me was in it, and I woke with a start. I shot up and regretted it. Everything ached. I stretched gently and an involuntary whine escaped me. Fletcher bolted up. He whirled around searching for danger. When he didn't see anything, he brushed against me.

I walked over to the Cub, shifted, and got dressed. He did so as well. There was a small one-man tent near where we had slept and since the doctor was sleeping in wolf form, I guessed that's where Bran had stayed the night. I was a terrible friend. I hadn't even helped her get settled last night, I'd just collapsed. The doctor must have helped her get settled before he had also drifted off.

I knew another long day lay before us. We had to get rid of the three aircraft and the bodies. We had left them all behind at Fletcher's cabin. We didn't want the bad guys, or any curious hikers stumbling across the mayhem left behind.

Dr. Burns had a Beaver—a larger aircraft than mine. It could handle Fletcher's gold and belongings, so the first order of business was to transfer anything personal from the helicopter to the professor's plane. Fletcher and I did that as the other two were waking. After eating, the planning began. It made sense to put most of the bodies in the helicopter, make it look like a true crash with multiple fatalities. Then, the rest could be pulled into the planes and made to look like normal crashes.

It took some doing, considering the doctor didn't have a winged form, to figure out how to crash the helicopter without killing him as well. It was tricky, but it amounted to me going with the doctor, dropping the helicopter low enough for him to leap out, then flying it into a mountain after I escaped. I worried since I had no experience with helicopters. The doctor assured me I could handle those simple in-flight maneuvers since I didn't have to take off or land, only crash. Crashing is surprisingly easy.

He thought he could survive a considerable fall if I dropped him low over open land. I couldn't even comprehend how much that was going to hurt. The plan was to crash the planes first. Then I'd fly to a nearby spot and the doctor would retrieve me with the helicopter. That way I could conserve my energy since I'd have to make it back to the doctor's property from the last crash site. Quite a distance for me in my current beat up state.

The crashing went smoothly. The worst part was maneuvering the bodies and strapping them into the pilot seat before I made my escape. Hopefully, when they were discovered, it would have been so long that it would look like a regular plane crash, pilot killed on impact.

The helicopter was a bigger mess. The professor gave me a brief lesson, and we were off. I had to fly back the full distance from this one, so I'd loaded up on calories and rested a few hours. As with the other crashes, I had to do it naked. We wanted to leave the least amount of evidence behind. I took only a shirt from one of the bodies and wore it for modesty during this flight. If anyone ever found the wreckage, they would wonder about how the shirt came off the body while it was strapped in, but so be it.

The bodies were strapped in the back, and one in the co-pilot's seat up front. I watched the doctor fly, memorizing as much as I could. When we were close to the spot where I was going to drop him, we switched places. I didn't bother buckling in. He stripped in the back, surer of regenerating his hurts in wolf form, and bundled his clothes into a small pack which he strapped to his back before his shift.

I had asked him why the big helicopter didn't have any parachutes. He told me because it had two engines and wasn't likely to crash. That made me worry about crashing it.

He laughed. "By the time anyone discovers it, no one will have any reason to suspect us."

While he shifted, I took the controls trying to hold steady as I lowered the helicopter down to the altitude he had insisted he could survive. The old wolf looked at me once and leapt out. I didn't watch him fall. I rose again and headed towards the place we had designated as our crash site.

Once the helicopter was locked in, I dragged a body up and strapped it in the pilot seat, stripped off the borrowed shirt, and dropped out. I stayed human until I was clear, letting my greater weight take me away from the rotor wash, then I shifted and flew away as the helicopter crunched behind me.

It hit the rocks and shale of the mountainside in an impressive poof of dust and screech of metal. I glided away. I only stopped from my long flight back to flutter over the area I thought the doctor might have landed, but I couldn't see anything or find him even with my sharp raven eyes. I didn't have the energy to spend much time searching, so I flew to a comfortable height, and let the wind guide me back to Fletcher and Bran.

We waited another day to see if the professor would make it back to us. He didn't. I made a sat phone call to dad.

"Pipe! Where are you?" he exclaimed. I hadn't missed a day of work without calling in before.

"I'm sorry. I'm sick. I'm staying at Bran's." It wasn't much of an explanation. He probably wasn't going to buy it for long. But I hung up before he could ask more questions. I was still angry at his secret keeping, and he must have known it because he didn't press or call back after I hung up. He had to have noticed my plane was missing. I'd have to have a story soon.

I flew Bran home first. I probably could have crammed both

Fletcher and Bran into my Super Cub together because she weighed so little, but I knew I was low on fuel. Plus, I had a lot to talk about with Fletcher. Bran and I were silent most of the way back to town. She had drawn in on herself. I knew why. A combination of the guilt over Mike and the others. Guilt about being taken as a fool and guilt over his death. I'm sure she was as sick about the killing of the others as I was, probably more so. My nature wasn't to dwell on things that were out of my control. Maybe it was the animal sneaking into the human—the tendency to live in the moment that came with my raven. I don't know. It was eating at her though.

"There wasn't another choice, Bran," I tried to sooth her.

"I know, Pipe. I just wish there had been another way." Her voice was small and hurt.

I nodded.

She could see the back of my head because she leaned forward and put her hand on my shoulder. "I'll be okay. I just need time."

"Time heals all wounds?" I asked softly.

"That's what they say."

I knew her though. She'd throw herself into work and avoid everyone. It would be a long time before she trusted another man. Hell, I hope *I* hadn't lost her trust. I felt a brief flare of panic at that thought.

"You haven't, Pipe," she reassured me.

"Thanks, Bran." I realized she had answered my worry without me saying anything.

"Hey, you can read minds." She laughed.

"No, I can't." Her old argument. "I just know you."

"Hmpf." I didn't believe her.

I dropped her off and told her to take my truck. It had been moved over and straightened up. Dad had probably thought I was just being rude parking like that. Well, I thought he was rude keeping things from me, so he'd have to deal with it.

I fueled up, checked over my Cub and flew back to get Fletcher. His problems were a little more physical than Bran's. The Silla Corp. knew about him. We didn't know how much of a head start he had. Would they be waiting for him at home? Would they try to capture him again? They didn't get any intel back that we knew of. Maybe the heli-copter pilot got something sent off, but there was no way of knowing what. We tried to come up with a plan on the way back where we knew no one could listen in.

"I think I might get a few days freedom before they realize I'm back," he argued.

"Why? Where are you getting that idea?" I fired back.

"They can't know what happened yet. They've got to think I'm still out here," he said stubbornly.

"Maybe." I shook my head. I didn't think so.

"I've got to go to my house and gather up my things at least." His voice was unsteady. I think the whole affair had thrown him for a loop. He had a new werewolf daddy, had dispatched terrifying enemies, and had learned things about himself he hadn't expected.

"Then what?" I knew he could disappear if he wanted. He had enough money. He could buy a new identity, skip town, and never be seen again. That made my stomach ache and my chest get tight.

"It depends on you." He looked directly at me.

"What?" I choked out.

"I'm not going anywhere without you." His voice was steady and sure. Truth.

I think my heart nearly leapt out of my chest. My face split into a huge grin. He couldn't see that, of course, sitting behind me.

"I don't know what we're going to do, but I do have somewhere you can hide out for a while," I said.

We took a cab back to his house, gathered up his belongings, which really were just his clothes and toiletries, and he took me home. We didn't see anyone following us, so I thought maybe he was right, and we did have a few days of freedom.

We slept a lot in the next couple of days. I was covered with bruises, and my face looked like I'd been beaten, which I had been. Fletcher and I hid his gold in dad's cave, and after a short explanation, we holed up there as well. It wasn't the most comfortable of places, but we were alone and safe. I needed to heal before I could return to work. We dropped his truck off and left it abandoned, title signed, and keys in it. Bran also took a couple of days off, recovering, and letting her new manager take care of things for once.

After the days of rest, I decided to finally check on Bran. I pushed open the door, and a bright female voice said, "Welcome to the Lunatic Fringe." I looked up to see a new employee that didn't know me. I smiled and waved and walked behind the counter and through the beaded entrance to the back. The girl moved as if to block me, but the manager caught her eye and shook her head. I walked in and shut the door behind the curtain. Bran was sitting at the computer working on the books, her back to the door. I shuddered. I didn't know how she could work like that. Especially after all we'd been through.

"Hey," I said.

She finished up what she was typing and turned around. "Hey, back," she said.

"Wanna Coke?" I asked and moved towards the fridge in the corner behind the door.

She stood up and stretched her back. "Sure."

I grabbed two Cokes and handed one to her. She walked around the small room a minute working out the kinks from sitting too long in a bad chair. She popped open her Coke. I plopped on the couch and propped my feet up on the table in front of it. I opened my Coke and took a slurp. She threw me a disgusted look.

"What's up?" I asked.

She shrugged. She had bags under her eyes, and I imagined she'd been torturing herself over Mike. I slurped again, louder, and more obnoxious.

"Please stop doing that."

"Doing what?" I slurped again.

"Ugh!" She knew I was trying to bounce her out of her funk. "That! You know I hate it!"

"Really?" I smiled and slurped. I could see the frustration on her face. The anger and hurt. She mimed throwing something at me. I didn't expect to be hit with a ball of heat. My Coke grew too hot, and I dropped it on the floor. It hissed and spat as it burbled out.

"What the hell!" I yelled and shook my burned hand. "That really hurt!"

She looked smug. I ran to the bathroom in the very back and ran my hand under cold water. I came back to Bran crying and soaking up Coke with a handful of paper towels.

I didn't do well around a lot of emotion. I hadn't grown up with it, and I wasn't the most emotional person I knew. I stood awkwardly for a moment, not sure what to do.

"Bran, what's wrong?" I finally asked.

She threw the towels in a corner and shook her head. "Is this about Mike?" Everyone here at the store thought Mike had dumped her, so they kept quiet and didn't bring him up.

She started to cry harder, and since she was trying to be quiet, she sobbed into her arm. Maybe giving her space for the past couple of days wasn't what she'd wanted from me. I wished I was better at this stuff. I knelt on the floor next to her and hugged her. She threw her arms around me and started apologizing.

"I'm sorry, Piper, I'm so sorry!" She said it over and over, sobs wracking her body. I was a little mystified why she was saying that. None of it was her fault.

I let her go on for a while. Then I pushed her back and shook her a little. "I'm only going to say this once—none of this is your fault. I'm sorry you lost someone you cared about. But nothing he did is your fault. Stop this feeling sorry about yourself right this minute!"

She sniffed and looked up at me. She was a mess. Her hair was falling out of its messy bun, her mascara was streaked down her face, and her eyes and nose were red. She had tears and snot smeared all over.

"I thought you would blame me for everything," she snuffled. "That's why you haven't come by."

"What? No! I was giving you space to grieve or whatever," I replied. Waving a hand to indicate the whatever.

"I felt a little bad at the time, but he kidnapped Fletcher, and he was going to kill us! I'm not going to grieve for him!" she said.

"Well, you are more important to me than any of that stuff," I said.

"I can't think of anything you can do that would make me stop being your friend." I shrugged, helpless. "Even stupid, murderous boyfriends."

Her expression lightened, and she looked as though a burden was lifted. "Thanks, Pipe."

I returned to Fletcher in the cave with a bag of greasy, fried food. I had some happiness due to me. The relationship building between me, and Fletcher filled an emptiness I had ignored for a long time. He took the food and tossed it onto the small table next to the couch. He pulled me into his arms and buried his face in my hair, breathing me in.

"Piper," he whispered with longing.

I returned his embrace. We kissed. After we made love, the food forgotten, I lay with him on our makeshift bed of camp pads and sleeping bags and gazed at him with love in my heart.

If he had to run from this, where would we be? Would our new love survive? Could we fight? What role would Dr. Burns, if he had survived his fall, play in our lives? What were the shadow winged really, and what did that mean for me?

I had more questions now than answers. But first I had to finish out this hunting season and take care of business. I had to help Bran get over Mike's betrayal and his ugly death. I had to help Fletcher do what he needed to do to protect himself, and we all had to figure out how to survive this new threat. Sounded like a typical raven mess.

END

Glossary of Terms

I'm including a simple pronunciation guide. Inupiaq is complex, with sounds that don't exist in English. These are *very* approximate English versions of the actual language.

Amaroq: (Ah-ma-rok) Inupiaq word for wolf.

Amaguq: (Ah-ma-gok) Inuit wolf god.

Animal Weres: A created race from an earth predator base and Sky Person technology. The animals could shift into a human form. No additional enhancements.

Atchu: (Aht-choo) Inupiaq for "I don't know."

Atiqlik: (Ah-tik-lik) Inupiaq word for a type of hooded blouse usually made from calico with a large pocket on the front. Unisex, although women may wear a version with an attached skirt.

Hróðvitnir: (H'ro-vich-nich) Icelandic for Fenrir.

Iminauraq: (Im-in-ar-auk) Inupiaq word for a mythical race of little people.

Qanuq itpich?: (Kan-uk-it-pich) Inupiaq for "how are you?"

Quyanaqpak: (Coy-un-ahk-pak) Inupiaq for "thank you."

Shadow Clan: Groups of shadow winged usually genetically related to an animal totem. For example, Raven Clan would consist of the Sky Person totem that represents raven, and his children, grandchildren, great-grandchildren, etc. from human/Sky Person lineage.

Shadow Winged: Any genetic mix between the Sky People and humans.

Shaman: A Native American magic user.

Sky People: The original Native American totems. They are powerful beings that came down from the heavens and subjugated the human race for a time. Identified by the animal clan they represent, i.e., Raven, Eagle, Wolf, Salmon, Orca, etc.

Tiŋiakpak: (Tin-e-ok-pok) Inupiaq for eagle.

Tornit: (Tor-nit) Inuit word for Bigfoot.

Totem: Sky People that lead a Shadow Clan, i.e., Raven, Eagle, Wolf, etc. Could be mis-identified as a god, particularly since they have godlike powers.

Tulugaq: (Too-loo-gok) Inupiaq for raven.

Urayuli: (Oo-ra-uly) Yupik word for Bigfoot.

Uvlaalluataq: (Oov-la-loa-tok) Inupiaq for "good morning."

Weres: A created race from a human base and Sky Person technology. Originally based on ice age predators but enhanced to be larger, stronger, faster, and more efficient warriors. Can shift forms into one enhanced predator.

Notes

Chapter 15

1. Story paraphrased from *First People: Native American Legends, Creation and Inuit Tale*
   http://www.firstpeople.us/FP-Html-Legends/Creation_An_Inuit_Tale-Eskimo.html

About the Author

Jilleen Dolbeare is the author of the Shadow Winged Chronicles, an urban fantasy series about a shape-shifting bush pilot in Alaska.

She loves riding horses, warm ocean beaches, and long walks in the mountains, none of which she can do in the Arctic, so she writes. Her activities are riding her four-wheeler on cold ocean beaches (often frozen or covered with ice), and long walks to and from work when it's 40 below— in the dark. She does keep her stakes sharp for those vamps that show up during the 67 days of night.

Jilleen lives with her husband and two hungry cats in Barrow, Alaska where she also discovered her love and admiration of the Inupiaq people and their folklore.

Piper's Logbook

Also by Jilleen Dolbeare

Made in the USA
Columbia, SC
01 July 2022

62631895R00198